Last Seen Alive

CLAIRE DOUGLAS

PENGUIN BOOKS

PENGUIN BOOKS

UK | USA | Canada | Ireland | Australia
India | New Zealand | South Africa

Penguin Books is part of the Penguin Random House group of companies
whose addresses can be found at global.penguinrandomhouse.com.

Set in 12.5/14.75 pt Garamond MT Std
Typeset by Jouve (UK), Milton Keynes
Printed in Great Britain by Clays Ltd, St Ives plc

A CIP catalogue record for this book is available from the British Library

ISBN: 978-1-405-92642-3

www.greenpenguin.co.uk

Penguin Random House is committed to a
sustainable future for our business, our readers
and our planet. This book is made from Forest
Stewardship Council® certified paper.

For Claudia and Isaac

Prologue

He had such pretty eyes; they were his best feature, the colour of the ocean. Now they are as glassy and lifeless as a china doll's, staring up at the darkening sky, empty, unseeing. The stone ornament falls from my open palm and spins towards his body, where it lands heavily against his thigh.

Fear takes hold of me so that, for a few moments, I'm rooted to the spot, staring at the dent in his skull and the arc of blood that has sprayed from the back of his head, staining the grass red. Then I kneel down beside him, my knees sinking into the damp lawn. I'm careful not to touch him. I can leave no evidence.

I glance up furtively. The building is over two hundred feet away, the windows opaque, some with curtains hanging open, others with the blinds rolled up. Was anybody watching? I'm already starting to think like a criminal. Was I seen at the bottom of the garden among the weeds and overgrown grass?

Was I seen killing my husband?

PART ONE
Cornwall

I

Jamie twists the dial on the radio up to full volume so we can hear the Stone Roses over the wind whistling past our ears. He looks like one of those nodding dogs as he moves his head to the music.

'God, I love this song.'

'You don't say,' I tease, and then grimace when he starts singing along.

He notices. 'What? I *was* the lead singer in a band when I was eighteen.' But he squeezes my thigh, a playful gesture that shows me he's not offended. 'You could've been our groupie.'

I'm tempted to remind him that he was with Hannah then. She would have been his groupie. But I don't want to dampen his mood. He seems happier than he's been in ages. I turn to appraise him, to admire his sharp jaw that curves into his long neck, the fine blond hair just visible above the buttons of his polo shirt, and I feel a flicker of desire. I place my hand where his still rests lightly on my thigh and we interlock our fingers. He catches my eye and smiles before his gaze snaps back to the empty lane that stretches ahead of us.

'I can't wait to see the house,' I say. 'I wonder what it's going to be like. I hope it isn't some kind of dive.'

He raises an eyebrow. 'A dive? I doubt that. Didn't Philip Heywood describe it as –' he puts on his telephone voice '– "an imposing seaside pile with panoramic views of the bay", or some such . . .'

I laugh. 'I don't think so.'

He takes his hand away and places it back on the steering wheel to navigate a bend. 'The Roseland Peninsula is supposed to be stunning.'

'The name certainly suggests so.'

'Apparently it's derived from *rhos*, Celtic for heath.'

'How do you know this stuff?'

He raises an eyebrow. 'Because I'm a geek.'

'You are.' But I'm smiling as I say it. I tug the collar of my coat further up my bare neck. It's been years since I've had long hair but I occasionally miss the warmth of it against my skin, especially in the colder months. The sunshine bounces off the bonnet of the car yet there is a chill in the air, despite the blue skies, reminding us that the threat of an April shower is ever present. I don't have the heart to tell Jamie to put the roof up. He needs this holiday just as much as I do. Our first nine months of married life haven't been easy.

I catch sight of our golden retriever Ziggy in the rear-view mirror, lounging across the back seat, his eyes closed, his tongue lolling out of the side of his mouth. It'd been a last-minute decision to bring the dog. Katie, Jamie's younger sister, had promised to look after him for us, but, as usual, she'd let us down at the eleventh hour.

I feel the drag of car sickness in the pit of my stomach as Jamie navigates another bend and I concentrate on breathing deeply, trying to push the nausea away, my nostrils desperately searching for the sea air that we'd been promised but instead finding the pungent scent of rapeseed from the yellow fields. My right arm feels heavy and itches beneath its cast, but at least it's given me a good excuse not to have to drive. Not that Jamie encourages me to get behind the wheel any more. Not since early on in our relationship, when I nearly killed us both by pulling onto a busy A-road and narrowly missing an oncoming lorry.

Eventually, a speck in the distance grows bigger, breaking up the monotonous country road; a tiny petrol station stands forlornly, like a lost child amongst the wild foliage.

'That must be the one,' I say, pointing at it in excitement, trying to remember the instructions that Philip Heywood had given me on the phone two days before.

Jamie pulls into the forecourt and switches off the engine, and the world appears to fall quiet for a moment. It's a welcome silence after the constant din of loud music and buffeting wind. Too much noise has always made me feel stressed and on edge, but Jamie loves to play music as loud as he can get away with.

He reaches over into the back seat and clips the lead onto Ziggy's collar. 'Do you want to go and get the key then, Libs? I'll fill her up as we're here. Then I'll take Ziggy over there so he can do his ablutions.' He

7

indicates a patch of unruly grass to the side of the shop. I agree, relieved to get out and stand on solid ground for a bit.

The guy behind the counter is barely out of his teens. He stares at me with a nonplussed expression on his acne-scarred face when I ask about the key to the Hideaway. 'I don't know nothing about a key,' he says while scratching a pimple on his neck. 'I'll get my manager. Name?'

'Pardon?'

He tuts, not bothering to hide his annoyance. 'What's your name?'

'Oh. Libby . . .'

'Surname?'

'Elliot . . . I mean, Hall. Mrs.' I'm so used to calling myself by my maiden name at work that I sometimes forget I'm now part of someone else's family.

He slopes off to the back of the shop, his long arms swinging like an ape's, and disappears through a grey door. The shop is small, the shelves piled high with cans of tuna, beans and plum tomatoes. I'm the only customer. I pick up some mints from the rack in front of me and scan the confectionery for something for Jamie. Something with coconut, his favourite. Then I watch out of the window as Jamie coaxes a reluctant Ziggy back into the car. Our Mini Cooper is the only vehicle on the forecourt.

The guy doesn't re-emerge and I feel the fluttering of panic that this is all some elaborate con and there is no key or house by the sea. Then a buxom woman with a mop of dyed blonde hair barrels through the door, key dangling enticingly from her chubby fingers.

'Elizabeth Hall?' she says in a thick Cornish accent.

I nod and she hands over the key, her face breaking into a smile. 'Aren't you lucky, going to stay at the Hideaway. Beautiful views. Not that I've ever stayed there myself. I didn't know they rented it out?'

I take the key gratefully. 'I don't know if they do, usually. We're doing a house swap.'

Her eyes widen. 'A house swap? What a great idea. So they're staying in your house while you're in theirs?'

I push my debit card into the machine. 'Yes. Although ours is a flat. In Bath.'

'I've heard Bath's lovely. I've never been.' She rips off the receipt and hands it to me as I retrieve my card. 'A house swap though. What a great idea.' Then her eyes sweep over my cast. 'Recovering from an accident, are you, love?'

I'd like to tell her to mind her own bloody business, and years ago I might have done just that. But those days are behind me; in my job I can't afford to lose my temper. So I swallow down my irritation. I can't tell her the truth – I'd be here all day answering questions.

'I slipped and broke it,' I say. It's only a half-lie. 'In the playground. I'm a teacher.'

She grimaces. 'Ooh, nasty. Did one of those little blighters push you over?'

I shake my head and force out a laugh, explaining

9

that I'd tripped over a skipping rope which had been left on the tarmac, all the while trying to extricate myself from the conversation by inching further towards the exit. 'Thanks again,' I say, waving the key at her and hurrying through the door before she can ask another question.

I spot Jamie through the windscreen, impatiently tapping the steering wheel with his fingers. We've had our fair share of rows lately, mostly over money, and I don't want to upset the fragile equilibrium that we seem to have found since the miscarriage. I slide into the passenger seat. 'Sorry about that. The woman wouldn't stop asking me questions.'

His expression darkens. 'What about?'

'Oh, my cast. The accident.'

'You didn't tell her?' His voice is unusually sharp.

'No, of course not.' I pull the seat belt over my shoulder.

'Good. We're supposed to be getting away from it all. Has she given you the key?'

I hold it up to show him. It's attached to a small glass heart that glints in the sun.

He visibly relaxes. 'Thank God. I thought it had all been a mistake. You know what they say? If it's too good to be true . . .'

I lean over and kiss the side of his face where his jawline meets his ear, his soft stubble grazing my lips. I love that he's excited about this. That he's regaining some of his former spark. That's what I'd loved about him when I first met him, his enthusiasm for life. He's a pint-half-full kind of man, but being made redundant, setting up on his own and constantly worrying about money has taken its toll, and I've noticed, over the last few months, that some of his brightness has started to fade, like a tarnished coin.

As we head down another narrow lane, thick hedgerows sprinkled with white blossom rearing up on either side, Jamie almost shouts, 'That must be it!' his eagerness bringing out his slight West Country twang. He points towards a house on the other side of a T-junction. I follow his finger. Surely he's mistaken? The house is huge, even grander than his mother's.

'That can't be it,' I reply as Jamie veers off the road and onto the driveway, gravel crunching beneath the tyres just as the nasal voice of the sat-nav informs us that we have reached our destination.

The car draws to a halt and Jamie switches the engine off. We sit and stare at the house in an awed silence, both of us taking in the detached, rectangular building with a round turret at one end; all traditional smoky-coloured stone and glass. A creeper grows halfway up the walls so that it looks like a beard. Trees and bushes in varying shades of green envelop the house as if they are embracing it. Beyond the property is a stretch of clear blue ocean sparkling in the distance. The only sounds are the cheerful chirruping of birds and the faint growl of the sea. I can smell the salt on the breeze, mixed with a trace of horse manure.

'It's quite remote,' I say, suddenly feeling a little over-whelmed. I grew up in the countryside – a little two-up two-down on a small council estate in North Yorkshire – but I'd spent the best part of the last decade in a city. I'm used to having neighbours. Being surrounded by people makes me feel secure, less frightened.

'It's amazing,' says Jamie, his face alight. 'I can't quite believe we're going to be staying here. Good call, Libs.' He takes a deep breath through his nose. 'Ah, smell that air. So fresh and clean. No pollution, no fumes.' Just cow shit instead, I want to say, but bite my lip. I can almost see the tension of the last few months ebbing away from him, transforming him back into the man I'd married.

A squirrel scrambles up a nearby tree and Ziggy barks, a deep woof that shatters the silence as he pulls against his restraint. Jamie laughs and leans over the back seat to unbuckle him, clipping the lead onto his collar. 'Come on, boy, I know you're dying to explore.'

Jamie jumps out the car and darts around to open the passenger door for me. 'Very chivalrous,' I say, try-ing not to flinch as I stand up.

He frowns. 'Are you all right, Libs?'

'I just can't wait to get this cast off, that's all. It makes everything so bloody awkward.'

'Not much longer, my little heroine.'

I thump his arm playfully with my good hand. 'Stop taking the piss.'

He kisses my forehead. 'I'm not taking the piss, you

are a heroine,' he mumbles. 'Don't you forget it.' Then he bounds away from me, dragged by Ziggy, and I follow with trepidation, half expecting the irate owner to come hurtling out of the house to tell us to get off his land. Noticing my hesitation, Jamie beckons me to the door, charcoal-grey aluminium, as clean and polished as the rest of the house. Philip Heywood told me on the phone that it has recently undergone a restoration.

Jamie's eyes are shining as he looks up from the piece of paper he's consulting. 'It is the right place, look,' he says, to reassure himself as much as me. He prods the paper with his finger, then indicates the slate sign with the words 'The Hideaway' carved into its face. 'Apt name. There isn't another house for half a mile. And it's not far from Lizard Point. I've always wanted to see the lighthouse.' He sounds like one of my six-year-olds.

I feel a stab of guilt that we've swapped our poky two-bedroom flat in Bath, with the animal hairs and the dog-food aroma, for this. It's not even a Georgian flat, as one might expect in Bath, but late Victorian.

'Do you think it was OK to bring Ziggy? I never thought to ask.'

Jamie's eyes widen in alarm. 'Shit, Libs. Why didn't you check? I have no idea.'

'I didn't expect the house to be so big and posh, that's why. Philip said there was still building work going on. I thought it meant it would be a bit more . . .' I pause, taking in the neatly tended plants and bushes that encompass the driveway '. . . unfinished.'

My fears are confirmed as soon as we step over the threshold. It's definitely not the sort of place to bring a dog. Everything is so white: the sofas, the rugs, the walls. I know we'll stain it somehow, with our messy ways and Ziggy's dirty paws. Apart from a pile of rubble near the tree in the far corner of the garden, there is little evidence that any building work has taken place.

I take the lead from Jamie, too worried to let Ziggy go, unable to shake the feeling that we are trespassing as I wander into the kitchen. It's huge and open-plan, with white gloss cabinets and marble worktops. Bifold doors open onto a wide garden that overlooks an expansive beach below.

'Look at this, Jay,' I call, my head in the American-style fridge, practically salivating at all the food. 'There's enough here to feed a family of ten.'

Jamie joins me to peer inside. 'Ooh, they have pâté, smoked salmon, a massive Stilton – and look at all those craft beers!' He grins at me. 'This is heaven!'

'Our fridge is practically empty,' I say, ashamed of the pint of milk and curled-up ham that I'd left behind. I never even thought about stocking it up.

'Don't worry about it, they've got more important things on their minds.' He drifts over to the kitchen island and picks up a lined piece of paper that looks like it's been ripped out of a notebook. 'It says here we can help ourselves to the food. Isn't that generous?' He doesn't wait for an answer as he tosses the note aside and wanders around the kitchen, touching appliances and tinkering with various knobs and buttons. 'Wow, this kitchen is fantastic,' he exclaims as a 20-inch TV pops up seamlessly from the island worktop.

I smile inwardly, knowing how much Jamie would love to have the money to spend on the latest gadgets.

'You can fiddle later,' I say, pulling him away from the spaceship-like coffee machine. 'Let's explore.' I take Ziggy off his lead. Jamie grabs my hand and we race around the house like over-excited teenagers, the dog at our heels, barking joyfully.

There are solid oak floors throughout, with an impressive floating glass staircase in the large, square living room that curves up to the second floor. Colourful abstract paintings adorn the chalky white walls and there is a huge head-and-shoulders shot of a woman who must be Tara Heywood in the living room, her head thrown back, her large brown eyes dancing. Upstairs I poke my head around the door of the first bedroom, which contains a sofa bed and a faded, antique dolls' house. Shelves along one wall are crammed with toys; not modern ones that my kids at school would play with, but old-fashioned and unsettling. Punch and Judy puppets are slumped against a china doll with one foot missing, and an ugly clown stands next to a stuffed weasel. Surely this isn't their daughter's room? It would have given me nightmares as a child.

The other two bedrooms are bigger and there is a traditional study with a leather-topped desk. I pad into the room. Bookshelves line the walls, although they are half empty; a few dog-eared romance novels, a classic-car manual and an encyclopaedia. I count three more stuffed animals: a ferret, a fox and a sad-looking rodent that looks a bit like a rat but could equally be some kind of mole.

At the end of the corridor, in the circular turret, is the master bedroom. It's the largest room by far, with an en-suite bathroom and a separate dressing room. 'Wow, this is bigger than our whole flat.' I stand and gawp at it in amazement – at the floor-to-ceiling windows, the four-poster bed with floating white muslin, the roll-top bath. There is another head and shoulders shot of Tara, black and white, her expression more serious this time. I go to the window and gaze out at the beach below. I can't see another soul. It's idyllic.

'I didn't expect it to be so modern, so opulent,' I say as Jamie comes to stand next to me. 'I thought it would be a quaint cottage or something.'

'Don't you like it?' Jamie looks astonished that I might not.

'No, it's not that. It's amazing. Like *properly* amazing, the sort of house you'd see in a film. It must cost millions. It's just . . . it doesn't seem a fair swap.'

He shrugs and puts his arm around me. 'It's what they wanted, remember. It was their idea.'

'I know . . .'

He sighs. 'God, Libs, this is a stroke of luck.' I face him, noticing the bags under his eyes, his grey complexion, and push down my uneasiness. The Cornish air will be good for him. And for me. I touch my stomach self-consciously and Jamie notices. 'We need this,' he says. '*You* need this. After what happened at school and then the miscarriage . . .'

Tears spring into my eyes and I blink them away. I can't think about it. I've come here to help me forget. To heal. 'Yes.' My voice is thick. 'It's a beautiful place. We're very lucky.'

'We'd better keep it tidy.' He pulls a face and I can hear the amusement in his voice. It's a standing joke between us, our mutual messiness, and we take great enjoyment out of accusing the other of being the worst.

I glance at Jamie; he still dresses like a student in his faded jeans, ripped at the knee. 'We should have taken our shoes off,' I say, looking pointedly at his scruffy Converse. 'And we're going to have to keep Ziggy's paws clean. We should've bought those dog socks we saw in that pet shop.' I giggle at the thought of Ziggy in fluffy socks. He'd never forgive us.

Jamie laughs, loud and heartily. It echoes around the house. I haven't heard that sound enough in the last few months and it makes my heart soar. 'Do you know what we need to do?' he says, a mischievous twinkle in his eyes as he grabs my hand.

'No, what?'

He inclines his head towards the bed. 'We're going to have to christen it.'

I raise an eyebrow. 'Really? What, now?'

'No time like the present.' He sweeps me up effortlessly – he is nearly a foot taller than I am – and carries me to the bed. We tumble onto the soft cotton sheets, our limbs entwined, and he starts kissing my neck in the way he knows I love. I wrap my legs around him, pressing my body to his, feeling more contented, happy, than I have in months.

We spend ages in bed, taking our time, exploring each other's bodies, just like we used to in the early days, before we got married, before things became complicated. Before his family's interference and Hannah's quiet, unnerving presence in our lives. Afterwards I snuggle up against Jamie's shoulder. It feels unnatural to have to lie on my left side, to avoid leaning on my cast. It feels so heavy and cumbersome. Less than two weeks, I remind myself.

I'm content for a while watching the sun going down, creating shadows across the lawn. Then I spring up from the bed, covering myself with a sheet, conscious that the windows have no curtains.

'Where are you going?' Jamie murmurs, gathering the feathered duvet around his armpits.

'To nose through Tara's wardrobe,' I say, raising my eyebrow playfully.

'Libs! You can't do that.'

'Oh, come on. Surely you're intrigued? Don't you want to know more about Philip and Tara Heywood?'

He shrugs, a lazy smile playing on his lips. 'Not really.'

'Well, I do.' I shuffle over to the en-suite dressing room in my makeshift toga. Ziggy follows me and stretches out on the fleecy rug in the middle of the floor.

The dressing room is about the same size as our bedroom back at home. A floor-length mirror hangs on one wall and a button-backed chair sits next to it. It's like a changing room in a fancy shop. This isn't even their main residence, just a holiday home. It makes me wonder what their actual home must be like. I reach up to flick through the clothes: long evening dresses, strappy sun dresses, floaty skirts, tops in silky fabrics. I take a long emerald dress from the hanger and drape it against my body, admiring myself in the mirror, although it's way too long for me and the extra material pools around my feet. I resemble a little girl trying on her mum's clothes. Or even a boy, with my short pixie cut. I return the dress and open a drawer of underwear. There are sexy thongs and high-end lacy basques. I recognise one I'd seen on an Agent Provocateur website. All very classy and out of my price range. Nothing tacky here.

I move to the shoes. They are on narrow metal shelves that pull out from the wall and are in every conceivable style and colour. All designer brands, some of which I've never heard of. I think of my tatty ballet pumps that I bought from Top Shop as I cradle a pair of patent red stilettos. Size 7, much too big for my size 4 feet. I put them back despondently.

'I can't even borrow her shoes,' I wail as I climb back into the four-poster bed. 'She's a giant. Or a supermodel.'

'Or an alien,' adds Jamie.

'A very beautiful alien,' I laugh. 'How the other half live, huh?'

He pulls me into his arms and says softly against my hair, 'Well, we're that other half this week, Libs. So let's enjoy it.'

2

I'd never have considered going on holiday if it hadn't been for the leaflet that came through the door a few days ago.

HOUSE SWAP URGENTLY NEEDED

My wife, Tara, and I are desperately looking for a place to stay for a week, maybe two. Your property would be ideal as we need somewhere close to the hospital asap to be near our precious daughter, who is undergoing a life-saving heart operation. We are willing to swap our beautiful, recently refurbished house in Cornwall with sea views. If you think you can help, please contact Philip Heywood.

His mobile phone number was written at the bottom of the page.

I dismissed it at first. I was in a rush to get to work. I'd been off sick for two weeks, ever since the fire and the subsequent miscarriage. My boss, Felicity Ryder, had insisted I take paid leave until after the holidays, but I wanted to go in for the last day of term to see my class and to wish them a good Easter break. I'd begun to care about those children. I felt responsible for their education, worried that the supply teacher hustled in to take over wouldn't understand their needs like I did. I also missed the school: my classroom walls decorated with the children's brightly coloured artwork, the camaraderie in the staff room, the shrieks of joy in the playground, gossiping with Cara, the young teaching assistant who worked alongside me, even the smell of disinfectant in the corridor. So I'd stuffed the leaflet in my handbag on my way out the door – and thought no more about it for the next few hours.

I'd been dismayed to see the evidence of the fire; the school hall had been redecorated and a new floor installed, but the burnt smell still lingered as though seeping through the fresh paint and the newly laid parquet. The dining room, where the fire was thought to have originated, was still out of bounds. When I pressed my face up to the glass doors I could see the blackened hole in the ground where the ovens had been. It was a depressing sight. The children had been told to bring in packed lunches until the kitchens were up and running again, and they sat, hunched over hummus, organic vegetables and cartons of juice, in the classrooms instead.

It was as the parents came to collect their children at the end of the day – congratulating me for my bravery and asking after Celeste – that the idea came to me. Mrs Hunting, Theo's mum, touched my cast lightly and told me I deserved to get away somewhere. 'You've had such a bad time of it, Ms Elliot,' she'd said, in the sort of voice you'd use on someone whose close relative had just died. 'It could have ended so badly. Celeste could have been killed in that fire if it wasn't for you. It doesn't bear thinking about.' I knew she was contemplating her own child too. I touched my stomach automatically, thinking of the one I'd lost.

The incident had been all over the newspapers, much to my horror. There was even a picture in the *Mail* of me playing the guitar, surrounded by kids, fringe in my eyes. It must have been taken when I'd first joined and was the only photograph the school had of me.

A story about a school fire wouldn't have made it past the local press if it hadn't been for the fact that I'd successfully led not just my year group, but Celeste Detonge, the granddaughter of a famous stage actor, to safety. We'd been the only year group in the building that day; Reception and Year One had been on school trips. Cara had started to panic as the smoke filled the school hall where we were practising our assembly, and I'd had to keep calm even though the screech of the alarms made the memories of another time, another fire, slam into me, winding me. But I'd forced down my own terror, instead concentrating on getting the children, and Cara, out of the burning building. Celeste had tripped and fallen and I'd rushed back in to the hall, the smoke clogging my throat, blinding me and making me trip over too. I landed badly but ignored the pain as I scooped her up into my arms and carried her to safety. I don't think I'm brave. I did what anyone would have done in the circumstances. I'm a teacher, a role that I love, that I live for. Those children are my first priority.

It was when I was having my arm X-rayed that the bleeding started. I'd been just days away from the twelve-week mark.

'Are you going anywhere nice this Easter?' Mrs Hunting had asked. 'You deserve a holiday after what you've been through.' Her sympathetic words made me realise how lovely it would be to get away somewhere. A proper break. Since Jamie had started his own business we had been strapped for cash. We hadn't been away since our honeymoon, and that had only been a five-day trip to the Isle of Wight. After what happened in Thailand I'd been too fearful to travel abroad, too scared to get on an aeroplane, convinced it would crash. So we'd had the odd long weekend or week away in England instead. It played on my mind on the walk home from school, that enticing line about a beautiful house in Cornwall with sea views. I imagined a little cottage somewhere, maybe in a fishing village like the one in *Doc Martin*. I thought the sea air would do Jamie good. He worked from home so he could take his laptop. By the time I arrived back at the flat I had convinced myself it was the answer to our prayers.

I could hear Jamie on the phone in our spare room, which he used as an office. I flicked the kettle on, made a fuss of Ziggy and started on dinner. It was difficult to cook with one arm in a sling, but Florrie, Jamie's older sister, had kindly made a batch of cottage pies and pasta sauces which I'd frozen. I grabbed a pie from the freezer and heated up the oven. Then, while the pie was cooking, I settled myself at the kitchen table in front of my laptop to google Philip Heywood.

It took longer than normal, having to type with one hand – it frustrated me how everything took twice as long – but then a list of Philip Heywoods popped up on-screen; a musician in the US, a biologist in Australia, a plastic surgeon in a private clinic in London. I clicked on the private clinic link and a photo came up of a respectable-looking man in his late forties with short, dark hair, greying at the sides, and a moustache. Could that be the same Philip Heywood? A bit more digging and I'd found his Facebook page, although the settings were too restricted to see more than two profile photos. One showed him on a deserted beach with his arm around a younger, very attractive woman with dark hair. His wife? And were they in Cornwall?

Jamie was still talking so I searched for 'Philip Heywood + Cornwall'. A photo came up of a local benefit in Truro; Philip was dressed in black tie, his arm around the same woman. She was wearing a strapless floor-length emerald dress, her hair a cloud of dark curls around her head and shoulders. The caption read: 'Avid supporters of the charity, surgeon Philip Heywood and his wife, Tara'. I studied their photo for a while, their wide smiles, their white teeth, their perfect skin. They looked like a successful, highly regarded couple. When their daughter became ill, they must have considered booking into a hotel, but found there wasn't one close enough to the hospital. Surely they could be trusted to live in our flat for a week or two if I was in their home?

I then searched for Philip Heywood and 'daughter'. A photo filled the screen of Philip, Tara and a girl in her early teens with a beautiful smile, sandy coloured hair and the distinctive features of Down's syndrome. I skimmed through the article, a small piece on his charity work. I was disappointed to note there was nothing more personal, no insight into his marriage or what type of father he was. All I could glean was that he was a very successful consultant who gave his time generously to various charities. But by the time I had finished reading my mind was made up.

Jamie didn't take as much convincing as I'd thought he would. I had my spiel ready: I was on holiday for two weeks anyway, it wouldn't cost us anything, he deserved a rest, he could take his laptop as I was sure there would be Wi-Fi, I had never been to Cornwall, the Heywoods looked and sounded respectable, their daughter had Down's syndrome and was obviously seriously ill if she needed a life-saving operation, we'd be doing a good thing . . . He sat opposite me, his long fingers entwined around a mug of coffee, not saying a word. When I finished he got up to put his mug in the sink, shrugged his shoulders and said, 'OK. If you sort it all out, then we'll go.'

I waited until we'd eaten dinner and Jamie was out

walking Ziggy before ringing the mobile number. Philip Heywood had a warm voice with a Yorkshire accent similar to mine. He sounded younger than I'd expected as he enquired which part of the north I was from. I didn't tell him, just made out I'd moved around a lot. 'A week in your flat would work out wonderfully,' he said, and I could hear the relief in his voice. We discussed where we would leave the keys – at the petrol station near his house for him, and with our upstairs neighbour, Evelyn, for us – and promised to ring each other if there were any problems. It was arranged for Saturday, two days later. I put the phone down full of excitement. How could anything go wrong?

3

I can see the stars punctuating the black sky through the large windows that take up almost all of one wall. It's like being in my very own planetarium. I lie in bed and try to spot Orion or the Plough, but I can't make out any constellations. It reminds me of those postcards that were all the rage when I was about eight, where you had to find a 3D picture hidden in the pattern. I used to give myself a headache trying to pick out the hidden unicorn or woman's face amongst the rows of triangles and squares.

I'm still finding it hard to believe we are actually here, in this beautiful house, with a beach at the foot of the garden. *A beach.* Happiness infuses me at the thought of the week ahead: romantic strolls along the shoreline with Jamie and Ziggy, relaxing in the beautiful garden with the sea views, pottering about the high-tech kitchen that looks as though it should be in an issue of one of those house-and-garden magazines I'm obsessed with buying. Now that it's quiet I can hear the rush of the sea crashing onto the rocks below. It's soporific. I haven't felt this relaxed since before the fire.

I wonder how the Heywoods are getting on in our flat. Are they disappointed with it? They must be if they are used to living like this. I think of Tara in her elegant clothes having to slum it in our bedroom with the second-hand pine furniture from Sylvia. Or are they so wrapped up in worry for their daughter that they couldn't care where they stay, just as long as they are close to the hospital, to her?

Jamie stretches lazily and says, half-heartedly, 'We'd better get up.'

'What time is it?' I shuffle away from him to glance at my watch. 'Shit. It's gone eight. What can we make for dinner?' I think of the fridge downstairs, bursting with food. 'I'm starving. And we haven't finished exploring.' I can't wait to have a further poke about their house. I've never done anything like this before; never stayed in an Airbnb or swapped homes. Even Jamie, who grew up in a leafy, middle-class cul-de-sac with his professional, university-educated parents, seems impressed by what he's seen so far.

I swing my legs out of bed, the floorboards warm beneath my feet (they must have underfloor heating). The suitcase is still in the corner of the room where Jamie dumped it earlier, and I rustle around inside it for my dressing gown. I can't go anywhere without it. Jamie can't understand why I want to wrap myself up in it at every available opportunity – he doesn't even possess one. I pull it around me now, snaking my good arm through the sleeve and letting the soft grey velour drape over my sling. It was one of the first things Jamie bought me, when we started going out together four and a half years ago. He'd stayed over in my little bedsit and when he clapped eyes on my threadbare towelling dressing gown with the pocket hanging off he'd taken the piss out of it. Two days later, on a cold Sunday afternoon, he'd surprised me with this one. That's when I'd truly fallen for him.

'Ziggy's going to need feeding too. The poor mite, we haven't left this room all afternoon.' When Jamie doesn't answer I turn around to see his naked silhouette groping the wall. 'What *are* you doing?'

'Looking for the light switch. I can't see a bloody thing. How did it get dark so quickly?'

'That's the trouble with being in the middle of the countryside,' I muse. No street lamps, no car headlights sweeping across the room as they pass outside our window. Not like our busy Bath street where you're just one of a crowd. Safe. Anonymous.

I start to snigger.

'What's so funny?' But I can hear the amusement in his voice. 'This is fucking ridiculous, Libs. I can't find the sodding thing.'

I blink, trying to encourage my eyes to adjust so that I can help him, but the darkness folds around us like smog. We both paw at the walls in vain, and my arm knocks against something hard, sending what I assume is an ornament to the floor with a thud.

'Shit!' I jump back, noticing a set of shelves above my head. I peer down at the object that's fallen. It looks like some kind of bird. I take a sharp intake of breath. Jamie is by my side in an instant.

'What is it?'

'It looks like a dead animal.' It's face down on the floor but I can see that it's large. And has feathers.

He crouches down and turns it over. 'It's an owl.' He gently picks it up and moves to the window, holding it up against the scant moonlight. I look at it over his shoulder, surprised to see that it's stuffed. Jamie gazes at it in amazement but it gives me the creeps with its staring, dead eyes.

'Put it back, Jay,' I hiss, as though expecting Philip or Tara to walk through the door any second.

'Oh, so it's all right for you to go through Tara's wardrobe, touching her shoes and trying on her dresses . . .'

'I didn't try on her dress. It was too long. I probably only come up to her armpits.' I give a snort of laughter, suddenly finding the situation ludicrous. I'm pleased to see that Jamie's grinning as he reaches up and places the owl back on the shelf, stroking its head tenderly. He's such a softy where animals are concerned, even dead ones it seems. 'Shouldn't you put some clothes on? You're standing in full view of the window.' I run my eyes over his lithe, rangy body dulled grey by the lack of light but I can still just about make out the fine blond hairs that travel from his belly button to his groin. I feel the deep stirring of desire. Today was only the second time we'd had sex since the miscarriage. Now, suddenly, I can't get enough of him.

He flexes his pectoral muscles as though he's in a

body-building contest and I laugh. 'We're in the middle of nowhere. Who's going to be able to see me?'

I roll my eyes in mock frustration. 'There must be another way to turn the lights on.'

'Of course!' he exclaims. 'It's sound-activated. I've seen people doing it in films.' He claps his hands together. Nothing happens. He claps again, twice, in quick succession and suddenly the spotlights overhead beam down on us, almost blinding us with their intensity.

'Is there a more ambient setting?' I ask, trying to blink away the black spots that are swarming in front of my vision.

'How the hell should I know?' He claps twice and we are once again plunged into darkness. 'Oh, fuck this. Why can't they have light switches like normal people?' He bends over to pull on the jeans that are slung over the bottom of the bed frame and then we make our way downstairs, fumbling our way in the darkness, Jamie walking purposefully in front of me, guiding me down the stairs.

When we reach the bottom, Jamie claps and immediately the spotlights blaze on. 'Surely there must be some sort of remote?' he grumbles, heading towards the kitchen. 'I feel like an idiot with all this hand clapping.' I follow him, Ziggy at my heels. As I round the corner I stop, my heart thudding. The front door is wide open, swinging on its hinges. I can feel the draught blowing around my ankles. I see the frown on Jamie's face as he goes to close it. He doesn't say anything. He doesn't have to.

'We closed that door,' I say, trying to keep the panic out of my voice.

He looks unconcerned but I know it's an act. Ever since the fire at the school he's been walking on eggshells around me, trying to convince me to talk to his mum or another therapist about the possibility of post-traumatic stress disorder. I know I haven't got PTSD though. How can I have when I've survived something far worse before?

'I couldn't have shut it properly. It must have swung open in the wind.' He avoids looking at me as he heads into the kitchen. I follow silently and sit at the island to watch as he opens and closes drawers in his hunt for a remote, my mind racing. How long has the door been open? We arrived at 4 p.m. Has it been open all that time? Anybody could have walked in off the street. Then I remind myself that there is no street. This isn't the estate where I grew up in Yorkshire, or our busy road in Bath that's nearly always full of traffic, people sauntering past, or kids coming home from one of the many schools in the area. Even in the dead of night the blue flashing lights of an ambulance or police car filter through the fabric of the curtains at our bedroom window.

'Yesss,' says Jamie triumphantly, holding up an electronic device. 'This is the bad boy I've been looking for.' He prods and presses at the buttons, causing the lights to flash as though we're at a disco at the working men's club my dad used to take me to when I was a kid.

The door has been open for hours. Somebody could be in the house.

The thought knocks into me, making me feel physically sick. Jamie will get cross if I mention it, I know he will. He'll say I'm being irrational and he'll start droning on about therapy again, and the happy, easy way we've been with each other since we arrived will be replaced by tension. I try to push the thought away, but it's in my head now, it's taken root and will grow if I don't find a way to stop it in its tracks. I used to be good at pushing such destructive thoughts from my mind. But since the fire I can't stop myself imagining the worst and I'm finding it harder and harder to remain positive.

Ziggy whines, staring at me beseechingly with his big brown eyes. 'Oh God, Ziggy, I'm sorry,' I say, jumping down from the leather and chrome bar stool. 'Jay, where did you put Ziggy's food?'

'Hmmm,' he says, not looking up.

'Ziggy's food? Where is it?'

'Oh, in the top cupboard, by the sink.'

The units are handle-less and I press my palm against the cool gloss doors to open them. I empty a packet of dog food into Ziggy's bowl, trying to avoid his nose as he immediately starts to guzzle it.

'Right,' Jamie says, 'got this thing sussed now. We won't be in darkness again, my darling.' He grins at me, then the smile slips from his face. 'What's wrong?'

'Nothing.'

'Libby, you look terrified. What's the matter?'

'It's the door . . .'

I can tell he's forcing down a sigh. 'What about it?'

'It was open for ages, Jay. I don't know, I just feel unnerved by it.'

He doesn't tell me I'm being paranoid. He doesn't have to – it's written all over his face. Wordlessly he leaves the room and I stand with Ziggy, wondering if he's gone off in a huff, although that's not like Jamie. He's usually so patient. I try not to play out scenarios in my head of Jamie being struck over the head by a burglar. All I can hear are the snuffling noises of Ziggy wolfing down his food. Eventually Jamie walks back into the kitchen.

'I've been around the whole house to put your mind at rest. Nothing. There are no intruders. Statistically we're safer here than in Bath. Although –' his face breaks into a grin '– I found a few more stuffed animals. The Heywoods like their taxidermy.'

The stuffed animals seem at odds with the modern furnishings but I shrug, trying not to show how relieved I am that there is no madman lurking in the shadows. 'I know I'm being silly . . .'

He snakes a hand around my shoulders and pulls me into him, kissing my hair. 'I understand. It's that fight-or-flight thing, Libs. After the fire, your senses are on high alert. But you have to switch off, now. You have to stop seeing everything as a potential threat.

That's one of the reasons we came away. I just wish you'd see someone . . .'

He sounds like Sylvia. 'Jamie. We're not all like you. Or your mum. I didn't grow up having my own fucking therapist.'

He moves away, holding his hands up in surrender. 'I know . . . I know. It's not how you were brought up. You keep telling me. Which reminds me, I need to text Mum to let her know we've arrived safely.' He reaches into his back pocket to retrieve his phone and looks at the screen. His face falls. 'Great, no reception.' He goes to the fridge and opens it. 'Anyway, what are we going to cook up for dinner? There's a plethora of organic delights in here. They've spoilt us.'

I smile but I'm not really taking in what he's saying because another thought has entered my head. I've never shared it with him because if I did he would frog-march me to a therapist himself. But I can't stop replaying it in my mind anyhow.

What if the fire at the school wasn't an accident?

4

I wake up early on Sunday, a white light flooding the bedroom. I'm never going to get used to the lack of curtains. My paranoia of yesterday evening is forgotten in the security of the bright morning with the tweeting of birds and the gentle roar of the sea. I'd tossed and turned for ages last night, unused to the complete darkness and crushing silence. By the time we'd gone to bed there was no longer any moonlight filtering in – it was as dark as if I was closing my eyes. Even as a kid I had to have a night-light. I could sense, rather than see, Ziggy at the end of the bed and I'd strained my ears for any sound, but there was nothing apart from the wind and the distant roar of the sea. No road noise, no planes in the sky, no voices from neighbours, no indistinct music. The silence stretched on and on. Coupled with the darkness it felt oppressive, as though we were the only people left in the universe. I was relieved when dawn arrived.

Jamie is snoring gently beside me now, Ziggy slumbering on top of the duvet, his heavy body deadening my legs. I gently push him away with my feet. 'Ziggy,' I hiss, 'you shouldn't be on the bed.' We allow him at home, but it feels wrong here on Tara's pristine white duvet cover. He ignores me, only shifting his body enough to allow me to swing my legs out of bed.

Above the bed is a huge wedding photo of Tara and Philip. They look so in love, so handsome, her in a sweeping full-length gown, him in a dapper well-cut suit and ivory-silk tie. She's looking up at him with such love on her face, and he's smiling softly down at her. Did Jamie and I look like that when we got married? So devoted? They appear a lot younger here than they do in the newspaper; there is no evidence of grey in Philip's dark brown hair and Tara's complexion is flawless, her brown eyes larger in her slimmer face. I imagine them to be at least fifteen years older than us, which would make them around forty-four but they can't be more than our age in their wedding photo. I want to know more about Tara, this beautiful privileged woman in whose house I'm living.

I kiss the top of Ziggy's head fondly, then wrap my dressing gown around me and head into the bathroom without waking Jamie.

I go to the loo, glancing enviously at the roll-top bath, the shiny chrome taps and the shelves of extravagant scented candles on the wall above. I've always wanted one of those candles, but they are way out of my price range. I imagine Tara luxuriating in the bath filled with bubbles reading a book on mindfulness while the room is pervaded with its exquisite scent. I wash my hands, then reach out and lift one from the shelf and inhale deeply. I can smell the mandarin and lime. Excitement makes my heart pound. Would any-one notice if I took one? There are at least six of them. More than she needs. Surely she won't remember how many she bought and she can't be that bothered if she's keeping them in her holiday home? I glance towards the door nervously, as though expecting Tara to be standing there. I can just about see the four-poster bed. Jamie is still asleep, one arm flung over his eyes. I look down at the candle in my hand. It's stealing, whichever way I look at it. I put it back reluctantly.

I rootle around in the cupboard under the sink, not sure exactly what I'm looking for. Just being nosy, I guess. I find a bottle of Tom Ford perfume in a tur-quoise blue bottle. I remove the lid and spray the lemony fragrance onto my neck and wrists. This must be what Tara smells like. Expensive. I replace it, noticing a large wash bag pushed to the back of the cupboard. I'm just about to reach for it when I hear Jamie calling.

'Libs, are you all right?'

I close the cupboard hastily and return to the bed-room. Jamie is leaning on one elbow, Ziggy still asleep at the foot of the bed.

'Why do you look so guilty?' He's smiling. 'You've not been trying on Tara's clothes again, have you?'

I feel myself blushing. 'Blimey, Jay, I've just been for a wee.'

He stretches. 'I ache this morning. This bed is too soft.'

'You sound like Goldilocks. I'm going downstairs to

make a cup of tea,' I say, walking towards the door, slightly miffed that he'd been closer to the truth than he realised with his jibe about Tara's clothes.

The morning sun streams through the French windows, giving the living room a clean, fresh look. I don't want to go home, I think as I wander over to the fireplace to touch a tall, fluted glass vase on the mantelpiece, recoiling when my hand brushes against a puffin next to another scented candle. The stuffed animals give me the creeps; they're so real-looking yet so obviously devoid of life with their staring, dead eyes. I can't imagine Tara would like them much. They must be Philip's idea. The soft chalk paint on the walls, and the rugs, throws and cushions would be Tara's influence, I'm certain of it. A woman's touch. Maybe Philip feels he has to have the stuffed animals as a token of his country lifestyle. He probably hates them really. They don't fit in with this house at all.

I flop onto the white linen sofa; it's L-shaped and I stretch myself out along the chaise part, resting my head against the feather pillows. I examine the patterned scatter cushions and finger the dove-grey cashmere blanket thrown over the back, wondering where she got them from and whether I could emulate the look in my own flat. If only we had more money to update our home. It could do with repainting and our sofa is one of Sylvia's cast-offs, too big and old fashioned for our flat.

I must have dozed off because I'm woken by loud

rock music. I sit up with a start, my heart racing. The TV on the opposite wall is blaring and I glance around for Jamie, thinking he must have come down and turned it on. Then I see him rushing down the stairs in his boxer shorts and a T-shirt, his hair standing up on end, Ziggy at his heels.

'For fuck's sake, Libs, you don't need to put it on so loud!' He has to shout to be heard over the music.

'I . . . I didn't turn it on . . .' I stare at the screen, confused. A heavy-metal band is rocking on a live stage, sweat pouring down the lead singer's face. 'It came on by itself.'

He's frowning as he wanders over to the TV. 'Where's the remote?' he shouts.

'I don't know. I didn't turn it on, like I've already said,' I snap. He knows how much I hate loud music.

It's so deafening that I have to leave the room. I go into the kitchen, my body trembling, and wrap my dressing gown further around my body as though it's soundproof. How did the TV come on by itself?

I feed Ziggy and make a cup of tea. It's easy with no kettle to boil – they have one of those instant boiling taps next to the sink. I can still hear the music from the next room so I wrestle open the bifold door and wander into the garden, the stone slabs cold beneath my bare feet. From outside I can see Jamie opening and closing drawers in the television cabinet, trying to find a way to turn the TV down. At least we don't have neighbours to complain about the noise. Ziggy seems unperturbed by the disturbance and joins me in the garden. 'It's all right,' I say, bending down to throw my good arm around his neck. He looks longingly at the lawn. 'Go on, it's OK,' I say, standing up again and watching as he trots across the dewy grass. I wander to the edge of the paving slabs and then stop. There are footprints on the lawn. Large. Man-sized. I swivel around to see if the side gate is closed. I remember noting that it was closed when we arrived yesterday as I wanted the garden to be secure for Ziggy. Now it's wide open, swinging in the breeze. I think again of the open front door yesterday and goose bumps pop up along my arms.

'Libs,' says Jamie for the umpteenth time as we stroll along the beach later that day, 'please stop being paranoid. I've told you . . .'

Blackened seaweed crunches underfoot. The beach is almost deserted, just the occasional dog-walker ambling past. Ziggy runs ahead of us, his tongue hanging out as he prances along the shoreline, getting his paws wet. It's windy and I've got a hat pressed onto my head. It feels heavy under the weight of its enormous bobble.

'Told me what? That those footprints could have been there for ages? I doubt that. It *has* rained in the last few days, you know. And what about the gate? And the TV?'

He sighs. 'The TV was on a timer. I've managed to

work it out now. I don't know why the volume was turned up so high. Maybe Philip and Tara like loud rock music.'

'They don't seem the type.'

Jamie stops walking and releases my hand. 'How do you know if they're the type? You don't know them. You have no idea who they are.'

I feel close to tears. 'What do you mean I have no idea? I know a lot about them already. I know they like nice things, they do a lot of work for charity, Philip is a consultant. A surgeon. Tara is . . . well, she's a home-maker. And a mother. She's beautiful and caring. They have a child who is seriously ill . . .'

'Libby,' Jamie says, gently coming towards me, 'I know you've spoken to him on the phone, seen their photos, rummaged through their belongings, read about him in the newspapers and we're staying in their home. But they're strangers.'

'I know that.'

'Good. Because they probably aren't perfect, you know. They still shit and piss like the rest of us.'

I push him away. 'Urgh, Jay, don't be crude.'

'I'm just saying. They're only human. Don't put them on a pedestal just because they're stinking rich.'

He's right, that's exactly what I've been doing. I've always been impressed by people who are high-fliers, who have luxury lifestyles, who have class. Maybe it's because I grew up with parents who were always scrabbling around for cash, or, in my mum's case, working extra cleaning jobs just to make ends meet. She was always talking about 'Mrs Haughton from the Big House' in awed tones, as though she considered her better than us just because she lived in a five-bedroom detached home. I take Jamie's hand silently and he holds eye contact for a fraction too long, but he doesn't say anything else about it. Instead we paddle in the sea with our trousers rolled up, then search for crabs in the rock pools.

When we get back to the house, windswept, with sand in our hair and on our skin, we tumble into the bedroom, shedding our clothes as we both head towards the walk-in shower, me laughing as Jamie grabs me around the waist and kisses my neck. I know he's trying to take my mind off my anxiety. It's what he does. What he's been doing ever since the miscarriage. Always trying to fix me.

I was devastated when we lost the baby. I think everybody was surprised by how badly I took the news. 'It was just cells,' Sylvia said. 'No bigger than a peanut.' 'You lost it doing a brave, selfless thing,' urged Cara. 'It's nature's way of telling you that something was wrong with the baby,' insisted Jamie's older sister, Florrie.

Jamie had never seen me collapse so emotionally before. He'd always admired my independence, he said. My strength. He loved to hear how I'd pulled myself from 'the gutter', as he called it, to get an education, to follow my dream of becoming a teacher. How I'd given everything up to go travelling to Thailand by myself after my parents died. But children are my Achilles heel. I love them. I love being a teacher to them and I so desperately want to be a mother to my own.

And now things are different between us. Jamie no longer sees me in the same light, I can tell. He's more protective. As far as he's concerned I'm now a frangible being with my broken arm and my empty womb. I get palpitations at loud noises when I never did before. I'm nervy, paranoid. Scared. I feel like I'm losing control, and it's turned my carefully orchestrated world upside down. The world I worked so hard to create.

5

There is a ringing in my ear. It's deafening, grating and monotone like a pneumatic drill, familiar – a fire alarm. Panic consumes me, pinning me down, crushing my chest. *Fire!* I need to escape. A cold sweat breaks out all over my body. I'm in the hostel. It's too hot. The darkness closing in, trapping me. I can hear the sound of running feet, shouts in a language I can't understand. Screaming. Smoke filling my nostrils and my lungs so that I can't breathe. I can feel arms around me, I try to shake them away. 'Get off! Get off!'

'Libby. It's OK . . . shh, wake up.'

My eyes snap open to see Jamie staring down at me, his face crumpled with concern, his hands on my shoulders. I'm on the sofa. In the Hideaway. I'm safe . . . I'm safe. I must have fallen asleep . . . but the noise, I can still hear it.

'It's just the smoke alarm,' says Jamie as if reading my mind. 'It's gone off in the kitchen. I was making some toast.' He smiles apologetically. 'I wanted some of their fancy pâté. But the alarm's too bloody sensitive. It will stop in a minute. I've pressed the button . . .' I pull away from his grasp and he steps back as though I've bitten him. 'You were having a nightmare. I was trying to wake you up.'

I shift my weight so that I'm sitting upright. 'I thought . . .' The noise stops and immediately my heart rate slows, even though I can still hear a faint ringing in my ears.

Jamie comes to sit next to me but doesn't touch me. I can see two overdone pieces of toast on a plate on the coffee table, the edges black.

'Libs, you're trembling . . .'

I have a nasty taste in my mouth and my top is clinging to me underneath my dressing gown, damp with sweat. 'I thought I was at the hostel,' I say, disorientated. I scan the room just to make sure I really am at the Hideaway and not in Thailand. Tara smiles down at me from the black-and-white canvas on the opposite wall, above the TV. Seeing her photo roots me in the present.

My chin quivers. I don't want to cry.

Jamie notices and pulls me into his arms. 'Oh, babe.' *Babe.* He hasn't called me that in years.

'It felt so real,' I whisper into his shoulder, my throat sore as if smoke really has been suffocating me. I pull away from him and get up, fumbling at my neckline. I can't breathe properly.

I walk shakily over to the French doors, turning the key to open one side and stand under the starless sky, cradling my broken arm. I've taken the sling off but the cast feels heavy. I flex my fingers. I can't wait to get the bloody thing off.

It's so dark outside, the kind of night sky you only

really see in the countryside, deep and thick and never-ending, untainted by pollution and street lamps. I take deep gasps of fresh air. I can taste the salt on my tongue, hear the roar of the waves from the sea below. Standing here like this, in almost total darkness, makes me realise afresh how remote we are. How far from civilisation. I suddenly yearn for our busy Bath street with all the people noisily going about their daily lives. It's too silent out here. Too still.

'You never talk about it. What happened in Thailand.' Jamie's voice makes me jump. I turn to see him standing in the doorway, back-lit from the muted living-room lights. Jamie had spent ages faffing with the remote to get the ambience just right.

'It's not something I want to relive,' I say.

He doesn't step into the garden. 'But you do. Relive it, I mean. You relived it just now. And you probably did when the school caught fire.'

'I just want to forget about it. To bury it. It's my way of coping.'

I've never really told him about what happened. To me. To Karen. He knows my friend died. He knows I was lucky to escape. It makes me worry, sometimes, the things I haven't told him. Because we shouldn't keep secrets from each other. Yet we do. I know that he's keeping things from me too. The way he felt about Hannah, for example. The loan he got from his mother that he assumes I don't know about. And that's fine. I understand. Because we love each other and we have to trust one another. I don't go in for all this therapy malarkey. I will never sit on a couch in a psychiatrist's office unloading myself when they ask, 'And how does that make you feel?' That just isn't me. As far as I'm concerned the past is the past. And it should stay there.

When I awake the next morning after a restless sleep, Jamie announces we should go out for the day. He doesn't have to say it but I know he wants to get me out of the house. Me freaking out over the smoke alarm last night was probably the last straw.

'We could go to St Mawes and see the castle? It was built by Henry VIII. Meant to be worth seeing,' he says over breakfast. 'Or do you fancy the lighthouse at Lizard Point?' He has a map spread out on the kitchen island and he's perusing it intently as he spoons Shreddies into his mouth. It always makes me smile how much he loves what I call kids' cereal. Frosties are a firm favourite of his too. He never goes anywhere without bringing his own.

'How far away is the lighthouse?'

'Should be an hour, max.'

I don't relish the thought of being cooped up in the car for that long. I can't shake the nausea I've been experiencing since last night, but I'd hate to burst his bubble. I'd rather visit the lighthouse instead of traipsing around a damp, crumbling castle. And it would be good for me to get out of the house, however much I love it.

We debate whether to take Ziggy but decide against it, although I feel a pang of guilt as he observes us with his big brown eyes as we're leaving. 'We won't be long, Zigs,' says Jamie. I blow the dog a kiss before Jamie closes the door. His expression is unsure as he faces me. 'Do you think he'll be OK? What if he shits on the furniture or something?'

'He *is* house-trained,' I laugh.

Jamie hovers by the door. 'I don't feel comfortable leaving him, Libs.' He returns the key to the lock and the door swings open again. Ziggy bounds towards us.

I roll my eyes in mock exasperation. 'Fine, but he'll have to stay in the car while we visit the lighthouse. Then we can take him for a long walk after.' Jamie darts back into the house to get the dog lead. 'And don't forget his water bowl,' I call after him as I bend down to stop Ziggy bolting.

It's colder than it was the day we arrived, with a slate-grey sky and an icy wind coming off the sea. I wrap my scarf further around my neck as Jamie lets Ziggy into the back seat. 'Don't put the roof down,' I say in a warning tone as I get into the passenger side. 'I'm freezing and I can't even put my coat on properly with this sling.'

'I wasn't going to put the roof down,' he says mildly, but darts a sideways look at me, as though assessing my mood. I want to scream at him: Stop walking on fucking eggshells around me! But I can't because I know it's coming from a place of love. I just hate being treated like some damsel in distress. I know I'm not helping myself with my fears that something terrible is about to happen, and I vow, as the car lumbers along the narrow lanes, to make an effort to pull myself together. To get a hold on these paranoid thoughts. I want Jamie to see me as the strong, independent woman he fell in love with. The woman who didn't take any shit. The woman who his mother once described, disparagingly, as 'quite feisty' after a heated discussion with Katie about the education system.

We don't speak. I stare out of the window as the country lanes rush by in flashes of green and grey. Over in the distant fields I spot sheep, their cotton-wool coats against the lush grass reminding me of a child's drawing. Jamie turns the radio up but he doesn't sing along.

Eventually he takes a right turn and I spot the light-house adjoined to an array of squat white buildings, their windowsills painted a fresh green. The car lurches over the bumpy tarmac, making me feel even more nauseous, and Jamie reverses into a space. 'Right,' he says, turning off the engine. 'Lighthouse first?'

'I'm dying for a Starbucks,' I admit.

He grins. 'No Starbucks here, I don't think. But we can try the café afterwards.'

'Yes, but will they do a caramel macchiato? I can't drink coffee unless it's syruped up, you know that.'

He squeezes my thigh. 'I'll do my best,' he promises, the tension between us forgotten. He swivels in his seat to address Ziggy. 'And when we come back we'll take you for a long walk, I promise.'

We amble around the lighthouse with the tour guide, a young, pretty girl with red corkscrew curls called Ruth. I feel claustrophobic in the small, circular room with nineteen other people. The car sickness still hasn't left me and the man standing next to me smells unclean. Jamie is fascinated as Ruth explains the history of the lighthouse, showing us to the top via a rickety staircase to see the panoramic sea views. I try to appear enthusiastic but I feel like I'm at work and this is one of our many school trips.

Eventually we are released back outside and I take deep lungfuls of the fresh sea air, trying to cleanse my system of the smell of unwashed bodies and old dusty memorabilia. My sense of smell is more acute than normal: the damp grass, the sea air, the coffee from the nearby café, the fruity shampoo of a passing woman. The only other time my sense of smell was this good was when I was pregnant. Could I be again? I rub my stomach instinctively, deep down knowing it would be unlikely. Before Cornwall, Jamie and I had had sex just once. I know it only takes one time for it to happen but I can't be that lucky.

I wander onto the grass, deep in thought, before realising that Jamie isn't with me. I turn to see him hanging about in the arched doorway of the lighthouse, in deep conversation with Ruth. He's listening closely as she talks, his eyebrows knitted together and a look of intense concentration on his face. He must say something funny because she throws back her head in laughter and touches his arm, running her fingers down his wool coat for longer than is strictly necessary. She has to be nearly ten years his junior but it's obvious she fancies him – the studious types always do. He's got that foppish, geeky look about him that some women – including me – find sexy, like a blonder, younger Jarvis Cocker. He's wearing a long coat over his scruffy jeans and a red scarf. He looks like a professor. Or a mature student.

I tear my eyes from them and begin to walk slowly towards the café, knowing that Jamie will eventually catch up with me. When he does he's breathless and his cheeks are flushed.

'Do you know,' he says, talking quickly in his excitement, taking my good arm and linking it through his, 'before they switched over to the computer system the lighthouse had to be manned by three men.'

'No, I didn't know that.' Jamie is always spouting random, often useless, facts.

'Years ago it was only two. But that changed. And why?'

I shrug.

'Come on, Libs. Humour me.'

I sigh. 'OK, why?'

I can see him mentally rubbing his hands with glee. 'Well, according to Ruth, a long time ago on a remote island off Wales, one of the two men on duty died of a heart attack or something. Anyway the other was left with the dead body, on his own. For months.'

By now we've bypassed the café, much to my dismay, reaching the cliff's edge, and I stop to ferret in my bag for my phone so that I can take a photograph of the bay below. The sky is overcast and the wind ruffles our hair and tugs the hems of our coats as though trying to take our attention away from the breathtaking views. The water is an angry-looking navy blue and the white frothy spray leaps off the rocks and smashes against the ragged shoreline. The noise of the wind mixed with the roar of the sea is deafening and we almost have to shout to make ourselves heard.

'He was worried the police would think he'd killed the man, so he kept his body as evidence and hung it out of the window,' Jamie continues.

'Urgh, Jamie! Why would he have to hang his friend's dead body out of the window?'

'Because there was no room in the lighthouse. It was too small. And the bloke was dead, Libs. He'd started to decay, to smell. Here, let me do that,' he says, taking the phone from my hand when he sees I'm having trouble.

I shudder. 'Thanks.' I wrinkle up my nose. The smell in the air is pungent; sea salt and fish. 'How did he hang him outside?' I ask. I can't help but feel curious even though I should know better than to encourage Jamie.

He beams, clearly enjoying himself as he imparts this piece of historical gossip. 'Well, he made a make-shift coffin, put his dead friend inside and hung it from the lighthouse.' He's always had a morbid fascination with the weird and wonderful. He's a regular subscriber to the *Fortean Times*. 'But the weather conditions broke the coffin apart, so eventually the man was left hanging there, decaying, banging against the window as though beckoning to his friend. Can you imagine that? Seeing your friend slowly rotting away . . .'

My stomach turns. 'All right, Jay. I get the picture. Why didn't the man get help?'

He rolls his eyes as if it's obvious. 'Because he couldn't leave the lighthouse unmanned, could he? He sent distress signals but nobody could come for months. The sight of his dead friend hanging there sent him quite mad, apparently.'

'Not surprised. Can we change the subject now?' I ask.

He grins at me, his eyes twinkling. 'Sure.'

'Is that what Ruth was talking to you about? While she was laughing at your jokes and generally being a flirt?' It slips out and I notice the ripple of surprise on Jamie's face.

He shrugs, good-naturedly. 'I've still got it,' he winks at me. 'What can I say?'

I push his arm playfully. 'Oh, you love it,' I laugh. 'As long as you remember you're mine.'

'How could I forget?'

We walk to the top of the grassy incline to get a better view of the sea and the jagged rocks below. The land juts out beneath us in a zig-zag shape. 'Is that a seal?' I say, nudging Jamie and pointing to a dark patch of sea where something sticks up from the water.

'Nah, just a rock,' says Jamie, squinting. He holds up my phone to take a few more shots. I'm aware of a surge of tourists chatting in French behind me. Over Jamie's shoulder I notice a man, perhaps in his late thirties, wearing an oversized grey fleece with a high collar that obscures his chin and a black beanie pushed down over his head. It reminds me of the tea cosy Mum used when I was a child. He has a camera with a zoom lens swinging from his neck, and a face as stormy as the sea below. There is something familiar about him. Now he has his camera angled in Jamie's direction, and he keeps lifting it to his eyes, as if he's paparazzi. Every time Jamie moves, so does the man – and his camera. Jamie's oblivious, filling me in on a documentary on seals that he'd seen last night after I went to bed. Something about the man is bothering me. Is he trying to take a photo of me? Of Jamie? I have a fleeting, paranoid thought that he's police, or a private detective, and my palms sweat. I gently steer Jamie further up the hill in an effort to make us inconspicuous among the throng of tourists.

I glance back at the café longingly. I'm desperate for caffeine but we can't stop now. I scan the faces behind me for the man and his camera. I can just about see his beanie over the shoulder of a tall woman. Is his focus no longer on us? Maybe he wasn't aiming his camera at us after all. I turn back to Jamie, relieved. Of course he's not some private detective. Who would even think about hiring one? And why?'

I'm just about to ask Jamie if we can go back and grab

a coffee when I hear him cry out and he stumbles into my side, knocking me forwards. It happens so quickly, I lose my footing on the uneven ground and trip. I'm so intent on trying to protect my broken arm that I find myself careering down the hill towards the cliff's edge. Blood pounds in my ears as I imagine plummeting onto the rocks below but I can't stop myself; it's like I'm on a treadmill and I can't get off. I hear somebody scream and I'm not sure if it's me. Then the next thing I know I'm being pulled backwards by the scarf around my neck and I feel familiar hands grabbing my waist.

'It's OK, Libs, I've got you,' says Jamie, his voice breathless with fear. 'I've got you.'

We're on the lip of ground before the land falls away; if I'd gone any further it would have been too late. My legs are weak and my throat hurts where Jamie has pulled the scarf. I let him lead me back up the hill so that we are safely on the pavement, then we sink to the ground together, like we are conjoined. I'm trembling all over. Horrified tourists gather around us, asking if I'm OK. An older man returns from the nearby café and thrusts a cup of tea wordlessly into my hands. I take it gratefully, my teeth chattering as I stammer out a thank you. His kindness, along with the shock, makes my eyes fill up.

'My God, Libs, you nearly went over the edge,' Jamie says, a tremor in his voice. 'I'm so sorry. I felt a shove in my back, pushing me into you.' He looks distraught.

'Don't worry, I don't think you were trying to kill

me.' I try to smile as I sip my tea, warming my hands against the cup.

'Not funny,' but he gives me a watered-down grin. 'Shit, that was scary.'

The tourists begin to disperse now they can see we're unharmed.

'Did you see who pushed you?' I say, feeling sick.

He frowns. 'Not really. A guy was standing by me. Big fella, broad, tall. But I'm not sure if it was him.'

'Was he wearing a beanie?'

Jamie frowns. 'I'm not sure. Why?'

'Before you fell into me I noticed a guy. He had a camera around his neck and he was taking photos.'

'So?'

'Of you. He had his camera trained on you, Jay.'

He shuffles and looks uncomfortable, his eyes sliding away from mine. 'Why would he be doing that?' he mumbles.

I let a beat or two pass before saying, 'I don't know.' I sigh and hand him my cup. He stands up and helps me to my feet.

'Look, Libs, it was an accident. There were too many of us standing together. You're not telling me you think this bloke did it on purpose, are you?'

I stare at the ground, my mind racing. 'I'm not sure. No, I don't think so. It's just . . . this guy was interested in you.'

Jamie smirks. 'Maybe he fancied me. Like Ruth, huh?' I can't help but laugh. 'Don't be an idiot.'

He wraps his arms around me. 'You feel freezing. Come on, let's go and get something to eat to warm you up. Then we'd better get back to Ziggy.'

I nod and allow him to guide me towards the café. But I feel uneasy as I scan the crowds and the stragglers who are making their way towards the lighthouse and the car park. It doesn't matter what Jamie says. I know I'm not being paranoid. There was something strange about that man and the interest he'd taken in my husband.

6

It's dusk by the time we get back to the Hideaway. From the lane I can see that the security lights have come on in the back garden, bleaching the lawn and throwing shadows over the trees and bushes so that they look as though they have been painted black.

Why are the lights on?

Jamie steers the car into the driveway, and immediately the front security lights come on. He switches the engine off and turns to me.

'Are you OK?' he asks when he sees I'm not making any effort to get out of the car.

'The lights are on in the back garden. I saw them from the lane . . .'

His brows knit together. I wonder if he's going to criticise me, tell me I'm being skittish. But he doesn't. 'Probably a cat or something,' he says. He opens the car door and Ziggy jumps out, kicking up the gravel as he scampers towards the house.

I follow, trying to ignore the sinking feeling I have inside. I pull my coat further around my body to stop the wind yanking at the fabric and look around me; at the bushes and trees that encircle the property, at the high walls. Was somebody in the garden? I go to the gate, the only access to the back, running my fingers along the rough wood as though I'm a forensic scientist. There is no lock. Somebody could easily have got in. Or come from the beach? I suddenly feel nauseous and can't work out if it's car sickness or worry.

'What are you looking for?' Jamie's by my shoulder.

I shrug. 'I have no idea. Evidence, I suppose . . .'

Jamie snorts with laughter. 'Evidence. What are you, Miss Marple? There hasn't been a bloody murder, Libs.' He sounds so unconcerned I find myself believing that there is nothing to worry about. He takes my hand, giving it a reassuring squeeze. 'Come on, let's go around the back and then you can see for yourself. Mum's got security lights in her garden and they're always coming on; it's usually because of the neighbours' cats.' He's talking in that fake jovial voice again, as though I'm an elderly person or a child that needs chivvying along. He leads me around to the back of the house, now in total darkness, the lights only coming on as we approach the bifold doors. He pulls the key from his pocket and unlocks them, sliding them open and going into the kitchen. I stay where I am. From here I can see the sea, grey and angry as it drains the last of the light. Everything looks a little drab in the twilight. I scan the garden, the rattan furniture, the patio. Nothing seems out of place. I wish, not for the first time, that the next house wasn't so far away.

I can see that Jamie is making us a cup of tea from the tap, the steam visible in the cool air. He looks so at home, so relaxed in the Heywoods' state-of-the-art kitchen. Ziggy is by Jamie's side, tapping his leg with his paw, wanting his tea.

I inhale deeply. Everything is as it should be. The light was set off by a cat, not an intruder. No more, no less. *Stop overthinking it, Libby.*

The next morning we are strolling along the beach, Ziggy at our feet, discussing Jamie's younger sister, Katie, who is having boyfriend troubles yet again. Jamie is the middle child of three, the only son, and his sisters are always giving him grief in one way or another; one minute they are overly protective and the next they are leaning on him when they're going through rough patches with the various men in their lives.

Jamie's father died when he was at university, before he met me. He'd been with Hannah then, his childhood sweetheart. The girl whose heart he'd broken, so his mother is constantly telling me. I sense Sylvia wishes her only son had married Hannah instead of me, which she proves by inviting Hannah – now a single mother with a little boy – over at every available opportunity, as if she is one of the family and not some ex of Jamie's from ten years ago. The fact that she's been Katie's best friend since they were about seven doesn't help.

Katie has never taken to me. I can tell by the way she speaks to me, cutting and disinterested; the way her eyes follow me around a room, silent and disapproving.

I try not to let it bother me, I know Jamie loves me, that any feelings he might have had for Hannah have stayed firmly in the past. And I feel sorry for her, she's had a rough time; she married a man who was a player, walking out on her when she was pregnant. She's quiet, with large, watchful eyes. It's obvious she still adores Jamie; it's written all over her face every time she looks at him. Sometimes, when I spot Jamie and Hannah together at gatherings, her four-year-old, Felix, wedged between them so that they look like a family unit, I experience a pang of insecurity and hurt that Sylvia can be so insensitive. It doesn't help that they all live down the road from us; sometimes the sheer force of their collective personalities and histories can be stifling. I can't help but feel an outsider. I don't have my own close-knit group. Jamie is all I've got.

But in Cornwall we are away from all that. It's just me and Jamie. I can breathe again.

It has rained in the night and the sand is still so damp that our trainers leave prints in our wake. We amble along hand in hand, Ziggy lolloping in front of us. The rear of the Hideaway is visible from the beach, although it's so high up that you have to navigate about a hundred steps cut into the rock face to reach our garden from here. I glance up towards the house and freeze, dropping Jamie's hand. My heart quickens. There's a man standing there. In our garden. Watching us.

'Jamie!' He's a little way ahead now, oblivious that I'm no longer by his side.

He turns towards me and retraces his steps. 'What's wrong?'

'There's someone in our garden. Up there, look!' The man has a camera around his neck. He holds it up to his face. I feel a burst of anger. How dare he!

Jamie looks up and squints. 'What the . . .?' He frowns. 'Who the fuck is that?'

The beanie. The camera. I realise with a jolt who it is. 'It's the man from yesterday!'

Jamie sprints towards the steps, his feet kicking up wet sand. 'Hey!' he yells, although his voice is snatched by the wind and it's doubtful the man will be able to hear him from this distance in any case.

'Jamie!' I call after him. 'Don't! Come back!' I'm unsure what to do. Should I ring someone? I fish my phone out of my pocket. But of course, there is no signal down here on the beach. Who would I call anyway? Who can help us? I lean down to hug Ziggy's neck. He's watchful, his ears forward, alert. The man, realising that Jamie is running towards him, suddenly backs away out of view. What if he attacks Jamie when he reaches the top?

Ziggy suddenly leaps into action, charging after Jamie, making light work of the steps so that he's beside him within seconds. I feel better knowing that Jamie has the dog with him. Ziggy is placid but he'd attack if Jamie was in trouble. They disappear into the garden.

I stand, rooted to the spot, mumbling a prayer to a God I'm not sure I believe in; *please God, please keep Jamie safe*. I'm too scared to move. So much for being a hero-ine, the irony. I feel exposed, standing on the empty beach by myself, with just the backs of a few houses high up on the hilltop for company. The imprint of Ziggy's paw marks dotted between Jamie's footprints is the only sign that I haven't been alone. Everything is too quiet, just the sound of the waves brushing the shoreline.

Eventually, after what seems like hours but can only have been five minutes at the most, Jamie reappears. He makes his way down the steps, Ziggy barking behind him, and I dart across the beach to meet them.

'Are you OK? Was it the same man as yesterday?' I rush into his arms and he kisses the top of my head. 'I was really worried.'

'You shouldn't be running with your broken arm,' he admonishes into my hair. 'By the time we reached the top he'd gone. I checked the grounds, nothing. He hasn't tried to break in or anything. I reckon it was a tourist, chancing his luck. The views *are* spectacular.' I can feel him grinning against my head.

I pull away. 'Why would it have been a tourist? It's too remote here for tourists, surely? It's got to be the same guy as yesterday. He was wearing the same hat.'

'Lots of people wear beanies, Libs . . .'

'Yes . . . but . . .'

He frowns. 'And *we're* tourists. Anyway, he might have driven past and wanted a better view. I don't know. But there's no sign of him now.'

'He can't have just disappeared! Where would he have gone? There isn't another house for at least a quarter of a mile. You would have seen him. Maybe he's still there, lurking in the bushes . . .' My voice rises with each word.

Jamie shakes his head and holds up his hand to stop my tirade. 'He might have been in a car and thought the place was empty . . .'

'But our car is parked in the driveway. Listen, Jay, if it was the same man who pushed you yesterday . . .'

'It can't have been.' He sounds calm but I notice a pulse throbbing in his jaw. 'Lizard Point is miles away from here. And nobody pushed me . . .'

'You said you felt a shove.'

'Yes, I did. There was a crowd. We were all standing close together. I don't think anybody deliberately tried to hurt me.' He has pity in his eyes as he looks down at me. 'I know why you're thinking this, Libs. I understand.'

I push him away. 'Please don't tell me you think this is all down to PTSD again, Jay!' I fling my arms up, exasperated, and then wince in pain.

'You should be wearing your sling.'

'I don't want to. And you're changing the subject . . .'

'There's nothing to worry about.' His tone is final.

I want to say more, so much more, but I'm aware I'll just sound like a nagging, neurotic wife so I keep my mouth shut as I shadow Jamie through the garden and into the house. Even though Jamie doesn't say it, I can sense he's disappointed that my neurosis since the fire hasn't stayed behind in Bath but has followed us on holiday. He was hoping this break would be a therapy of sorts. And maybe this *is* all down to post-traumatic stress. Maybe I am imagining that it's the same man from yesterday. I don't know what to think.

I'm not normally an edgy person. I've always thought of myself as a risk-taker, driven, independent. Capable.

I didn't have the best childhood. The truth is, my father was an alcoholic. He'd always had a problem with drinking, preferring to spend most evenings down the pub, frittering away my mother's hard-earned cash. I'd sit with her in front of the television in our sparsely furnished living room, eating meat pie and chips off trays on our laps while we both pretended we weren't waiting on tenterhooks for him to come bursting through the door, unnaturally jolly and smelling of booze and fags.

Then, when I was fourteen, Mum died and everything was just that little bit worse. My grief-stricken father stopped working altogether and I had to support us both with my meagre earnings from weekend jobs. When the drink eventually killed him I left it all behind to go travelling alone. All I had wanted was to get as far away from Yorkshire, my village and my old existence as possible.

When I returned from Thailand after the hostel fire, I moved to Middlesex and worked hard to get my PGCE, funding myself by stacking shelves in supermarkets and pulling pints behind the bar. Anything to have a better life than the one fate had dealt me, and determined not to end up like my put-upon mother.

What would she think of where I've ended up? I like to imagine she would be proud of me.

I hardly ever talk about that time. Jamie doesn't know the half of it. He doesn't need to. It would be too depressing for him to hear about my childhood, so different from his. He probably wouldn't understand. How could he?

I lost touch with everyone the day I took that flight to Thailand nine years ago. A fresh start.

By the time I met Jamie in a pub in Bath when I was nearly twenty-five, I felt I'd already lived a long life. I'd recently moved to the area after getting a teaching job and I hardly knew anybody. I'd stood at the bar with my colleague, Cara, scowling at any man who dared look in my direction, barriers firmly up, when Jamie came over and asked to buy me a drink. He wasn't put off by my surliness, and with his floppy blond hair and kind eyes he reminded me a little of my first love. Jamie later told me he saw straight through my no-nonsense attitude to the scared little girl underneath. 'You looked so fragile, trying to make out that you didn't give a shit, that I wanted to protect you,' he said.

I'd found his confidence, his optimism, reassuring. Jamie Hall, with the large, boisterous, bickering family in that sprawling house, with his private-school education. Such a different life to the one I'd had. Everything began to fall into place. Despite my upbringing I was one of the lucky ones. I was a survivor.

7

I can feel Jamie's eyes boring into me as I dry the wet sand off Ziggy's paws with one of the old towels we'd brought with us. I try not to look at him, concentrating instead on dealing with the dog.

Eventually I can bear it no longer. I snap my head up. 'What?'

'You,' says Jamie. His arms are folded across his chest, his jaw set as though preparing himself for a fight. He's still wearing his coat. He leans against the kitchen island. 'This can't go on. I'm going to speak to Mum. Get her to recommend a therapist.'

'I don't want you talking to your bloody mother about me,' I insist, releasing Ziggy and standing up. The thought of Sylvia knowing about my problems and using it against me later on makes my blood boil. I brush past him to hang the wet towel over the radiator.

'Libby,' he begins, with that determined look on his face I know so well, 'something isn't right with you. I know I'm not a shrink. But you're seeing danger everywhere – you have been since the fire. Take that man today. It could have been anyone, yet you're assuming it's the same guy that was at Lizard Point yesterday.

The security light is on in the back garden and you automatically believe there's an intruder . . .'

'But someone *was* in our garden!' I interject. 'Today. That person could have been there yesterday too.'

He raises his hand. 'I know, but this house is usually empty. The man ran away as soon as he saw us. It doesn't have to mean anything sinister. He was just using the garden to get a better look at the beach.'

Or at us?

Jamie's not convincing me but I can't say anything without sounding paranoid. Instead I shrug off my coat and drape it over the back of one of the kitchen chairs.

'Please.' He comes towards me. His cheeks are still red from our walk. He places a hand on mine. It feels cold. 'I want you to relax and enjoy this holiday. God knows, we both need it.'

I feel a lurch of guilt. The miscarriage affected him too, yet all the sympathy went to me and Jamie never complained. 'I'm sorry,' I mumble. 'I hate feeling like this.'

'I can understand exactly why you're feeling this way. But please let someone help you . . .' He means his bloody mother. I bite my lip so hard I can taste the metallic tang of blood. He's a good man. The best. He truly cares – about me, about his family, even though there are times when I wish he had more backbone when it came to his demanding mother.

'Maybe it was too soon to come away,' I say, going over to the hot tap. I retrieve two cups from the overhead cupboard. 'Do you want a cup of tea?'

'Please.' He watches me in silence for a few moments as I place teabags in the mugs and turn on the tap. Then he goes to the fridge for the milk. He places it on the counter wordlessly.

'Thanks.' I smile up at him. His eyes are still heavy with concern. The silence between us is starting to feel uncomfortable. 'Maybe it's too remote here and it's making me feel jittery. I don't know . . .' I say, handing him the mug. I can't bear to look him in the eye, to see the disappointment on his face. Jamie's more relaxed than I've seen him in ages and here I am, ruining our holiday. Outside I can hear the crash of the waves, the squawk of seagulls.

I can hear his disappointment when he says, 'But you can't let that man make you feel like that, Libs.'

I shake my head. 'I know. I'm sorry. I'm ruining it for you,' I say in a small voice.

'You'll never ruin anything for me. I love you. And we have Ziggy here with us. He'll protect us.' He chuckles. 'His bark sounds worse than his bite anyway. He'll scare away any intruder.'

I smile tightly.

'And haven't you noticed? This place is like Fort Knox.' He sounds like I do when I'm trying to reassure one of the children in my class that monsters or vampires don't really exist. 'The Heywoods are obviously security savvy. Look, by the door, there's even a camera. You can see anyone who might be lurking outside. Not –' he adds hurriedly when he notices the horror that must be evident on my face '– that there is anyone lurking outside.' My eyes dart to the security screen that Jamie's talking about. It's divided in half, one camera trained onto the front driveway and the other onto the back garden. But there are areas where it won't have access; all those hidden crevices and dark corners. I've noticed the camera before but if anything it makes me feel more nervous. What would I do if I did notice somebody trying to break in? The phone reception is sketchy here and I've not seen any landline phones.

'Sweetheart,' says Jamie, 'if you really can't relax here – and after all that's one of the reasons why we came – then we should go home.'

'But the Heywoods . . .'

'Sod the Heywoods. They'll have to find somewhere else to stay. You're more important to me, Libs.'

I think of Philip and Tara and their seriously ill daughter. I can't do it to them. And for what? Because a man was bird-watching on the premises when he shouldn't have been? It's very unlikely to be the same man from Lizard Point the day before. They just had a similar style hat on, that's all. I'm being ridiculous. I can't ruin this holiday. I love it here, and so does Jamie.

'It's fine. Maybe I'll talk to someone when we get home. Get some counselling or something.' I smile non-committally, knowing, deep down, that it will never happen. I grew up in a family where nobody aired their dirty linen in public. My mum was of the old-school mentality, her mantra being 'put up or shut up'. Which she did, never complaining about her lot in life or the throbbing pain in her leg and then her chest as the thrombosis travelled to her lungs and killed her. Jamie's mother, on the other hand, thinks it's much healthier to express every feeling she has, which she does, frequently.

'I'm not going to let anything bad happen to you, I promise,' Jamie says seriously. I glance at his long, rangy frame, at his skinny but toned arms protruding from his T-shirt. He isn't exactly tough-looking.

He follows my gaze. 'All right,' he laughs, flexing his bicep, 'I know I'm not exactly Arnie.'

'"I like you just the way you are,"' I say, quoting his favourite film, *Blade Runner*. It's one of our things: our special sayings from the films we both love, that are important to us. He'd taken me to see the director's cut after I told him I didn't like science-fiction. He was determined to change my mind. And he did.

'Right!' He leaps up from the sofa, his mood brighter, more hopeful after our little talk. 'I'm going to get my laptop and do a bit of work. It looks like it's going to rain so shall we stay in tonight?'

I glance out of the doors; the sky's grey, the clouds bunched together in mutiny. We've stayed in all three nights we've been here. Usually I love it, relaxing in the luxurious surroundings, eating off the pristine dining table that can easily seat ten, sipping wine from the chiller cabinet while darkness falls outside, turning the windows opaque and making me feel as though there is nobody

73

else in the world but us. But for once I fancy going out somewhere. 'We could drive to Portscatho? We've not explored the area yet and it's the nearest town.'

He pulls a face. 'To be honest, I'm knackered. And I do need to catch up on a bit of work while I'm here. Why don't we just eat the food from the fridge? It's free.' He grins. 'I can cook up those gourmet sausages if you want? The sell-by dates are still good on them.'

'If you're tired, I'll cook . . .'

He shakes his head. 'You never let me do it. I did use to be quite good . . . once . . .' He takes his coat off and gathers mine from where I'd left it, strewn over the back of the chair, throwing me a look. 'I thought we were going to try and be tidy? I'll hang these up.' He wanders out of the room.

I'm frying up the chunky sausages on the fancy hob which pops up from the island when Jamie returns, carrying his laptop. He looks distracted as he balances on a bar stool opposite.

'What is it?' I ask over the spit and hiss of the sausages.

'Nothing.' His finger stabs at one of the keys, his plain gold wedding band glinting as it catches the over-head light. It still thrills me to see it, that symbol of our marriage. His brows are knotted together.

'It doesn't look like nothing . . .' I try to keep my voice even.

'My laptop was turned off. I was sure I'd left it on earlier. Maybe it ran out of charge . . .' His voice trails

74

away as the computer screen lights up at the press of the 'on' key.

My stomach tightens. I prod the sausages. Some of the oil flies out and hits me in the face. 'Ow!' I rub at it, already feeling a small pin-prick of sore flesh on my cheek.

His head shoots up. 'Are you OK?'

I nod. I don't want to say it. I don't want to think it. But I do anyway. 'Do . . . do you think the laptop has been tampered with?'

I can see I've pissed him off. His whole face darkens. 'For fuck's sake, Libby. We talked about this earlier. You're joking, right?'

I want to laugh and say, 'Of course, just a joke.' But I don't. I can't.

I must look sheepish because he sounds exasperated as he adds, 'Please don't tell me you think that man has broken into the house?'

'But shouldn't we check?' I can hear my hysteria rising like the tide in a storm, threatening to flood its barriers. I swallow to collect myself. I add, more calmly, 'You said yourself, he simply disappeared. Maybe he disappeared in here?'

He closes his laptop. 'How? There are no windows broken. No doors kicked in.'

'You don't have to sound so irritated. I can't help the way I feel, Jay.'

He takes a deep breath. 'Fine. Come on, let's have a look around, put your mind at rest,' he says. I can see he's trying really hard to be patient, to humour me. I take the frying pan off the hob and put it to one side and then let Jamie lead me upstairs, Ziggy at our heels. I follow him around the house, feeling a little foolish as he makes a great show of checking that all the windows and doors are secure.

'See, everything is locked,' he says when we are back downstairs, standing in the hallway. 'Can we eat those sausages now?'

My eyes flicker to the door next to the kitchen. 'Does that lead to the basement?'

'I think so . . .'

I raise an eyebrow.

'You want me to look in the basement?' he asks in disbelief.

'We might as well.'

He laughs. 'Are you just being nosy, now, Libs? You don't really think there's an intruder in the basement, do you?'

I shrug, non-committally. I suddenly have this over-whelming need to look in Tara and Philip's basement. It's the only part of the house we haven't seen.

With a theatrical sigh Jamie turns away from me and tries the door handle. He rattles it unnecessarily. 'It's locked.'

'Now I'm even more intrigued. Why would they lock the basement?' I tease. I march into the kitchen, remembering the row of keys that hang from a metal holder attached to the wall by the fridge. 'I think this is it,'

I say, returning with a small single key. Jamie takes it from me and tries the lock; the door swings open.

'You first,' I say as he takes a step over the threshold.

A smell wafts up to greet us, mildew and damp, making me realise that even though the house has been modernised to within an inch of its life, it's probably very old. There's something else too, pungent, like the slightly metallic smell of blood. I can taste it in the back of my throat. I cover my nose with my sleeve. Stone steps lead down to the cellar and to Jamie's left there is a light switch. He flicks it on and we both watch as the room is illuminated by a bright ceiling light, like the sort you get in hospital theatres. Ziggy butts against my legs but I pull on his collar to keep him from going into the cellar.

I gasp, my eyes blinking in the sudden brightness, dots forming in front of my vision. The cellar looks like a crime scene.

The room is square with a low ceiling and no windows. Set up in the middle of the stone floor is what looks like a mini operating table. Latex gloves, a scalpel, a large serrated knife and some kind of animal hide are strewn haphazardly across it. Hanging up next to it is a rubber apron.

Jamie screws up his nose while I try not to gag. 'It stinks in here,' he says, his eyes going to a bucket in the corner. My stomach heaves at its contents. 'Is that the –' he gulps '– the innards?'

I breathe into my sleeve, trying to inhale the scent of

cherry-blossom fabric conditioner instead of blood and guts. I recall the stuffed animals upstairs. I'd assumed Philip had bought those hideous creatures.

'Urgh. He's a bloody taxidermist. You'd have thought he'd tidy it away, knowing we were staying. It's pretty gross.' But he descends the remaining steps anyway, his fascination with anything macabre winning out. He creeps over to the animal skin on the table, as though he's worried he'll spook it.

'It's dead, Jay, it's not going to bite.'

He swivels his body towards me and pokes out his tongue. Ziggy pushes past me and trots over to the bucket in the corner. Jamie grabs his collar. 'Oh no you don't,' he says firmly. Then he turns back, peering down at the carcass on the operating table. 'I can't make it out. Is it a cat? God, Libs, I hope the animals didn't suffer.'

I tremble, still hovering on the steps. 'They would already have been dead. Unless Philip Heywood is some sort of animal serial killer . . .'

'Don't even joke about it,' says Jamie.

'Let's go, it's freaking me out.'

He indicates a large freezer in the corner. 'Do you think the animals are in there? Ready to be worked on?' He pulls the door open and something large in a plastic bag falls out and onto the hard floor with a thud. Ziggy pulls away from Jamie to push at it with his nose. It's a badger, the plastic bag tied at its neck, as though it's been suffocated. I scream, making Ziggy's ears flatten against his head.

'Jay, put it back, please.' I start to feel panicky and claustrophobic, even though I'm only halfway down the stairs. I have visions of more animal corpses tumbling out of the freezer. Jamie picks up the bag and shoves it back, shuddering with the effort. Then he hurries over to me, Ziggy at his heels. 'Sorry, sweetheart, but it's strangely fascinating, don't you think?'

'Not really, no.'

Before Jamie can get to the stairs he stumbles and his leg kicks against something, sending it scudding into the middle of the room. It looks like a large metal suitcase. He stops to rub his leg, his eyes going to the case. My heart falls when I see it has piqued his interest.

'Jay, come on,' I call.

'Hold on.' He's unclasping the catches on the suitcase.

'Now you're the one being nosy,' I say, trying to keep my voice light. But my body feels heavy with dread. What is he going to find now?

The suitcase opens and I can hear Jamie's sharp intake of breath. 'Oh my God, Libs. You'll never guess what they've got here. Surveillance equipment. Cameras and shit. Looks like bloody expensive kit. Wow. Why have they got all this? *Who are they?*'

8

'Do you think they're spies or something?' says Jamie as he locks the basement door. I'm feeling unsteady on my feet.

'We're not in some espionage TV drama,' I say as I reheat the sausages, my stomach turning at the thought of eating anything after seeing those animal carcasses. My mind is working overtime. Why would the Heywoods have all that equipment? And why would they keep it here? It must be worth thousands. As I turn the sausages over in the pan I look about me, wildly. Are there cameras hidden around this room? Around this house? Are we being watched? You hear about things like this: nanny-cams so that parents can spy on the women they've hired to care for their babies, and I once read in one of those true-life magazines about a woman whose landlord had deliberately hidden a camera in her bedroom and filmed her and her boyfriend having sex.

No, Tara wouldn't do that sort of thing. She's classy. Beautiful. She's not sordid and cheap. But Philip? Maybe he has some kind of fetish that she doesn't know about? Maybe he gets off on filming unsuspecting people in the showers and the loos.

*

Later that night when we're getting ready for bed, I spend ages in the bedroom, examining their ornaments, the stuffed owl, the photograph on the wall, for hidden cameras.

'Do you think they could be in the lights?' I say, looking up at the spotlights in the ceiling.

Jamie sighs. 'I'm sure they're not secret pervs.'

'It's a bit weird though, isn't it? Having all that stuff in the basement?'

Jamie steps out of his jeans and tosses them on the chair by the window. 'At least it's in the basement. Proof it's not being used.'

'Why have they got that kind of stuff anyway?' I wander into the en-suite to use the loo. As I sit there and look up at the shelves with the row of expensive candles I notice something else. Something long and thin with a hole at the end. I'd mistaken it earlier for an ornament. But what if it's something else? What if it's a camera and Philip is filming me on the loo?

'Jamie!' I cry and he comes rushing into the bathroom.

'What! What is it?'

I point to the object. 'That. Up there on the shelf by the candles. What is it?'

'Why can't you get up and have a look yourself?' he says grumpily. 'I thought something had happened, the way you cried out.'

'I'm worried it's a camera. I can't get off the loo.' I pull my fleecy pyjama bottoms higher to try and cover myself from the camera's prying eye.

'Oh for crying out loud . . .' But he reaches up anyway and grabs it. 'Do you mean this?'

I nod. 'Oh God, it's a camera, isn't it? He's probably been filming us having sex and in the showers and everything. It's disgusting . . .' My face is burning.

'It's an air freshener,' says Jamie.

'What?' *What?*

'An air freshener. Here.' He thrusts it under my nose. It smells of lavender. Jamie rolls his eyes but a smile tugs at his lips.

'I've never seen such a fancy air freshener,' I laugh as Jamie reaches up and puts it back. He leaves the room, his shoulders shaking with mirth. He won't let me forget about it as I get into bed and cuddle up next to him.

'You wally,' he sniggers. 'Honestly. Philip Heywood isn't some secret perv. Will you stop it now?'

'Yes,' I say, nuzzling against his chest.

'Good.' Jamie claps twice and the room descends into total darkness.

The next morning, I leave Jamie and Ziggy sleeping peacefully and pad into the kitchen to make myself a cup of tea. I stand at the doors in my pyjamas, sipping my tea and feeling uplifted. There is nothing to worry about. Jamie's right. I can relax.

In the distance the sea glistens and I watch as a flock of birds fly in a graceful formation towards the sun. It's worlds away from where I come from. We might never get the chance to stay in such a stunning house ever again. *Oh Tara, you're so lucky to have all this.*

I move away from the doors and busy myself making toast, enjoying a little fantasy in my head that this house is mine, that this is our way of life. How am I ever going to return to my two-bedroom flat in Bath after experiencing this? It's already Wednesday. We only have three more full days here. I glance around at the white walls, at the glass shelves, the bespoke cabinets. Nothing is out of place. It really could be a photograph from a glossy magazine. When Jamie gets up I'll persuade him to go into town and buy some flowers to sit on the island; I imagine something white and pure like lilies or roses. The house deserves some frivolity. There must be a glass vase here somewhere. I think about lighting one of Tara's expensive candles. Would she mind? Maybe she'd expect us to? She left them out after all. I go to the living room and pick one from the mantelpiece. Then I return to the kitchen and rummage around in the drawers for a light. A small box of matches is tucked down by the side of the knives and forks. I can tell the candle hasn't been used yet but I light it anyway and immediately the room fills with expensive scent.

I open the bifold doors. It rained overnight and the air smells as clean as freshly washed laundry. I retrieve my mug and sit at the garden table. The chair isn't completely dry and I can feel the water seeping into the seat of my pyjama bottoms but I'm determined to sit out here, to feel like I'm on holiday. I hear the scratch of Ziggy's paws on the tiled flooring and turn to see him plodding through the kitchen. He plonks himself next to me, his head in my lap. There's no sign of Jamie.

'Daddy can't still be asleep?' I ask while rubbing Ziggy's velvety ears.

It's nearly 10.45 and I expect Jamie is sitting cross-legged in the middle of the four-poster bed, tapping away on his laptop, catching up on emails. He'll start to feel anxious if he's behind with work, especially as he no longer has a boss to chivvy him along.

Not wanting to disturb him, I stay in the garden, my eyes closed, the sun warm on my face, the sound of the waves crashing against the shore below. I can smell the sea from up here, mingling with the candle's fragrance and a faint trace of something else, a muskiness mixed with sweat.

Then two things happen simultaneously: a twig cracks underfoot and Ziggy barks. My eyes snap open just in time to see the back of someone disappearing down the steps that lead from the garden to the beach. I stand up so quickly that my chair topples backwards.

'Oi!' I shout. Has someone been watching me? I run across the lawn, Ziggy following me, barking manically, the damp grass soaking the hem of my pyjama trousers and my slippers. Fury makes me forget to worry for my safety. I peer over the gate; a man is making his way down the steps. He looks different from the one yesterday, older, less stocky, and with skinny bow legs. He has a flat cap pulled down over his forehead and is wearing a waxed jacket and jeans. He's holding a walking stick, although he looks fit and able. I stare, shocked by his audacity, and can only watch as he scampers across the sand. I wonder what he's doing and where he's going. Is he using our garden as a cut-through to the beach instead of walking further down the road? Is he a neighbour? Why do strangers around here feel like they can just wander onto someone's property? I wonder if it's because the house is empty half the time.

I retreat into the house, shaking from the adrenaline and shock. I race through the kitchen, into the living room and up the glass stairs. Jamie is still fast asleep.

'Jamie!' I shake him awake. It's nearly 11 a.m. now, unheard of for Jamie to still be asleep at this time.

His eyes open straight away and he sits up, looking about him in shock. 'W— what's going on?'

I fill him in through halting breaths.

'Maybe he's a neighbour, there's another house a quarter of a mile or so away. Ring Philip . . .' He falls back against the pillows, looking exhausted.

'Are you OK?' Jamie's normally an early riser; even at weekends he's up long before me, tinkering with his laptop or out for a run with Ziggy. He's untidy and disorganised but he never likes lounging around in bed during the day. His hair is standing up on end, he has bags under his eyes and his skin is pale, with beads of sweat glistening on his forehead and dampening his fringe.

'I feel really sick and groggy. Like I've got a hangover. My mouth feels like the bottom of a parrot's cage.'

'Nice,' I laugh. Then I frown. 'You didn't drink much last night.' I touch his forehead; his skin feels hot and clammy under my fingers.

'My head is killing me. I'm going to stay here for a bit if you don't mind, Libs.' He pulls the duvet up around his chin and turns over with a groan.

'Do you want me to get you anything? Painkillers? Water?' I say, concerned.

He grunts a no from under the covers so I leave him to it, trying to ignore the anxious feeling in the pit of my stomach. I'd picked at my food last night, and I hadn't touched the sausages, or the beers he'd been drinking. They'd been sealed, straight from the fridge. I wonder if they'd been off. Or maybe he's coming down with a bug. I've known Jamie for nearly five years and in all that time he's only been ill once after too much to drink.

I return to the kitchen, pour some granola into a bowl and perch on one of the bar stools to eat it. I try calling Philip, not expecting him to pick up, suspecting he's at the hospital with his daughter. As predicted it goes straight to voicemail. I don't leave a message; instead I stare at the phone in my hand, debating whether I should have bothered him.

I potter about the kitchen for a while, but the quietness unnerves me so I fiddle with the knobs on the radio again. I've already tried to fathom how it works but

I can never manage to tune in to a station; instead it emits white noise and, irritated, I turn it off.

I have a view over the garden from the sink as I wash my mug and, as I glance up, my stomach flips. The same man as earlier is walking through our garden. I tap on the window with my knuckles but he ignores me, strolling down the side of the house. I hurry to the front door just in time to see him rounding the corner of our driveway and heading to the lane beyond. I call after him but it's too late, he's gone.

I'm furious as I head back into the kitchen and I try Philip's mobile again. This time he picks up.

'Hello,' he barks. He sounds irritated, as though my call has interrupted something important; it's at odds with the soft way he'd spoken to me the other day.

'Philip Heywood? It's Libby Elliot . . . I mean Hall. I'm staying in your house.'

'Libby.' His voice immediately softens, although he seems distracted as he asks how things are going at the house.

'Great . . .' An image of the dead animals and his surveillance equipment flashes through my mind. I feel as though I know too much about him, as if I've eaves-dropped on an intimate conversation between him and his wife. What has he gleaned about us by staying in our flat? That we can be slovenly, that we're not successful or rich, that our lives, in fact, are opposite to theirs? I swallow. 'Erm, it's just that a man keeps coming into the garden, I think he's using it as an access to the beach.' I describe the man from this morning, even though I'm not sure if it's the same man as yesterday.

'Oh that's just Jim, a neighbour. Ignore him. He's a bit of an oddball, always out looking for fossils or trying to spot marine life.' He laughs. 'He keeps an eye on the place when we're not there and we let him use our access as he can't get to the beach from his bungalow. He's not very good at minding his own business.' He laughs again but it sounds forced. 'Listen. I'm glad you called actually. There's been a change of plan . . .' He hesitates. 'My daughter is coming out of hospital earlier than we expected.' He sounds rushed now and there's an edge to his voice. 'I know, I know, it's great news. So we'll be going back to our place in London tonight, tomorrow at the latest. I'll leave the key with your neighbour, shall I?'

London? I frown into the phone. So why would they need to go to a Bath hospital for the heart operation if they live in a huge city like London? I feel myself blush at the thought that he obviously can't wait to hotfoot it out of our flat.

'That must be a huge relief,' I say. 'I'm so glad your daughter is getting better. I hope the flat's been OK?' My uneasiness makes me gabble.

'Excellent, thanks. Great for the hospital. Please don't rush to leave our house though. I've arranged for the cleaners to come in on Saturday, so stay until then if you like. Just drop the key back at the petrol station on your way home. Thanks again . . . *Libby*.' He accentuates my name, as though trying it out. And then the phone goes dead.

I stare at it, perplexed. Could his daughter really have made a miraculous recovery after a life-saving heart operation? And if they leave our flat, how can we stay here? It's supposed to be a swap. Then it crosses my mind that he might be lying to me and has found somewhere more salubrious to go. That must be it – otherwise there's a lot that doesn't make any sense at all.

9

I'm relieved when Jamie says he doesn't want to leave, because I don't either. Not really. I'll miss the house. I'll miss living like Tara.

'It's only Wednesday. Our agreement was until Saturday. I don't care that they want to go before then, that's their decision,' he says from between the covers. He looks strangely feminine in the Heywoods' four-poster bed amongst all that white muslin, like some New Romantic from the 1980s.

'Is it a bit weird though?' I ask, settling on the edge of the mattress. 'If we're still here and they aren't in our flat? It's not exactly a straightforward swap then, is it?'

'I don't care,' he groans. 'I feel really rubbish, Libs, can you leave me in peace?' He tugs the duvet up over his head so only a crop of fair hair pokes out the top.

'Charming,' I say mildly, getting up and going to the dressing room. I never did unpack our suitcase, knowing my clothes would look shabby hung up next to Tara's like poor relations. I pull a denim dress over my head and push my feet into a pair of Birkenstocks. When I leave the room, I make sure to close the door loudly behind me, annoyed that Jamie isn't planning to get up, that a precious day of our holiday will be wasted.

But by the time I reach the kitchen to give Ziggy his breakfast, guilt gnaws at my insides. Jamie isn't a layabout. He must really feel unwell to still be in bed. The day stretches out in front of me, long and dull. We've hardly spent any time alone since Jamie became a freelance consultant and I'd ruined the day before worrying about intruders.

I'm on my hands and knees, rifling through their small stack of DVDs in a wicker box by the TV, thinking that I'll kill two hours watching a film. But there's nothing I fancy that we haven't already seen before, and the others are either French erotica or full-on horror. Not my kind of thing at all.

When I hear the clunk of the letterbox I freeze and Ziggy starts barking manically, charging towards the front door. I get up to follow. The postman must have been as a few envelopes dangle from the letterbox. 'All right, Ziggy, quieten down,' I say, pushing past him to grab the post. There isn't much. A few fliers; one for a new restaurant opening up locally and another for an arts fair in the next town. There's also a glossy brochure from a Scandinavian company I've never heard of. I flick through the pages as I wander into the kitchen and sit at the dining table, immersed in the brochure. I want everything in it, the sofas, the dining tables, the chairs, but the prices are astronomical. I close the book, feeling despondent.

Ziggy is turning circles in the kitchen, a sign he needs the loo. 'Come on, Zigster, let's go for a walk.' I clip the lead onto his collar. I know Jamie doesn't like me taking

Ziggy out by myself with one arm in a cast – Ziggy's large even for a golden retriever and is more than strong enough to pull me over if he became startled. But the prospect of going for a walk on that lonely beach by myself is unbearable. And I feel an urgent need to get out of the house. As beautiful as it is, there is something unrelaxing about being in someone else's home with nothing to do but lie on their pristine sofa, worrying that even my body touching it will leave a mark. At home I'm always so busy: working, marking papers, writing reports, preparing lesson plans, washing, tidying, cooking, cleaning. I thought I'd love just 'being', no demands upon my time, no interruptions, but – and I hate to admit it even to myself – I'm slightly bored.

At weekends Jamie and I usually take a stroll into Bath or along the canal. We browse the boutiques or galleries, gaze at the artwork that we can never afford. At home we are always surrounded by people going about their daily lives, not necessarily interacting with us but they are there. I never knew how lonely it would feel being this isolated. Maybe it reminds me too much of my childhood, stuck in that village with nobody but my father for company. I was cut off from everyone back then. Friends didn't bother with me, boys never asked me out because everyone knew I always had to look after my dad. The only people I ever saw were the same group of youths on the green opposite our house, drinking cider and smoking, hanging around the swings and spraying graffiti on the nearby garages. The sort of teenagers in hoodies that you would cross the road to avoid. The ASBOs, my dad called them. He would hurl abuse at them when he staggered home, drunk. Once, in retaliation, they sprayed graffiti on our front door, a crude drawing of a penis. They were harmless enough though. They could've beaten my dad to a pulp, but they never did.

I go out the front door instead of opening the bifolds up again, as I'm unsure how to lock them from the outside. 'Now, you need to be good,' I tell Ziggy in a stern voice as we head out. 'No running off, I've only got one good arm, remember. And you've got to come back when I call you.' Ziggy stands by my side, head cocked, looking at me with his brown eyes as though he can understand everything I'm saying.

The weather is unpredictable; one minute I can feel the sun on my back, the next the sky darkens and the temperature abruptly drops. I feel a little apprehensive about seeing Jim lurking about and am relieved when there is no sign of him. As I descend the steps to the beach I wonder, idly, where this Jim lives. I remember passing a few detached homes along the lane before we reached the Hideaway the other day – I can see the backs of some of them from the beach – but they are few and far between, broken up by green vegetation and the jutting cliff's edge. Could it have been him who I'd seen watching us yesterday?

Sylvia would no doubt say I'm having delusions brought on by the stress of the fire. She usually has an answer for everything.

I let Ziggy off his lead and watch as he bounds across the beach. I follow, the wind whistling in my ears, the sea roaring. I've never been to Cornwall before, let alone the Roseland Peninsula, but, from what I've seen of it so far, it's beautiful. As I stand breathing in the fresh sea air, I feel guilty for my earlier thoughts of boredom. We're lucky to be having this holiday.

Ziggy dashes towards the shore, his tongue lolling, his ears fanned back, his legs kicking up sand. I pick my way across the beach, stepping over stringy wet sea-weed and rock pools, feeling exposed, the only one here. Thank goodness I have Ziggy with me. He had been Katie's. She'd bought him as a puppy, despite everyone advising her against it – Katie isn't known for being responsible. But, headstrong as always, she refused to listen and brought the puppy home to her studio flat in the centre of Bath. She called him Zippy and treated him like a baby. But as he started to grow so did her doubts, until eventually, sick of not being able to stay out late, or sleep over at mates' houses, she told Jamie that she was going to take Zippy to the dogs' home. Jamie was incensed. I'd never seen him so angry with her; she's usually got him wrapped around her dainty, French-manicured little finger.

'We can't have the dog,' I had said when he got home that evening and told me all about it, knowing that's what he was angling for. 'We live in a flat too, Jay.'

'The garden . . .'

'Which,' I'd interjected, 'belongs to Evelyn, not us.'

'She might let us use it.' He looked hopeful.

I made a noise through my teeth. 'She might but I'd feel bad about asking her. It's not fair to put her in that position. I'm sure she wouldn't really like a dog shitting all over her grass and would be too polite to say.'

'I don't know why,' he said in a voice that wouldn't have been out of place on a sulky teenager. 'It's not like anyone would ever notice. Her garden's a bloody eyesore. I've offered to mow the grass but she won't hear of it.' He had his fists clenched by his sides and he looked like he was going to cry. I loved the fact that he was a big softy at heart. I'd seen him try to hide his tears at animal programmes on the TV. 'I can't let her give the dog away,' he said in a small voice, running his hands through his mop of unruly hair. 'That dog's become a member of the family.'

I went to him and put my arms around his waist. 'Oh, Jay.' He had to lean over quite a way to rest his head on my shoulder.

Of course I gave in. We were all smitten with the dog. So Zippy – or Ziggy as Jamie renamed him – came to live with us. 'I can't let the poor dog be called Zippy,' he laughed, but really it was just because he'd always entertained the idea of naming a pet after his hero, David Bowie. That was over two years ago now and neither of us can imagine our lives without him.

Jamie. My heart aches for him as I stroll along the beach. I miss trying to keep pace with his long strides, the feel of his warm hand in mine. I have to try to stop being so jumpy, so paranoid, and enjoy what's left of this holiday. I know it would make Jamie so happy if I went to his mother for help, and part of me would love to ask Sylvia about my symptoms and whether I am suffering from PTSD, but I know I never can; it would turn into a therapy session and she might extract more from me than I'm ready to give.

I stop to look up at the Hideaway, at the full-length windows and the round tower. Jamie's in there, lying in bed feeling awful. I need to make sure he's OK.

I call Ziggy, who's prancing about on the edge of the shore, splashing about in the cold water, and we head back towards the house.

Just as I'm walking up the stone steps, I feel a presence and glance up to see Jim standing over me, a stern look on his face. I stop, my heart pounding. 'Christ,' I say, instinctively cradling my broken arm, 'you gave me a fright.'

'Who are you?' he growls in a strong local accent. He has binoculars around his neck and his weathered face is screwed up in annoyance. He's leaning on a cane, flat cap pulled over his eyes, and I notice there's a bald spot on the felt collar of his tweed jacket.

'Me?' I can feel myself bristling. Bloody cheek. 'I'm Libby. I'm staying at the Hideaway for the week. With my husband, Jamie.'

'I don't remember Mr Heywood mentioning you were coming to stay. This place has been empty for a few months. Building work has been going on,' he says, scowling at me. 'This isn't your property. It belongs to Philip and Tara.'

I swallow down a sigh. 'I know,' I begin patiently. I wonder if he is, as my mum used to say, a sandwich short of a picnic.

'Why are you here?' He pushes the front of his cap back and assesses me with startling blue eyes. I long to tell him to get lost and mind his own business but know I can't be so rude. I remind myself of my teacher's training, to remain calm and professional at all times. To not lose control.

So I smile politely as I fill him in on the house swap. 'They needed to be near the hospital. For their daughter.'

His pale eyes narrow. 'Daughter? They don't have a daughter.'

I stand up straighter, gripping Ziggy's lead. He's straining, trying to get away. 'What do you mean? Of course they have a daughter.'

'They don't have children.' He leans on his cane. 'Philip has never mentioned anything about you staying here. He was here a month or so ago, overseeing the building work. Why didn't he tell me then? He's never done anything like this before. I look out for this place, you know. When he's away.' He begins pacing, as though talking to himself. His agitation is making me nervous.

'Feel free to ring him,' I say. 'It's all above board. It was only agreed last week.'

97

He stops and glares at me and I realise, in that moment, that he probably doesn't even have Philip's number. He's just a local busybody who can't keep his nose out. He mumbles something under his breath and turns his back on me to walk away.

'Oh,' I call as he's about to step onto our grass, 'could you please stop walking through our garden? Just while we're staying here. We leave on Saturday. Thanks. I'd really appreciate it.'

He swivels around to stare at me, his eyes cold. 'It's not your garden. So I'll do what I like. I take orders from Mr Heywood, not you.' And he waves his cane at me threateningly. His anger makes me recoil. I open my mouth to say something else but he stalks off. I can't help but stick my fingers up at his retreating back. My heart thuds in anger as I watch him cross the garden and disappear around the side of the house. 'What an arsehole,' I mutter under my breath. I want to run after him and tell him that if he trespasses on our property again I'll call the police, but then I remind myself that he's right, it isn't my property. It's Philip and Tara's house. If they're happy for him to wander around their grounds then what can I do?

I go to find Jamie. 'You'll never guess what!' I exclaim as I run into the master bedroom. 'I've just had a stand-off with that Jim. He says the Heywoods don't have a daughter. Why would he say that . . .?'

I stop at the sight of my husband, prostrate in bed. He's deathly pale, a sheen of sweat coating his face and body. The room smells musty, of sweat and vomit. 'Jamie . . .' My stomach lurches. I hurry over to the bed. 'Jamie!' I shake him and his eyes blink open.

'Libs . . .' he croaks. His mouth sounds dry and raspy, his lips are cracked. 'There's an orange string bag under the bed . . . get rid of it . . .' His voice grows weaker as his eyes flicker shut. I stare at him in horror, at the blue veins that criss-cross his eyelids, at his waxy pallor.

'It's OK,' I soothe, stroking back his hair. 'It's going to be all right, don't worry.' I concentrate on keeping calm so that I can remember my first-aid training, like the day little Maya Price collapsed at school with suspected meningitis, or when Finlay Ward crashed headfirst into a tree and knocked himself out. I can tell my husband needs urgent medical care, but I don't know where the nearest hospital is, and worse, even if I did I can't drive him there. I flee downstairs to get my mobile from the kitchen island. Without even thinking, I dial 999. I have no choice. Jamie's clammy skin coupled with his delirium means he's probably dangerously dehydrated from the stomach bug.

I'm surprised that the ambulance only takes fifteen minutes to arrive. Jamie is stretchered into it and I jump in. As the doors slam shut I notice Jim hovering in the bushes near the driveway, staring after us with those pale, hostile eyes.

IO

I hold Jamie's hand all the way to the hospital, murmuring words of comfort while the paramedics attach him to a drip and he retches into a cardboard bowl. The journey takes about twenty minutes and I begin to feel sick myself as the ambulance swerves around bends and down narrow lanes. Then I sit, shell-shocked, in the waiting room of the hospital as Jamie is wheeled away, dread growing in the pit of my stomach with every passing minute.

Logically I know that Jamie will be OK, that it's just a stomach bug, or maybe food poisoning, but I've heard horror stories of dehydration leading to failing kidneys and even, in rare cases, death. Before I can push it away, the image of life without him flashes through my mind. Both my parents died before I'd even hit twenty. I have no grandparents, aunts or uncles. Jamie is my only family, my everything. I couldn't bear it if he was taken away from me too.

Catastrophising, that's what Jamie's mum calls it. She'd caught me doing it once over the wedding with my 'What ifs?' 'What if it rains?' I'd asked. 'What if I faint at the altar?' 'What if I'm ill on the day?' She'd reprimanded me in front of Jamie and her daughters as if speaking to a child, and I'd bristled. I felt like one of my pupils being ticked off. Then, when she noticed that my face was flushed with embarrassment, she gently told me it was because of my upbringing and a symptom of both my parents dying when I was still young. She'd tried to psychoanalyse me then, but I'd pulled the drawbridge up, as though I was a castle that needed protecting.

I sit on a hard, plastic chair kneading a tissue with my good hand while trying to bite back my panic, to hold back the tears. The waiting room is packed, an air of anticipation seeming to hang over everyone, evident in their worried faces, their wringing hands, their jiggling legs. Nurses scuttle in and out with files pressed against their chests. Jamie will be fine, I reassure myself. But I can't get the image of his pale, sweaty face and his delirious talk of bags hidden under the bed from my mind.

Eventually a young woman with a slightly harassed expression approaches me, her small heels clip-clopping on the tiled floor. Her brow is creased and my heart beats faster as she gets closer. I notice a child's sticker on her cardigan, a lion with the words 'I'm Brave' underneath.

'Mrs Hall?' I can only nod and stand up to shake her proffered hand. 'I'm Dr Carter. Your husband is going to be fine. We've run some tests and he has E. coli, which has led to dehydration . . .'

'Food poisoning?' I remember the sausages he'd eaten last night. I hadn't been able to stomach them after finding those dead animals in the basement. 'He ate sausages last night for tea. Do you think they caused it?'

Dr Carter has an attractive face with nut-brown hair piled into a messy topknot and thin, wire-framed glasses that give her an intimidating appearance, although she looks about my age. 'Possibly,' she says. 'Contaminated meat or . . .'

'Can I see him?'

Dr Carter's smile lights up her face. She looks like she could be fun outside of this hospital, somebody I'd like to go for a drink with. 'Of course,' she says, touching my shoulder lightly, and I follow her into a private room.

Jamie is sitting up in bed, a tube snaking from his arm to the drip at his side. He still looks pale but more like his normal self, orange string bags forgotten.

'You gave me a fright,' I say, trying to hug him, which proves awkward with my arm in a sling and him attached to the drip.

He kisses the top of my head. 'Sorry about that,' he says into my hair. 'But, Christ, I've never felt so ill in my life.'

Dr Carter is at my side. 'We're going to keep him in overnight, just to observe him, but he should be fine to go home in the morning.'

I stare at her, my mouth falling open. 'Um . . . overnight?' My whole body grows cold at the thought of spending the night alone in that huge, secluded house. I meet Jamie's eyes. He looks worried.

'It's OK, Doc,' he says, sitting up straighter and trying his best to look less ill. 'I'm feeling fine now. I've always had the constitution of a fox. Or is it a horse?'

He grins at me over her shoulder then switches his gaze back to hers. 'My fault for not drinking enough water. Surely I can be allowed home?'

She shakes her head, taking the chart from the end of his bed and scribbling something onto it. 'Sorry, Jamie, but you can't. You still need lots of fluids. Is there a problem?' She looks up at me with her clear eyes. She seems so calm, so together. Professional, like I was a couple of months ago. I can see myself through her eyes; a jumpy, nervy woman in her late twenties who's so clingy and neurotic that she can't spend a night away from her husband.

I swallow. 'No. No problem,' I say, plastering a smile onto my face.

'Great.' She pushes her glasses further up her nose and returns the chart to Jamie's bed before breezing off, already thinking about her next patient.

Jamie squeezes my hand. 'Are you sure, Libs?'

'I don't have much choice.' I notice a flash of concern cross his face and add, hurriedly, 'I'm a big girl, Jay. I lived alone before I met you. It never bothers me staying in our flat when you're away with work. And I have Ziggy with me. I can't leave him there alone. He needs feeding . . .' I take a deep breath. 'Everything will be OK.'

He's still frowning. 'The Mini is still at the Hideaway. You'll have to get a taxi. Are you sure you'll be OK?'

'Don't worry, Jay. I'll be fine.'

11

It's gone 7.30 p.m. by the time the taxi drops me off outside the Hideaway. I pay the driver then climb out of the car, my heart sinking as I stare at the house, dark and unwelcoming. I think of that basement, with its animal skins and surgical implements and I shudder. I'm not helping myself with my gruesome thoughts. The house isn't threatening. It's safe. Tara wouldn't live here otherwise, I tell myself. It's obvious she likes the best things in life, the little luxuries.

As I step onto the driveway the security light flashes on, momentarily bleaching the surroundings. From the corner of my eye I can see something hanging from the nearest tree. Something bone-white and sinister. I cry out.

'Are you all right, love?' the driver calls as I stand, rooted to the spot. His window is wound down, his arm leaning against the frame, his sleeve rolled up so I can see the long dark hairs sprouting out of pale flesh. I run over to the car and point up at the tree with a trembling finger.

'Look, that up there. What is it?' It resembles a disfigured skull, its jaw hideously jutted open as if it has died screaming.

He squints. He has a kind face, the sort of face my grandfather might have had if I'd ever known him; laughter lines and a grey bristly beard. 'Looks like a sheep's skull to me, love.' He sounds unperturbed, as if he encounters animal skulls hanging from trees on a regular basis.

'I'm sure it wasn't there earlier,' I say, my throat dry. I would have noticed it, surely?

He shrugs. 'It looks like it's been there a while. Quite weathered, ain't it?' He grins and then winds his window up. I want to beg him not to leave me alone but I steel myself. I'm being paranoid again. That skull has most probably been there for years. It doesn't mean anything. I watch as the taxi drives off, its tail-lights winking in the dark night until it rounds the corner out of sight. I shiver as I realise I'm totally alone, with just the crashing waves and the desolate beach for company. And Ziggy, I remind myself. At least I've got the dog.

I can't get into the house quick enough. I fumble with the key in my eagerness to insert it into the lock. I push the door open and Ziggy bounds towards me, nearly knocking me off my feet. I clap twice to turn the lights on, feeling silly, but I can't remember where Jamie put the remote. The lights flood on overhead, making me feel more secure, even though the house still has that lonely air about it. Can I really stay here on my own all night? I bend down to hug Ziggy, my mind whirling. What if I paid to stay in a hotel? But could I take Ziggy? I can't leave him alone. He pushes his nose into me, his way of telling me he's hungry.

The house is cold and it feels too quiet, so I switch the television on just to have some background noise. I concentrate on giving Ziggy his dinner. I'm too scared to take him for a walk at this time of night – that's usually Jamie's job – so I let him into the garden and I sip a mug of tea while he darts about the lawn, setting off the security lights, which just emphasise the darkness of the boundaries; the shrubs and hedges where somebody might be hiding.

When Ziggy is back inside again I make sure to double-lock the doors. I wish, not for the first time, that the Heywoods had curtains. I hate the thought that I can't see out of those huge windows, but somebody might be outside looking in, watching me, maybe the man from Lizard Point or that weird Jim creeping about. I remember our conversation earlier, about the Heywoods not having a daughter. Why would he say such a thing? In all the worry over Jamie I didn't have the chance to talk to him about it.

To take my mind off the fact that I'm alone in the house, I start to dial Jamie's number, then realise, in all the confusion, we left his phone behind. I run upstairs to get it and see if it needs charging. A lump forms in my throat as I glance at the bed, at the sheets all twisted into knots, the dip in the mattress where Jamie's body had been. I sit on the edge of the bed and touch the sheets, still damp from his sweat. My eyes fill with tears but I shake them away. I have no time for self-pity. Jamie will be fine. It's just one night on my own and I wouldn't think twice about it in Bath. I have to, as Jamie would say, grow a pair.

I pick up his phone from the bedside cabinet. There's a message. From Hannah.

> I've been thinking about it. I know you won't tell anyone but can we talk . . .

I'm tempted to open it to see the remainder of the message. My finger hovers indecisively over the text. I trust him. I have to. Unfortunately for me, Hannah is part of our lives. I don't particularly like her but she's wormed her way in with his family; she's not going anywhere, so I have to live with it. And, if I open it, he'll be able to tell and then he'll think I'm even more paranoid and neurotic than he does already. I don't want to be one of those wives who's always checking up on her husband, constantly suspicious. My mum was like that with my dad, never trusting him, always worrying he was out drinking instead of working, constantly checking his pockets for receipts. I saw how unhappy it made her, how the doubt and suspicion aged her.

And now I'm the doubtful, suspicious one. The nagging worry about the man at Lizard Point is suddenly back. Was it him we saw here yesterday? Did he follow us? His camera was angled at Jamie, I'm sure of it. Could he have been paid to take photos of us? But why? Again, I wonder if he's a private detective. He didn't seem interested in me though. He definitely seemed focussed on Jamie. Although what if it is about me?

The tears come out of nowhere so that I'm rocked by them, my shoulders heaving. I'm not even sure what I'm crying about. Jamie, the miscarriage, or that other pregnancy a lifetime ago. I cradle my stomach; the loss is so acute it's painful. Ziggy jumps up onto the bed and sits silently beside me in comfort.

I wipe away the tears and stare down at the phone in my hand, my eyes focussing on the words *I know you won't tell anyone*. What does she mean? What is she asking Jamie to keep from me?

Hannah being in our lives sometimes unsettles me, that's true; the way she studies Jamie when she thinks nobody's watching, her face full of longing. It irks me how she uses him as a sounding board, how she acts like she's the daughter-in-law, instead of me. Sometimes, when I look at her blonde hair or her tall, wide-shouldered frame, so different from my small-boned, petite body, I wonder what their sex life was like, whether he prefers her figure, her larger breasts, her longer legs. I don't want to have these thoughts and, on the whole, I don't let my mind go there.

I know you won't tell anyone.

What are they keeping from me? Maybe it's something to do with my thirtieth birthday in June, or a surprise for Sylvia. It doesn't have to mean something underhand, does it? It doesn't have to mean they're having an affair. I push the text from my mind. I'll try and get it out of Jamie tomorrow. If he has nothing to hide then he'll tell me, won't he?

Unless he has got something to hide.

I slap my palm against my forehead. *Stop it, stop it*, I tell my brain. I have to think the best of Jamie. He likes women, it's true. He's comfortable with them, having two sisters. But it doesn't mean he'd cheat on me. Especially not with an ex-girlfriend. He was the one who'd ended things with her all those years ago after all, not the other way around.

I consider calling Sylvia to let her know that Jamie's in hospital. I go as far as scrolling to her name, but something stops me. She's so over-protective about her son that she'll only worry unnecessarily. Jamie's going to be fine.

I prowl around the place, unable to settle; my thoughts oscillate between worrying about the skinned animals in the basement, to thinking about that sinister skull in the tree and then going on to the text from Hannah. I'm giving myself a headache.

Ziggy follows me as though sensing my unease. I toy with the idea of turning all the lights off. It means the house will be in darkness, but at least I'd be able to see out. If I keep them on then I'm completely visible to anyone looking in. Neither option thrills me but I keep them on, mainly so that I don't bump into things.

Why do I feel so scared being here by myself? I can hear Sylvia's voice in my head, loud and clear as though she's standing in the room, telling me it's just the shock of the recent fire together with my errant hormones after the miscarriage. Surely, though, most people would be a little unnerved by a taxidermist's basement or an animal skull in a tree?

I have to put it in perspective. Instead of wasting energy focussing on negative thoughts, I can use this time constructively. With Jamie in the hospital I have free rein to have a nose about without worrying that he's judging me. I look around, suddenly panicked by the idea that there might be a hidden camera somewhere. Why would Philip have all that surveillance equipment in the basement otherwise?

I scan the room, trying to pick out objects that might contain a camera, but there is nothing apart from that sad-looking stuffed puffin, a few photographs of Tara and an empty vase. Before I can talk myself out of it, I'm down on my hands and knees going through the sleek sideboard underneath the TV. There is a key in the lock and the door opens when I try it. The insides are disappointingly sparse but I find one of those photo books you can make yourself online. I grab it eagerly, flicking through the pages, taking in the photos of Tara and Philip on various holidays and days out. I'm surprised not to see any of their daughter.

Jim's words echo in my mind. *They don't have a daughter.* But that makes no sense. I shove the photo album back and take the next one. It's less interesting; numerous snaps of this house in various states of disrepair.

Wow, I think, my eyes flickering over each one. This house was a wreck when they bought it.

I'm just about to go upstairs to check out the spare bedrooms when I hear a loud crash from above. I freeze, the album slipping from my lap. What was that?

Ziggy's ears prick up and he jumps from the floor.

There's someone upstairs.

My mouth is dry and my heart knocks against my chest as I stand up slowly. I feel panicked, uncertain. What do I do? I frantically search around for something, anything, that I can use as a weapon and my eyes fall on the poker by the fireplace. It's shiny, not that heavy, more for show than anything else, but I reach for it anyway, feeling more protected just having it in my hand. I creep up the stairs, Ziggy at my heels, all the while terrified of what I'll find when I get to the top.

There is a shrieking sound coming from inside the smallest bedroom.

I stand at the door and push it open tentatively. '*Ziggy*,' I hiss. He turns to me and whines. My chest hurts where my heart is pounding so much. I incline my head and Ziggy wanders in first. I peer around the door frame tentatively. In the middle of the room, next to the sofa, is an old-fashioned toy clown rolling around on the wooden floor, cackling as though it's alive. It's one of the ugliest things I've ever seen, eyes mad and staring, mouth grotesquely large, nose hooked like a witch. It must have fallen from the shelf and set itself off. The noise travels right through me. I find clowns repulsive and always refused to watch Punch and Judy shows as a child.

I drop the poker and, suppressing my revulsion, pick up the toy, trying not to panic at its continuous cackling. I frantically try to find the off switch and manage to locate it at the back of its neck, relief coursing through me as the noise stops, like a baby who has fallen asleep after a bout of screaming. I notice that one of its pointed ears has cracked in the fall and I feel bad for their little girl that her hideous toy is damaged. I prop it back up on the shelf and turn to leave the room when something in my peripheral vision makes me start. Curled up next to a fluffy pink unicorn is a chocolate-brown Persian cat, its eyes firmly closed despite the commotion.

I tip-toe over to it, my hand held out in front of me. 'Hello, puss,' I say gently. What is it doing here? Philip never mentioned a cat. We've been here for nearly five days and we haven't noticed it before.

The cat doesn't flinch. I perch next to it to stroke it. I recoil. It feels cold and hard under my fingers. Of course, the thing is stuffed. But it looks so real. Had it been their old cat? Why haven't I noticed it before?

I carry the poker to bed, Jamie's absence pressing down on me like a physical weight. I feel so lonely, so vulnerable staying here by myself. Finding the clown and then the cat was a shock, and afterwards I had to run to the toilet to be sick. Now, as I lie in bed I feel miserable and worried that I've also got food poisoning, even though I didn't touch the sausages. I toss and turn, my heart racing every time the security light comes on outside, worrying that there might be someone skulking around the garden, waiting for the opportunity to break in and murder me in my bed. I can hear something banging in the wind and I'm reminded of Jamie's sinister story of the lighthouse, the coffin knocking against the glass. I pull the duvet further over my head like I'm a child hiding from the monster under the bed.

I shiver every time I think about the clown and all the other ugly toys in the smallest bedroom. What a strange choice for a child.

But surely it means that they do have a daughter, doesn't it?

12

I eventually fall asleep sometime in the early hours of the morning. I don't wake up until 10.30 a.m., tired and muddy-headed.

Even without a broken arm I wouldn't want to drive the Mini, so I book a taxi for 11.15 and then jump into the shower, hoping it will revive me. As I'm drying myself I remember the cupboard under the sink and the wash bag that I'd been interrupted from nosing through by Jamie. Gathering the towel under my armpits I bend down and open the cupboard, feeling a twinge of guilt for snooping. It's what anyone would do, I tell myself. I'm just trying to find out more about the Heywoods. After all, they've been staying in our flat too. It's perfectly reasonable, isn't it, to want to know more about the people who have been living in your home?

I pull the wash bag from the back of the cupboard and it falls to the tiled floor, spilling its contents everywhere. I'm disappointed to see nothing more interesting than old Chanel lipsticks, tissues and a broken make-up brush. Damn it. I begin picking through the detritus and I'm just about to stuff everything back into the bag when I notice a strip of little white pills nestled between an eye-shadow case and a make-up sponge. I peer at it more closely, squinting as I read the back. Anti-depressants. They must be Tara's. I replace them, a mixture of guilt and sadness tugging away at me as I push the bag to the back of the cupboard. Tara's depressed. The realisation hits me hard. Her life, from my view, seems so wonderful, so privileged. I should know by now that nothing is perfect, despite how it might appear from the outside.

I'm struggling into my jeans and a baggy cardigan when the taxi arrives. I gather up some clean clothes for Jamie and then dart through the pelting rain to the waiting taxi, my feet wet inside my ballet pumps. Just as I'm about to get in, I see Jim standing by our gate, his arms folded on top of his walking stick, an obstinate look on his weathered face. Fury curdles inside me. I hold my hand up to the taxi driver, indicating for him to wait, and then storm over to Jim. 'What are you doing here?' I hiss. 'What did I tell you yesterday?'

He holds his nerve, replying defensively, 'I don't take instructions from you.'

'Philip has let this place out to me and I'm telling you to get lost. If you're here when I get back, then I'm calling the police.'

He straightens up, pushing his shoulders back and jutting his chin out. 'I'm not scared of you. You shouldn't be 'ere.'

I don't know what makes me do it – lack of sleep or fluctuating hormones, maybe it's the stress of spending last night in a state of high alert – but, propelled by a surge of adrenaline, I prod him hard in the chest, throwing him off balance so that he falls back into the gate. 'Don't fucking mess with me,' I spit. 'I've had enough of this shit. All right?' And then I turn and flounce off to the waiting taxi.

My shoes squelch as I walk down endless corridors to find Jamie. He's sitting up in bed, chatting to a pretty nurse when I walk in. He's still wearing the ugly hospital gown and his face brightens when he sees not just me but the plastic carrier bag full of clothes. I'm relieved to see that he's no longer wired up to a drip.

The nurse smiles at me from across the bed. She's young, with one of those timeless faces that remind me of actresses in the old Hollywood films, maybe Ingrid Bergman. 'I'll just get the papers so that you can be discharged,' she says bustling off. Jamie watches her leave and then turns to me, his bright expression vanishing. 'God, Libs, are you OK? You look like you haven't slept all night.'

'That Jim was standing by the gate when I left the house this morning. I told him to piss off. I'm so angry, Jay. What is his problem?'

His eyebrows almost disappear into his hair and he grins. 'That's the Libby I know and love,' he laughs. 'I'm glad you told him.'

I laugh too. 'You should have seen his face.'

'Maybe we should call the police?'

I shake my head vigorously. 'No, no, I don't think we

need to do that. We just need to let him know he's not going to win. He's obviously not all there.' I tap the side of my head. 'He told me the Heywoods don't have a daughter.'

'Really? What a strange thing to say.'

'I thought that. The little bedroom. It has a few toys and things in it. But . . . there are no photographs of a child or a young girl. Unless they come away without their daughter? Maybe they use it as a bolt-hole or something. An adults-only space?'

Jamie shrugs as though he couldn't care less and I sink onto the chair next to his bed, exhaustion washing over me.

'Are you sure you're OK?' he asks. 'You look a bit pale.'

'I've been throwing up,' I say miserably, suddenly feeling dowdy and unattractive after standing next to the beautiful nurse. A spot swells on my chin and I press it self-consciously.

'Aw, sweetheart.' He climbs out of bed and I stand up so that we can hug. He knows how much I hate being sick. It's one of the hardest things that I find about being a teacher, trying not to panic when a stomach bug sweeps around the school like the plague.

I pull away from him. 'I've probably caught it from you . . .'

His mouth twitches. 'Can you catch E. coli?'

I pull a face. 'Of course you can. And I need to blame someone.'

He laughs and holds me closer to him. The nylon

gown is warm against my cheek and I can feel the cushion of his hairy chest underneath it. I sag against him, relieved that I don't have to spend another night in that house alone.

'Let me get my clothes on and then we can get out of here,' says Jamie, turning to wiggle his bare bottom at me through the slit in his hospital gown. I can't help but giggle.

'You're an idiot,' I laugh. But he's my idiot. And he's coming home.

As we're heading back to the Hideaway I tell Jamie about the sheep's skull in a low voice so the taxi driver can't hear us.

'It freaked me out a bit,' I admit. 'Finding it when I did. It was odd, really. As though I was meant to see it then.'

'What do you mean?' There's an edge to his voice.

I hesitate. It's been playing on my mind, but to say it aloud will make me sound neurotic. 'Well, I never noticed it before, only last night when I was about to spend the night alone.'

'It's just a coincidence,' he says with finality, resting his head on the back of the seat. He still looks a bit peaky.

I don't like to say any more so I fall silent for the rest of the journey. The rain is coming down in sheets, and the sky is charcoal. Even the trees look threatening with their gnarled branches stretching out towards the car like bony fingers.

The lane is deserted as the taxi pulls into the drive-way. There is no sign of Jim. Maybe my words have frightened him away or, more likely, he doesn't want to hang around in the pouring rain. As we rush to the front door, coats pulled over our heads, we can hear the sea roaring in the distance as it angrily thrashes against the shore.

The dash from the car is enough to soak us so I immediately run upstairs and change into my pyjamas, even though it's only early afternoon, and wrap my dressing gown around me as we huddle on the sofa.

'It's nice to be back,' says Jamie, turning on the TV. 'Not fun having to spend part of your holiday in hospital.' The room is dark with no sunlight flooding through the windows, and I snuggle up next to him, thankful that he's here with me. 'I'm quite looking forward to going home though, Libs, aren't you? It's been nice living someone else's life for a while but I'm looking forward to getting back to reality.'

I smile non-committally and pull the cashmere throw over us. It's cold in here. Jamie, as though reading my mind, gets up to light the wood-burner. I feel the same about returning home. I've been feeling uneasy since Lizard Point. Tara's life has morphed in front of my very eyes now that I know about the anti-depressants. Of course I realised that not everything was hunky-dory, what with them having a seriously ill daughter. It normalises her somehow; makes me realise she's not immune to the things that plague us mere mortals, despite her wealth and beauty. She's just like the rest of us.

'Oh, I've got your phone,' I say, suddenly remembering as Jamie sits back down. I reach into the pocket of my dressing gown and hand it to him. I notice how his eyes eagerly slide over Hannah's message and how his thumb quickly swipes the screen so that he can read her remaining words. His fine eyebrows knot together and then his eyes find mine. I can see something registered there, something dark. Anger, maybe. Or fear.

'Everything OK?' I ask.

He nods, smiles, but it doesn't reach his eyes. 'All fine.'

I'm intrigued to know what the message says and why he seems troubled by it, so much so that I'm unable to concentrate on the TV. *To Catch a Thief* is on, a film we've seen numerous times before, and usually it's as familiar and comforting as a cup of tea. Not today. The words *I know you won't tell anyone* roll around inside my head. Is Hannah's text some kind of threat? That would explain the fear I'm certain I saw in Jamie's eyes. But how can I bring it up without making it obvious I've seen the text?

Jamie pulls me further into him, his legs resting on the coffee table, crossed at the ankle. His thick socks are baggy at the toes and look too big for his feet. The fire flickers, warming the room, and soon my eyelids feel heavy, my body relaxing knowing that Jamie is home, safe and well.

When I open my eyes Jamie's no longer next to me. The film's still playing, Grace Kelly's beautiful face lighting up the screen. I sit up, fear spreading over my body like a rash. Where is he? I kick the throw off my legs and wander into the kitchen. Jamie's leaning against the bifold doors, surveying the weather as Ziggy prances about on the lawn.

'What are you doing?' I shiver. The doors are open slightly, enough for Ziggy to get back in, and I pull my dressing gown further around my body.

'Ziggy needed a pee. We should take him for a walk really but I'm still a bit weak.' He looks cagey and I notice the phone lit up in his hand. Had he been calling Hannah?

'Oh, right . . .' I say, thrown. 'Well, we need to get some food too, I no longer trust what's in the fridge after you were poisoned.'

Jamie shoves the phone into the back pocket of his jeans. 'I wasn't poisoned on purpose. Unless you poisoned me. You cooked the sausages, after all.'

I thump his arm. 'You could have cooked them yourself.'

'You always do it for me. You probably think I'm not capable.' He doesn't smile as he says it and the barb hovers between us so that the atmosphere in the kitchen feels laden.

'Of course I do. You're a good cook.' There was a time, so Florrie informed me once, when Jamie had ambitions of being a chef, until his mum talked him out of it. Sylvia wanted him to be a doctor like his father. Computer studies was a compromise. 'Maybe they were out of date. We should have checked.' I wrestle the fridge doors open. 'All this food,' I say in dismay. 'Pâté, Stilton, milk . . . we can't trust any of it.'

Jamie sighs. 'You're being paranoid, Libs.'

'I wish you'd stop saying that – it's really condescending,' I snap. 'Look, this pâté is well out of date,' I say, picking it up and examining the packaging. It's partially opened. 'Didn't you say you had some on toast the other evening?'

He doesn't answer so I slam the fridge door and whirl around to face him. His attention is no longer on me, but on Ziggy, who's walking towards him, his coat sleek with rain, his paws and legs splashed brown with mud, leaving prints on the wooden floor. In his mouth he's carrying what looks like an old rag, or a piece of clothing that he's dug up from the garden. He drops it at Jamie's feet and we stare down at it. Shock renders me speechless because I recognise it straight away. It's one of Tara's expensive basques, torn and covered in blood.

13

Jamie insists on calling the police, despite my pleas.

'It doesn't mean anything,' I protest, but even as I say it I know I'm lying. Of course it must mean something. The basque is torn in such a way that it looks as though it's been violently ripped from a body. And the blood . . . is it Tara's?

I feel sick as we wait for the police. Jamie paces the room. 'This just feels so wrong, Libs,' he mutters over and over. Ziggy stares up at him, unaware of the drama unfolding thanks to his find.

'I know,' I say in a small voice. 'But I don't want to get involved.'

He spins around, his eyes blazing. 'So what do you suggest we do? Go back to Bath and pretend we haven't found it? And what the fuck are we going to find when we get back to our flat? Philip Heywood could be some kind of psycho who's killed his wife, for all we know.'

A loud knock on the door makes us both jump. Jamie goes to answer it and I sit on the sofa, my knees jiggling, wishing I'd got dressed before the police arrived. Grace Kelly's face is frozen on the screen in a smile. I get up and turn the TV off.

Two uniformed officers walk into the room bringing

with them the smell of rain. One officer looks like he should still be in school. They tell us their names but I forget them straight away. I can barely concentrate.

The older one, with straight brown hair and an unremarkable face, asks us to show him the underwear. We troop after Jamie to the kitchen. The basque is still by the bifold doors where Ziggy dropped it. The material is a light colour, maybe cream or pale pink, it's hard to tell, it's so soiled with blood and dirt.

'Have either of you touched it?' asks the older policeman while the younger one picks it up with tongs and places it into a plastic bag.

I shake my head and Jamie says, 'No. Like I said on the phone, our dog dug it up from the garden . . .' He looks puce.

The older officer retrieves a notebook from the pocket of his jacket and flicks it open. 'I'm going to have to take a statement.'

'Of course,' says Jamie.

'This isn't your house?'

'We're doing a house swap. With a Philip and Tara Heywood,' explains Jamie.

'Do you know them?'

'We've never met. My wife organised it after they put a note through our letterbox.'

The officer turns to me with a sceptical look on his face. 'That's a rather unusual way to go about things.'

I can feel myself blushing. 'Well, I . . . we needed a holiday . . .' I say lamely.

Jamie turns to me, frowning, as the police officer consults his notes and I throw my hands up as if to say, *I panicked*.

'So, you're saying this house belongs to a Philip and Tara Heywood?' he continues, glancing up at Jamie.

'Yes.'

'And I assume you have details for them?'

'I do,' I say. I disappear into the living room to get my phone and then trot back to the kitchen, reeling Philip's number off, and the policeman scribbles it down. I can feel the tension coming off Jamie like steam. I have to concentrate on keeping my hands and legs still. I want to run. Run far away from this place.

'Have you spoken to Tara Heywood at all?' he says, looking from Jamie to me.

'No . . . I've just spoken to Philip. On the phone,' I say.

'So you've not seen Tara?'

'I've not seen either of them. It was all conducted by phone after the leaflet came through the letterbox.'

'Right. Of course.' He rubs his hand over his chin. 'Obviously we're going to contact the Heywoods but unfortunately you can no longer stay here. Are they still at your property?'

'No,' says Jamie. 'Philip spoke to my wife yesterday to say they were leaving.'

'So you can return to your flat?' His eyes are hard as he assesses Jamie.

'Well . . . yes. It looks that way,' says Jamie.

'That might be for the best. But we will need to talk

to you again. And you'll need to give us the key to this house and your address in Bath.'

Jamie gives the officer our address. The younger policeman has peeled back the bifolds and is standing in the garden, looking down at the hole in the ground where Ziggy must have found the basque. The rain is so heavy that a mist has formed, thick and grey, so that I can no longer see the steps that lead to the beach. What will they do now? Will they get a team in and comb the garden, looking for further evidence of a crime? I think of the implements in the basement, the scalpels and knives. Philip is used to skinning animals. He's a surgeon. Has he hurt Tara? Have we been living in the house, oblivious, while all this time she's buried somewhere in the garden?

Jamie is unusually quiet on the drive home. The rain is so heavy that the wipers are on full speed and they squeak as they pan back and forth. We're both in shock, silently reeling from what we found back at the house. The other things – the taxidermy in the basement, the surveillance equipment, the skull in the tree, the footprints, even Jim – are bad enough. But the underwear . . . the blood. Every time I recall it, a chill runs through me.

I worry about Jamie driving the three-hour journey when he's still ill. He's tried to convince me in the past to get back behind the wheel, to practise, gain confidence, but I've refused. I've told him I'm scared of having that responsibility. I can't be in charge of a machine that could potentially kill someone.

It's dark by the time we pull into our street. Jamie manages to find a parking space right outside our building. I'm relieved to be home, but my stomach clenches every time I think of walking back into our flat. What have the Heywoods left behind?

The pavement is polished with rain. I get out of the car and stand staring up at the familiar creamy Bath-stone walls with the blackened stain around the middle so it looks like the house is wearing a belt. Evelyn's lamp glows from behind her lace curtains. I can just about make out her silhouette, sitting in the chair by the window, her knitting needles no doubt clacking away. It's reassuring to see her. She barely sleeps, so she told me once. I peer over the railings to our basement flat. The windows are dark, I observe with relief. The Heywoods must have already left — if Tara was ever there that is. It did cross my mind earlier to ring Philip's mobile but when I voiced it to Jamie he told me to let the police handle it.

I stand with Ziggy as he sits on the wet pavement under the street lamp, his tail wagging half-heartedly. The raindrops shimmer under the light. Jamie drags our suitcase towards me. 'Home again, home again, jiggety jig,' he says. It's something we always parrot whenever we've been away for longer than a day. Like a talisman. I know he's hoping it will be lucky now, as he adds, 'You definitely think they've left?'

'I bloody hope so. Oh Jay, what a nightmare.' He leans

in and kisses me tenderly, his eyes tired, and then he takes a deep breath, as though bracing himself. I squeeze his hand in reassurance as I follow him down the stairs gingerly, expecting Philip Heywood to come storming out of our front door at any moment, maybe with a scalpel.

Jamie throws me a wan smile as he turns the key in the lock. My heart is in my mouth, terrified of what we might find. He pushes the door open and I follow with apprehension, surprised by how narrow our hallway is, how cramped our living room and kitchen, even though in the past I've always thought they were generous for a two-bedroom flat. After living at the Hideaway for five days I've become used to all that space.

I let Ziggy off his lead and he charges in and out of the rooms, happy to be home.

'Everything seems in order,' says Jamie with relief, standing in the middle of the kitchen and glancing around at the wooden Ikea units. They look tatty after the slick gloss of the Heywoods' designer kitchen. My eye goes to the chip in the black laminate worktop, the missing tile above the cooker and the white paintwork that needs freshening up. Everything is how we left it.

'It smells different,' I say. A scent hangs in the air that wasn't evident before. Not perfume exactly, more incense. And there's an empty glass on the worktop. I pick it up and examine it, noting the lipstick on the rim. A dark purple smudge. So a woman has been here. Tara? I place the glass in the sink, not sure what to think.

Jamie leaves the room and I flit around the kitchen,

opening and closing the cupboard doors, even peering into the dishwasher: all as we'd left it. Apart from the glass, nothing is out of place. I find Jamie sprawled on our shabby sofa that's covered in dog hairs, looking more relaxed than he ever did on the Heywoods' furniture. But his pallor is grey with exhaustion. I perch next to him, worried.

'Are you all right?'

'Just tired.'

'I'll make a cup of tea.' I leave him lying there watching an old episode of *QI* and go to our bedroom. I stand in the doorway, assessing the room, wondering about the couple who have slept in our bed. I feel violated somehow, knowing they have stayed here, feeling as though our lovely flat, our sanctuary, has been tainted by something unseen, almost as though an unsavoury spirit has pervaded the place, changing the energy. I run my hand over the duck-egg-blue duvet cover. It looks rumpled, as though recently used.

In a sudden frenzy I pull the cover from the duvet and rip the sheets from the bed, bundling it all up and shoving it into the washing machine. I put clean linen on the bed and then slump to the floor, my broken arm aching. My eye catches something on the floor by my bedside table, and I bend down to pick it up. It's a silver necklace, a St Christopher, its fine chain sliding between my fingers. I frown, a memory blooming and then fading in my mind so that I can't quite grasp it. I drop the necklace into the pocket of my cardigan.

Our guests have looked after the place, there's no doubt about that. It's almost as though they haven't been here. If it wasn't for the glass, the rumpled bedding and the strange smell in the air, I'd have assumed the place had been standing empty. Then I remind myself that they probably haven't been here much anyway, spending most of the time at the hospital with their daughter.

I'm contemplating whether to get the vacuum cleaner out or if it will disturb Evelyn above us when I remember Jamie's cup of tea. Then I hear a shout coming from the spare bedroom. I dart in there.

'What is it? What have you found?'

Jamie is standing over his desk, shaking his head in confusion. 'I think they've stolen my work folder. It's gone – the client list I was building, their names, how much they owed me . . .'

'Don't you have records on your computer?'

'Of course I do.' He sounds exasperated. 'But I also made hard copies. They've obviously been in here, rifling around . . .' He bends over and starts pulling at drawers and rummaging through the endless paperwork that he's never got around to sorting out.

'Why didn't you lock the drawers?' I ask in dismay.

He stands up and runs his hands through his hair in frustration. 'I didn't think. What the hell are they planning to do with my folder?'

I'm trying not to panic because that would tip Jamie over the edge. He doesn't often lose his rag but his illness compounded with the long drive and the shock of what has happened on holiday is taking its toll. We should have locked the desk or hidden our paperwork. Everything important is in this study: our bank statements, our mortgage details, our deeds for the flat.

The filing cabinet is heavy as I haul the drawers open, my heart in my mouth. *Please let everything be in order,* I will as my fingers flick through the papers. I'd suggested the house swap in the first place to give Jamie a break but it has only succeeded in making him more stressed. 'Jamie,' I cry when I find the folder he's looking for, 'it's here.'

He's by my side in an instant. I hand it to him and his whole body visibly relaxes. 'Oh, thank God,' he says. 'I was so sure I'd put it in my desk drawer.'

'It doesn't look like anything has been taken, Jay, don't worry.'

But later, as we lie in bed listening to the comforting sounds of the Bath traffic outside our window and the occasional ambulance siren, I know that my fears at the Hideaway weren't solely down to PTSD. There had been reason to worry. The strange things that took place there, the man at Lizard Point, the bloodied underwear in the garden, maybe even Jamie's food poisoning. It was all connected somehow.

And despite Jamie's protestations to the contrary, after the way he over-reacted about his folder I know that deep down he thinks so too.

14

The next morning, I leave Jamie in bed to recover and knock on Evelyn's front door. It occurred to me during the night, when I woke up in a cold sweat, that she would have met Philip and Tara when they came to collect – and give back – our spare key.

Evelyn's weathered face breaks into a huge grin when she sees me standing on her doorstep. She seems to have aged in the week since I last saw her. Evelyn is tiny, not even five feet tall, and walks with a stoop. Her silver hair is always tied back into a neat bun at the nape of her neck. 'Libby, my love, come in,' she says, beckoning me over the threshold. I step into the hallway. I love Evelyn's flat; it's the two floors above ours, with original Victorian cornicing, high ceilings and patterned floor tiles in the hallway, creams and browns with a blue flower at the centre of each square. Not to mention the huge garden which would be perfect for Ziggy. Jamie confided in me once that he hoped by the time Evelyn was ready to 'move on' we would have enough money to buy her place. I know his 'move on' was really a euphemism, but the thought of Evelyn dying is too upsetting to think about.

I follow her into her elegant front room – she calls it

the drawing room – and sit down on one of her Louis XVI-style chairs. 'I thought I heard you come home last night,' she says after offering me a cup of tea, which I decline. I've completely gone off tea.

'I hope we didn't disturb you . . .'

Her eyes twinkle. 'Not at all. You know me, never sleep. Did you have a lovely holiday?' She leans forward in her chair and studies my face. She has this way of looking at you so intently it feels like she can read your every thought.

I find myself telling her everything then, the words spilling out of my mouth in my desperation to unburden myself. She flinches when I describe finding the torn, bloodied clothing. When I'm finished she looks at me steadily. 'My goodness,' she says eventually. 'That's quite some holiday.'

I burst out laughing. I can't help it. It feels like a release.

She laughs too and then her face grows serious again. 'It all sounds very strange, Libby, particularly the clothing. Do they think it's Mrs Heywood's blood?'

I fidget. 'They haven't said yet. But it looks like the kind of thing she'd wear. I . . .' I try not to squirm under her unwavering gaze. 'I noticed some similar items in her drawer.' I haven't been explicit about what clothing we found. I feel uncomfortable talking about basques to my eighty-year-old neighbour.

'The thing is, Libby my love, you knew nothing about them before you let them stay in your flat, did you?'

I grimace. She notices.

133

'Oh, I know it's what you young people do nowadays. With all this Air Nub nonsense . . .'

I assume she's talking about Airbnb. I don't correct her.

'But I don't know,' she continues. 'You're letting strangers into your life, aren't you? With all their funny ways. All their baggage – and I'm not just talking about their suitcases.'

'I'm worried, though, Evelyn. About Tara. Obviously I'm going to assume something violent has happened. Wouldn't you?'

'Well yes, of course . . .'

'Did you see them, both of them, I mean? Did they both come to pick up the key on Saturday?'

'Yes, a man came. Youngish. Older than you. Maybe mid-thirties. I couldn't say exactly. When you get to my age everybody looks young.' She chuckles and sits back in her chair, folding her pale hands in her lap. The veins criss-crossing her skin are a lumpy blue-green. My heart goes out to her, imagining her sitting in this room day after day with only her memories and the many photographs that line the mantelpiece for company. I make a vow to myself to come and visit her more often. As far as I'm aware she never has any visitors. She'd mentioned a nephew once. I remember because she described him as her only living relative, who was 'unlikely to procreate because he's a homosexual'. She'd whispered the word 'homosexual' as though it wasn't supposed to be spoken aloud, reminding me that we were from different eras despite the fact that she's one of my closest friends.

'Was a woman with him? His wife?' It isn't until I ask that I realise how desperately I want her to say yes. The thought that Philip has killed Tara at the Hideaway and buried her in the garden for my dog to find is too horrific to contemplate.

She shakes her head, silver tendrils of hair bouncing around her jawline. 'No, he turned up for the key alone, although a few days later, the Wednesday I think . . .' she squints as she tries to recall it. 'Yes, it was definitely a Wednesday because the recycling men came. Anyway, I saw a woman outside. By the bins. It was quite dark.'

'Oh, thank goodness,' I say, exhaling with relief. So Tara was with him, which means she's still alive. But if it isn't Tara's underwear that we found in the garden, then whose is it?

Her expression darkens. 'You know, he never returned with the key. In fact, I got the sense that he was hardly at your place. No lights were ever on, apart from that first night.'

'Maybe they were at the hospital. They might have been able to stay the odd night with their daughter?'

'I suppose. I did hear a bit of a noise. I'm sure it was yesterday but it might have been Wednesday . . .' She frowns. 'One day merges into another for me.'

'What sort of noise?'

'A bit of shouting. A sort of scuffle. Banging. I think

they might have been having an argument. I heard a woman's voice.'

'It could have been about their daughter. Stressful time, I'd imagine.'

'Perhaps . . .' she says, but I can tell by her expression that there is something she's not telling me.

I crane forward in my seat. 'What is it, Evelyn?'

She shakes her head again as if to dispel any unpleasant or uncharitable thoughts about Philip Heywood. 'Nothing, really. He just seemed a bit odd, that's all. A bit agitated. But of course, he was probably worried about his daughter.'

I fill her in on his phone call and how he'd left earlier than planned. 'Maybe he forgot to leave the key in his hurry,' I say, trying to swallow down my alarm that he still has access to our flat. Maybe I should have drawn up a contract. I'd been too trusting, assuming there would be no issues if it was a swap.

She nods in agreement but her kind eyes are troubled – or maybe puzzled, I can't quite work it out. It's as though she's trying to access a thought or concern that is just out of reach. But I don't want to probe too much, just in case it has nothing to do with Philip Heywood at all.

As I go to leave, kissing her papery cheek, she places her crinkly hand on my arm and says, her voice serious, 'I would get those locks changed, Libby, love. Just to be on the safe side.'

The locksmith is here within hours and I relax a bit, knowing Philip Heywood can't get in. I try to ring his mobile a few more times but each time it just rings out. I can't resist searching the Cornish newspapers to see if there have been any developments, any arrests made, or any bodies discovered, but each time there's nothing about Philip Heywood, Tara or the Hideaway. I consider googling him for his office number but I'm worried that it will look as though I'm stalking him, and he has his daughter to think about. He's bound to be tied up looking after her. After all, as far as I know, he hasn't done anything wrong. Anyway, it's up to the police now.

15

'There are no such things as coincidences,' Sylvia says when we visit her on the first Sunday we're back. 'I'm glad you left when you did.'

We are sitting around her large dining table eating a roast dinner. Jamie began telling them all about the holiday, but he'd recounted it in a witty, breezy way, not revealing how anxious we've been feeling about it since we arrived home three days ago. He doesn't mention the food poisoning, wanting to keep the story light. I can tell he thought it would be a funny tale to regale his family with and he doesn't anticipate Sylvia's horror – although he should have done knowing how over-protective she can be.

'I can't believe you found dead animals in their basement,' interjects Florrie's husband, Richard, through a mouthful of roast potato. Jamie gets on quite well with Richard – but then Jamie gets on well with everyone. I think Richard is a bit immature. He's the sort of person who falls about laughing if someone steps in dog poo and I've heard Florrie moaning to her mother that he stays up half the night playing on the X-box and can't get up for work the next day. There's something a little sleazy about him too, the way his eyes linger too long on your breasts, or how he can't quite meet your eye. When Katie wears short skirts, which is more often than not, I notice how his gaze sweeps over her legs.

Florrie nudges him in the ribs and scowls. He glances at me and pulls a comical face.

'And I can't believe,' says Sylvia in her cut-glass accent, turning her flint-coloured eyes on me, 'that you let my son languish in hospital without telling me.'

There's a collective intake of breath around the table. Florrie puts her knife and fork down with a clatter, Katie's wine glass freezes at her lips and Richard looks at me with a smirk on his face as though he's a kid at school delighted that I've been told off by the teacher. Hannah sits quietly at the end of the table, opposite Jamie, her large eyes watching me. Her little boy, Felix, and Florrie's son, Jacob, are the only ones unaffected by Sylvia's exclamation.

The chicken I'm chewing feels like rubber in my mouth. I swallow painfully. 'I . . . I didn't want to worry you.'

Her finely shaped eyebrows, so like her son's, knit together. 'It's a mother's job to worry. Thank goodness Hannah told me.'

Hannah? I meet her cool, challenging gaze. How did Hannah know? And then I remember the text message she sent Jamie. With all the drama of leaving the Hideaway and fleeing back to Bath I'd forgotten to ask him about it. I can just imagine his text, apologising for not replying sooner because he'd been in hospital, discussing their secret and keeping it hidden from me. I feel an intense dislike for her then.

'Mum, leave her alone,' says Jamie mildly. 'I'm thirty years old. You don't need to know my every movement.'

Sylvia's face softens. She has an attractive face when she isn't being judgemental, with striking grey eyes framed by her blonde fringe. She always dresses well, thinking it important to accessorise; she likes chunky jewellery and is never without a wristful of bangles. These jangle now as she pours gravy over her chicken. 'But you were in hospital, Jamie, love. What if something had happened?'

'I had a bit of food poisoning, that's all. And that's not the worst of it. We found –' he lowers his voice so as not to frighten the children '– some clothing. Underwear. Ripped and covered in blood. Ziggy dug it up. We called the police. They're taking it very seriously.'

There's a stunned silence.

'Blimey, what a holiday,' proclaims Richard eventually, sitting back in his chair. 'Finding sexy underwear in the garden and having the shits.'

'Hardly sexy,' I mutter, appalled at his crassness.

'Richard!' Florrie prods him again. She seems to spend her whole life being embarrassed by her husband.

'Mummy, what does "the shits" mean?' asks Felix, glancing up at Hannah with the same big eyes. Hannah looks furious and glares at me, as though it's my fault.

'Uncle Richard said a bad word,' she says, turning her attention to her son.

The name jars but I push it out of my mind and distract Felix by asking him to show me the new cuddly seal that he's brought with him. He's soon telling me all about Snowy and Richard's words are forgotten. I'm rewarded by a grateful – and rare – smile from Hannah.

For the rest of the afternoon I watch the interaction between Jamie and Hannah, scrutinising them for signs that they are keeping something from me. They disappear at one point and I find them in the kitchen. I can tell by their body language that they are having a heart-to-heart. She's standing with her back against the worktop and he's so close that their shoulders are touching. She looks pretty in a knee-length floral dress, long boots and a denim jacket. He has his arms resting loosely across his stomach, his legs crossed at the ankle and they are talking in murmurs. As soon as I walk in they spring apart, Hannah reaching up to the cupboard to get a glass and Jamie inexplicably opening the microwave.

'What's going on?' I say, my voice cold. Hannah glances at me, her face a picture of innocence.

'What do you mean?'

'Well, why have you disappeared in here?'

'We're just having a private conversation,' she says and I want to slap her smug face. 'That's still allowed, now that he's married, isn't it?' She smiles sweetly, then brushes past me and out of the room. Probably running to tell it all to Katie and they'll gossip in the corner like two teenagers instead of the twenty-eight-year-old women they are.

Jamie can't meet my eye as he closes the microwave door. He's empty-handed.

'What's she playing at?' I hiss.

Jamie shakes his head. 'Libs. I've known her for years . . .'

'I don't care. She wants you for herself.'

'She doesn't see me like that any more . . .'

I groan. 'Are you that naïve . . .?'

'And even if she did, it doesn't matter. She's just a friend. That's all. You should know this by now, Libs.' He strides over to me. 'She's just got a problem she wants some help with, that's all. You do trust me, don't you?'

I sense an undercurrent of irritation beneath his jovial tone. I've always been secure in his love for me, even though I've sensed that his family don't like me much, except maybe Florrie. So why do I feel this way now? This fear that I'm about to lose him, that everything is unravelling? Is it because of what happened in Cornwall? Or the fire and the miscarriage? I'm not sure.

'You told me yourself, Hannah really loved you. She thought you were The One, Jay.'

He looks down at his feet and shuffles, clearly uncomfortable. 'We were kids . . .'

'You broke her heart . . .'

'We were too serious, too quickly. Then we went to different universities and things . . . well . . . you know how it is.'

'You cheated on her!' The realisation suddenly hits

me. He's never admitted that to me before but it's in his expression: the downcast eyes, the sheepish smile. Guilt.

'I . . .' He shuffles and glances down at his Converse. 'I'm not proud of that.'

'Why have you never told me before?'

'Like I said, I'm not proud of it.' He lifts his head up but doesn't smile or make a joke. I'm pleased he's not trying to make light of it.

I stare at him. He's capable of cheating. Jamie Hall, who I've always thought was so black and white. So *moralistic*. So well bred. He is no better than my father. Than Harry.

'Libs, why are you staring at me like that? As though you don't know who I am. Jesus, it was a lifetime ago. I was young and stupid. I wasn't in love. Not like I am with you.' He moves towards me. 'Please don't make a big deal about this.'

I swallow and try to compose myself. 'I'm not . . . I just . . . I don't know.' How could I not have known this? We've been together nearly five years. Did he keep it from me deliberately? I think back to all those early conversations, intertwined on my single bed in a shabby bedsit, where we were finding out about each other. About past relationships.

He pulls me to him, wrapping his arms around my waist. 'It was different then. *I* was different. I would never do anything like that to you. I hope you know that. I don't care how Hannah feels about me. It's you I love. You I married. You I want to be with for the rest of my life.'

'I'm glad to hear it,' I say. From beyond the doorway I catch a flash of floral, a swish of blonde hair. Has Hannah been standing there this whole time, listening? I lean into him and rest my head on his chest, trying to ignore my unease.

It's a cold day with a crisp blue sky and a low sun. After lunch I sit in the conservatory, enjoying the warmth filtering in through the glass, watching Felix and Jacob, wrapped up warm, sprinting up and down the vast lawn, Jamie and Richard running after them. Hannah and Florrie look on adoringly, their arms folded. Being back here, with his family, it's easy to forget the events of the past week, almost as though we've never been to Cornwall.

Despite the years we've been together, I still can't get over how large this house is, that this is where he spent his childhood. So different from the two-up two-down I'd grown up in. They even have a coach house at the bottom of the garden where their guests sleep. Sylvia is always having friends to stay over. I sense she likes it best when her house is filled with people and laughter and chatter, and despite the fact that she annoys me at times, I feel for her, not having her husband around any more.

I watch as Jamie dribbles a ball and Felix runs after him, laughing, his arms outstretched. Jamie cheated on

Hannah. I still can't believe it. It's as though he's shifted slightly in my perception, like catching sight of him through one of those fun mirrors at a fairground.

'Don't you want to go out and join them?' A voice makes me jump. I turn to see Katie reclining against the door frame, an insolent expression on her face. She has the same dirty blonde hair as her mum and Jamie, whereas Florrie is dark, like their dad. Katie is a pretty girl, all long arms and slender legs, but there's something restless about her, as though she doesn't really know where she belongs, boomeranging from one job to another, one boyfriend to another and one home to another. She's recently moved back in with Sylvia, and is jobless once more, even though she's only two years younger than me. Sylvia has never said it – she's intensely loyal to all three of her children – but I know that she worries about Katie, her lack of direction. I would have given anything for the privileges and the expensive education that she obviously takes for granted. Even though Florrie is the archetypical bossy older sister, I prefer her to Katie. Florrie's more down to earth, more solid, even if we don't share the same taste in men. Not that Richard is a bad bloke, he's just a bit of a prat at times. Katie, on the other hand, is manipulative, playing her role as the baby of the family to suit her needs. But not with me. I can see straight through her.

I turn to her with what I hope is a 'don't mess with me' look on my face, the kind I give my pupils when they play up. She ignores it and sits down opposite me on one of the rattan sofas. She swings her legs around so they are hanging over the arm. There is a wedding photo of me and Jamie above her head, Florrie and Katie flanking us, resplendent in pale blue. I remember how much of a diva Katie had been about the wedding, how she'd refused to wear blue as it 'washed her out', how she accused me of trying to make her look bad, as though it was all about her. I'd bitten my tongue, of course, although I refused to change the colour of the bridesmaids' dresses. Jamie informed her firmly that she either wore the colour I'd chosen or stepped down as bridesmaid. Not for the first time I wished I'd had my own sister to stand by my side on that day, to fight my corner. It's hard sometimes, standing up to the Hall women.

Katie is quietly assessing me with her cool gaze. 'You're so quiet sometimes, Libby. Who knows what goes on inside your head? You should be out there with your husband instead of letting him play daddy to Hannah's kid.'

I fix a smile on my face, unwilling to rise to the bait. 'It's nice for him to spend some time with his family and I'm still feeling a bit off colour.' I touch my stomach to illustrate my point. 'And with my arm . . . you know . . .' I lift my cast and pull a disappointed face. 'Don't want to fall over when the cast is coming off next week.'

She chews her lip thoughtfully. 'Hmmm, I suppose

you don't want to play with kids when you're looking after them all day.'

'It's not that, I love kids . . .'

'But it must be weird,' she continues relentlessly, crossing her legs at the ankle and wiggling her toes. Her nails are painted a dark purple. 'To see your husband with his ex-girlfriend. I remember how in love they were once upon a time. First love. That's a powerful thing, isn't it? We all thought they'd get married. Funny how things turn out. Don't you think?'

I wonder if she continues to see Hannah just to wind me up. It's true they've been best friends for years but Hannah, now a mother, has outgrown Katie. It's always struck me as odd how Katie parades Hannah around the house like some kind of prize pig.

'Well, I've been seeing them together for five years, so I'm used to it,' I say pleasantly, my tone belying my irritation. I'm like a tennis pro, the way I bat away her digs. I've had enough practice over the years. It's as if she knows exactly what to say to get to me, but I never show her how much her words sting.

It had been strange at first, knowing Jamie's ex was still a part of the family. Hannah had been heavily pregnant – and still married – when I first met her and I'd quickly realised that I'll never have the sort of relationship with Sylvia that they share, the sort of relationship that I'd hoped for, had craved. I assumed, before I met Jamie's mum, that she would fill the void my own mum had left behind when she died, that

Sylvia would become a sort of surrogate. But of course it isn't as simple as that. Sylvia couldn't be more different to my own mother. It's as though she doesn't feel I'm quite good enough for Jamie, that I'm not the daughter-in-law she'd been hoping for, with my northern accent, my preference for a pint of lager over a glass of wine, my chipped nails, my clothes stained with marker pens. I'm not what she calls 'well turned out'. Once I saw her looking with distaste at the tattoo of a winged bird on my upper arm. She doesn't like that I'm competitive at board games, that I don't iron Jamie's clothes (I don't even iron my own clothes), that I have three piercings in my left ear, that I'm not constantly on a diet or talking about food or baking. My saving grace is that I'm a teacher. I can almost hear her telling her friends at the Women's Institute that at least I have an education. Hannah, on the other hand, fills that void, with her posh girls' school education, and her family money, even if she is now a divorced single mum. Jamie confided in me once that Hannah's family were 'utter snobs' and he never really liked them because they were so disinterested in Hannah, putting all their efforts and ambition into their Oxford-educated son instead. They moved to Jersey a few years ago and, so Jamie tells me, Hannah hardly sees them.

Katie frowns now, twirling a section of her hair around her finger. 'Yes, well I wouldn't like my husband being so close to his ex. But then we're different, aren't we?' She smiles sweetly and jumps up from the sofa, bored that she isn't getting a rise out of me. I long to tell her to grow up, but I pick up a magazine from the coffee table and start leafing through it instead. I can sense her watching me by the door but I keep my eyes on the page, pretending to be engrossed in the private life of a soap star.

'I know you think I'm pretty thick.' Her words cut into the silence.

I'm so shocked, the magazine slips from my lap and onto the stone floor. I snap my head up. 'No, I don't. I think you're actually very clever.' It's true, she is. She just uses her intelligence in the wrong way, by being sly.

'I might not have a degree, like you, but I know about people. And I know about you. You like to think you're so together, so strong, but you're like a swan; on the surface you're elegant and in control but underneath it all your legs are desperately kicking to stay afloat.'

'Katie . . .'

'It doesn't mean you're weak to show that you're not perfect, you know?'

'I know that. I don't think I'm perfect. Far from it.' How can she know that most of the time I feel like an imposter?

She narrows her eyes as though wanting to say more, but thinks better of it, tossing her hair back and flouncing out of the room.

Outside the window, Sylvia is handing out tea from a circular tray, the steam rising from the assorted collection of bone-china mugs. Jamie and Hannah are in conversation on the edge of the group. She's leaning into him and laughing at something he's saying and it irks me that even after our earlier conversation he's still indulging her. She sees me watching and smirks. I feel a spark of anger. She should be careful who she messes with. I've put everything I've got into creating my life with Jamie and I won't let her, or anyone else, ruin it for me.

16

Two days before Good Friday I finally have the cast removed. I almost skip home from the hospital, ecstatic that I'm no longer restricted by the sling, that I can now take Ziggy for walks again, or go for a run, or play badminton, all the things I'd enjoyed before the fire.

Evelyn is sitting at her window as I descend the steps to our basement flat and I give her a wave. She waves back and I vow to pop over to see her later. I fumble with my key; the new lock is a bit stiff and the door seems to resist as I push it open. I soon realise why. The post has arrived and it's clogging up the hallway. I bend over to pick up the junk mail that's dropped through the letterbox – ten times the amount we usually receive. I flick through it, frowning. All are addressed to me and seem to be from companies selling everything from the mundane to the obscure to the downright rude. I throw them onto the worktop and a lewd advert about a penis enlargement kit glares up at me. I screw it up and shove it in the bin, surprised when I see what's underneath it: the same catalogue that was in the Hideaway, with all that expensive Scandinavian furniture. Surely I didn't order this? Or did I? I throw it onto the sideboard, where it skids across the wood, only stopping when it knocks against an ornament.

The Buddha. What's that doing here? I haven't laid eyes on it for years but I couldn't bring myself to part with it so kept it hidden away. Did Jamie find it and put it out? I study the Buddha's calm face, his relaxed pose, turning it over in my hands. I can't look at it without thinking of everything that happened. It has to go. The door to the spare room is firmly shut and I can hear Jamie talking on the phone, something about infrastructure and databases. I still don't really understand what he does, even though he's always trying to explain it to me. I carry the Buddha into the bedroom and shove it to the back of my wardrobe, underneath a pile of summer clothes.

When I return to the kitchen I switch the kettle on, desperate for a cup of tea and still missing the instant tap at The Hideaway.

Ziggy springs up from his bed. 'Sorry, boy, I've not said hello yet,' I say, enjoying the freedom of hugging him. I bury my face in his fur. He needs a bath. In fact, I think as I stand up, this whole flat smells of dog. I light the candle on the pine sideboard at the dining-room end of the kitchen, taking deep breaths of the mandarin scent. The candle really cheers up the room with its flicker and crackle. It doesn't have quite the same effect as it did in The Hideaway, but the smell reminds me of the Cornwall house: expensive and exotic.

Jamie pads into the kitchen. He hasn't shaved for a

few days, the stress that had lingered around him like bad aftershave before Cornwall is back, and not for the first time I worry that becoming self-employed is too much pressure for him. He's holding a parcel by the tips of his fingers, as though he's loath to touch it. It knocks against his leg as he walks.

I wave my right arm at him. 'The cast's gone!' I say, feeling euphoric.

'That's great news,' he replies, beaming at me, his eyes twinkling.

'What have you got there?'

His face closes up. 'It's for you. What have you been ordering? I haven't made my first million yet,' he jokes. His eyes go to the candle. 'And where did that come from?'

'I, um . . . I bought it cheap from the charity shop,' I lie. 'Must have been an unused gift or something . . .' He won't approve if I tell him the truth, that I took it from The Hideaway. I'd justified it to myself that, as we'd used it when we were on holiday, Tara wouldn't have expected us to leave it behind. Jamie might not see it that way though.

'I've not ordered anything.' I take the parcel from him. It's large and heavy, the name of a well-known catalogue company emblazoned down the side of the orange plastic envelope. 'I don't even have any catalogues.' I rip it open.

'What is it?' he asks, going over to the kettle and pouring the boiling water into two mugs.

I frown. 'It looks like some kind of bag,' I say as it slides from its packaging. It's large, ugly, the type of backpack a student might take travelling. 'I definitely didn't order this.' I double-check the name on the front, hoping there has been some mistake and it's meant for one of the neighbours, but it's definitely addressed to me.

Jamie places a mug of tea on the table in front of me. 'Going somewhere, Libs?' he laughs. But it's not funny. Cold fingers creep down my back. Why have I been sent this? I dump it on the table and then ferret inside the packaging to find the order form.

'This is weird, Jay. It appears I have an account with them. Look . . .' I wave the piece of paper under his nose. He narrows his eyes and takes it from me. 'I've never set up an account.'

'It's obviously some sort of error,' he says with a dismissive shrug, handing me back the form. 'Just ring them and tell them. Send the bag back.'

I sigh. 'But it's such a faff.'

'I know, Libs, but these things happen.' Cradling his mug, he wanders out of the room. I stuff the bag back into its packaging and refasten it.

The sky darkens and it starts to rain as I walk to the post office. The niggling feeling about the bag stalks me. Does it mean something? Is it personal? I remember walking those dusty, sun-baked streets in Thailand with a similar bag on my back weighing me down. I'm so distracted I almost bump into a woman with a baby strapped to her front. I apologise and she smiles in that tired yet euphoric way that new mothers do and my heart twists. I would have been nearly four months pregnant by now. Would I have had a bump? A glow? And the other one. The first.

The streets are busy with families enjoying the last week of the Easter holidays, wrapped up in waterproofs, the streets a sea of umbrellas. The traffic is starting to build up as I get closer to the high street and lights are coming on in the windows I pass, despite it only being 4 p.m.

The amount of post I'd received that morning plays on my mind as I queue at the post office. All those advertising round-robins and promises of 15 per cent off from companies that I've never even bought anything from. Why would they suddenly send me stuff?

Just getting rid of the bag makes me feel lighter. As I round the corner to our street I sense somebody close behind me. I stop and turn abruptly. A woman is snapping at my heels. Her face is obscured by her umbrella, but I see long straggly hair and clunky biker boots. I walk on more slowly, but she doesn't go around me, she slows too. Is she following me? I stop and stand aside to let her pass, annoyed that she's invading my space. She strides past, not giving me a second glance.

When I arrive back at the flat, Jamie is out with Ziggy so I retrieve my laptop from the living room to conduct what has become a daily ritual of scrolling through Cornish websites for news. As usual there is nothing.

It's dusk by the time I've finished and Jamie is still

out with Ziggy, so I put a pan of pasta on the hob. I feel jittery and anxious, the parcel and letters still at the back of my mind. I can hear Evelyn's radio on upstairs. She always has it turned up too loud but I find it comforting. Later in the evening the radio will be replaced by the TV and it won't be long before I'll hear the theme tune to one of the many soaps she watches.

I strain the pasta over the sink, my gaze going to the window and the pavement above. Ziggy's sitting under the street lamp and I can just make out a pair of legs next to him. I lean over the sink to get a better view. Jamie's talking to a man in a pinstriped suit and dark overcoat. I vaguely recognise him from one of the big houses further down the road, a three-storey detached home with its own driveway. I've seen him getting into a flashy sports car. His wife is an attractive woman, younger than him and very glamorous, never without lipstick and several coats of mascara on her long lashes, her glossy dark hair always blow-dried in loose waves. The glow of the lamp-post illuminates the fine rain that falls softly onto Ziggy's coat. Why is Jamie standing there talking in the rain? I can see that the man looks furious and he's waving something in Jamie's face.

I run to the front door and open it just in time to see the man striding away. Jamie's expression is closed as he descends the steps with Ziggy lolloping close behind. The rain has darkened Ziggy's golden coat and his fur is furrowed between the eyes so that it looks as though he's frowning.

'Was that the guy from down the road? What did he want?' I ask as soon as Jamie steps over the threshold. He shrugs off his coat and hangs it on the peg while I rub Ziggy down with an old towel.

'Yep. Martin. Such a twat.'

'What did he want?' I repeat when it's obvious Jamie isn't going to volunteer any more information.

'Oh, it was nothing.'

I feel my hackles rising. 'It didn't look like nothing.'

He stalks off into the kitchen and I follow. The sieved pasta sits on the side, growing cold. I return it to the saucepan and add some of the tomato sauce I'd defrosted earlier. I begin stirring the pasta so vigorously that sauce spits over the side and onto the hob with a sizzle.

Jamie comes up behind me and wraps his arms around my waist. 'Don't be mad, Libs.'

'Then why can't you tell me what it's about?'

He sighs, his breath hot on my neck. 'It's actually a bit embarrassing. Crossed wires, it has to be.'

I swivel on my heels to face him. 'What do you mean?'

'Martin accosted me as I was walking home with Ziggy. Said I'd been sending his wife love letters . . .' He has the good grace to blush.

'What?' I drop the wooden spoon in shock and we both watch as it clatters to the floor, splashing tomato sauce onto the cabinets. I tut heavily and grab a dishcloth from the sink, wiping the floor and the cupboards.

Jamie side-steps me and turns down the hob. 'I know. It's ridiculous. Well, they weren't really letters.

More like cards. Romantic cards.' He gives a disbelieving laugh. 'I don't even know his wife. Didn't even know her name until today. It's Anya, apparently.'

'But you've seen her? This Anya? Even you can't have failed to notice how attractive she is.'

'Well . . . yes,' he says helplessly. 'I suppose she is attractive. But I've only ever said hello. Sometimes we pass each other when she's out running and I'm walking Ziggy.'

I can feel the heat flood my face. I think of Jamie cosying up to Ruth at Lizard Point or chatting with Hannah, their bodies touching. He's a bit of a flirt, I've always thought so. 'So he showed you one of the cards?' I say, still scrubbing the floor.

'He practically shoved it in my face.'

I stand up to rinse the cloth under the tap, trying to remain calm. I think of Katie's swan analogy. She's right. That's me. Beneath it all I'm kicking furiously, trying not to drown. 'And was it your writing?'

'Of course it wasn't. Libs . . .' He grabs my arm and swings me around to face him. 'You don't think I'd do anything like that, do you?'

'No . . . no, of course not . . .' I look past his shoulder.

'You don't sound too sure.'

'I am. It's just . . .'

'It's just what?'

I raise my eyes to his. We've been married for nine months. That's all. And together four years before that.

Long enough, surely? But how well do you ever really know someone? And he'd cheated on Hannah.

I can't help the words that slip from my lips. 'I saw the text Hannah sent you.'

'The text Hannah sent?'

'When you were in hospital. I didn't read it all. It popped up on your phone.'

'I thought you were cool about Hannah now. I thought you understood. She's just a friend . . .'

My face grows hot with anger. 'You know how she feels about you and guess what? I think you like it.'

His eyes widen in surprise. 'What?'

'You like the attention. Would you be so understanding if my ex-boyfriend was invited to every fucking family dinner? If I stood next to him in the garden having cosy little chats, if he sent me texts asking me to keep secrets?' I'm so angry that spittle is flying from my mouth. I'm usually careful to control my temper in front of Jamie – in front of everyone – but all the fear, the resentment, that's been building up is erupting out of me.

Surprise registers on his face but I'm on a roll now. 'And don't say I'm paranoid or bloody irrational. I can't stand it when you say that. It's so patronising. And yes, I am jealous. I'm jealous of the fact that you put her feelings before mine. That your family seem to like her more than me, that when we're around your mum's house I feel so redundant, so unwelcome –'

'My family have *always* welcomed you.'

'No they haven't. The only one who is nice to me is Florrie.'

There is a stunned silence. I've run out of steam now so I throw the wet cloth into the sink.

Eventually Jamie speaks. 'Libs, I'm sorry. But you have to trust me. I trust you.'

A pang of guilt rips through me. 'I've not given you any reason not to,' I mumble.

'There's lots I don't know about you. You never talk about your childhood. You never even want to go to Yorkshire. You never tell me anything about your parents. You keep everything bottled up, even what happened in Thailand. I know you haven't told me the full story there.'

'What do you want to know?' I glare at him, my hands on my hips.

'I think you were badly hurt by someone. Someone you loved.' He moves towards me, his eyes soft. 'I think your friend's death has really affected you, has made you anxious about taking risks, trying anything new. You try to hide from anything that you deem dangerous, like flying, or driving a car. But you can't . . . look what happened at the school. An accident that you couldn't have prevented even though you spend your life trying to assess risk.'

'Don't try and psychoanalyse me, you sound like your mother. All I want to know is, did you send Anya those letters?'

He backs away from me, his body heavy with

disappointment, the softness in his eyes gone. I watch his face carefully to see if he's lying.

'No, I didn't. But it hurts me that you even have to ask.'

He looks sincere. I move towards him, my hand outstretched, a sorry on my lips, but he walks out of the room.

I can't sleep that night. I toss and turn, the sheets twisting beneath me, hot with anxiety. All I can think about is Martin accusing Jamie. After we rowed I apologised over slightly burnt pasta, and he'd reassured me it was a case of mistaken identity, that he would never cheat on me or hurt me. But Martin must have a reason to think it was Jamie. And even though I believe Jamie when he says he hasn't sent them, it unnerves me to think that someone wants Martin – and possibly me – to think that Jamie has.

17

The next day another parcel is hanging out of our letterbox from the same catalogue company. I recognise the garish orange wrapping instantly.

'Don't open it,' warns Jamie as I sit with it in front of me at the kitchen table. He's standing by the kettle. His eyes are tired. He was up until 1 a.m. working. 'You know you didn't order it so just return it.'

'I need to know what it is. I can't help but think these parcels are personal.'

He hands me a mug of tea. 'Why?'

'I don't know. But the Heywoods . . . they stayed here. They had access to our information. How do I know this isn't down to them?'

He opens his mouth to tell me not to be paranoid, but when he notices my expression he shuts it again. I tentatively tear open the plastic. It looks like some kind of wig, long and golden-brown. What can this mean?

'What is it?' Jamie peers over my shoulder.

'A wig. Why would anyone send me a wig?' I touch my own hair self-consciously to check that it hasn't started falling out.

He doesn't say anything and when I swivel around in my chair I notice he's moved away from me and is looking out the window. He has his back to me so I can't see his face but from the rigidness of his body I can tell he's tense. 'Jamie? Are you OK?' It's then I notice the phone pressed to his ear. I didn't hear it ring. He walks out of the room and to his office, phone clamped to his ear. It must be a work call, I think, as I pick up my own phone and dial the catalogue company. Or Hannah? I push this thought away.

The woman I speak to is helpful, informing me I'd opened an account last Thursday at 10 a.m. – the day we were returning from Cornwall – and had ordered the bag and the wig online twenty minutes later. I try to keep the frustration out of my voice as I inform her that there is some mistake, that I haven't opened an account or ordered anything. 'Please can you close it?' I ask. 'And if someone tries to open another account under my name can you let me know? It's very important.' She assures me she'll do as I ask but I feel unsettled as I put the phone down. Why would someone do this to me?

When I return from the post office – soaked through from a downpour because I'd forgotten my umbrella – a man I don't recognise is sitting drinking tea at the kitchen table with Jamie. He's wearing a Columbo-style mackintosh, with dark patches on the shoulders and back where he's been pelted with rain. He looks to be in his late fifties with a stern face and thick bifocal glasses perched on his nose.

'Libby.' Jamie pushes back his chair when he sees me.

His face is devoid of colour, making his stubble look more prominent. His whole demeanour is tense. 'This is DS Byrnes. He's got some news. About the Heywoods.'

I slide into a chair wordlessly. My eyes dart to Jamie to try and ascertain his emotions, but his face is closed, his lips pressed together so tightly that they turn white. I brace myself for news of Tara's murder. Spending time in her home, amongst the decor that she had chosen, the photographs on her wall, with her beautiful clothes hanging in the wardrobe, I feel her loss even though I've never known her.

I can't bear the tension any longer. 'Is she dead?' I blurt out.

'Who?' asks DS Byrnes, frowning.

'Tara Heywood?'

'Why would you think that she's dead, Mrs Hall?' His voice is calm but I can hear the note of suspicion. Is it directed at us? Does he think we have something to do with Tara's death?

'Because . . . because of the clothing. That we found in the garden . . . the blood . . .'

He stares at me in a way that makes me feel on edge, as though I've done something wrong.

'No, she's not dead. Both the Heywoods are alive and well, you'll be pleased to hear. We've finally managed to locate them. They've been away . . .'

'Well, yes . . .' I frown. Of course they've been away, I want to shout. They've been here.

He carries on as if I haven't spoken. 'They live in

London. Where they've been for months.' He peers at me over the rim of his thick glasses. 'They have never heard of you or –' he inclines his head in Jamie's direction '– Mr Hall. They know nothing about the house swap. In fact, they were under the impression that their Cornwall home was empty.'

I can tell by Jamie's body language that he's already been told this news. Shock renders me speechless for a few seconds. DS Byrnes assesses me coolly.

'But . . . but I don't understand.'

'Neither do we,' he says in the same grave voice. 'Can you tell me, from the beginning, everything that happened that led to this so-called house swap?' I notice he has an A4 notepad and pen in front of him. He clicks the end of the pen with his thumb and presses it against the paper, turning to me expectantly.

Jamie leans across the table and gives my hand a reassuring squeeze. 'Go and get the leaflet, Libs.'

I leap out of my chair and hurry into the hallway. I'd shoved the leaflet in the top drawer of the unit by the door just in case I'd lost Philip's number or there had been a problem. Not that I'd been expecting anything like this. I rummage through the drawer, taking all the papers out and rifling through them. But the leaflet is nowhere to be found.

With a sinking feeling I return to the kitchen. 'I can't find it,' I say. I can see the dismay written all over Jamie's features. 'It said that they were looking for a house swap, that they needed to be near the hospital as their daughter was undergoing life-saving surgery. He gave his phone number. I spoke to him. He was from the north, like me . . .'

DS Byrnes smiles to himself as though he's party to a joke nobody else can understand. And that's when I realise: there's no proof that the person we spoke to was Philip Heywood.

I sit down with a sigh. 'Look,' I begin, trying to remain calm as I reiterate the facts, 'I spoke to a man on the phone. He said he was called Philip Heywood. I googled him. He seemed respectable. He came to get the key from my neighbour upstairs. You can check with her. Her name's Evelyn Goodwin. And a woman was seen here too. A glass was left with a lipstick mark on.' I curse myself for washing it and not keeping it as proof but I'd had no reason to think I'd need to. 'They had been here.' I can hear my voice rising in desperation. 'And they do own the Hideaway because I looked it up before we went, just to be sure.'

He clears his throat. 'It's true, they do own that property but they've been at their home in London since the end of February. Neighbours have corroborated their story. The Heywoods don't have a daughter. They don't have any children.' He takes his glasses off and leans towards me. 'I don't know who was staying in your flat last week, Mrs Hall, but it certainly wasn't the Heywoods.'

18

I half expect DS Byrnes to arrest us, but instead he stands up and stuffs his notebook back into a briefcase, telling us he'll be in touch, as though he's a travelling salesman, not a detective. 'I'll be back in the next few days to interview your neighbour,' he says.

We sit at the table in stunned silence after he leaves, unable to take in what we've heard. I can't get my head around the notion that we've been conned, that someone has used Philip and Tara's home to swap with ours. But why?

Jamie puts his head in his hands and groans. 'What have we done?' His head shoots up, his eyes narrowed. 'We let strangers into our home and we don't even know their real names. They could have done anything while they were here. Rifled through our personal stuff. They could have bank details, credit card numbers . . . they were obviously in the study. I could tell that my folder had been moved.' He throws his arms up into the air. 'We're fucked!'

'No we're not. We need to cancel all our cards, check any accounts that have been opened in our name,' I say calmly. 'We've been unlucky, that's all. Lots of people do house swaps. Maybe the Heywoods are lying to the police. Have you thought about that? Maybe he *has* killed his wife and is trying to frame us.'

He sighs. 'Why would he even do that?'

'I don't know,' I admit. 'He needs someone to pin the blame on?'

He takes a deep breath and I can see he's making an effort to control his frustration. He spreads his hands out in front of him on the table. 'OK, here's what we know. Somebody – either the Heywoods or someone else – posted a leaflet through our door asking to swap homes. Were we targeted on purpose or did they do a leaflet drop along this road and we were the only ones to bite?'

I frown. 'I don't know. Does it make a difference?'

'Of course it does, Libs. Don't you see? If we were the only ones to receive a leaflet, then they wanted our particular flat. And if that's the case it's obviously personal.'

I'm appalled at the thought. 'I can't get my head around any of this. It doesn't make sense. Why would somebody want to use our flat? You think they used the Heywoods' house to get us out the way? And if it wasn't Philip and Tara it must be someone they know, someone who has a key!'

His eyes light up. 'Or someone who knew they were away a lot. Maybe they had a key cut without Philip and Tara knowing?'

'Like that Jim? He was really weird, following us about, or that other bloke at Lizard Point. He was definitely acting odd.'

'Or maybe Philip and Tara aren't as innocent in all this as they make out? Maybe their neighbours are covering for them and Philip killed his wife. Or they've both killed someone else?'

Despite our situation I smile at Jamie, feeling closer to him than I have since Cornwall. Because he's finally admitting that something is very wrong. He's not dismissing me as paranoid. This is actually happening to us.

He smiles back, a little uncertainly. Then he stands up, pushing his chair away in a sudden fit of frustration. 'We're just going around in circles, aren't we?'

We are. I have to do something constructive. I can't sit here ruminating any longer. 'I'm going upstairs to see Evelyn,' I say, also standing up. It's only 5.30 p.m. Not too late to go calling.

Jamie looks quizzical. 'Why?'

'Because she handed our key over to the man who called himself Philip Heywood and I also want to see if she received a leaflet too. I never thought to ask before.'

He pulls me into his arms. 'It will be all right, please don't worry, Libs. I know what you're like. After everything . . .' He trails off. He doesn't have to finish. I know what he's trying to say. It has been a traumatic few months, and now this. He brushes my hair back from my face and I lean against his chest. I've always felt safe before, wrapped in Jamie's arms, but this time I'm not sure if even Jamie can stop the unease that

169

has settled like dust into every layer of my being. I fear I'll never feel safe again.

Evelyn opens her front door cautiously, peering out with round, frightened eyes. When she sees it's me standing there she visibly relaxes. But even as she ushers me into the hallway, urging me to get out of the rain, she still wears that pinched, worried look on her face.

'Are you OK?' I ask.

She nods and waves her hand dismissively. 'I'm fine, don't worry about me. Just a hint of indigestion.' She rubs her floral blouse with a fist to illustrate her point, although that doesn't explain her fearful expression when she opened the door.

I follow her into the drawing room and watch as she makes herself comfortable in her usual seat by the window. I sit opposite her. I don't want to worry her, but I fill her in on what the detective told us earlier.

'So the man who came to get the key? What did he look like?' I ask her gently.

She has a cup of tea next to her, which she brings to her lips with an unsteady hand. 'Like I said before, he was mid-thirties. He looked a bit older than your Jamie, but not much.'

I recall the photo of Philip Heywood on Google, his dark hair flecked with grey and neatly combed into a side parting, his trim moustache, the shoulders of a pinstriped suit visible in the shot. He looked to be in his late forties, at least.

'Did he have dark hair and a moustache?' I can barely keep still; my whole body jangles with anticipation like the bracelets on Sylvia's wrists.

She frowns, replacing her teacup on the side table carefully. 'No . . . no, definitely not a moustache.' She picks up her knitting – it looks like the beginnings of baby booties in a soft lemon wool and the sight of them fills me with longing. I'd only just begun telling people I was pregnant, before the miscarriage. The twelve-week scan had been days away. We'd been so excited, Jamie and I, so looking forward to being parents. We had such plans. And the pregnancy had gone well. I'd experienced no side effects, no nausea. I cradle my stomach. There is still a slight bulge. My periods aren't back to normal, my body out of sorts and hormonal. It has only been five weeks, after all. Evelyn was so kind to me afterwards. She'd been a midwife when she was young, she told me, and had seen it all before. I wonder who she's knitting them for before my mind snaps back to thoughts of Philip. Evelyn pauses from her knitting and assesses me, eyebrows raised. 'It was hard to tell, really, because he was wearing a hat.'

'A hat?'

'Yes, one of those ugly ones you young people like to wear nowadays.' She gives a short, sharp laugh. 'Like a tea cosy.'

'Do you mean a beanie?' I manage.

'Yes, that's it, a beanie. He had one of those on. And a woolly, fleecy thing.'

171

It's the same man, it has to be – the man from Lizard Point, the man who had been watching us on the beach near The Hideaway. Who was he and what did he want?

Evelyn carries on knitting, the needles clacking. Radio 2 is on in the background and Simon Mayo is chatting to a guest.

I swallow down my nausea. 'Did you . . . did you ever receive a leaflet through the post? Asking if you'd do a house swap?'

She glances up at me over her needles, which are still moving at speed. 'No. I didn't get anything like that.' She stops knitting and looks serious. 'Do you think this man is responsible for all those strange things that happened to you on holiday?'

I shake my head. 'I don't know. I think so. He's obviously not Philip Heywood. I don't know who he is.'

'Like I said before, I didn't get the sense he stayed very long in your flat.'

That's probably right. After all, he couldn't have been in Bath for very long if he'd followed us down to Cornwall.

'Long enough to do something,' I admit with a regretful sigh. 'I just wish I knew what.' I stand up to leave. 'I'd better get back. But please promise me, Evelyn, if you notice anything *weird* . . . anyone hanging around our flat, will you let me know?'

She stands up too. I'm short but she only reaches my shoulder. 'There is something . . .'

'What? What is it?'

'I've noticed . . . men. Not always the same man, but different men. Lurking around outside. They've not done anything. It's as if they are waiting . . .'

'Waiting?'

'Yes. I'm not sure what for. But it has frightened me a little bit.'

Was that why she'd been so reluctant to open the door earlier?

'You know,' she says, folding her knitting away and placing it on the side table. 'I do see some strange things sometimes, sitting here all day.' She takes one of my hands; her skin feels like tissue paper, thin and fragile. 'Please be careful, Libby, my love. You've always been so good to me.'

'Evelyn, you're scaring me now. What strange things do you see?'

She blinks, as though inwardly debating whether to tell me. And then, 'I've also seen a woman hanging around outside.'

'A woman?'

'It might be nothing. I'm not sure. It's probably just a coincidence . . .' She sighs. 'Just be careful, be aware, that's all I'm saying. When you get to my age you realise there are a lot of strange people out there, people who think nothing of hurting others. And some of them can be the closest person to us.' She smiles regretfully. 'My husband didn't always tell me the truth. I wasted so many years with him. Just make sure you get the truth, Libby, my dear.'

As I return to my flat, looking over my shoulder for the shadowy, nameless men or the faceless woman that she talked about, I have the distinct, unnerving impression that she'd been trying to warn me about Jamie.

19

As I close the shutters before bed that evening, I see a figure on the other side of the road. It's too dark and too far away to tell if it's a man or a woman, but by their height I think they must be female. Their features are masked by the dull light but I can make out that they're leaning against the garden wall of the house opposite and smoking a cigarette. Who would be hanging around at this time of night? Is this the woman Evelyn was talking about?

When I look again, ten minutes later, the person has gone.

I hardly sleep. Evelyn's words spin around and around in my head, refusing to be dislodged, like a wayward sock in a washing machine. Every time a shadow passes across our Roman blind, or the sound of a bin clatters in the street, I wake up with a start, my heart pounding, my nightwear clinging to my sweaty skin. What was Evelyn trying to tell me? Was she insinuating that Jamie wasn't to be trusted?

Suspicion swells inside me. I so desperately want to think the best of Jamie but I can't stop the nagging voice in my head telling me that Anya is beautiful, that Jamie's by himself in the house all day and has plenty of opportunity for an affair, that he's cheated before. How would it have started? Had they bumped into each other while he was out walking Ziggy? Most people stop to stroke or coo over our dog, and Jamie is handsome, friendly. And we've had our problems these past few months. Has Jamie's head been turned by Anya? Had they got talking and then realised their mutual attraction? Did they fall into bed together, unable to stop themselves?

My thoughts are running away from me like an excitable toddler. I know, deep down, that Jamie loves me. And he's too disorganised, too moralistic to conduct a double life. But then Hannah's text message pops into my head along with the little voice reminding me that he is keeping something from me; something Hannah doesn't want me to know.

Is Hannah behind the house swap? Did she send me the backpack and the wig? That doesn't make sense. Why would she? And what about the bloodied clothing we found in the Heywoods' garden? If it doesn't belong to Tara then whose was it?

On Saturday I offer to take Ziggy for his morning walk. Jamie pauses from tying the laces on his trainers to look up at me. 'It's the only exercise I get,' he says, sounding disappointed. 'I sometimes run with him. I'm stuck behind a desk all day.' Is that the only reason he's so desperate to go? Or is he hoping to bump into Anya?

'Let's go together then,' I suggest. He seems surprised but he doesn't object as we amble down the street. In fact, he seems happy to take my hand in his. It's a sunny day, unusually warm for April, and I'm only wearing a thin jacket over a T-shirt and jeans. I purposefully lead him past Anya's house, hoping to spot her. I'm not sure why. Maybe I want to see how Jamie reacts if we bump into her. If he really has sent her romantic cards, if he really does have a schoolboy crush on her, I will know by the way he acts around her. Martin's car is in the driveway – a black, shiny BMW – but there is no sign of either of them, much to my disappointment. I wonder, as we head to the park, whether Martin actually believes his wife has been unfaithful. Maybe she really is having an affair. Maybe there's another Jamie and he'd jumped to the wrong conclusions?

We spend Easter Sunday with Jamie's family, like we always do. It's times like this that I miss having a family of my own to spend the holidays with. I watch Hannah, noting the many times she tries to engage Jamie in a private conversation. Could she have hired some man to pretend to be Philip Heywood to drive a wedge between me and Jamie? But that's just too bizarre. Surely she's not capable of that kind of manipulation?

I observe her bustling around Sylvia, helping set the table and placing pretty, ditsy napkins on plates. My offers of help were batted away earlier by Sylvia, with a slightly harried expression.

I also study Katie as she flits around the house in her too-skimpy clothes, acting like the teenager she still thinks she is, her hair in ropes around her shoulders, a strand woven around one of her fingers. She has a new boyfriend with her, someone else to squeeze in around the oval dining table and for Sylvia to fuss over. He's older, handsome in an obvious kind of way, with too-white teeth, dark hair and a square Desperate Dan jaw. His name's Gerard and they'd met 'through friends', apparently. 'He went to Sheffield uni, didn't you, Gerard?' Katie says over the roast duck. 'Like you, Libby.'

Gerard, who's sitting between Katie and Hannah and opposite me, Florrie and Jamie, grins inanely. 'I certainly did.'

There's something about him I don't like. He seems too pleased with himself, with his top-of-the-range car and his job in 'events management'. He assesses me then with his hooded eyes. He resembles a crow. 'What year did you graduate?'

'Um.' I prod a roast potato with my fork. 'Two thousand and eight.'

'Ah. Two thousand for me. I'm a little older than you.' That made him ten years older than Katie. He looks like the type of man who thinks it's a status symbol to have a younger woman on his arm, as though Katie is a flash motor to brag about. 'What course did you do?'

'English Lit.' My mouth has gone dry. Gerard's too nosy for my liking.

'Me too. Do you remember Professor Peterson? He was a right one, wasn't he? I'm sure he had narcolepsy, because he seemed to fall asleep as he talked. Either that or his lectures were so soporific he bored himself.' He laughs at his own joke and I grin along, chewing my potato. Katie can't stop stroking his arm and gazing adoringly at him. Richard, who's sitting at the head of the table opposite Sylvia, watches them with interest over his glass of red wine, as though he hopes they'll start having sex right there and then.

Jamie and I had agreed before the meal not to mention the disturbing developments and our fears about the Heywoods to Jamie's family. We still hope there will be a simple explanation for it all. Although as time goes by I'm at a loss to know what that could be. Gerard is staring at me expectantly, another question about our university days already forming on his lips. He opens his mouth. 'And do you remember . . .'

I need to change the subject, quickly. I don't want to be engaged in conversation with Gerard any longer. 'Florrie!' I cut right across him in my best teacher's voice, clear and confident. 'I really love that top you're wearing. Where did you get it?'

I return to school on Tuesday, welcoming some normality, some routine back into our lives. I'm delighted to be teaching again, to interact with my class and to gossip with Cara. I'm so busy over the next few days that I push everything else to the back of my mind, where it sits there, niggling away at me like an ache.

I'm tired as I trudge home from work on Friday evening. It's been a busy day; a Year One child threw up outside the receptionist's office, a parent came in to complain that her son wasn't being moved up the reading levels quickly enough, and I've had to get to the bottom of why one of the Year Twos deliberately ripped up a library book in a fit of temper. After so many restless nights, I can hardly think straight. The rain begins to fall as I turn into our street, cementing my bad mood. I see Evelyn sitting in her chair by the window. It's prematurely dark because of the weather but she doesn't have a lamp on. I wave but she doesn't wave back. My mind is foggy with tiredness. All I want to do is convince Jamie to get a takeaway and flop in front of the telly to watch *The Affair*.

My heart falls when I see DS Byrnes sitting at our kitchen table. He stands when he sees me. He's wearing the same beige mackintosh and I can see a stain down the front that looks like brown sauce. He has a mug in front of him, the one with a triangular chip at its rim that we should have thrown away years ago. I can't believe Jamie has given it to him.

Jamie pushes back his chair, relief on his face. 'I've told DS Byrnes everything we know,' he says before I've even sat down. I drop my bag by my chair and shrug off my jacket. The air in the kitchen feels oppressive, with a faint tang of spicy noodles which Jamie must have cooked for his lunch.

'Right.' I glance at Byrnes. 'Jamie's told you that we think the man at Lizard Point is the same person who pretended to be Philip Heywood?'

'Yes. He's filled me in on everything. We are trying to ascertain who might have had a key to the Heywoods' property.'

'Do you think –' I gulp '– that a murder took place there?'

'I can't reveal that at the moment, I'm afraid, Mrs Hall. Although I can say that the clothing has been examined and it doesn't belong to Mrs Heywood. The blood isn't human either.'

'Not human? You mean . . . it belongs to an animal?'

'Yes. We think it must have been put in the garden to frighten you. We are also trying to discover whether this is something personal against yourself and Mr Hall or whether it's a scam.' He clears his throat. 'Have you noticed anything missing from your property? Jewellery or any other items that could be worth something?'

I frown. 'No, nothing.' It's one of the first things I did when returning from Cornwall, not that we have much in the way of valuables.

'And you've changed your locks?'

I nod. 'As soon as our upstairs neighbour told me that Philip Heywood – or who we thought was Philip Heywood – hadn't returned the key.'

'That's great. I'll be in touch when we have any more

information.' He inclines his head towards Jamie. 'Thank you, Mr Hall, for the updated statement. That's very helpful.' I almost expect him to doff his hat at us, if he was wearing one. There is something reassuringly old-fashioned about him.

Jamie sees him out and I switch the kettle on, smiling to myself when I hear Jamie bounding into the kitchen. 'Isn't it good news?' he asks.

'There didn't seem to be any news. He just wanted more information from you, didn't he?'

'Yes, but I think he believes us. He said he's going to speak to Evelyn, and she'll confirm that a man came to pick up the key from her and what he looked like. Honestly, for a while there, Libs, I thought we might get arrested for murder or something.'

I laugh, although it sticks in my throat. All I can think about is that someone deliberately soaked a woman's underwear in animal's blood to scare us.

About twenty minutes later, Jamie is ordering a take-away and I'm pottering in the kitchen when I hear the sound of knuckles rapping urgently on our front door. I can see from the kitchen window a flash of DS Byrnes' beige coat, the rain falling heavily onto his head and shoulders. I curse under my breath, wondering why he's back again so soon. Maybe Evelyn has revealed something he needs to ask us about? I shuffle to the door in my too-large slippers, my dressing gown wrapped around me. I'd changed out of my suit the minute the detective left. I feel bloated and uncomfortable.

I open the door and let him in out of the rain, a gust of cold air in his wake. He stands in the hallway, his eyes narrowed, making them look even smaller behind his thick glasses. 'I'm so sorry to bother you again, Mrs Hall, but I can't get hold of your neighbour. I've been knocking for ages and I can see her in the window. But she's obviously too scared to answer. I was wondering if you would come with me. Maybe if she sees you then she'll answer. I know some old people don't like to open the door when it starts getting dark.'

I swallow down a sigh and grab my raincoat from its peg, kicking off my slippers and shoving my feet into a pair of wellies. I don't get the chance to tell Jamie where I'm going as I follow DS Byrnes to Evelyn's door.

Most windows along the street are illuminated by the soft glow of lamps or overhead lights, but Evelyn's flat is shrouded in darkness. I can see her in the window. I lean over the railings to tap on the glass, careful not to fall onto the sharp spikes or to lose my balance. I imagine landing with a sickening thud outside our kitchen window, Jamie finding me prostrate on the pavement outside our front door.

'Evelyn, it's only me,' I call, but my voice drifts away into the rush-hour traffic building up along the main road.

'Who lives above Mrs Goodwin?' says DS Byrnes.

'Nobody.' I tap the glass again, trying not to lose my footing. 'It's a two-storey house. The basement where we live was converted and sold separately.'

Why isn't Evelyn answering me? And why is her head slumped back against the headrest of her favourite chair? 'She can barely make the stairs any more but she's lived here more than forty years.' I turn to him, trying to quell the worry lodged heavily in the pit of my stomach. 'I think something's wrong. I can't see properly over the railings but she doesn't look like she's moving. She could be asleep? But she's eighty . . .'

'Understood. I'm going to have to break in.'

'What the hell is going on?' Jamie is suddenly standing on the pavement, in the rain, watching us. 'You'd disappeared. I was worried.'

I fight back tears. 'Evelyn's not answering the door, Jay. Can you go and get the spare key?'

DS Byrne looks relieved not to have to break the door down. 'You have a key? Why didn't you say?'

'You didn't ask.' We'd swapped keys just in case either of us ever got locked out. Although she doesn't go very far nowadays. I pull the coat around me, shivering.

Jamie's back within seconds. He darts up the stairs to join us, turning the key in the lock deftly, the heavy front door swinging open. I run past him, the others close behind.

I know, before I even enter the room, that she's dead. But I rush to her anyway, my insides twisting with grief to see her sitting in her favourite chair, the yellow baby booties she'd been knitting on the floor by her feet, her beautiful blue eyes staring into nothing, her hand on her chest as though, as death approached, she'd been willing her heart to keep beating.

20

I spend most of Saturday in bed, crying; Jamie can't understand why I've taken her death so hard. How can he when he is constantly in the bosom of his heaving, loving family? He only knows what it's like to be loved unconditionally. I haven't experienced that type of maternal love in a long time – and it wasn't as though Evelyn loved me, we only knew each other for two years, but I could tell she cared about me, that she was on my side. She was the closest thing I had to a grandmother and now she's gone.

Her last words to me play on a loop in my mind. She'd implied that I shouldn't trust my husband. Why would she say that? I think again of those cards Martin accused Jamie of sending to Anya. The secret he shares with Hannah. What had Evelyn been alluding to? I dismiss the thought straight away, feeling disloyal to Jamie for even entertaining the idea, but it keeps creeping back into my head, needling away at me. I've always been so sure that Jamie would never cheat on me, that he takes our marriage vows seriously. He is a black and white kind of guy, no grey areas for him. It can be infuriating sometimes but that's why I love him. Yet what if I'm wrong? What if I'm one of those women who's blind to what's going on under her nose?

Is everything that's happening to us now because of Jamie? What's that saying? Hell hath no fury like a woman scorned. Who has Jamie scorned?

The thought of losing him is so painful it makes me feel sick. He's the only person I have left.

He walks into the room, carrying a tray of tea and toast. *Would he be so kind to me*, I reason, *if he was having an affair? Guilt*, insists the voice inside my head. *Guilt is why he's bringing you breakfast in bed*. I'd read a book only the other week, about a marriage where the woman finds out that her husband has a secret life; that he isn't what he'd seemed. It's too common, there are always stories about it in newspapers and magazines under screaming headlines of 'Love Rat' or 'Love Cheat'.

And Jamie has kept things from me before.

The loan from his mother for one thing. He doesn't think I know about that, but I overheard them talking in low voices. He'd been unable to set up the business without her help. I still don't understand why he couldn't just tell me. Pride, I suppose. And he knows I'd hate the thought of owing his mother anything.

'Are you all right, Libs?' he says now, placing the tray across my lap as though I'm a patient in hospital. He sits on the edge of the bed. 'I'm so sorry about Evelyn.'

A tear snakes out the corner of my eye and I grab the tissue from beneath my pyjama sleeve. After constantly sniffing as a child due to hay fever, my mum always made me carry a tissue. It's a habit I can't break, and in a strange way it makes me think of her, knowing that she cared about me in her own way. 'Thank you for this,' I say, indicating the breakfast, the tissue damp and starting to break up between my fingers. He opens his mouth as if to say something but then closes it again. I know what he's thinking; that this isn't just about Evelyn, it's about losing my mum too. I sense him contemplating whether to bring up counselling again.

I take a sip of tea, assessing him over the rim of my mug. He rubs his eyes. His blond hair is damp from the rain and he looks ruggedly handsome in his old Primal Scream T-shirt and jeans. I yearn to reach over and kiss him but something stops me. He's smiling at me but it's too set, too fake.

I put the cup down. 'What is it? What's wrong?'

His smile slips. 'It's been a stressful few weeks and I didn't want to worry you with this,' he says, looking down into his lap. It's then that I notice the bank statement in his hand. 'But I've spoken to DS Byrnes and we think it must be the same person who's responsible for opening the catalogue accounts under your name. And all those annoying pamphlets and circulars you keep receiving.'

I'm angry that he went straight to DS Byrnes instead of talking to me about it first. The tips of my fingers tingle and I resist the urge to snatch the letter out of his hand. 'What does it say?'

His voice is strained when he replies. 'Our bank account has been emptied. And someone has opened a four-thousand pound credit card in your name and spent all the money.'

I fall back onto the pillows, fresh tears forming in my eyes. 'Oh God.'

'I know. Luckily our account wasn't that flush at the time. They only took seven hundred pounds.'

'Only!'

'It could have been worse.'

'And the credit card?'

'That's a bit more difficult. We're going to have to prove you didn't open it. They had all your details. National Insurance number. Bank account numbers.'

I push the tray aside, suddenly losing my appetite, and jump out of bed, pulling my dressing gown on. 'Who would do this to us, Jamie? Why go to such lengths?'

'Someone seriously fucked up, that's who,' says Jamie darkly. 'Do you know anyone like that, Libby? Anyone from your past?'

I round on him, my cheeks burning. 'Do you?'

'The bag, Libby. It was a backpack. Could it mean something?'

'Why? Why does this have to be something to do with me? This could be about you. A woman who you've scorned, perhaps? There seem to be a few.'

'Not this again,' he mumbles, his face crestfallen. 'Why won't you believe me?'

My anger vanishes as quickly as it arrived. 'I'm sorry,' I say, going over to him. 'It just doesn't make sense, Jay. None of this makes sense.'

Has someone organised this whole house swap just so they can get into our flat and rifle through our things to steal enough details to get a credit card in my name? I've read newspaper articles about the elaborate lengths scam artists sometimes go to. But why us? Why not one of the bigger houses down the street? There are many more valuable houses in Bath, like Martin and Anya's, for example. Why choose our small basement flat?

Unless it *was* personal.

Jamie plants a kiss on my mouth. It feels perfunctory rather than loving. Why do I feel that these events are forcing us apart rather than together? He stands up and stretches his long legs. 'You've had a shock with Evelyn's death, I'll sort this out. It will be all right.'

I'm touched by his optimism; it's like having the old Jamie back, the one I'd first met, who had taken a broken, defensive girl with enough baggage for a year's holiday around the world, and breathed life back into her as though he were a paramedic. I can't reconcile that Jamie with the one that Evelyn warned me about; the one who keeps secrets, and tells lies, who maybe has affairs with a married neighbour. But our personalities are multi-faceted, aren't they? Maybe those traits are part of him and I'm only beginning to realise.

I can hear him clattering around the kitchen, emptying the dishwasher and putting the crockery and glasses away. Usually he has to be reminded to empty the dishwasher. He obviously wants to keep busy, I tell myself, pushing away any disloyal thoughts that it's guilt galvanising him.

'I'm popping out, Libs,' he calls from the kitchen. 'I'll be a few hours. See you later.' Before I can answer I hear the front door slam. Where's he going? I rush to the kitchen window and pull aside the blinds, but there is no sign of him, the pavement above empty and slick with rain. Ziggy whines and I turn to see him lying despondently on the wooden floor, his head between his paws, looking up at me with his big brown eyes. Jamie usually takes Ziggy when he goes out. I crouch down to comfort him. 'I'll take you for a walk. Let me just have a shower,' I say, kissing the top of his fluffy head, inhaling his comforting, doggy scent.

I'm just about to go back into the bedroom when I notice Jamie's laptop on the kitchen table. He usually keeps it in the study. He very rarely works weekends. He's still starting out, so he doesn't have that many clients. In fact, he complained only a few nights ago that he isn't as busy now that two potential clients have pulled out, deciding to go 'another way'. It worried him; I could tell by the creases in his forehead as he told me, trying to appear casual with his legs stretched out in front of him and his laptop resting on his knees, yet his voice gave it away. It had been tinged with panic; questions of how would we cope financially left unspoken.

I don't know what makes me do it. It's something I'd never have considered in the past. Maybe it's what Evelyn said, her last words to me still fresh in my mind. I lift the lid of his laptop. He has a picture of the two of us as his wallpaper, Ziggy squashed between us, our arms around his neck. It was taken last summer, a few weeks before we got married, in his mum's garden. It's the same photo I have on my phone. We both look tanned, my dark fringe swept to the side, a contrast to his dirty blond mop, our eyes shining with happiness, our smiles wide and sappy with love, the top of Ziggy's fluffy head reaching to just under our chins. A lump forms in my throat. I snap the lid shut. What am I thinking? I can't spy on my husband.

A knock at the door shatters the silence and Ziggy leaps to his feet, emitting a deep bark. I go to the door, opening it halfway, conscious that I'm still in my dressing gown. A man is standing in front of me, good-looking, in his early twenties.

'Yes?'

'I'm looking for a Jamie Hall,' he says in a foreign accent I can't quite place.

'He's not here at the moment. Can I help?'

There is something about the man's expression that unnerves me: cocky, arrogant, his body language too familiar. 'He said he would meet me here. But he didn't say anything about a three-way.' His eyes travel to my bare legs as though following an invisible line, stopping where the velour dressing gown meets my calves.

'What are you talking about?'

'The advert . . .' he says, frowning, suddenly unsure of himself. He lowers his voice. 'The sex?'

I close the door in his face, my heart pounding. The sex? In the middle of the afternoon? In broad daylight?

'You bitch!' he shouts through the door, and then there's the sound of his boot kicking the wood. Ziggy begins barking furiously.

'If you don't leave right now I'll call the police,' I scream back, fleeing into the kitchen so that I can watch as he strides up the steps to the pavement above. I see him pause when he reaches the top and then stroll on as if nothing untoward has happened.

Evelyn's words flash through my mind. *I've noticed . . . men. Not always the same man, but different men. Lurking around outside . . . It's as if they are waiting . . .*

I open Jamie's laptop and google his name, already having an idea of what I might find. I have to scroll through numerous Jamie Halls until I find what I'm looking for, and, despite my suspicions, my mouth fills with saliva when I click onto the lurid porn website advertising Jamie's services.

21

I pace the flat, unable to settle. I ring Jamie's mobile but there's no answer. Where the hell is he?

I try to keep busy to ward off my unease. I shower, dress and take Ziggy for a walk via Anya and Martin's house. It's a Saturday but Jamie left in such a hurry this morning that I can't help the flame of suspicion that flickers in my mind. Is there some truth to Martin's accusations? No smoke without fire, right? Is Jamie with Anya at this moment? As I approach their house I notice Anya in the driveway, pulling dandelions out of the front garden. Martin's car isn't on the drive. Even weeding she looks glamorous, a scarf tied around her dark hair and wearing skinny jeans that hug and flatter. I hesitate by the entrance. Dare I approach her? As if sensing my presence, she stands up and turns around, her eyes widening when she notices me.

'Can I help you?' she asks, walking towards me. Her voice is soft and well modulated but her eyes are wary. She's wearing gardening gloves with a pretty floral print. I try to work out her age. She can't be more than thirty at the most. But the way she holds herself, with a kind of self-assurance, reminds me of some of the mothers at the school.

I can feel myself blushing. 'Um . . . I'm Libby. Jamie Hall's wife.'

Recognition dawns. 'Ah. I see.'

'I . . . actually I don't think you do. Could we have a quick chat?'

She frowns, her gaze taking in Ziggy, as though worried he'll mess up her front lawn. I notice she's wearing red lipstick, which enhances her olive complexion. She reminds me of Nicole Scherzinger.

'I don't think there is anything to chat about. Do you?'

'My husband didn't send you those cards!' I exclaim. I don't know why it's so important for me to tell her, maybe it's pride. I don't want her to think my husband has a crush on her. 'I don't know why you think he did . . .'

A smile plays on her lips. 'Maybe because he signed them.'

'Saying what? Jamie Hall? Don't you think that's a bit weird, including his surname?'

She looks unconvinced, as if she's used to being sent romantic cards and mementos from lovesick admirers.

'Do you even know Jamie?' I blurt out. I wait, my throat dry, for her response. Ziggy pulls on his lead and I pat his head to reassure him.

Anya appraises me with kohl-rimmed eyes, and then shakes her head. 'We've never spoken,' she admits, 'apart from a brief good morning.' Relief surges through me. Thank God. 'But,' she adds, 'I've seen him around quite a bit. He's cute.'

She watches me for a reaction but I charge on: 'The

thing is, we think we're victims of some type of scam. The police are investigating. We did a house swap. Now things are missing and weird stuff is happening. Jamie didn't send you the cards but we don't know who did. I just . . .' I pause, my heart racing. 'I just wanted you to know that.'

She shrugs. 'Fine.' She transfers her secateurs from one hand to the other. 'Is that all?' She raises a perfectly groomed eyebrow. They are so perfect, in fact, that they look like they've been tattooed on.

'Yes . . . thanks . . .' I mumble.

'Good. Nice to meet you,' she says and then turns on her heels – she's actually wearing heels to garden in – and struts back down her driveway.

I've only been back in the flat half an hour before Jamie walks in. He has a streak of dirt on his face and dark patches on the knees of his jeans. What has he been doing?

'Where have you been? I rang your mobile, you didn't answer.'

He can't meet my eye. He snaps the kettle on and then leans against the counter, playing with his phone. 'Helping out a friend. Why?'

'Because while you were out a man turned up here. Asking for you. He wanted sex?'

His head whips up so fast it's actually comical. 'What?'

'Yes, that's right. He was looking to have sex with you. And then I realised why.' I lift the lid of his laptop. The porn site is still on the screen. Jamie rushes towards it, his face ashen. The website is explicit, advertising 'bisexual Jamie Hall' who is 'up for anything with either sex, particularly hard-core bondage'. In the photo he looks so young and handsome, in jeans and a white shirt. He must have been about nineteen. *Hannah.* The photo would have been taken around the time they'd been going out. Has she done this? I dismiss the thought immediately. Hannah loves Jamie. Why would she do something so horrendous?

'I've never seen this website, you do know that, don't you?' he says, gripping the edge of the table as if to moor himself to the room.

'Of course I do,' I say, shocked that he could think I'd doubt him about this.

'Where did they get my picture?' He shakes his head. 'I can't believe a guy turned up here. Christ, Libs, anything could have happened to you.' He turns to me, his eyes full of fear. It upsets me to see him like this. It's usually me who's afraid. 'I don't think we should stay here at the moment.'

I sigh. Ever since that man turned up I've been thinking the same. I've googled my name and nothing has come up. But that doesn't mean I'm not somewhere on the web, offering my services. 'But where would we go? We can't afford to stay in a hotel. Especially now.'

'I think we should move in with my mum. Just for a bit . . .'

My heart sinks. 'Or we could stay in the coach house

at the bottom of the garden?' I say, liking the idea much more than sharing a house with Sylvia and Katie, regardless of how much space they have.

His cheeks colour. 'Ah, well Hannah and Felix are staying there at the moment. She couldn't afford the rent on her place any more and . . . don't look at me like that, Libby.'

I swallow down my anger. 'What?'

'She's been having financial trouble. That's what she didn't want me to tell you. She's embarrassed. Her ex isn't paying child support, she's only got that part-time job in the estate agent's. It doesn't pay much. She couldn't keep up the payments on the flat she was renting. And . . . well, I've been trying to help her.'

'Financially? Jamie, we haven't got much money ourselves.'

He sighs. 'I know that. But I said I'd have a word with Mum, who then offered Hannah the coach house rent-free.'

'That's incredibly generous of Sylvia. But why didn't you tell me?'

'Because I knew that you wouldn't like it.'

'Is that your philosophy on our marriage then? You keep things from me that you know I won't like? What else are you keeping from me?'

He runs a hand over his face and groans. 'We can't keep going over this again . . . we've got more pressing things to worry about. Like this fucking website with my name and our address all over it.'

'Just get it taken down then,' I hiss. 'You're in IT. I'm sure you can find a way.' I push my chair back so hard that it crashes to the floor. We both stare at it in surprise. I'm about to flounce off but Jamie stands and grabs my arm.

'Libs. Please don't . . .'

I burst into tears. 'This is a nightmare, Jamie. I feel like we're in a nightmare.'

He cradles me to him. 'I know.'

'And Evelyn's dead,' I sob into his T-shirt. 'I can't believe she's dead.' Then a thought strikes me. I stand back; the neck of his top is wet with my tears. 'Is that where you were this morning? Helping Hannah move?'

He nods sheepishly.

'So you left me here, crying over Evelyn, to go and help Hannah move?'

'I'm sorry. I'd promised, and I didn't know Evelyn was going to die. I was only gone for a few hours. She just needed some help moving the heavier stuff.'

'And she couldn't get a removal van?'

'She couldn't afford it.'

'You should have told me, Jay. I could have helped too. But Hannah wouldn't have wanted that, would she? She wants you all to herself.'

He looks shamefaced. 'I'm such a prat. Libby, I'm so sorry. I should have told you. I don't know why I didn't. I was going to and then Evelyn died and you've got enough on your plate. I just thought . . .'

I pick the chair up off the floor and sit down on it

heavily. I want to hurl abuse at him but I feel so tired that all I can do is sink further into my chair. What is the point in arguing about it now? He's right, we have more pressing matters to worry about. Like the website. 'What are you going to do about this?' I say, pointing at the offending page still showing on the screen.

He sits down next to me. 'Somebody must really hate us, Libs, to go to all this trouble. That's what scares me.'

We decide to move in with Sylvia the next day. I don't relish the idea but agree with Jamie that it's for the best. Just until this whole nightmare is over.

My heart is heavy as I fold some clothes and belongings into a suitcase. The sunshine of yesterday is forgotten and now rain hammers on the windows outside. Ziggy is turning in circles, desperate for a wee.

'I don't fancy taking him out in this,' says Jamie, watching the downpour out of our bedroom window. 'Another bloody April shower.'

'Just take him into Evelyn's garden,' I suggest. It's visible from our window. She'd offered, in the past, for us to take Ziggy out there, but we didn't like to. It didn't feel right somehow, even though it's an eyesore, overgrown with weeds and bushes.

'Do you think Evelyn would mind?'

Tears spring into my eyes. I can't get used to the fact that she's no longer upstairs, sitting in her favourite chair, knitting. I pull a tissue from my sleeve and shake my head, my throat restricted by tears.

'I'll take him quickly before he pisses on the carpet,' says Jamie with a rueful smile.

He calls the dog and I hear the clink of the lead as he snaps it onto Ziggy's collar and the front door opening and closing. I fold clothes, wondering how long we'll be away for, when I hear Ziggy bark. I glance up. I can see them outside so I knock on the glass and wave. The garden is on our level which meant Evelyn could only access it from a raised patio area outside her kitchen, or from a side gate at ground level. It would have made more sense for the garden to have been sold along with the basement flat but, if it had, it would have bumped the price up and then we wouldn't have been able to afford it.

What will happen to Evelyn's flat now and who will buy it? It won't be the same having new neighbours, I think sadly as I watch Ziggy bound across the wet lawn. Jamie is standing with his back to me, his hood pulled up. He's wearing his green parka that makes him look like a student. We need a garden. I touch my stomach. My periods are so irregular that I don't dare hope I might be pregnant, but the nausea, the heightened sense of smell, makes me determined to do a test to find out. Should we consider putting the flat on the market? With Evelyn's place up for sale, someone might buy the whole building and turn it back into a house. If we moved further out of Bath we might be able to afford a small house with a garden for the same price we could get for the flat. It would mean a longer commute in the morning, unless

I moved schools. Either way it would be a fresh start and a garden for Ziggy and possibly a baby. It's something to think about.

I'm startled by a cry coming from outside. It's Jamie, an edge of panic to his voice. I rush to the window. He's standing towards the end of the garden now, a lone figure, the weeds brushing his knees. He's bending over, as though winded. Ziggy is by his side, staring down at something. What's wrong with Jamie? Is he ill again? I run into the hallway, push my feet into my wellies and charge around the side of the building and into the garden, the rain immediately soaking my long-sleeved T-shirt so that it clings to my body.

'Jamie!'

He stands up, waving his arms. 'Don't come over here. Stay there!' he shouts in alarm. I don't listen to him of course. Oh, how I wish I'd listened.

I wade through the wet foliage to join him and there, sprawled out amongst the weeds, is a body. It's almost concealed by the long, wet grass but I can make out that it's a man, his blotchy face staring up at the colourless sky, his eyes open, unblinking. His head is bare, showing a wound to his temple, his short dark hair matted with blood. Even though his top is soiled with mud I can tell it's a fleece. My hand flies to my mouth and I grab Jamie's arm as my legs collapse beneath me.

22

Jamie and I sit on Sylvia's overstuffed sofa unable to speak, gripping the mugs of tea that she'd thrust into our hands the minute we arrived. The only sounds to be heard are the ticking of the large grandfather clock and the wind that rattles the leaded windows. Hannah is on the other sofa, next to Sylvia and Katie. Their eyes are round with horror as they stare at us. It's almost funny to see their identical expressions: their slack jaws, arched eyebrows and bloodless pallor.

The duck-egg-blue walls are oddly calming, as is the hypnotic ticking of the clock. I've eventually stopped trembling and now I just feel numb. Ziggy is slumped across my feet like a furry pair of slippers.

'Do they know who this man is?' says Sylvia eventually, getting up to draw the heavy curtains.

'Not yet,' replies Jamie. Both their voices sound far away, as though coming from the next room.

'And I'm assuming they don't know how long he's been there?'

I feel Jamie shrug.

I tilt forward to put my mug down on the glass coffee table, my limbs so heavy that even this small act is a huge effort. 'I think I'll go to bed,' I say, getting to my feet unsteadily. Ziggy jumps up and follows me, as though relieved to get away from the oppressive atmosphere.

I can sense their eyes on me as I leave the room. Sylvia's voice floats after me in a loud whisper. 'Poor thing, she's still in shock, two dead bodies in two days. It's going to take her a while to get over this.'

The spare room smells musty and has an unused air, although it's neat and tidy, with a white-painted dressing table in the corner and pale-green flowered curtains at the windows. I crawl in between the crisp, white sheets, still fully clothed. I'm freezing, and feel as though I'm coming down with flu. It isn't even nine o'clock but I can't face anyone. I just want to shut my eyes and fall into a deep, oblivious sleep where I don't keep seeing Evelyn's face, serene in death, or the man's bulging, colourless eyes, the gash to the side of his head.

Jamie and I had been frozen for the first few minutes, unable to do anything except stare at the dead man, oblivious to the rain that soaked through our clothes or Ziggy standing quietly next to us. I half expected the man to jump up and tell us this was a sick joke. But of course he hadn't. The air had been strangely still and quiet; even the rain was soundless, as if the world was holding its breath, waiting to see what we would do next.

Jamie was the first to act, pulling the phone from his pocket and calling the police. Within ten minutes two detectives had turned up. Then it took hours to explain to them all that had happened. We had to keep repeating every detail: the leaflet, the house swap, how we thought the dead man was the same person at Lizard Point and the Hideaway, and everything that had happened since we came home. Jamie kept telling them to speak to DS Byrnes from Devon and Cornwall police. 'He knows everything,' he insisted.

'I'll call him,' said one of the policemen, DC Gardener, who was young, cocky and very unhelpful. He'd taken one look at the suitcase on my bed and decided that we were some modern-day Bonnie and Clyde, about to do a moonlight flit. Eventually, after speaking to Byrnes on the phone, they allowed us to go to Sylvia's – but not before making sure they knew exactly where they could get hold of us.

I'd been relieved to leave the flat. As we drove away in the Mini, I glanced back once at the building where we had been so happy, where Evelyn had lived for over forty years, and which now looked dark and forlorn, police tape fluttering in the wind.

Days pass. Jamie works from Sylvia's conservatory and I'm relieved to return to school, despite Sylvia insisting I should take a few days off, that I'm still recovering from the shock. But I want, *need*, to throw myself back into work, to keep my mind off everything that has happened. I sense Sylvia eyeing me disapprovingly every time I move and I know she's disappointed that I'm not 'processing' my grief and fears. That I'm just burying them instead.

On the Wednesday I'm called into the head teacher's office. Felicity Ryder is a stern woman, twenty years older than me with small blue eyes in a formidable face. She has dark-red hair that is so stiff it doesn't move when she walks. I often wonder how much hairspray she must use to keep her hair so intact. When she smiles it transforms her into the warm, witty person she really is underneath her strict facade.

'Can you sit down please, Libby,' she says from the other side of her desk. She has glasses that she wears on a cord around her neck as she's always losing them. She puts them to her face so she can read what's in front of her. I take a seat opposite. She looks up and stares at me for a couple of seconds as if trying to work me out. Then she closes her eyes and runs her hand over her forehead. I've seen her do it countless times when talking to teachers or parents and it's never normally a good sign. I hold my breath, waiting.

'I've received a call. It's from a concerned parent. And –' she adds when I open my mouth to ask their identity '– I can't reveal who, as you well know. They are saying that you are under investigation at the moment and they don't feel comfortable about you continuing to work in the school.'

I feel as though somebody has punched me in the stomach. 'They?'

'There are a few. They've been talking. You know how it is.'

I most certainly do. There's a cliquey bunch of

mothers I've often seen hanging around the playground, standing in a huddle, gossiping in their Lycra. I bet it was them.

'I'm not under investigation. A body was found in my garden. We'd recently done a holiday house swap . . .' I throw my arms up in the air. 'It's a very long story. I don't even know where to start.'

She folds her arms across her chest and peers at me over her glasses. 'Well, I suggest that you try, Libby. Because from where I'm sitting it doesn't look very good and this school has its reputation to protect.'

'Suspended! She's suspended me,' I cry as soon as I walk into the conservatory, where Jamie is tapping away on his laptop. I notice he has three empty mugs in front of him. Somebody has obviously been keeping him topped up with caffeine.

He looks up. 'What? Why?'

'Parents complained. They knew about the body we found. They don't want me teaching their kids until it's all been resolved and I'm found to have had nothing to do with it.' I sink onto one of the chairs in disbelief. 'Shit, Jay. This could ruin my career.' My mouth is so dry I can hardly swallow.

Jamie jumps up and comes to sit beside me. He grabs my hand. 'Don't worry, they'll find out you've got nothing to do with it soon enough and then you can go back to teaching. It will be fine.'

'Or my reputation will be in tatters. We found a dead

body in our bloody garden! They're not going to think it was Evelyn, are they? Even if she was still alive. She was eighty years old. Oh God . . .' I clutch my chest. I can hardly breathe. Not being able to teach feels like my soul has been ripped from my body. I'd changed my life to make it happen. I defined myself by my job. And I'd do anything for the school. I had put myself in danger to protect a child without giving it a second thought. They said I was a hero. They'd wanted to give me a bloody award but I'd shied away from it, not wanting any more attention. And now this. If I can no longer teach I don't know who I am.

I wonder if this is what it's like to have a heart attack; it's what killed Evelyn. DS Byrnes had telephoned to inform us after specifically requesting the information from Avon and Somerset Police. Had this been what it was like for her? This tightening, as though being squeezed in a vice, this pain? My heart is racing so much that I'm convinced I'm going to drop down dead. 'I can't breathe . . .' I say, gripping Jamie's arm. 'My chest, it hurts . . .'

'Mum!' Jamie cries. 'Mum, it's Libby!'

Sylvia darts into the room and pushes Jamie aside. 'Put your head between your knees. No, your knees!' she urges, forcing my head down. 'Breathe through your nose, and out your mouth . . . through your nose . . . out your mouth . . . nose . . . mouth . . . that's it, good girl.' Her voice is soothing as I concentrate on what she's saying and my heart rate slows, my extremities stop tingling.

'I'm sorry,' I say, reclining against the cushions. 'I don't know what happened.' Jamie's face, from behind his mother's shoulder, is pale and full of concern.

Sylvia pats my hand but says, sternly, 'You had a panic attack. You need to look after yourself.' She turns to Jamie. 'You both do. The sort of stress you've been under in the past few weeks is going to take its toll.' She rubs my arm affectionately. 'I'll go and make a cup of tea.' She gets up and brushes down her skirt. I watch her go, wishing that a simple cup of tea really would make everything OK.

It's ten days after we found the body when the police turn up.

That morning, the sound of someone mowing their lawn filters through the open windows and the breeze smells fresh, of flowers and cut grass. For the first time this year it feels as though we are on the cusp of summer.

I'm about to take Ziggy into the garden when there's a rap on the front door. Two policemen stand on the step, the sun shining on the hills of Lansdown behind them. DS Byrnes shuffles awkwardly, looking slightly sweaty in his mac. He introduces the man standing next to him as DI Hartley from Avon and Somerset police. He holds up his badge with an air of authority. I stand back to allow them over the threshold, clutching hold of Ziggy's collar to stop him darting out the door. Byrnes looks grim-faced as he perches on the arm of the sofa. Hartley is younger but more serious-looking, with a craggy face, closely cropped hair and eyes that suggest he's seen it all over the years.

Sylvia, never normally one for tact, makes herself scarce. Luckily Katie is out, and Hannah and Felix are ensconced in the coach house. Jamie drifts in from the conservatory, a sheen of sweat dampening his fringe and a distracted expression on his face.

'DS Byrnes. Good to see you, do you have news?' he says, his eyes lighting up. He thrusts his hand at DI Hartley and introduces himself. Hartley shakes it warily. 'Would you both like a drink? Water? Coffee?' They both decline. Byrnes is avoiding eye contact, which puzzles me. My heart starts to thump.

'We've not come with great news, I'm afraid,' says Hartley. He hasn't joined Byrnes on the sofa, but is standing very formally by Sylvia's drinks cabinet. He's wearing a jacket that is much too heavy for such a hot day. It gives him an intimidating air, which is probably why he wears it. 'We have an identity on the man found in your garden.' His eyes find mine. They are cold. 'His name was Sean Elliot. He was one of the builders working at Philip Heywood's Cornwall property. He was murdered. He was struck over the head with a blunt instrument.' He pauses, his eyes narrowing, the flicker of a sneer on his lips as though he's taking enjoyment in this. 'Does the name mean anything to you?'

'I've never heard of him,' says Jamie, frowning. 'You don't know him, do you, Libby?'

I shake my head and address Byrnes, who's sitting silently. 'My maiden name is Elliot. But I don't know a Sean Elliot.'

Hartley smirks as though expecting me to say this. I make up my mind there and then that I don't like him. 'I think you're lying, Mrs Hall,' he says.

I can feel myself blushing with indignation. 'Now wait a minute . . .'

Jamie is unusually quiet. I can sense him watching me.

Hartley consults the piece of paper in his hand. 'It seems, Mrs Hall, that you knew Sean Elliot ten years ago . . .'

'Ten years ago?' I do a mental calculation. In 2007 I would have been twenty.

I notice Jamie frowning.

'According to this,' he holds up what looks like a marriage certificate, 'you married Sean Elliot in 2007.'

I turn to Jamie. All the colour has drained from his face. I shake my head. 'No . . . I, no, that's not . . .'

'Elizabeth Hall, I'm arresting you on suspicion of murder,' he says. 'You do not have to say anything but it may harm your defence if you do not mention when questioned something you later rely on in court. Anything you do say may be given in evidence.'

'No, you've got this wrong,' I cry as Hartley takes my arm. 'Please, Jamie, you've got to believe me.'

Sylvia comes rushing into the room. 'What's going on? Take your hands off my daughter-in-law,' she insists, her face flushed. She puffs herself up to her full five foot five inches and blocks the doorway that leads to the hall. I'm heartened to see that she's trying to stick up for me.

'Please get out of the way,' says DI Hartley coldly, and Sylvia's face falls. Without a word she moves from the doorway.

'It's OK,' I try to assure them as Hartley frog-marches me from the house. 'I'll explain everything when I get back. Please, it's a mistake, that's all . . .'

'I'll drive to the station and wait for you,' says Jamie, the colour coming back into his cheeks as he springs into action. 'It will be fine. Just tell the truth.' But I can see the disappointment in his eyes when he looks at me, can almost hear his thoughts. *My wife is a bigamist. A liar.*

The last thing I see as the police car speeds away is the shocked faces of my husband and mother-in-law huddled together on the front step and, despite Jamie's words, I know that nothing will ever be the same again.

I sit alone in a small, stuffy room, waiting. All this waiting and on the hottest day of the year. I haven't even been offered any water.

What will become of me? How will I explain it all? One way or another I'm sure to get prosecuted. I've tried, I really have, to be a good person, to make up for what happened in Thailand, to live a good life. To re-invent myself. But now it's all going to come out and I'll lose everything.

That backpack. I tried to find out, without telling Jamie, googling all those people I'd travelled with: Lars, Harry, Emma and the others. It had crossed my mind that they could have been messing with me, that maybe they had found out my secret and were trying to black-mail me.

There is still so much that doesn't make sense to me but one thing is obvious: this isn't about Jamie at all. This is about Thailand. About me. And about Karen Fisher.

PART TWO
Thailand

23

Karen Fisher was dead. That's what I'd always believed. Last seen alive in Thailand nine years ago.

It was May 2008 when I fled grey, drizzly England and arrived in the colourful city of Bangkok. The air was hotter than I'd ever imagined, the type of heat that rushed out from an oven when you opened the door, humid and all-encompassing, hitting me in the face as soon as I stepped off the plane. And the smells: food cooking on the pavements, sweet and pungent; the river, stale with an undercurrent of fish; animal dung and traffic fumes. It was like another world. I was used to living in North Yorkshire, with the moors and the trees and the quaint city of York on my doorstep, even if I had spent a few years living in a high-rise tower block stained with graffiti and despair. Before Sean took me away from all that. I'd been to university in Sheffield and thought that frenetic. But Bangkok was something else.

I remember the first few days after I'd arrived, walking around as though in a daze, gazing in wonder at the palace and the huge golden reclining Buddha, at the busy river ferries crammed with people, at the traffic that zoomed past in six different lanes, tuk-tuks weaving in and out of cars and vans as though the drivers had a death wish. I even spotted an elephant trudging along a pavement, led by a man who smiled toothlessly and gestured to people as he passed. I took it all in, giddy with happiness and relief. I had escaped.

After spending a week in Bangkok, I'd decided to try my luck in the south. I fancied lounging around on the beaches, taking a dip in the warm, jade-coloured sea, snorkelling among the coral, or diving off a boat in the middle of the ocean. I could do anything now, and that thought alone propelled me forwards. I wanted to experience everything, I wanted to live.

The overnight train was stuffy, with cramped seating that converted into beds. A guy was lounging on one of the chairs, earphones plugged in, his foot tapping to some tinny dance music I could just about decipher. He had blond dreadlocks and a T-shirt with stains around the armpits. It was going to take all night to travel down to Trang and I wasn't looking forward to the journey, but it was a lot cheaper than a flight and I had to make my money last as long as possible. I didn't relish the thought of sitting next to someone who looked like they might not have washed for weeks. Behind him a couple in their thirties sat munching on egg rolls.

The carriage was airless despite the little rectangular windows that were flung open. I could see knots of people congregated on the platform, most of them with backpacks and maps and perplexed expressions on their faces. As I ambled along the aisle I stopped to let a teenage girl heave her backpack into the compartment overhead. Somebody was pushing into me, forcing my own bag into my kidney, and I spun around irritably. A blond, preppy guy with a smug face stared back, his mate's head popping up over his shoulder like a jack-in-the-box. 'Get a move on,' said the guy in a plummy accent, his friend gurning at me. I swore at them, using the c-word, enjoying the way they shrank back in alarm. They hadn't expected such vile language from a girl my size, I thought, as I walked further down the carriage. They didn't know that I'd lived on the type of housing estate they only saw in gritty urban TV dramas. I was used to looking after myself. Act like a hard nut and people will leave you alone – that was Sean's motto. I'd learnt a lot from him.

I spotted a space at the end of the carriage. A girl about my age was already next to the window, facing forwards, flicking through a magazine. There was an empty seat opposite her. I contemplated it, but it meant I'd be going backwards when the train started to move. I'd rather have her seat. She glanced up from her magazine with clear hazel eyes as I approached. She looked like she'd just arrived in the country; there was a freshness about her in her cotton blouse and denim shorts. Her skin was pale with a few freckles across her nose and she had mousy hair that came just past her shoulders. The perfect companion to share this journey.

'Do you mind if I sit here?' I indicated the brown leatherette seat opposite, acid-yellow stuffing bursting out of a rip in the arm. It didn't look particularly comfortable for such a long trip.

She beamed. She had dimples in her cheeks on each side of her mouth. 'Sure. You're English, right? Yorkshire?' She had a similar accent, although her tone was harsher than mine. I nodded. We had that in common, at least, not that I wanted to make small talk. I planned to spend most of the journey sleeping.

I hoisted my backpack up onto the shelf above our heads. It weighed a ton; my spine felt like it had been crushed by it over the past two weeks.

'I'm Karen,' she said, extending a slim, pale hand rather formally. I shook it before sitting on the chair facing her.

'Elizabeth,' I said. 'Although everyone calls me Beth.' At least at home I was always Beth, and that's what Sean called me. I reached into my pocket, pulled out a hairband and gathered what was left of my dark hair away from my sweaty neck. The window was open, yet I couldn't feel the benefit.

Karen raised her head from her magazine. 'It'll get cooler once the train begins to move,' she said as if reading my mind. She must have noticed the beads of sweat that had formed around my hairline, trickling into my eyes. It was six o'clock in the evening and yet the heat was relentless. Karen went back to her magazine and I studied her; her slender neck, her protruding collarbones. What was her story, I wondered? Maybe I would speak to her after all. But first I needed her to swap seats.

I cleared my throat to get her attention, while fiddling with the corner of my T-shirt in what I hoped was a self-conscious but endearing manner. She looked up. 'I get terrible travel sickness,' I said. 'I've taken a pill but it would really help if I could sit forward facing. Would you mind?' I smiled sweetly.

I noticed a trace of surprise in her expression which she tried to cover up. 'Of course, no worries.' She got up quickly, clutching her magazine to her chest. So obliging. That was a good sign. I stood up too; she was tiny, even smaller than me. We did a kind of side shuffle to change places. I could tell she wasn't entirely happy with our swap, but she was either too well mannered, or too cowardly, to say. She had an aura of containment about her, as though she was used to being on her own. She settled into her new seat. My leg knocked against something and I was irritated to see her backpack by the window. She'd need to get rid of that. 'Ow,' I said, rubbing my leg theatrically.

'Oh, God, I'm so sorry. I'll put it in the overhead compartment.'

I smiled in thanks and watched as one of the guys I'd sworn at earlier offered to help her lift it. She epitomised a damsel in distress with her large doe eyes and her petite stature. I assessed her critically. She was pretty, I had to concede that, but her mouth was slightly too large and her nose too long to be considered beautiful. And of course she had those cute dimples. That helped. She sidled back into her seat, flushed but not smiling. If anything she seemed embarrassed and a little infuriated by the attention. I reappraised her. That was interesting. I got the sense that she was running away. Like me.

I needed to find out more about her. We could be kindred spirits, her and me. I was happy to travel around Thailand by myself but it would be more fun to have a companion.

'So, Karen,' I began, 'what's your surname?'

She lifted her eyes from the magazine, looking puzzled. 'Fisher. Why?'

'Just wondered.' I pretended to consider her name. 'Fisher? Hmmm, I don't know any Fishers. Are you meeting anyone at the other end, Karen Fisher?'

She smiled, but it had a hint of reservation behind it. 'No. I'm travelling alone.'

'Me too.'

'And you're Beth . . .?'

'Elliot.' I prayed she didn't know Sean – his family were notorious in my part of town.

She frowned. She looked like she longed to get back to her magazine but I sensed she also didn't want to appear rude. She fixed a smile on her face, trying to mask the effort it was costing her. 'Whereabouts in Yorkshire are you from?'

'Not far from York,' I replied. 'Except with none of its quaintness . . .' I hesitated. I didn't want to tell her too much.

It transpired that we had grown up only twenty miles

from each other and we chatted about our home towns for a while. I could almost see her unfurling like a flower at the beginning of spring and, as the train pulled out of the station, I found myself relaxing. The heat was less oppressive now that the train was moving and I could, at last, feel the warm breeze from the open window. I closed my eyes, liking the way the air fluttered against my face.

It was a few hours and a few cans of lager into the journey when she told me that both her parents were dead.

'Same here,' I said, thinking of my mum and dad, although I didn't reveal the details. 'I'm an only child. They were older parents, religious.' She nodded knowingly, her eyes sad, and I got the feeling there was something she wasn't telling me. 'What made you decide to come away?' I asked.

'I hated my life,' she replied, surprising me with her intensity, and I noted a hardness, a bitterness to her expression. 'It was going nowhere. No qualifications. No prospects.'

'You didn't go to uni?'

She shook her head. 'Family circumstances,' she said non-committally. 'I had to get away otherwise I'd go mad.'

I took a swig of lager. 'Same here. I finished my degree just before coming here. Sheffield uni. But I was stuck in an abusive relationship with this guy.' I swirled my finger near my head to indicate how much of a psycho he was. 'I met him when I was vulnerable. Isn't that always the way?' The alcohol had made me loose-lipped. I didn't want to say too much. 'What about you?'

She shook her head, her fine hair falling about her face. 'No. Nobody special.' I could tell she wasn't about to be drawn so I dropped the subject. Instead I asked her where she planned to travel and we talked about our journeys so far. I found out that she'd only been in Bangkok for two days. We discussed our desire to island hop for a few months. By now the sky had darkened, the strip lighting buzzed overhead, and the carriage was a hive of activity as seats were converted into beds.

'Shall we make our beds?' she said, her eyes lighting up, which made me laugh. It was like a giant sleepover; there was something strangely exciting about it. I realised that the overhead compartment converted into a bed and the seats we'd been sitting on could be laid flat so that they joined up. 'It's like bunk beds,' she laughed. 'Do you want the top or bottom?'

'Bottom, if that's OK?'

She nodded, appearing pleased. An orange nylon curtain concealed the two of us from the rest of the carriage. 'This is cosy,' she said, the overhead bunk creaking as she manoeuvred herself into her nightwear. I pulled a long T-shirt from my backpack. It was creased and smelt damp but I put it on anyway, having to contort my body in the cramped space. I unwrapped the sheet provided from its cellophane bag. It was crisp and white and felt cool against my skin. I lay there, the sheet pulled up to my chin, trying not to be afraid of the rattling train. In the darkness it felt like it was going too fast; I started to worry that we would go hurtling off the tracks. How safe were trains in Thailand?

'Are you OK?' asked a disembodied voice from above. Then Karen leaned over so that her upside-down face was showing, her hair splaying out in front of her. 'I don't think I'm going to get any sleep. Do you?'

'I'm worried we're going to derail,' I admitted.

'Derail? Seriously?' Her face had turned red where all the blood was rushing to it. 'I didn't think you were afraid of anything, Beth Elliot. You with your tough-cookie image.'

I laughed. 'Tough cookie. Is that what you think?'

'I saw the way you handled those blokes earlier.' Her eyes flashed with admiration. 'You're someone not to be messed with.'

She was right about that.

24

When we disembarked from the train the next morning, blurry-eyed and hungry, we stuck together, an unspoken agreement between us, both of us relieved to have found a companion.

It's funny how quickly relationships are forged when you are travelling; people you might not have met, or been interested in getting to know, in your everyday life suddenly become indispensable. You sleep together, eat together, wash together, spend all day sunbathing or swimming together, and it forms a kind of intimacy that I'd never had with a woman before. I didn't have many mates back home; most girls at school had given me a wide berth thinking I was too mouthy, too weird. University was different, but having a possessive, abusive husband put paid to forming any close friendships. Most people I met couldn't believe I'd got married so young and I was immediately elevated into the 'old before her time' category and never invited to go out drinking or clubbing with them. Not that I would have done anyway, it wasn't worth the grief when I got home.

But I'd escaped Sean and my past. In Thailand I was fun Beth, exciting Beth. I could see it in Karen's face as I downed pint after pint in the beach bar, or went skinny-dipping in the sea at night: admiration. We were the same age but I could tell that she looked up to me. Maybe her upbringing had been more sheltered than mine.

We were like snowballs, Karen and I, collecting people as we went, so that by the time we'd passed through Trang, Krabi and Nopparat Thara beach and arrived on Koh Phi Phi a few weeks later, there was a small group of us hanging out together: Emma, a statuesque redhead from Ireland with the palest skin I'd ever seen, sullen Lars from Finland whose eyes were too close together, and Harry and Dylan from New Jersey. Dylan and Emma were both on a gap year before starting university, Lars was a few years older than me and had jacked in his dead-end job to go travelling, and Harry had recently finished a medical degree and was taking six months off before looking for work.

We partied hard, often falling into bed at 4 a.m. During the day we swam in the clear jade waters, or sunbathed on the pure white beaches. I had a bit of a crush on Harry, with his foppish blond hair and dimpled smile. He towered over me and Karen and out of the three lads he was the most charismatic. Lars was too moody, although Emma seemed to like him, and Dylan was constantly going on about the size of women's chests in their bikinis. Karen and I agreed that we thought he was handsome – dark curly hair, brown eyes and a buff, tanned body – but ultimately, we said regretfully, he was a sleaze. Dylan's tongue practically hung out every time Emma was in his eye-line, but she showed no interest in him, much to his disappointment.

I felt safe in a crowd. Despite knowing that Sean had no clue as to my whereabouts, that he would never have guessed I'd taken a plane to Thailand of all places – he knew I hated flying – it still sent shock waves through me when I saw someone who resembled him; a tall, stocky frame, or striking blue eyes which could be as warm and inviting as the Indian ocean one minute and as icy as the Antarctic the next.

Karen was the quietest of our group. She would often sit and watch us, her eyes dark by the light of the camp fire as the rest of us drank and swore and sometimes snogged. I wondered what went on behind Karen's large hazel eyes. Was she nursing a broken heart? She didn't seem interested in men; if anything she seemed to want to disappear, getting irritated if anyone tried to chat her up. I attempted to find out a bit about her, but apart from revealing that her parents had died when she was young, she was closed about her life back in England. I didn't ask too many questions and neither did she, which suited me fine. Yet, because we had spent the first week together before being joined by the others, I felt a connection to her.

'What will you do after this?' I asked her one night. It was late and we had joined a party on the beach. She sat away from the others, clutching a can of lager, her slim legs crossed. There was a slight breeze coming off the sea and I could smell coconut oil and sand.

She shrugged. 'I don't want to go home. I'd quite like to go to Australia after this. Maybe work in a bar. Earn some money so that I can keep travelling.' She seemed sad as she talked. 'What about you? Do you fancy Australia?'

I was touched that she might want us to travel there together. 'I've got a place at teacher-training college for this September,' I said. 'Middlesex. But I'm going to defer it.' I'd made up my mind earlier that day while lying on the beach, the sun on my skin, the sand in my hair. It was paradise. I didn't want it to end.

She giggled. 'I don't blame you. Who wants to go back to depressing, grey England when we have all this?' She widened her arms as though encompassing the beach, the sea, the palm trees swaying. Lars and Emma were running along the shoreline with a group of people I hadn't met, shrieking and darting in and out of the sea.

'Exactly,' I replied. 'I'm not planning on going home. Ever.' Karen was the first person I'd told about my place at college. Sean didn't even know. Middlesex was to be my escape, except things escalated sooner than planned so I'd fled to Thailand instead.

Karen laughed, her teeth glowing white in her tanned face. 'Still running away?'

She knew I had escaped an abusive relationship but I hadn't revealed anything else. To talk of it all would make it real, and here I could be somebody else. I wondered if she felt that way too. In Thailand we were living in the moment, we were who we decided to be that day. I suspected we were both shedding the skins of our past, like the snakes we sometimes spotted in the long grass by our hotel.

'Did he hit you? Your ex?' she asked, concern flashing in those big eyes.

I was suddenly ashamed I'd been that person, that woman. That I'd put up with it for so long. That I'd married the bastard. He'd been charming. Older, richer – although I later found out the money came from dodgy dealings and ripping people off. But I hadn't known that at first. I'd been flattered that he'd shown an interest in me, an unhappy fifteen-year-old girl living alone with her father. He'd been twenty then and dapper, driving around in his Jag, with his chunky Rolex watch (which I later found out was fake) and his well-cut suits. He thought he was a gangster but I'd been impressed. It soon wore off.

'Yes,' I admitted in a small voice. 'He hit me.'

She shook her head sadly, fiddling with the top of the lager can. 'I know I've only known you a few weeks. But shit, Beth, you're the last person I'd imagine would fall for a man like that.'

'There isn't a type who ends up with abusive men,' I snapped, the familiar white flame of fury flickering inside me. I was shocked at her naivety. My first impression of her had been right. Prissy little bitch. 'It can happen to anyone.'

Even in the dark I could sense her embarrassment. 'I'm sorry, I didn't mean . . . I just think that you're so feisty. I've seen the way you unleash that tongue of yours on people.'

Unleash? She made me sound like a monster. I wondered, then, if she was a little scared of me. Maybe not scared, exactly, but wary. I hoped so.

'I got my own back on him, don't worry about that,' I said, pulling my legs up to my chest. I watched the party unfold around me, Emma dancing suggestively with Lars, Dylan's eyes roaming over the gyrating bodies of the women, Harry, who kept stealing glances at us. I hoped he'd come over.

'Really? How?'

I tried to sound nonchalant. 'At first I gave as good as I got until I realised that to fight back would make it worse. He put me in hospital once . . .'

She flinched.

'. . . so I hit him where it hurt the most. I emptied our joint bank account and ran away.'

Her eyes widened. 'Bloody hell, Beth.'

I was angry with myself. I'd said more than I should have. I'd learnt the hard way that to reveal too much was to leave yourself open. If Sean ever found me I had no doubt he would kill me.

I changed the subject. 'I know!' I exclaimed suddenly, making her jump so that she spilt lager down her legs. 'Why don't we get a tattoo?'

It was only a ten-minute walk to the other end of Ton Sai village, where I was sure I'd seen a sign advertising tattoos, yet it took us much longer as Karen kept pausing at the stalls, rifling through purses and sarongs. She seemed unable to say no to the traders who shook jewellery or towels in her face. It began to irritate me, so every time she stopped I huffed and sighed loudly. She threw me an apologetic smile from behind her hair, putting down whatever she'd picked up to trail after me. She was so eager to please. The stifling heat was making me bad-tempered and by the time we'd reached the tattoo parlour I wanted to punch somebody in the face, preferably Karen.

The parlour, if you could call it that, was actually a one-room shack on the edge of the village. A slim Thai man with a scarf tied around his neck stood over a young lad with a very hairy back, etching a heart onto the skin of his shoulder blade.

Karen paled. 'Do you think it's safe?' she whispered in my ear, taking in the scraggy-looking dog with one leg missing that had flopped to the floor in the heat; the man's dirty grey T-shirt with a sweat patch in the shape of a moth down his back. She shot a fearful glance at the images of various tattoos slapped onto the makeshift walls.

'It will be fine,' I assured her, although I had misgivings.

When the hairy-backed man vacated his chair, Karen stepped forward, brushing the hair from her face. I noticed a sheen of sweat above her top lip. 'Um . . . tattoo, please . . .' she said, her voice raspy between her dry lips. After a bit of haggling we agreed a very cheap price.

The man gestured to the pictures on the wall and asked us to choose a design. Karen stared at them, her brow furrowed. 'I don't know . . . I can't decide . . .'

'Oh for fuck's sake,' I said irritably. 'I'll go first.'

Karen stared at me with round eyes. 'Oh, OK . . . sure . . .' She fumbled in her bag for her water bottle and took a large swig.

I side-stepped her. I'd made up my mind before we'd even arrived. I knew exactly what I wanted: a winged bird in flight. Freedom. I made myself as comfortable as I could on the hard stool and pointed to my arm. 'Right here, please.'

An hour later, my new tattoo scabbing over and throbbing, I was leaning on Karen as we ambled back to the hotel, our flip-flops smacking against the dusty ground. By the time we reached our resort, we were both sweating in our shorts and T-shirts. One of the scabs had opened up and little globules of blood had collected around its edges. I sat on the bed in the room we shared and dabbed at it half-heartedly with a wet wad of tissue.

'I feel such a wuss,' said Karen, slumping onto the bed opposite. She had bailed at the last minute as I knew she would. Every time the needle touched my skin she blanched. At one point I thought she might pass out.

'And so you should,' I chided. 'I thought you were

tougher than that, Karen Fisher. And a Yorkshire lass too. I'm disappointed.'

I was half joking but she looked stricken. In that moment I could tell that she thought she'd failed me, that she was a lesser person in my eyes. A coward. For once in my shitty little life I was the one in a relationship where I held all the power and the feeling was intoxicating.

The next day Karen disappeared. It was unusual for her to go off without telling me where she was heading. I wandered down to the beach with the others, hoping to catch her, but she was nowhere to be seen.

'Where's Karen?' asked Harry. He was hunched over his snorkel, adjusting the straps, his legs stretched out, long and tanned beneath his shorts. I couldn't take my eyes off them.

I shrugged, slapping sun cream onto my arms. I'd hoped Harry would offer to do my back but he seemed distracted. 'I have no idea. She'd left before I woke up this morning.'

'Do you think she's moved on? Without us?' He sounded worried and I wanted to ask why he cared so much.

'I don't think so. Her stuff is still in our room.'

'That's good. I like Karen,' he said matter-of-factly, slipping the snorkel over his head. Then he jumped up and sprinted into the sea. I watched as his lithe body dived in between the waves, my stomach curdling with jealousy.

An hour later Karen was back. She walked across the beach gracefully, a new red sarong tied around her waist, a beach bag slung over her shoulder. She waved at me. She was beaming. It was only as she got closer that I noticed the tattoo.

25

It pleased me, that tattoo, what it signified. I'd reached the ripe old age of twenty-one and never experienced what it felt like to have a best friend. Getting married young to a possessive man will do that to you. Sean always said he was my best friend. He hadn't wanted me to go to university and tried to make me give it up; he was terrified I'd meet someone else on my course, but I refused to leave. He couldn't make too much of a fuss, what with the lecturers and that university counsellor hanging around. He was a coward underneath it all, as bullies usually are.

Harry was the first man I'd fancied since Sean. He was everything Sean wasn't: self-effacing, clever, softly spoken, his New Jersey accent warm and friendly, his body graceful, like a ballet dancer. Sean was so cocky, a Jack the Lad, a working-class man made good (a phrase he rattled out often). Brash, with his gold jewellery and handmade suits.

As the weeks had turned into months our little group – Emma, Lars, Dylan, Harry, Karen and me – had become like a family. I could have told Karen how I felt about Harry, of course, but that wasn't the type of friendship we had. We didn't open up to each other about our feelings. She was like me in that way, closed and practical. We might have felt deeply about things but we didn't like to show it, as if admitting our emotions made us weak. We were both used – in different ways – to hiding our feelings from the ones closest to us.

After the conversation on the beach, I watched to see if anything was developing between Harry and Karen. I began to notice little things, like how they would always end up sunbathing next to each other on the beach, or perched at the bar together. If he wanted to go into the village, he always asked her to walk with him. He laughed a lot at her – quite honestly crap – jokes and seemed to find her witty. He told her once, while I was in earshot, that she had a dry sense of humour which he 'loved'. That comment pissed me off for days. Her behaviour changed too: sitting that little bit too close while sipping their cocktails so their knees touched; flicking back her hair, raking her fingers through it and curling it demurely behind her ears as she talked to him, head on one side.

One evening, we had trekked en masse through the village and up the steep incline to watch the sun set over the two bays of Phi Phi. As we navigated the narrow, twisting paths, I had to keep stopping to take a swig from my water bottle. The air was humid, my vest top clinging to my skin, my trainers rubbing my feet. I was stuck at the back of the group with Dylan, who had his earphones on. I noticed that everybody had paired up: Emma and Lars, Karen and Harry, which left me with Dylan. I wasn't his type at all – my boobs weren't big enough for a start – and he paid me no attention, which was fine by me. I think he and Harry had only hooked up because they both came from New Jersey, but they were so different. Emma and Lars were holding hands as he helped her up the rickety pathways, and I glanced at Karen and Harry ahead. They were laughing, turning to chat with Emma and Lars, and I had a horrible, paranoid thought of them becoming a foursome. I wasn't interested – and neither was Dylan – of making it six, so where did that leave us? Suddenly our group was becoming more couply and it left a nasty taste in my mouth. I washed it down with water.

The views from the top were breathtaking. We sat on the flat, warm rocks to watch the sun going down behind the bays, the two curves of sand reminding me of butterfly wings. The sun looked like a huge orange ball, staining the sky pink and red, and reflecting in the shimmering sea. We all fell silent as we watched. Karen leaned her head on Harry's shoulder, then, as if remembering she was in company, sat up straight again, tossing her long hair back. But I'd noticed the intimacy, the frisson of electricity that had passed between them.

'Isn't it stunning?' said Harry. Karen was sitting between us and I longed to push her out of the way. What was it about her he liked? We weren't that dissimilar; both brunettes – although hers was more mouse – both short, both lean. OK, she did have a pretty face whereas mine was more masculine, more angular. But still, I could look attractive when I made an effort. I lit a cigarette and saw Karen's eyes flash. She didn't approve of me smoking. I leaned across her and offered one to Harry, who took it gratefully, and I threw Karen a triumphant look.

'A doctor who smokes,' she said disapprovingly, staring straight ahead. 'Very incongruous of you.'

'Ooh, incongruous,' mocked Dylan next to me. 'Have you swallowed a dictionary by any chance, Karen?'

I nudged him in the ribs, hard, enjoying his groan of pain. 'Grow up,' I hissed. He was like the annoying little brother I never wanted.

We walked back down the hill, me silent, brooding, the others giggling and stumbling as we navigated the rocky pathways in the dusk. The smell of smoke drifted towards us from a nearby bonfire. A group of locals sat around a hut, colourful washing blowing in the faint breeze from a makeshift line.

Dylan struck up a conversation with me about that night's activities, which involved getting hammered in the bar. 'I can't wait to get a couple of pints down me,' I said with feeling; I was planning on getting wasted.

'You're a bit of a hard nut,' laughed Emma in her soft Irish accent. 'You can drink me under the table and that's saying something.'

'I'm not a big drinker really,' said Karen with regret, grabbing hold of Harry's arm as she stumbled over a rock.

Emma laughed. 'I've never seen you pissed, Karen.'

'She's too much of a control freak,' I offered for Harry's benefit. 'And she doesn't smoke.'

'I had a girlfriend at medical school who used to get wasted every weekend,' said Harry. He had the type of voice that people automatically listened to, strong and confident, as if he'd grown up with parents who were interested in everything he had to say. 'She'd be nearly comatose after puking up everywhere. It wasn't very attractive in the end, not to mention what she was doing to her liver, binge-drinking like that . . .'

'Not very attractive?' teased Emma. 'But it's all right for men to get off their faces?'

'And it's all right for you to smoke and fuck your lungs up?' laughed Karen, prodding him good-naturedly in the side. 'But at least your liver's pristine.'

'Well, yes, that's different.' He tickled her and she fell against him, giggling. 'But it's not very attractive who-ever gets off their faces,' added Harry mildly, throwing an arm casually over Karen's shoulder. 'Not to the extent where you're incoherent, talking shit and puking every-where. And she was like that every weekend. It just got embarrassing.'

It was easy to spike her drink. It didn't take much, just the benzodiazepines I'd picked up in Bangkok. It's amazing what you can buy over the counter at the chemists there. I'd gone in for diazepam, to help me block out the nightmares I had about Sean tracking me down, but when I saw the rows of little blue, white and yellow pills lined up in jars along the shelf like sweets, I knew I had to make the most of it. So I'd bought some of each.

That evening, I mixed them all together to make a fine powder. Later, we were all standing with our backs to the bar, chatting, and I positioned myself next to Karen. Her cocktail was behind her and she turned every now and then to take a sip. She usually spent all night harbouring two pints of lager. I'd only ever seen her a little bit tipsy. It was easy to tip the powder into her drink while she was flirting with Harry.

It didn't take long for all those drugs to get into her system. It started with the dancing, something Karen never did; she told me once she was uncoordinated. She was right about that. Despite having a body like a dancer she moved like an elephant, unwieldy and inelegant, knocking into people; her clumsiness astonished me. Dancing was something that came naturally to me. I made sure I was next to her and Harry, remembering some of the moves from a salsa class I'd taken with Sean (before he got jealous when the dance teacher used me as an example and insisted we stopped going). I gyrated next to Harry as he did a sort of shuffle, looking embarrassed as Karen flung herself around, arms flailing above her head, her usual inhibitions forgotten.

'This isn't Ibiza, love,' one bloke called to her when she stumbled into him, standing on his leather-thonged foot. I heard him mutter under his breath, 'Bloody druggies.'

I could see the shade of humiliation in Harry's eyes. Eventually he took her arm, telling her that she'd had enough and should get some water. I followed them, pleased to note how sweaty and unattractive she looked, stumbling and clutching on to him as though she would fall if left to her own devices. Harry led her back to the bar for a glass of water, which he made her down, concern etched on his face.

'Wow,' I said unnecessarily, 'I've never seen Karen so pissed.'

'It must be the heat. She needs to keep her fluid intake up.'

'I feel dreadful,' she groaned, still leaning heavily against Harry. Then her body convulsed and she threw up everywhere. I jumped back in alarm as it splattered to the floor, but Harry held on to her, calmly rubbing her back and holding her hair out of her face. Karen was like a ragdoll sagging between us, each of her arms around one of our necks as we half carried, half dragged her to our bungalow. We laid her down carefully on her bed. By now she was out of it, mumbling incoherently to herself, her eyes closed, a sheen of sweat covering her face like cling film. She had vomit down the front of her dress, which had ridden up, exposing her knickers.

Harry knelt on the cold tiles, straightening her dress and mopping her brow with a wet towel he'd got from the bathroom. 'You need to keep her cool, make sure she drinks fluids and turn her over onto her side if she's sick again.'

I felt a flicker of panic as he got up. 'Where are you going?' I'd imagined us spending the night together, playing doctors and nurses to Karen, having intimate chats over her prostrate body.

He frowned. 'I'm going back to the bar . . .' he said as if it was a stupid question.

'You're leaving Karen with me?'

He looked doubtful. 'Well, I thought she might be embarrassed if she knew I'd seen her like this. And you're her closest friend here.'

Closest friend? I liked it. He came over to where I was sitting on the edge of my bed. He towered above me. I had a sudden, overwhelming urge to pull his cargo shorts down and make him forget all about Karen bloody Fisher. He leaned over and squeezed my shoulder. 'You're a good friend,' he said. 'Let me know if she takes a turn for the worse though. Hopefully she'll sleep it off.'

She did take a turn for the worse. I made sure of it.

26

Karen spent the next few days in bed. I popped in to see her in between bouts of sunbathing, snorkelling and drinking, wafting incense sticks around in an effort to get rid of the smell of sickness and sweat. Harry came with me sometimes, but he seemed detached, distant. Maybe it was the doctor in him taking over but it was as though he no longer saw her as Karen, the object of his affection, but a patient.

She was still feeling too sick to come with us all to the Emerald Cave. We had a fantastic day, Harry and I larking about, pushing each other off the boat, taking it in turns to dive into the sea. I imagined what it would be like without Karen around. I enjoyed her company but when she wasn't there Harry's attention was on me instead.

I was on a high when we arrived back at the resort. I had a drink with the others at the bar, pretending not to notice as Harry slunk off. When I returned to the room Karen was sitting up in bed, looking happier. On her bedside table was a sleek ornamental Buddha about six inches in height. I picked it up. It was beautiful and heavy, carved out of onyx. 'Where did you get this?'

'Harry bought it for me,' she said. 'To cheer me up.'

Why hadn't I thought of doing something like that?

I put it back, feeling despondent. She'd only been absent from the group for less than a week, but the dynamics had already started to shift; I was no longer stuck with Dylan but had become Harry's companion. It was me he would seek out if he wanted to go into the village or for a swim. Now Karen was better I was worried things would revert to the way they had been before.

Sure enough, when we left Koh Phi Phi a week or so later and travelled by boat to Koh Lanta, where we rode elephants and snorkelled through the brightly coloured coral, I noticed Karen and Harry growing closer again. Every time he was in the vicinity her mouth would tilt up into a smile, accentuating her dimples, and they would gravitate towards each other, linking arms and wandering off together, their heads bent in conversation. I wondered if they were shagging. I never lowered myself to ask, and there were certainly no giggly admissions from Karen. She wasn't the type. I wondered if it was time to move on without them, make some new friends. It was easier to do that here. Especially as the old ones were beginning to feel like dead wood. I felt my power diminishing with both Karen and Harry, and I didn't like it.

'I'm thinking of going back to Bangkok,' I said one evening a few weeks later. The weather had begun to get windier, with frequent heavy showers, and although the heat was more comfortable than it had been back in May, it wasn't quite so much fun diving and sunbathing.

The resort we were staying in now was right on the beach, although the one-bedroom chalet I shared with Karen was basic. We had laughed in shock at the hole in the ground that was the toilet. We were sharing one of the hammocks dotted about the beach, facing each other, our legs entwined, sipping cocktails. The sun had gone down and fairy lights were peppered about overhead. It had rained earlier but the air was warm, the wind rippling over the dark sea. In the distance we could see the others at the beach bar; every now and again their chorus of laughter would reach us.

Karen's eyebrows shot up as she sucked her cocktail through a straw. The liquid was a vivid pink – berries and watermelon mixed with vodka – staining her lips. She swallowed. 'You want to leave Koh Lanta?'

'I'd quite like to go to the north. Then maybe on to Nepal. Or Burma.'

I could tell she was considering the idea. She licked her lips. 'That does sound like it could be fun.'

'I love it here,' I admitted, throwing one of my arms in the air and glancing around at the long stretch of white sandy beach, the sparkling waters, the palm trees nodding in the breeze. It really was paradise; one long holiday, one extended party. A young guy in a beach hut next to us was having a massage from a dainty Thai woman, who was practically sitting on his back as she busily kneaded his shoulders. 'But it's been a few months now. Time to move on.' My heart beat fast behind my vest top. If I was honest with myself I wanted her to come with me, but not the others. I toyed with the stem of my glass, watching the array of different emotions pass over Karen's face like disco lights. She was weighing up whether to leave Harry or to leave me.

She took a swig of her drink. 'When are you planning to go?'

'In a few days. Do you want to come too? Or are you happy to stay?' I tried to keep my voice even, to show I was indifferent whatever she decided to do.

She sighed. 'I'm not sure. Let me think about it.'

'Of course,' I smiled sweetly. She looked relieved, but I wasn't worried. I would make sure she chose me.

I spent ages getting ready the next evening. There was the usual party down on the beach; I could hear music and laughter and the tinkle of glasses from my open window. I studied myself in the small speckled mirror. I'd lost over a stone living off rice and fish for months, and was more svelte, more tanned, than I'd ever been. My dark hair was glossy and I looked healthy and attractive. I applied some red lipstick and slicked my hair back off my face. It was growing out of its pixie cut and needed reshaping.

We'd started drinking early and I already felt a little sloshed as we made our way down to the beach. 'I'm worried about drinking too much,' Karen said. 'After last time. I still feel embarrassed to think of it. And I still don't understand why the alcohol affected me so much.' It was dark now and the steps were decorated with little lanterns so we could find our way. There was a string of fairy lights hung around the bar, giving it a festive atmosphere. I spotted Harry standing with Lars and Dylan on the beach, his head swivelling around when we walked in, but he didn't come over.

'What's wrong with Harry?' I asked as we queued at the bar. 'He has a face like a slapped arse tonight.'

Karen's mouth twitched. 'Oh Beth. You're wicked. I told him we might be leaving. He doesn't want to come as he's already been to the north.' I remembered him telling us when we first met but I said nothing, just nodded sympathetically as she continued, 'I think he wants to carry on travelling with Dylan and Lars. They hooked up in Vietnam and have been together ever since.' She sighed. 'Emma's going to stay with them too. Harry asked if we want to go with them. What do you think?'

'Where are they headed next?'

'I think they want to fly to India.'

'India? I don't think you'd like it,' I found myself saying. 'You'd get Delhi-belly and there's people shitting in the streets. Plus, it's a long way from here.'

She looked miserable and stared at her hands. 'I know it's far, but I have always wanted to see the Taj Mahal.'

'And it's all right for them,' I added. 'They've seen Thailand. But we've only just started, Karen. And what about Vietnam, Laos? I'm not done with South East Asia yet. It would be a shame to cut it short. You must do what you think best, but I'm leaving for Bangkok tomorrow.'

We were interrupted by the cute barman asking what we wanted to drink, and after ordering cocktails we floated off towards the beach, caught up in a throng of other partygoers. Emma came bounding towards us, pulling me and Karen to where she was standing with Lars and Harry. Dylan was chatting up a busty blonde over in a darkened corner.

Harry looked handsome that night. The sun had bleached the ends of his hair and coloured his skin to a golden hue. I longed to touch him, to kiss his full mouth. Karen was also looking at him with longing. The difference was, he was returning her look of lust.

Harry. What was his story? Everybody had a story. The music was pumping, some dance tune that pulsated in my ears. I knocked into Harry on purpose so that his drink spilled. 'I'm so sorry,' I said, taking his glass as he looked with dismay at the sticky liquid dribbling down his thigh. 'I'll get you another.' Karen was chatting to Emma and hardly noticed me hurry to the bar. It was easy to slip the drugs into Harry's drink with nobody around to see.

When I returned, Harry smiled at me and took the drink gratefully. 'Cheers, Beth. You didn't have to do that.'

'It was my fault,' I said, staying by his side. Somebody

turned the music up and a new crowd surged onto the beach. Karen and I got separated so that I was left alone with Harry. I saw him glance about, trying to spot Karen, but I grabbed his hand, moved us further into the crowd. He was still holding his glass but I was pleased to note that he'd downed most of it. 'Dance with me,' I said in my most sensuous voice, moving my body suggestively to the music. He began swaying half-heartedly as the crowd enveloped us so that we were in our own little bubble. His pupils were huge in his face. This was my chance, I thought. This was my chance to show her. I just hoped she was watching. I reached up and pulled him closer, grinding myself against him. I saw the surprise in his eyes, but he placed a hand on one of my hips and I reached up and planted a lingering kiss on his mouth, my hands finding that lovely blond hair at the nape of his neck, taking in the smell of him, like lemons. I felt him stiffen at first, shocked at my forwardness, but then he went with it, relaxing into the kiss, his tongue finding mine, lost in the moment like I knew he would be. It went on for ages, his hips grinding against mine as he grabbed my arse, pulling me so close that I was almost sitting on him. His drink spilled down the back of my top but I didn't care. I ground into him, feeling him harden against me. I was good at seduction – Sean always said so. Eventually, as though waking from a trance, Harry pulled away from me, his eyes widening in horror as it dawned on him what he'd just done.

'Oh God, I'm so drunk,' he said, as if that made

everything all right. I could see his head swivelling around like a meerkat's as he tried to spot Karen in the crowd. 'I need to take a piss,' he added before staggering off.

When I turned around I caught Karen's eye, and by the hurt that flickered on her face I knew that she had seen everything.

The next morning the two of us travelled to Bangkok alone.

I'd pleaded ignorance of course. Said it was all him. That he was a sleaze, just like Dylan. She was so angry she never even said goodbye to him and we left before he got up. I admired her for that. She was stronger than she first appeared, although I noticed that she packed the Buddha he'd given her.

Maybe I should have realised how much she loved him. I can see that now, in hindsight. I can see that I made a terrible mistake in what I did. But I was young and hot-headed. Resentful. I'd wanted to punish her for being the one that Harry had chosen.

How was I to know that she would end up punishing me?

27

Things had changed between us. On the train back to Bangkok I sensed her taking sneaky peeks at me from behind her book – some soppy rom-com – as though trying to figure me out. But she had my measure, surely? She knew what she was letting herself in for when she first heard me hurling the c-word at those guys; when she agreed to swap seats; when she got a tattoo to show me she wasn't a coward. She'd wanted to impress me, to please me. She must have known I liked Harry too, but she hadn't wanted me to have him. Oh no, she could be selfish when it suited her.

It was the end of August by now, and rain drummed on the roof of the train. We didn't speak much as we sat opposite each other, so different to how it had been three months previously; no excitable laughter or getting-to-know-each-other chatter, no drinking cans of lager or banter. Karen read her book with a sullen look on her face and I stared out of the window, following the raindrops with my eyes as they snaked down the glass. When it was time for bed, we made up our bunks wordlessly. Karen climbed to the top and I didn't see or hear from her again until the morning.

I would miss Harry too, I wanted to tell her. But it

was for the best; if I couldn't have him then she couldn't either. I lay there in the dark, the occasional light flashing past and the low hum of conversation from the other passengers keeping me awake.

By the time we reached Bangkok she had begun to bore me with her sulky silences. I started to think I was going to have to cut her loose. I didn't sense her admiration any more, just her disapproval. It reminded me too much of Sean.

We trudged around the city for most of the day, visiting the Grand Palace and the Reclining Buddha, even though we'd both seen them before. We were aimless, really, engrossed in our own little worlds, missing Harry and the others but not wanting to admit it to each other. The sky was overcast by the afternoon, the weather humid. We took a boat down the river to see the houses built on stilts. I was amazed as the fish jumped up, mouths gaping open for the food the guide threw them, before disappearing back into the murky water. Karen sat staring into the distance, her eyes full of sadness, ignoring everything around her.

Karen answered my questions in a monotone as we stepped off the boat, pretending to be engrossed in the architecture. I wanted to tell her to get over it, that he was just a guy, but I acted like there was nothing wrong between us as I studied my guide book. 'This hostel sounds cheap,' I said as we veered down a dusty residential side road in a less salubrious part of town. 'If they've got space, shall we stay here tonight, and then we can travel north tomorrow?'

She lifted her shoulders in a half-hearted shrug. 'Sure.' She glanced up at the building. It was narrow and set back between two shopfronts, with large glass windows and a bonsai tree wilting by the entrance.

She shadowed me through the hallway and stood, examining the mosaic-tiled flooring while I enquired about rooms.

'We are not busy tonight,' said an attractive Thai woman with a beaming smile. She had glossy dark hair swept up in a bun and coral lipstick that didn't look quite right on her face. She led us up two floors and down a corridor to a narrow room with two sets of bunk beds. A fly buzzed at the open window between the bunks. There was no air conditioning. The room felt muggy and the walls seemed to tilt inwards. I said we'd take it.

Karen collapsed onto one of the lower bunks. She had dark rings around her eyes and her face was pale. She curled up on top of the sheets, still fully clothed, her knees tucked up into her chest.

I told her I was popping out to the 7-Eleven on the corner, promising to be right back. When I returned, armed with bags of crisps and cans of fizzy drinks, she was sitting up, staring into the distance, hugging her knees, a look I couldn't quite read on her face. I offered her a can and she took it without a word; it hissed and bubbled as she opened it.

I went to the loo. When I came back she was fast asleep, her eyes fluttering behind her lids, the Coke can by the side of the bed, opened yet untouched. I picked it up and drank it, not wanting it to go to waste, and settled down on the bottom of the bunk opposite. On the window sill between our beds sat her Buddha. On impulse, I picked it up and shoved it into my backpack. She had to stop looking at him, mooning over Harry. I was doing her a favour.

I must have fallen asleep too, because when I opened my eyes I was sprawled out on the bed, still fully dressed. I'd been sleeping heavily and felt groggy, wondering what had woken me. It was so dark it was as if my eyes were still closed and there was a funny smell in the air, thick and cloying. I could hear shrieks coming from the corridor and the pounding of feet.

I sat bolt upright, hitting my head on the bunk above and blinking as my eyes adjusted to the darkness. My whole body felt lethargic. Somebody was hammering on the bedroom door as though trying to break it in. What was going on? Then the door burst open, smoke filling the room, curling around the bed posts, thick and black, stinging my eyes and making me cough. A fireman was standing in the doorway. He shouted to me in Thai. I tried to get up but my legs felt heavy and gave way so that I fell to the floor. 'Karen!' I called. 'Karen! Get up!' The smoke was so dense that I couldn't tell if she was out of bed or still asleep. I tried to get to my knees, the smoke jamming the back of my throat, threatening to choke me. I couldn't breathe, I was losing the edges of my vision. Suddenly I felt hands grab me and scoop me up, somebody speaking. A man's voice. Calm. I realised it was the fireman; he was carrying me down the corridor. My lungs were working overtime as I tried to inhale but there was no air, just the acrid smoke, like a thick duvet rammed down my throat. I was suffocating. And then we were heading towards an opening, a rectangle of black sky just visible through the smoke, and finally I was taking deep, desperate breaths of fresh air.

The fireman clattered down a metal stairwell with me slung over his shoulder. A group of teenagers were standing on the ground, gawping in fascinated horror as he dropped me to the pavement. I crumpled onto the hot tarmac and stared as the fire ate away at the top floor of the hostel like some ravenous beast.

Karen. Karen was in there.

'My friend!' I pointed in the direction of the hostel. He ran back inside just as one of the windows exploded with a popping sound, glass splintering and raining down on us. There was a cry. The group cowered, covering their heads with their hands while I looked on in dismay. A policeman yelled at us in Thai, then in English: '*Stand back!*'

It was utter chaos after that. More fire engines turned up, lurid yellow, screaming to a halt outside the hostel, and I was ushered into an ambulance, dazed and still coughing. As the fire worsened, I could only watch, wrapped in a scratchy blanket the colour of horse dung, shivering despite the heat. After a while I was taken to a hospital, where I was checked for smoke inhalation. When the doctor asked for my name I lied. I didn't want to reveal my real name in case it made the newspapers. I could just imagine the headline: 'British backpacker survives hostel fire in Thailand' – and then Sean would know where I was. I had no documents on me, no details – they would have gone up in smoke along with everything else.

I could hardly sleep that night. My chest felt heavy, as though the smoke was still in my lungs. I thought of Karen. Had she managed to escape?

The next morning, I was discharged. I had to fill out forms, which I did in a fake name. I went back to the hostel. It was unrecognisable, the top floor completely burnt out, blackened, and seeming to shimmer in the heat, the lower floors covered in ash. Officials were picking their way through the wreckage. My belongings had been destroyed. When I asked if an English girl had been found, a harassed-looking policeman with a notebook shook his head sadly. He took down my details, saying they might want to interview me for the investigation. But I never heard any more from them.

Over the next few days, I rang around all the hospitals to find out if she had been taken in, or was having treatment, but each one said the same thing: no Karen Fisher had been admitted.

Eight died in the fire that night, three members of staff and five backpackers. There were seven survivors and two missing. Luckily the hostel had been relatively empty, otherwise there would have been a lot more casualties. There was no mention of my name. Or Karen's. Most things had been obliterated in the fire, no records survived, just bodies found, blackened and burnt.

I was lost in the days and weeks that followed, numb, going through the motions as I contacted the British Embassy, applied for a new passport in my maiden name of Elizabeth Davies – a way of escaping Sean permanently. I'm not too proud to admit that I missed Karen; I missed her companionship, somebody to have a laugh with, even her crap jokes.

It's funny how life can change direction so suddenly, as though everything is being engineered by a higher being. My dad was a vicar, and both he and my mum spent their time trying to instil Christ into me, so that even now I can't quite shake the belief that there might be something in it, even though I'd rebelled against it as a teenager, running away from home at fifteen and living in a squat with a group of like-minded people until I met Sean.

I'd told Karen my parents were dead, but the truth was my mum left. She'd left my dad and she'd left me. I haven't clapped eyes on her since I was twelve. She would spend ages sitting on the edge of my bed in the evenings, before she ran out on us, spouting words from the Bible at me, telling me that I needed to cleanse myself of sin. I often wondered if she'd done the same, after she fucked off with the man from our local church. Or maybe those rules didn't apply to her. My dad blamed me, saying I was difficult, a spoilt, only child. I wasn't 'quite right', he said, because I didn't conform to the way he lived his life as a pillar of the community, in our quaint chocolate-box village. After Mum left he was always getting called in to school because I'd played truant or got caught smoking behind the bike sheds. When I was seen kissing Theo Masters in the boys' loos my dad had been furious, branding me a 'slut, like your mother!' We rowed and I'd stormed out. I never saw him again.

As a kid, I imagined God like a puppet master, hovering above us all, pulling our strings, deciding which way our lives would go as though on a whim.

Marrying Sean so young had been an escape. He was desirable because he was older, suave, well-off, with his own flat. He had his own construction company. I'd been impressed by him, but I'd jumped from one disaster to another.

When Karen had said I was a tough cookie she hadn't known the half of it.

28

I'd only been back in the country a couple of days – the first time in nearly ten years – when I saw her photo. I was flicking through a copy of the *Mail on Sunday* that had been left behind in a café, some greasy spoon in Huddersfield. It was a few weeks out of date, middle of March 2017, but I began reading it anyway. It was the name in the caption I recognised. Because it was my name: Elizabeth Elliot. What a coincidence, I thought as I sipped my coffee and re-read the story of a teacher who had saved the life of a pupil in a fire. A teacher with the same name as me. Not that I was a teacher – I never did take up my place at the teacher-training college. It wasn't what I really wanted to do. I'd stayed on in Thailand for a few years instead. Then I travelled around the world, working in bars and restaurants, always moving on after a few years. Then I met a Spanish man, Matteo, fell in love, and we were happy living in Barcelona, until everything went tragically wrong three months ago.

I'd only returned to England because my dad had died, and only to see if the bastard had left me anything. I was his only child, his next of kin, and I needed money since I'd run from Matteo.

It didn't dawn on me at first. It wasn't until I took a closer look at her picture, noticing those large hazel eyes and the smudge on her right arm in her sleeveless blouse; her matching tattoo, almost blurred if you weren't looking for it. Her hair was different, darker now and cropped, with a sweeping fringe. The same style as mine had once been, as it was in my old passport photo.

I couldn't believe what I was seeing. Karen Fisher? How could it be her when she'd died in the fire? I peered more closely at her face, at the dimples as she smiled down at the children at her feet. It was a surreal moment. When you spend nearly ten years thinking that someone has died and that it was somehow your fault, well, I went into a kind of shock. I sat there, shaking, feeling as though I'd downed too many cups of coffee. A waitress had to come over to check that I was all right.

Why was she using my name? What did it all mean?

I wanted, needed, answers.

It wasn't hard to find her address. Amazing how easy it is to find details from a newspaper article. Teacher. Independent school. Bath.

I took the early morning train to Bath. I'd never been before but the pretty Georgian buildings and the twee little parks turned me cold. It reminded me of York, of my unhappy childhood. Of course Karen would end up somewhere like this; I couldn't imagine her slumming it in Sheffield or Birmingham or any

261

other urban, cosmopolitan city. She wasn't cool enough. She was too vanilla. For the whole journey her deceit churned in my mind, around and around. She let me believe she was dead. Was she trying to escape me? Maybe she'd been rescued and ended up in hospital? But I had rung around all the hospitals. She'd never been admitted.

I waited outside the school that wet day at the end of March, obscured by my umbrella. I recognised her straight away despite her change of hairstyle. From a distance she could have passed for me, I suppose, or for what I used to look like. My hair was nearly down to my waist now, my face brown and weathered from spending too long in the sun, so that I looked older than my twenty-nine years. Karen, though, looked fresh-faced and, more annoyingly, she looked happy. She had a coat slung over her shoulders, one arm in a sling, and she was holding a polka-dot umbrella. She almost skipped through the school gates, choruses of, 'Goodbye, Ms Elliot, have a lovely break,' echoing in her wake from pupils and parents alike. I followed her as she made the ten-minute journey home by foot. I saw her enter a basement flat in a wide, busy street and watched from the pavement above as she kissed a tall, handsome man with blond hair in their kitchen. My life had turned to tatters and yet she had everything.

I stayed in a little bed-and-breakfast a few streets away and did some more research on my phone. I found out that she'd taken up my place at Middlesex to do a PGCE. She didn't have a degree of her own, I remembered, so she'd clearly had to pretend to be me to use mine. My purse, passport, National Insurance number ... everything had been in my backpack. I'd thought it had been destroyed by the fire. Yet Karen must have had them all this time.

I'd never hated anybody so much in all my life as in that moment. The anger was so deep, it swelled and grew so that I felt pregnant with it.

The bitch had stolen my life. And I was determined to get it back.

29

I made enquiries at the school, found out that they were on their Easter break. I skulked around outside her flat, but it was always in darkness, although I once noticed the old biddy from upstairs watching me from her bay window. I wondered if they were on holiday, whether my journey had been wasted. Then a stroke of luck: on the Wednesday I saw a light flickering on in the window below the pavement. It was mid-morning and rain hung in the air, the sky the colour of the nicotine stains on the ceiling of the squat I'd lived in. I descended the steps, ready to confront her, hoping her bloke would be at work. I knocked on her door, my heart hammering, wondering what I would do when I saw her, what I would say. I heard footsteps padding down the hallway, a low, deep cough, and I froze. It sounded like a man. I was about to turn around and run back up the stairs when the door was wrenched open. And there, standing in the doorway, was Sean.

We stared at each other, our faces mirror-images of shock. He looked different: older, more weathered, less groomed. He'd been handsome once, with a charm I hadn't been able to resist. Until I'd finally grown up and seen through to the bully he really was. The suits and long wool coats he used to favour were now replaced by jeans and a fleece. His eyes were harder than I remembered, his body stockier and more muscular, as though he'd been pumping steroids.

He found his voice first. 'Beth?'

I nodded, fear cutting into me, wondering why he was in Karen's flat.

'What the fuck are you doing here? You're supposed to be in Cornwall!' he growled.

'Cornwall?' I could barely breathe, let alone speak, and the word came out in a squeak. Before I could react further he'd grabbed me by the throat, dragging me into the hallway and slamming me up against the wall, his fingers pressing into my windpipe. He kicked the door shut with his foot. 'Yes, Cornwall,' he spat; his breath smelt of coffee and I flinched. What had I ever seen in him? He repulsed me.

'Please . . . I can't breathe . . .' I spluttered. He released the pressure on my throat and grabbed my upper arms instead, his fingers pressing into my flesh. There would be bruising later.

'You're supposed to be in Cornwall,' he repeated, his teeth clenched. 'With your prick of a husband.'

'I don't have a husband . . . except you.'

He shook me then, so hard that I bit the inside of my mouth. I could feel the iron taste of blood on my tongue. 'Don't lie to me, you stupid bitch. What the fuck are you doing here?'

'I'm not lying!' I yelped. 'Please. I don't know what you're talking about. I've come to see Karen Fisher.'

He stopped shaking me. 'Karen Fisher?'

'She was a friend I met when I went travelling,' I said, trying to wriggle from his grasp but he gripped my upper arms tightly. 'I saw a photo of her in the newspaper . . .'

'That was you in all the newspapers,' he hissed.

'No, it wasn't. I thought . . . I thought she'd died, in Thailand. But she took my identity. She's pretending to be me. I don't know why . . . I don't . . .'

His eyes flashed. 'So you don't live in this flat with Jamie Hall?'

'I've never heard of Jamie Hall.'

'Then what are you doing here?'

'I came to confront Karen.'

He staggered backwards as though I'd been the one to deliver the blow. 'For fuck's sake,' he groaned, putting his hands to his head, stalking up and down the hallway. 'For fuck's sake!' I couldn't understand why he was so agitated.

'What have you done, Sean? What have you done with Karen?'

He always was a manipulative bastard. I'd been too young to see it then, but in that moment terror shot through me. Had he hurt Karen?

He leapt on me then, grabbing my hair and dragging me into a bedroom. 'I've been looking for you for years. Nine fucking years. You stole ten grand from me. Did

266

you think I was going to let you get away with that? And then that photograph. I thought I'd found you. And now you're telling me it wasn't you at all but some other stupid cow pretending to be you?' Spittle was flying out of his mouth as he shouted, his face so red and angry that his eyes bulged. 'I want to kick the shit out of you. You've ruined everything . . .' His eyes glinted and I could see right to his rotten core. I always knew that Sean would kill me if he saw me again. I'd betrayed him, tricked him, stolen from him and run off. I knew he'd never forgive that. Which is why I'd kept away all these years. He raised his arm, his meaty hand clenched into a ball, and I cowered, protecting my head, awaiting that first blow. It took me back to when we were married, although he was careful then to hit me where the bruises wouldn't be seen.

A vibrating buzz emanated from him and he paused, lowering his arm in surprise, taking his mobile from the back pocket of his grubby-looking jeans. They would once have been designer. Had he fallen on hard times? He frowned as a name flashed up on the screen. His mouth twisted into a sinister smile. 'Well,' he said, glancing at me, 'look who's ringing.'

I stared at his thick neck and the tattoo on his arm. My name had once been inked on that left bicep, but now I could see it had been turned into an ugly, green snake.

He positioned himself between me and the door as he talked into his mobile in a fake jovial voice, something about a man called Jim trying to spot fossils. Then he cleared his throat. 'Listen. I'm glad you called actually. There's been a change of plan . . .' He hesitated, shooting a glance in my direction. 'My daughter's coming out of hospital earlier than we expected. I know, I know, it's great news. So we'll be going back to our place in London tonight, tomorrow at the latest. I'll leave the key with your neighbour, shall I?'

What was he talking about? What daughter? And then he smirked again. Whatever he was up to he was clearly enjoying himself. '. . . Just drop the key back at the petrol station on your way home. Thanks again . . . *Libby*.' Libby?

'Who were you talking to?' I asked him as he slipped the phone back into his pocket. He grinned, looking ghoulish in the half light.

'It seems your friend Karen Fisher is calling herself Libby. Not Beth.'

'Why are you speaking to Karen? What's going on, Sean?'

He stared at me as if seeing me for the first time. 'I don't like to admit it but I've been had. She looks more like you than you do. What happened to you? You look like shit.'

My guts twisted. Even after all these years his words hit a nerve.

'I thought I'd have a bit of fun with you before fucking up your life. But that's gone tits up now, hasn't it?' He emitted a cynical laugh. 'You've even messed up that pleasure. Now I'm going to have to think of something else for you.'

What had he been planning to do? Knowing Sean, it was obviously something warped.

I played for time. He always was arrogant. He'd enjoy filling me in on what he was going to do. 'Were you going to kill me?'

'Of course I was going to fucking kill you. Do you think I'd let you get away with making a fool out of me? With stealing my money.'

My mouth was dry but I asked anyway. 'How?'

'I was following you – or someone I thought was you – in Cornwall. Watching *her* and her weedy husband. I pushed him when they were visiting a lighthouse. Didn't plan to hurt him then, just wanted to freak them out, but she nearly went over the edge of a cliff. I thought there was something different about you. Your walk, your laugh. But it has been ten years.' He shrugged and grinned nastily. 'I came back here to steal your bank account details so I could get my ten grand back, plus interest. Oh, and I poisoned some of the food in Cornwall. In the fridge. Covered your underwear in animal's blood and buried it in the garden. But I fucked up. Got the wrong person . . .'

'My underwear?'

'That expensive basque I bought you, remember? I kept it. All these years. I knew I'd be seeing you again. That eventually I'd find you. I treated you well, took you away from that disgusting squat you were living in. Bought you nice things. And this is how you repay me?'

'Treated me well?' Despite my fear I couldn't keep my mouth closed. 'You beat me up. You abused me. You took advantage of me, my age, my vulnerability . . .'

The punch when it came was unexpected and knocked me back against the bed; it felt like my cheekbone was about to explode. I could feel nearly ten years' worth of pent-up frustration and anger in the force of that fist. Then he straddled me and I hit out at him, but my blows were as ineffectual as water. He flipped me over so that I was on my front and grabbed my arms roughly behind my back. I could feel him tying something around them, cutting into my flesh. 'I'll be back for you,' he said, getting up off the bed. And then he left me there, in the dark, my eye throbbing where he'd punched me.

As soon as I heard him slam the front door I worked on loosening my ties. I sat up against the wooden headboard and ran my wrists against the sharp edges, gradually sawing away. He'd used some kind of thick tape – did he carry it around with him? Nothing would surprise me with that psycho. I was sweating as I toiled away, and my wrists were rubbed raw, but I eventually managed to cut through the tape. Sean had been too cocky. He'd forgotten that I'd had enough practice at this when we were married.

I jumped up, glancing around the bedroom that Karen slept in; modern and clean, with Scandinavian oak furniture, her dressing table cluttered with different potions and perfume bottles, a photo of her and her husband sitting proudly amongst the mess. Sean had called him Jamie. Jamie Hall. I needed something hard, heavy, something to use as a weapon for when he came back. I opened her wardrobe, hoping to find a sharp stiletto heel or a heavy book to smack him with. But there were only trainers and ballet flats. No heels at all. And then I spotted something shoved in the corner of the wardrobe among some summer clothes and hand-bags. Something familiar. I leaned in and grabbed it; the stone was cold under my fingers. The Buddha that Harry had given her. Why had she kept it? Did she still yearn for him? The one that got away?

I thought we'd be OK, Karen and me. Two strong women escaping our pasts without the need of a man. But she'd betrayed me. The thought of teaching Karen a lesson gave me the impetus and the strength I needed. That's the thing about me and Sean, we were more alike than he realised. Perhaps that's what had attracted us to each other when we were young. We would have made a great team if we weren't constantly trying to outdo each other with our power struggle to come out top. Then I thought of Matteo; kind, loyal Matteo, with his big brown eyes that always looked sleepy. My heart twisted with longing for him. He'd kept the darkness at bay. He had made me want to be a better person. But he'd seen through me in the end too.

The room was drenched in darkness. Where was Sean? I daren't leave the bedroom in case he suddenly came back. I pocketed the Buddha – it was heavy enough to use as a weapon if needed. I didn't want to risk the front door so I wrenched open the bedroom window and climbed into the garden. The light was dwindling, casting shadows on the overgrown grass. I wondered what was beyond the garden. Would it be easy to escape? Before fear could kick in I sprinted across the lawn. Then I heard a bellow and turned my head, stumbling in my eagerness to get away. Sean was clambering out of the window. I ran for the bushes, but he was so quick he was soon only an arm's length away. I forced down a shriek of terror and darted behind a large bush, my hand reaching inside my leather jacket for the Buddha. I crouched down, my breathing shallow, my heart beating so ferociously I was worried he would be able to hear it.

'I know where you are, you stupid bitch,' he called, sounding amused. He peered around the bush. I screamed and swung the Buddha at him with all my might, smacking him in the temple, relieved and horrified as the ornament made contact with his skull. He staggered, his shocked eyes finding mine as he went crashing backwards like a tree being felled.

Fear took hold of me so that, for a few moments, I was rooted to the spot, staring at the dent in his skull and the arc of blood that had sprayed from the back of his head, staining the grass red. Then I knelt down beside him, my knees sinking into the damp lawn, careful not to touch him. I must leave no evidence.

I glanced up furtively. The building was over two hundred feet away, the windows opaque, some with curtains hanging open, others with the blinds rolled up. Was anybody watching? I was already starting to think like a criminal. Was I seen at the bottom of the garden among the weeds and overgrown grass?

Was I seen killing my husband?

So I was a murderer. It had been surprisingly easy, killing a man. The moment my fingers encircled that ornament I knew I'd wanted to do as much damage as possible. I wanted to kill. I felt no guilt, no remorse. And now he was out of the picture. For the first time since I was sixteen the threat of him no longer hung over me. He'd taken enough of my life and I wasn't going to let him take any more.

I stayed in Karen's flat that night, too scared to leave. But it spooked me, the thought of Sean's body at the bottom of her garden. How long before it was discovered? I was terrified that someone – maybe that old crone upstairs – had seen me. I snooped around, of course, saw that everything was in my name: her bank details, her credit cards, her driving licence. There was nothing that betrayed who she really was. So she had even been lying to that husband of hers. I was shocked by how effortlessly Karen had stepped into life as Elizabeth Elliot. Clever to use Libby instead of Beth. Maybe she felt that sounded posh, more in keeping with her new middle-class life. Perhaps she felt she could disassociate herself from what she had done if she used a different name.

How had she survived the fire? I couldn't understand it. I was the last person to be rescued from the hostel and I had been lucky. Nobody had been rescued after me – that's what the fireman said. So how could Karen Fisher be here, pretending to be me?

Unless she wasn't in the hostel that night. Unless she'd already left.

A hundred questions filled my head as I pocketed her bank statements. It would be easy to access her money – she was complacent enough to have a four digit number scribbled onto a piece of paper in the filing cabinet: her pin. She was obviously using my National Insurance number. She really must have thought I was dead to do something so audacious.

And then it hit me so hard that I had to sit down on her sofa; I thought I'd been the one in control. But she had been more cunning, more daring, than I'd ever given her credit for.

I spent ages washing the Buddha, making sure to wipe away any traces of my fingerprints from its surfaces, its creases and dents. My stomach turned at the sight of Sean's blood. Then I put it on her sideboard, where she'd be able to see it. All this fuss, I thought. All this fuss about Harry and she'd hidden the Buddha away as though it meant nothing.

I prowled around her flat, examining the photos of her and Jamie at various events or holidays; they looked happy together, usually joined by a big, dopey-looking dog. I was relieved to see there was no evidence of children.

Oh Karen. She had no clue that I was already married and that when she'd tied the knot under my name with her precious Jamie she was committing bigamy. *A bigamist.* It tickled me, to think that. Her one mistake.

And when Sean's body was found, as it inevitably would be, Karen would get the blame. And then the whole sorry tale would come out. What would Jamie think when he found out the truth about his not-so-perfect wife? All I needed to do for now was stand back and watch as her whole world imploded.

30

I took a perverse enjoyment out of spying on them when they returned from Cornwall; their disintegration as they realised that someone had stolen their credit cards and emptied their bank accounts, their paranoia as they wondered who was behind it all, the fear eating away at their relationship. I opened an account at a catalogue company in my name and sent Karen items to jog her memory of our time in Thailand: a wig the colour and style that her hair used to be, a backpack similar to the one we'd both carried.

And then there was the old biddy who lived upstairs. A few times she spotted me hanging around while Karen – *Libby* – was at work in the job that should have been mine. Karen never saw me though. She was too engrossed in her own smug little world.

I didn't know what my plan was exactly. All I could think about was that Karen must have left me behind in that hostel. And she needed to pay.

One afternoon, I was hovering in the alleyway between her building and next door. I was waiting for Karen to get home from work when I heard a tap on the bay window and the old lady's face peered over her net curtains, beckoning me in. I was intrigued, and a little afraid. It had started to rain and I was getting impatient and cold in my thin jacket, so I'd made my way tentatively to her front door. She opened it only partially, as though she was scared of me. It made me wonder what she had seen from her windows. Had she seen me killing Sean? I dismissed this idea at once. If she had seen me then she wouldn't be inviting me into her home, would she?

'Are you looking for someone, love?' she said, not unkindly. 'I've seen you before. Can I help you with anything?'

Nosy old bat. The lie slipped easily off my tongue. 'I'm Libby's sister,' I said, smiling politely. 'But we've sort of lost touch. I don't know whether I'd be welcome . . .' I shrugged, averting my eyes shyly and shuffling my feet, staring down at her Victorian floor tiles. She'd opened the door then, as I knew she would, and invited me inside. My hands were so cold that they burned with chilblains in the too-warm house. She fussed around, making a cup of tea while I stood in her large sitting room, gazing around in wonder. It was cosy, with knick-knacks covering every surface and gilt-edged plates on the wall. Old-fashioned but homely, the sort of place I would have loved to have grown up in, instead of the sparsely furnished vicarage with pictures of Christ above the beds. My eyes went to the array of photographs on the mantelpiece, all showing her in another life; various stages of being young, happy and in love. She'd been pretty once, the black-and-white photos reminding me of actresses from old films, with her pin curls and her dark lips. An old-fashioned radio sat on a shelf, the male presenter talking in dulcet tones. I found his voice soothing. She noticed me looking and turned it down with a self-conscious smile. 'I always have it too loud, but it's company.'

I found myself nodding. I wondered if she was lonely. Like me.

'I'm Evelyn,' she said. 'Please, take a seat.' She indicated the chair by the window. She had a tea-tray on the side table next to her with a teapot and two china cups. Was she expecting someone? She offered me tea and I nodded, blind-sided, while she poured and then handed me a cup. As I sat there, numb and unsure as to what I was hoping to achieve, she reached over and took my hand, her eyes going to the bruise on my cheekbone. 'Libby has never mentioned a sister . . .' she said.

'Oh. A family rift. A long time ago. Has she told you much about her family?'

She shook her head. 'No, not really. She said once her mum had died. Libby is very private. But she's a lovely woman, she would welcome you, I know she would. Don't be afraid, my dear.'

I felt a punch of jealousy to my gut. A lovely woman? Hardly. This Evelyn was like a grandmother and by the way she spoke about Libby, her eyes shining with pride, I realised how much she must care for her. All I wanted – all I had ever wanted – was for someone to care about me in that way. Maybe my mother had once upon a time, before unhappiness had seeped into her, changing her, making her bitter. And my father had always been hard. He loved God but not much else. I had never known a happy home with laughter and love. I imagined Evelyn would have made a good mother, a good grandmother. The fight began to abate as I sat there. And I realised I was afraid. I thought of my depressing hotel room with its single bed, how alone I felt, nothing but a few belongings to show for my thirty years of life. I yearned in that moment for my baby. For Matteo.

She leaned forward, her eyes kind. 'What happened?'

And I found myself telling her, about escaping a violent man, falling in love for the first time, having a baby, and how they were both taken away from me in the cruellest of ways. And now I was left with nothing while Libby had everything. Everything that should have – could have – been mine. Her pale-blue eyes smarted with tears and she gripped my hands in her knotted ones. 'Oh my love,' she said, and her face was so full of sympathy and kindness that I felt tears prick my eyes too. 'And Libby knows nothing about this?'

'We . . . er . . . fell out before then. When we were young. Over a boy. A silly argument.' I shrugged. 'You know how these things can escalate.'

She sat back in her chair and picked up her knitting. I watched, mesmerised, as her needles flew back and forth, the soft lemon wool dangling onto her lap in a ball. And then I noticed what she was knitting. Tiny little booties.

'Is somebody having a baby?' I said, thinking of my own stillborn baby, the pain in Matteo's eyes as realisation dawned that we wouldn't be playing happy families after all. My dad's voice in my ear telling me this was God's punishment for being wicked.

Her eyes lit up. 'They're for Libby.'

'Libby?' The words stuck in my throat and I placed the cup and saucer down on the side table with a shaky hand.

She nodded. 'She hasn't told me, officially. But I know.' She smiled enigmatically. 'I can tell when a woman is pregnant. I was a midwife, you know, a long, long time ago.' She gave a girlish giggle but my whole body was rigid with shock, fury inching its way through my veins. She must have noticed, as she added hurriedly, 'Oh my love, I'm so sorry, that was insensitive of me after your loss.'

I stood up hurriedly, knocking the side table over in my haste. My tea cup clattered to the ground, sending cold tea down the legs of the table and puddling onto the wood flooring. Evelyn dropped her knitting at her feet, the wool unravelling.

'Oh my love, it's a shock . . . I'm sorry . . .'

'I need to go. I can't do this . . .' I stumbled away, blinded by tears. It wasn't fair. Karen didn't deserve any of this. She had everything I wanted.

Just as I was about to leave the room I heard a groan. I turned back to see Evelyn clutching her heart, her face a strange colour, like putty. 'Evelyn. Evelyn!' I ran over to her but she slumped forward, a gurgle coming from her lips. I gently lifted her head, but her eyes were already lifeless. Just like Sean's. A cold feeling crept into my heart and I slumped to the floor next to her chair. The only person in months to show me kindness was dead.

I sat with her until it grew dark, then sneaked out of her flat by the back door.

My dad had been right about me. I was bad through and through. I had the devil in me. I destroyed everything I touched.

PART THREE
Bath

31

Hartley's expression is smug as he slaps a photograph on the table in front of me. It's a black-and-white print of the man from Lizard Point, but taken years ago when his face was less ravaged and he'd looked attractive. So this was Sean Elliot. Beth's ex. In all the time we were travelling together she never once mentioned that she was married to him, or even what he was called. She'd drip-fed me information about him so that I was aware he was abusive and that he'd put her in hospital, but that was all. I could understand why she'd never said more about him. Thailand had been her escape, as it had been mine; a place where our pasts hadn't mattered. Or so I had thought.

Beth. I'd tried not to think about her over the years because to do so would cause my stomach to flip with guilt.

When I first met Beth I'd really liked her; I thought she was sparky and I admired her courage. When she said she had a place at teacher-training college I have to admit it shocked me. I couldn't see her as a teacher. She seemed so tough and streetwise, with her hard face and her foul tongue, but it was obvious she had a bit of a chip on her shoulder. She didn't take any shit and I'd felt safe travelling with her. She could be manipulative, I cottoned on to that quite early on. But then the business with Harry and what came afterwards made me realise that she was actually a nasty piece of work.

What had her husband been doing in my flat? He was obviously the one who had arranged the house swap. DS Byrnes said he was a builder working on The Hideaway, so he would have had access to keys and must have cut one for himself. But why go to all that trouble?

'Do you recognise this man?' asks Hartley in an impatient tone, bringing me back to the present. Another detective – a woman this time – sits next to him. She's young, in her early thirties, and has very straight, glossy blonde hair in a bob. She doesn't speak.

I shake my head, tears springing to my eyes, mumbling 'No comment' like my duty solicitor advised me to do. He sits next to me, reassuring in his suit, his briefcase open on the table.

I am in too deep. I took Beth's identity without a thought for her past or the future repercussions it would cause.

How can I ever tell them the truth without losing everything?

My life as Karen Fisher had been bleak. When my mum died I was left with my dad – a raging alcoholic. He never hit us, he wasn't a violent drunk, alcohol just heightened his emotions. I believe he really did love my mum, in his own way. They rowed, usually about his drinking, and once an affair with the local barmaid, but when he was sober – and he could be, for long stretches at a time, before relapsing again – he was the loveliest man in the world. He'd surprise her with flowers, or trips to Scarborough or Whitby. She loved it by the sea. He made her laugh and would sneak up on her while she was chopping vegetables in the kitchen and snake his arms around her waist, nuzzling her neck. She would bat him away with a 'get off, you silly bugger,' but I could tell by the way her eyes lit up that she enjoyed it. They never had much money and my dad was forever in and out of jobs due to his drinking. We lived in a small village in a two-up two-down. It wasn't much but Mum kept it clean and tidy and it was furnished with little knick-knacks and cushions that she had made. That's why I'd always loved being at Evelyn's place – its warmth and clutter reminded me of home.

But then my mum died and everything changed. My dad was desperate without her. He'd go out most evenings, drinking, rolling in late and collapsing onto the sofa, a big, heavy mass, reeking of alcohol and cigarettes. I tried to keep our home looking nice, as my mum had done, but when Dad was on a bender he'd come in drunk and smash things up. He never threw anything away, so empty cans, fag butts and half-eaten crisp packets would be strewn all over the floor. I was forever clearing up after him. I ended up missing school to nurse him as the drink took its toll on his health. I loved him and I wanted him to get better, I couldn't bear to lose both my parents.

Even though I did well in my GCSEs – especially considering I'd missed so much school – I knew A levels and university were out of the question. Dad was on benefits but they didn't stretch very far and I needed to work. So I left school at sixteen and took any job I could find. The pay was terrible as I wasn't qualified for anything. I had no choice but to watch my friends leave our small village for the big cities and universities like Manchester, Leeds, Bristol and Cardiff, places I could only dream of going to, and I soon lost touch with them all.

Then, when I was twenty, my dad's liver finally gave out. He was only fifty-three when he died. I had no other family; my parents hadn't kept in touch with their own families – I sensed there was a rift when they got married – so I'd never known any aunts or uncles or grandparents. The house I'd grown up in was put on the market, but my dad owed so much money in unpaid mortgage fees that I only got a few thousand out of the sale. Not knowing what to do with my life I decided I needed to get away from the place where everyone knew my sad history. I had nothing and nobody to keep me in Yorkshire. I'd always been a loner, slinking through life hoping nobody would notice me, or feel sorry for me.

I bought the first available flight, which happened to be to Thailand.

On the night of the fire I'd watched, rigid with shock, as flames licked the hostel and gusts of smoke surged out of the windows, knowing that Beth was trapped in there. It was chaos; fire engines and an ambulance wailed to the scene, then came shouts from the firemen as they darted in and out of the building, or tried to put out the fire with huge hoses. The air was scorching; black smoke drifted up my nostrils and down my throat. I felt sick. Where was Beth? She must still be in bed – she had been out of it when I left. I grabbed a fireman, screamed at him that my friend was still in there, but he just shook his head sadly.

I staggered away, unable to witness it any longer, and found another hostel to stay in. But I couldn't sleep; I just lay there, too horrified even to cry.

I returned the next morning. The hostel was a burnt-out shell. I was told that eight had died. They couldn't tell me if Beth was among them. *Not yet*, said a policeman in halting English, *not until their bodies have been identified*. I rang around a few hospitals, asked if an Elizabeth Elliot had been admitted, but nothing. It wasn't until I was ensconced in a hotel room a few streets away, shocked and nauseous, the smell of smoke still strong in my nostrils, that I realised, in my hurry to flee the hostel, I'd picked up Beth's backpack instead of my own.

It had been a snap decision. When I saw everything that was in her bag – her wallet stuffed with cash, her passport and her National Insurance card – I thought about using them as a means to keep travelling, rather than having to hang around waiting for the embassy to issue me another passport. I had no doubt that my possessions had been destroyed in the fire.

I sat on the bed, my head reeling, wondering what to do, her stuff laid out in front of me on the orange blanket. And then I saw it, the Buddha that Harry had given me. What was it doing among her things?

Then my eye went to the letter.

It was from the teacher-training college, offering Beth a place on their one-year PGCE course in English. They had included all the information about the course, and details on placements and funding for the £9,000 fees. How hard could it be? English was my best subject at school. But I hadn't been to university, I hadn't coped with doing a degree. Beth had scribbled on the letter in pen, reminding herself to ring them to defer. Had she done it?

I pushed the thought from my mind, telling myself I'd never get away with it. They would have met Beth for an interview. But how long ago? We didn't look dissimilar. And if I cut my hair and dyed it darker then I could pass for her, couldn't I? They would only have met her once. A passing resemblance, that was all it needed to be. We both came from Yorkshire, so had similar accents.

No, I couldn't do it. I wasn't brave enough. I dismissed the idea and tried to sleep. But a little voice in my head kept probing and prodding, telling me that I had to do it. What were the options otherwise? Go back to university and do a degree myself? But that would take years, and by the end of it I'd be in so much debt that I'd forever be trying to pay it off. I thought of my parents, of the life they'd lived. I wanted more.

The next day I rang the college and said I was interested in starting in September after all. Then I went to a local salon and had my long hair dyed a rich chocolate brown and chopped into a pixie cut so that I resembled Beth's passport photograph. I liked my new haircut; it showed off my big eyes and accentuated my cheekbones, so as the years went by I ended up keeping the style.

Every now and again I'd experience bouts of doubt that would make me stop in my tracks, my heart pounding, my mind whirling. What was I thinking? What if I got caught? What if Beth had survived the fire and took the place on the course herself? And then I'd convince myself that she was dead. She had to be. There was no way she could have survived. And if she had, by some miracle, managed to escape, then she would have continued to travel up north. She couldn't leave the country until she had a new passport. She was having doubts about being a teacher, she'd told me so herself. And the course was only a year. Not long to pretend to be someone else.

Now that the idea had formed in my mind I knew I couldn't dismiss it. I had to go through with it. The prospect of being a teacher, of working with kids, excited me. I'd have a future, something to look forward to.

It was so risky but at the same time I felt compelled to do it. As if this was my one chance. What was the worst that could happen? I asked myself. If they found out that I wasn't really Elizabeth Elliot I'd get chucked off the course. But I had to try. I had to find a way to scrape back some semblance of a future because I couldn't afford to continue travelling for ever. And then what? What awaited me back at home? Factory jobs and stacking shelves, minimum wage and no career prospects? I couldn't even type. Whatever Beth's background, and she hadn't told me much, at least she'd had the sense – or luck – to get some qualifications. I would work hard, I promised myself. I would keep my head down. It was a year – less, really, if you thought about holidays.

And so I did it. I became Elizabeth Elliot. Libby. And then I met and fell in love with Jamie, and after a while I began to forget that I was ever called Karen Fisher.

32

When I'm eventually released from the police station I'm relieved to see that Jamie has hung around for me. His whole body is tense and rigid as he sits bolt upright on a grey plastic chair in the airless waiting room, and he looks like he hasn't slept for a week. He's unshaven and his hair is a tangled mop, as though he's been frantically raking his fingers through it. He has bags under his eyes and his white T-shirt is stained. As soon as he sees me he's up on his feet, rushing towards me.

'Libby, thank goodness. Are you OK? Have they charged you with anything?'

I shake my head, tears springing to my eyes at the look of concern, *of love*, on his face. *He thinks I'm a bigamist but he's still here, standing by me. I don't deserve it.* He slings an arm over my shoulder and steers me outside to where the car is parked. I'm surprised to see that the sun is going down already, although the air is still humid. I must have been in the station for hours.

I slide into the passenger seat and my body starts to shake in delayed shock. I need to tell Jamie everything, but will he ever forgive me? He sees everything in black and white and I've lied to him since the day I first met him. I married him under a false name. Thanks to the duty solicitor I've not had to reveal anything to the police yet, but it will only be a matter of time.

I study Jamie's profile as he drives, his straight nose, his full mouth, his left ear with the kink at the top. He's a funny, messy geek. And I can't lose him. He must have a million questions swirling around in his brain but he hasn't asked me any. His mouth is set in a grim line and I reach out and touch his thigh, the denim rough against my fingertips. 'I really love you, Jamie. You need to know that.'

He stiffens, and when he speaks it's as though his throat is restricted. 'You're scaring me, Libby.'

'I'm so, so sorry.' I take my hand away and fold it into my lap.

His chin crumples and I can tell he's trying not to break down. He's thinking the worst, I know it. He's thinking I married a man and never told him. Does he also think I'm a killer?

When we get back to Sylvia's, she fusses around me, making sure I'm comfortable on the sofa, offering to make tea, her bangles jangling as she positions a cushion behind my back as though I'm a patient and not a murder suspect. I can tell she's desperate to know what's going on, it's written all over her face. Jamie sits motionless by the window, looking out onto the street. He hasn't said a word since we got back from the police station. Ziggy is sprawled at my feet and I reach down to stroke him, reassured by his presence.

What will the Hall family do when they find out the

truth? Will they chuck me out? Where would I go? The worry of it makes me feel sick.

'Where's Katie?' I ask Sylvia as she moves towards the doorway.

'Oh, she's out. With friends.' Sylvia gives an unconcerned shrug and I feel lighter knowing Katie isn't here, with her probing, judgemental attitude. I wait until Sylvia has disappeared into the kitchen before turning to Jamie.

'We need to talk.'

He doesn't look at me but continues gazing out of the window. The street beyond is empty, the trees shadowy and moving slightly in the breeze, the last of the sunlight filtering through the branches, bright, like a flash torch. It's so quiet I can hear a bird tweeting outside.

'Jay . . .?' I try.

'I know,' he says coldly, his head snapping around so that he's facing me. 'I know we need to talk. But I don't know if I'm ready to hear what you've got to say. It's going to change everything. Christ, Libs. You're already married? To that . . . that man?' He runs a hand over his face in exasperation. 'Why didn't you say? In Cornwall? You must have recognised him. How could you have married me when you knew you were already married to him? My God, is our marriage even legal? Are you even my wife?'

I lean forward. 'Listen. I can honestly tell you that I've never seen that man before our holiday in Cornwall.' He makes a disbelieving sound through his teeth but I hurry on. 'It's true, he was married to Elizabeth Elliot. But that's not me.'

Jamie stares at me.

'Elizabeth Elliot is not my real name. My name is Karen Fisher.'

His eyes grow rounder with every word I tell him so that by the time I've finished the whole story they look like they are going to pop out of his face.

There is a stunned silence. Eventually he says, 'You're telling me that you stole another person's identity and used it to get out of Thailand and start teacher-training college?'

I nod.

'And the real Elizabeth Elliot?'

'She's dead.'

He looks like he's about to throw up. 'How?'

'When we were in Bangkok, there was a hostel fire. I –' I hesitate, twisting a tissue in my hands '– I managed to get out. But she was still in bed.'

He looks at me, aghast. 'You didn't try and save her?'

I shake my head. 'No . . . it wasn't like that. I was already outside when I realised the hostel was on fire. I was . . .'

I have to tell him the truth. That I was trying to escape her.

He frowns. 'You were what?'

'I . . . I was running away from her.'

I've never admitted this to anyone before.

His eyebrows shoot up so they are almost hidden

by his fringe. 'What? But why? I thought you said she was your friend?'

'I found out that she had done something awful to me. It's a long story, and it's not important now. I just knew I could no longer trust her and I didn't want to continue travelling with her.'

'So you buggered off in the middle of the night, leaving her to die in a fire?'

'I've carried the guilt with me for years.' I hang my head.

He rakes his hands through his hair. 'Christ, Libby . . .' Then he stops and gives a humourless laugh. 'That's not your name, is it? It's *her* name.'

'She called herself Beth . . .'

He stands up so suddenly that I shrink back against the sofa. 'I don't give a fuck what she called herself!' he shouts. 'I can't believe I'm hearing this. I just . . . I can't . . .'

He storms out of the room.

Sylvia comes in with a tea tray, the cups rattling as she walks. 'Everything all right?' she asks too brightly as she sets the tray down on the coffee table. I get up and dash past her without answering.

I find Jamie in our room, lying on the bed and staring up at the ceiling, his face expressionless. The curtains are open but the room is in shadow, the light a grey-white on his face.

I stand over him. 'Jay, you have to understand, I did it because I needed to change my life. My life was shit . . .' Tears fill my eyes.

He groans. 'I just wish you'd told me. I feel like I don't know you . . . that's the thing that hurts the most.' He sits up to face me. 'You've lied to me. For five years.'

'My background, everything I told you about my parents, is true . . .'

'But you've hardly told me anything about them. You've always been so cagey about your background. Now I know why.'

'I told you my mum died of a blood clot. That's true. I just . . . I lied about going to university . . .'

'And your name. For Christ's sake.' He shakes his head. 'Why couldn't you tell me? You made me feel bad for hiding the fact that I was helping Hannah, that I'd cheated on her at uni –' he gulps and makes an effort to continue '– and all this time you were hiding this huge thing from me. I knew you were keeping something from me. I thought it was odd you never wanted to go to Yorkshire, that you never really talked about your parents, or Thailand. But this . . .?' He throws his arms up in the air. 'All this deceit. I'm finding it hard to reconcile myself with the fact you're capable of all this.'

I perch on the edge of the bed. Tears and snot are streaming down my face and I brush at my eyes angrily with my sleeve and try to blow my nose with a disintegrating tissue. 'Would you have understood?' I sniff. 'I couldn't tell anyone. And I wasn't hurting anyone, Jay. I didn't know that Beth was married. We were only twenty-one when we met. So young. Beth didn't want that place on the course – and I'm a good teacher.

I'm . . .' I sob into my hands and eventually I hear the bed creak and feel Jamie's arms around me. 'I'm so sorry,' I say, burying my face in his T-shirt. 'I'm so, so sorry.'

When I wake up the room is completely dark and still. Too still. I can already sense that Jamie isn't with me. My fears are confirmed when I turn over and see the space next to me is empty. I'm fully clothed, but the air has turned colder. I grab a cardigan and creep downstairs so as not to wake Sylvia or Katie.

Jamie is sitting in one of the rattan chairs in the conservatory in the dark, staring out at the garden bathed in moonlight; it looks magical. He's wearing the same grubby T-shirt as earlier and the Wallace and Gromit boxer shorts I bought him last Christmas. I sidle into the seat next to him and take his hand in mine. He lets me. And we sit like that, for hours, not speaking.

33

A clean break. That's what Jamie wants. No more lies. And the only way to do that is to tell the truth and suffer the consequences.

The next morning, as we sit around the breakfast table with Sylvia and Katie, I fill them in while Jamie silently butters his toast. Katie gawps at me openmouthed. 'I knew it!' she says, dropping her knife in excitement. It clatters onto her plate. 'I knew there was something *off* about you.'

Sylvia's eyes radiate disappointment. It's painful and I lower my gaze. 'I'm sorry,' I mumble. Another apology. It doesn't seem enough, somehow.

'You took a dead girl's identity!' Katie stares at me incredulously. 'How low is that?' She turns to Jamie. 'Surely you're not going to forgive her for this? She's lied to you for years. What else has she lied about? How can you ever trust her again? She married you under a false name. She's a bloody bigamist.'

'No, Katie, she's not.' Jamie's voice is a warning.

'Well,' she says hotly, 'she can't be trusted. And surely it's an offence to pretend to be someone else? I can't believe you're standing by her. You're a mug.' Her eyes flash dangerously as she turns her attention to me. 'And you're a criminal. I hope you're going to tell the police. If you don't, I will.'

Sylvia places a manicured hand on her daughter's arm. 'Katie. You're not helping.'

She shrugs her mother off and jumps up. 'Why should I want to help that stupid cow? I'm going out.' She grabs her denim jacket from the back of the chair and storms out of the room. A few seconds later we hear the front door slam.

I stare at my plate miserably.

Sylvia's voice, when she speaks, is clear but gentle. 'I'm sorry about Katie. She's always been hot-headed. And she's fiercely loyal to her brother. I do agree with her, though, Libby. You do need to go to the police. I'm going to call my lawyer, OK? She's the best in Bath.' She reaches across the table and squeezes my hand. 'You're family. And we love you and we will support you in this. Won't we, Jamie?' She shoots a look at her son, then gets up and breezes out of the room, leaving me staring after her, speechless.

'I always thought your mum hated me,' I say later as we walk along the Bath streets to the meeting with her lawyer.

Jamie has showered and looks handsome and much younger than his thirty years in smart jeans and a short-sleeved linen shirt. As we dressed this morning my heart swelled when I saw him pick out his outfit, realising he was making an effort. For me.

The sun is shining, the sky a clear pale blue with the occasional gauzy cloud. It's the sort of beautiful spring day where you feel nothing bad can happen, and I feel optimistic that we can get past this, that Jamie can begin to forgive me. We can move forward, being honest with one another. I know I'll lose my job, that I may never teach again, and it devastates me, but losing Jamie terrifies me more.

'My mum can be a bit of a dragon, but she's loyal. Like me.' He takes my hand and squeezes it gently. He stops then, in the middle of the pavement, so that a woman with her head down almost bumps into him. She tuts loudly as she glides past.

'What is it?' I ask. His face is so serious I worry he's going to say he's changed his mind, and the day darkens just that little bit. He takes my hands in his and his voice, when he speaks, is urgent. 'You have to promise me something though, Libs. No more lies.'

I swallow. 'I promise. No more lies.'

We reach the lawyer's office and are buzzed straight in. Melanie Finch is in her early fifties, tall, thin and glamorous, with sleek dark hair and a white streak at the front that reminded me of Anne Bancroft in *The Graduate*. She sits making notes on a leather-bound pad while I tell her everything as clearly as I can. Jamie holds my hand the whole time. After I've finished she sits back in her chair and appraises me.

'Will she be prosecuted?' Jamie asks.

She blinks at Jamie and then addresses me in her

calm, well-spoken voice. 'Yes, you will most likely be prosecuted because you used the identity of a dead person for your own gain.'

My mouth goes dry. 'Will I go to prison?'

She frowns. 'It's doubtful for a first-time offence. You'll probably get a suspended sentence, maybe community service. I can't promise that, of course, as it really does depend on the judge. But, Libby, there is a worse potential charge hanging over you. A man was found murdered at the bottom of your garden. You, and possibly Jamie, are likely to be suspects.' She consults her notes. 'I see that DI Hartley has interviewed you already. I'm glad to see you haven't given him any information yet.' She frowns. 'It states here that the victim was last seen alive at midday on Wednesday fifth April and estimated time of death is anywhere between midday on the fifth and six p.m. the following day. Do you remember where you were?'

Relief washes over me. 'Yes,' I almost shout. 'We were in Cornwall. Wednesday the fifth was the day Jamie got sick and he was rushed to A&E. We were at Falmouth Hospital that day. You can check. We couldn't have murdered Sean. We didn't get back to Bath until the evening of the sixth.' My voice rises in excitement.

Melanie Finch smiles. 'I will check it out, of course, but that's encouraging news.'

The police want to question me again the next day and Melanie accompanies me to the station. She's advised me to admit everything.

DI Hartley and his colleague, DS Trott, sit in silence, the tape whirring while I explain all that's happened. 'Sean must have orchestrated the house swap in order to do something awful to me – thinking I was Beth. That's the only explanation I have as to why he'd do such a thing.'

'And he ended up dead. How convenient,' says DI Hartley with a sneer.

'Maybe he had enemies? But Jamie and I were in Cornwall that whole week. Staying in Sean's boss's house. And on the day Sean was killed, we were in hospital. Jamie had food poisoning, you see . . . from the food that Sean had provided . . .'

Melanie pushes a piece of paper across the desk. 'I have confirmation here from Falmouth Hospital,' she says, 'but feel free to check it for yourselves. The worst my client has done is commit identity theft.'

DI Hartley glances at me smugly, obviously relieved I'm not walking away from all this without some kind of punishment. And it's true: my career is ruined. The thought of no longer being able to teach breaks my heart. I'm back to square one. And then I think of Jamie, my husband, the love of my life, and how he's standing by me and I realise that, no, I'm not back to square one at all. It's just a different kind of future than the one I had envisaged, that's all.

Jamie is waiting for me outside the police station and I fall into his arms, feeling so much lighter.

'Does that mean I've got to call you Karen now?'

'I hope not. I like the name Libby Hall.'

'We're not legally married, you do realise that?' He stoops to kiss me. 'It means we're just going to have to do it again.'

'Just us this time. A quiet affair.' I throw my arms around his neck. 'Just you and me.'

A new beginning. A fresh start. We can finally put the past behind us.

34

The weather holds as April turns into May. It's not until I look at the calendar on my phone that I realise – I've not had a period for months. They were all up in the air after the miscarriage, but surely I should have had one by now? It could be the stress of the last few weeks, and I don't dare hope as I sneak out to Boots to buy a pregnancy test.

When I get back I call for Jamie and he follows me into the bathroom, his eyebrows raised questioningly, a hopeful expression on his face. And then we're hovering over the little white stick as the pale blue line becomes a cross. Positive. Jamie's eyes light up as he glances at me and with a cry of joy he picks me up and whirls me around and I laugh, catching my heel on the bathroom door.

Over the next few days I oscillate from being wildly, deliriously happy to anxious and sad. I've had no choice but to resign from my job. I write a letter to Felicity, explaining that my circumstances have changed and I feel I am no longer able to teach. I tell her I have a criminal record now and that I lied about my qualifications to get on the PGCE course. I can't bear to think about how it will look for the school when the news gets out – as it surely will when the case comes to court. I can imagine the newspapers will be all over it. I avoid calls from my teaching assistant, Cara, unable to face talking to her, preferring to hide away from it all. Knowing I can't run away. Not this time.

Hannah made reference to my deceit only once, the day Jamie and I found out about the baby. She studied me coldly as we were standing in the garden, near the coach house. Felix was rolling around in the grass, enjoying the sunshine, and I had my hands on my tummy, unable to stop the smile spreading across my face every time I thought about the baby. We call it Peanut as we are convinced that's how big it is, although we don't really have a clue. We've decided to keep the news to ourselves for now, until we are past the twelve-week mark. So Hannah knew nothing about it as she said, quietly but with a steeliness that I've never noticed before, 'You'd better never hurt him again.' It had shocked me.

I met her gaze; it was challenging, confrontational. Territorial. 'I won't,' I said firmly, before walking away from her.

I am now as restless as Katie, both of us wafting in and out of rooms without purpose. Sometimes Hannah and Felix join us, usually when Felix is home from school and she's finished for the day at the estate agent's where she works. Not that Hannah ever talks to me. I sense she only comes over because she wants a babysitter for her son. So I spend my time with Felix while Hannah seeks out Katie. The two of them are always together, heads bent next to each other, in the conservatory or walking around the garden, deep in discussion or heading towards the coach house, Felix usually forgotten. I'm sure they are talking about me.

On the odd occasion I've found her in the kitchen with Jamie, chatting over a cup of tea. Her face closes up when I come in, as though she's a robot who's run out of batteries. It seems that only Jamie and the Hall family can fire her up. When I see the two of them together I have to remind myself that it's me he loves, that we are having a baby together. But I can't shake the feeling that Hannah would have been a better wife to him than me. That she wouldn't have lied to him like I have.

We've been living with Sylvia for nearly a month when I receive a call from Melanie Finch. At first I think that she's ringing about a court date, but I'm ecstatic when she tells me, in her crisp, calm voice, that an arrest has been made.

'It seems that Sean Elliot had a lot of dodgy dealings and was wanted by some very shady characters. A man that Sean owed money to was seen in the area around the time Sean was killed. You and Jamie are free to go back to your flat.'

I put the phone down, feeling relieved. We can go home. I run to tell Jamie the good news. As much as I've enjoyed staying at Sylvia's – more than I thought I would – I'll be happy to escape Hannah's hostility and Katie's quiet disgust. She is still barely speaking to me.

I deserve her contempt, I know I do. But Jamie and the rest of his family have forgiven me, so why can't she?

That night as we're lying in bed, Jamie turns to me in the dark, raising himself up onto his elbow. His hand traces my stomach where it now gently bulges. 'You do realise we're going to have to sell the flat, don't you, Libs?'

I nod, although I'm not sure he can see me in the dark.

'We can't afford it now that you're no longer working. I'm not making as much as I'd like yet, but we have a bit of equity. We'll have to move further out. Maybe one of the villages on the Bristol side. We can get more for our money there.'

The prospect of a bigger place away from here fills me with excitement. Maybe somewhere with a garden for Ziggy and Peanut. 'I think that's a good idea. A fresh start.'

He props himself up further. 'What about the estate agent where Hannah works? They could give us a valuation.'

I don't want to involve Hannah, but I agree nonetheless. If Jamie had asked me to run around the garden naked, I'd do it to make him happy. To keep the equilibrium.

By the weekend we are back in our flat. It smells the same, a slight dog odour mixed with damp washing and something sweet, a sort of exotic incense. Ziggy is pleased to be back in the place where he can, once again, lounge all over the furniture, which he isn't allowed to do at Sylvia's.

'It feels weird being back,' I say as I slump next to Ziggy on the sofa. 'Everything has changed.' *We've changed*. We'd left in such a hurry that we'd not had time to clean up the dirty cups on the coffee table and now green spores of mould cling to the tea at the bottom. It's obvious by the mess that the police had a good rootle around. Jamie's work cabinet has been emptied, a pile of files left on the floor. The cupboards in our sideboard are yawning open. Melanie told us they had taken some items away for further tests and the flat now has the air of a burglary about it. Strangers have been rifling through our things. I'll be glad to sell it.

Jamie's standing at the window looking onto the street above, and I know he's probably worrying about who's out there; nameless, faceless men who might be staking us out, thanks to the porn site. The police have managed to deactivate the site but it hasn't allayed our fears; our address has been out there for too long. He sighs. 'So much has happened. I can't get my head around it.'

'I know I keep saying it, but I'm sorry, Jay. And it could all have been so much worse.'

'What do you mean?' I notice the doubt flickering in his eyes as though he's expecting me to reveal another secret, another lie, and it makes me feel sad. I've caused this. Will things ever go back to how they were?

'Sean. What he could have done to us. Whoever

killed him did us a favour.' I shudder at the thought. He'd been here, in our home. What had he planned for us? He'd stolen money from our account and he'd sent cards to the neighbours, pretending to be from Jamie. He had been a twisted individual. For the first time I realise how it must have been for Beth. No wonder she scarpered over five thousand miles to Thailand to escape him.

'I think he might have killed us,' Jamie says, his face troubled. 'That's why he was watching us at The Hideaway. The underwear was obviously some kind of threat.' He frowns and then answers his own question: 'I guess we'll never know.'

Something wakes me in the night, a sudden, heavy thud coming from the flat above. I sit bolt upright in bed, my heart pounding, my skin hot beneath my night clothes. Jamie continues to snore beside me. I listen carefully to the comforting sounds of our home: the buzzing of the fridge, the clanking of the pipes, the occasional whoosh of a car outside. Was I mistaken? I strain my ears. Nothing. I'm just about to settle back under the duvet when I hear it again, as though something has been dropped overhead. My first thought is that Evelyn's flat is being burgled. I nudge Jamie awake.

'Jamie,' I hiss. 'There's someone upstairs.'

He groans and reaches for his phone, the screen lighting up the room. He blinks furiously as his eyes adjust. 'Urgh, it's four a.m.'

311

'Did you hear it? That noise. Someone's in Evelyn's flat. Oh God, should we call the police?'

He's wide awake now. His hair looks comical, standing up on end. I'd laugh usually, but adrenaline is pumping around my body so fast I feel dizzy. He tilts his head to one side, just like Ziggy does, and listens. 'I can't hear anything.'

My heart is still thudding and I press my hand against my chest, willing myself to calm down. It can't be good for the baby. 'I heard a crash.'

He runs his hands through his mad hair. 'There's no one living in Evelyn's flat. Why would somebody be up there?'

'Burgling her?'

I peel the duvet back and get out of bed. I stand at the window, peering through the curtains. The street beyond is dark, the rose bush outside our window scratching the glass in the wind. I don't know what I expect to see but there is nothing except a black cat sauntering across the main road and a dustbin lid on the pavement. Is that what I'd heard? A dustbin lid clattering to the ground? But it had sounded like it had come from overhead. Maybe it was my imagination, a symptom of missing Evelyn, of knowing that the flat above is no longer filled with her presence, her little quirks, like the too-loud radio and the tunes from her favourite soap operas drifting through the ceiling. Sometimes I forget she's not up there, pottering around, making cups of tea or knitting.

'Come back to bed.' Jamie's voice is thick with sleep. 'It was probably an animal or something.'

I curl up beside him. His body feels warm and he's soon fast asleep again, while I lie in the dark, wide awake. Evelyn's flat is also on the market. Apparently there was a nephew somewhere who made that decision. But as far as I'm aware all her photos and furniture, her ornaments and clothes, are as they were when she died. I long to go up there, to be amongst her things, in her comfortable sitting room where I always felt safe. Was someone up there now? Or am I being paranoid again? After everything that has happened over the past few months, I assure myself, it really isn't surprising.

We spend all Sunday frantically cleaning the flat, trying unsuccessfully to rid the sofa and rugs of the smell of dog. I light candles, hoover, dust, tidy. It takes three hours. But when it's finished I feel a sense of achievement. It's finally ready. Tomorrow we can contact an estate agent and begin the process of moving.

Jamie takes Ziggy out for his walk while I finish wiping down the kitchen. I also have a doctor's appointment the following day. I've calculated I must be about six or seven weeks pregnant, which would explain the queasy feeling I've experienced since Cornwall that isn't just down to anxiety. I try not to think about what we will do for money now that I'm no longer able to work as a teacher and I push away thoughts of how much I miss my class and the school, determined to remain upbeat.

I'm lucky, I know I am. Things will work themselves out, I feel sure of it. I find that I'm humming to myself as I wipe down the worktops, and I switch the radio on, scanning the channels for something that I can dance to. Despite everything, I'm feeling positive. This is a good day. The sky is a hazy blue, it's warm but not as hot as it has been. I feel closer to Jamie than I ever have now that there are no lies between us. He still calls me Libby, which is the way I want it. Karen feels like another person now.

I'm jigging along to Justin Timberlake when I hear the front door slam. It must be Jamie, back early from his walk. I dart into the hallway, happy to see him and wanting to show him how pretty the flat looks now it has been decluttered and cleaned, but his face is pinched with worry.

'What is it?' And then I notice Ziggy. He's slumped on the floor, his eyes sad. I bend down to him. 'Ziggy, are you all right, boy?' I ruffle his head but he hardly moves. He lets out a sorrowful whine and my heart contracts.

Jamie unclips his lead, but he doesn't stand up again, instead he crouches so that he's at my level and says, 'I think we need to take him to the vet, Libs. There's something wrong with him.'

Ziggy suddenly makes a choking sound and my face grows hot with panic as he starts convulsing, his eyes rolling back in his head.

'What's happening?' I cry, standing up.

'It looks like he's having a fit. We need to get him in the car. Come on, the vets are open twenty-four hours.'

Ziggy is so heavy that it takes both of us to carry his shuddering body to the car. We lay him on the back seat and I run back into the flat to get a towel and blanket. When I return Ziggy is no longer convulsing but is still. Too still. I climb into the back seat with him and place my hand on his tummy, reassured when it rises and falls. 'He's unconscious. Quick, Jay. We need to get to the vets, right now!' I yell.

Jamie looks ashen. He pulls away from the kerb at speed, and as I glance up I'm certain I see a shadow at the window, as though someone is watching us from behind Evelyn's yellowing net curtains.

35

Beth

I've been watching and biding my time.

I've seen the police come and go, and Sean's body carried out in a bag. I've witnessed forensics comb the garden and the flat. And when I was satisfied the police wouldn't return, when the team dispersed, I moved into Evelyn's flat. I had no choice. I need to make my money last and the bed and breakfast I've been staying in for the past six weeks is too expensive. I must get around to visiting my dad's solicitor to find out if the bastard has left me any money. Seeing Karen's photo in the newspaper distracted me from all that.

And then, yesterday, there they were, tripping out of their car all smiles and laughter and cheesy banter as they led their big dopey dog into their flat. Slipping back into their lives as effortlessly as pulling on a pair of favourite jeans.

So they've allowed her to come home, which means they aren't treating her as a suspect. I know they won't be looking for me. I'm like a ghost, a spook, the way I come and go, leaving behind no trail. I've paid for everything in cash – *her* cash.

It's easy to do damage to someone who thinks I'm dead.

I haven't got many belongings. I left most of my things behind in Barcelona. I've just got a bag of clothes, my passport and my phone. And the photo. I look at it every night. It's my only reminder of her, my beautiful princess. I sleep upstairs in one of Evelyn's spare rooms, which she never used, by the look of them. There is a thick layer of dust everywhere, on the picture rails and coating the carpets. The air is stale and musty.

A 'For Sale' sign has been erected outside the window. It's a bit of a risk, staying here when prospective buyers could descend at any time, like magpies picking their way through that nice old lady's things and cawing over the period features. But it's a small price to pay to be near to Karen.

Because there is more damage to inflict, more pain to cause. She hasn't even begun to suffer enough.

On Sunday I hear a commotion. I rush to the window, pulling aside Evelyn's net curtains just in time to see Karen and Jamie heaving their dog into the back seat of their car. I'm not a fan of dogs – I prefer cats myself; dogs are too needy, too desperate to be loved for my liking. I want Karen to be tormented, believe me, but even I wouldn't wish suffering upon her dog. It's just a defenceless animal at the end of the day.

Karen turns towards the window, her eyes full of pain and unshed tears, and quickly I withdraw into the shadows. Out of sight. Just how I like it.

36

Libby

We are told Ziggy is in a critical condition. I can't stop tears rolling down my face as I kiss him goodbye on the velvety bit between his nose and mouth, where his whiskers grow. My favourite bit. 'I love you,' I whisper to him. 'We'll be back tomorrow.'

My heart feels like it's going to break seeing him lying there on the vet's cold, metal table, a tube in his paw, his eyes closed. 'I don't think I can bear it if he dies,' I sob, not caring that snot is running from my nose and merging with the tears dripping off my chin and onto my cotton blouse.

'He's not going to die,' Jamie insists. He grabs my hand; his feels hot and sticky in mine. 'He's going to be fine.' I can tell he doesn't really believe it by his tight smile and his fake joviality. His eyes are red and he's unable to tear them away from our beloved dog.

Our vet, Owen, comes in wearing green scrubs and holding a towel. He's quite young, although he has an air of calm and authority about him. He's been Ziggy's vet ever since we've had him. 'He'll be in good hands here overnight,' he says. 'Please try not to worry. We'll do all we can. This should flush the poisons out of his system. I'll ring you if there is any change.'

Poison?

I grip Jamie's arm tightly as we walk back to the car. 'He's been poisoned, Jay. Who would do such a thing?' I think of the shadowy figure I'm certain I saw in Evelyn's flat. Why can't I shake the feeling that someone is still watching us, despite Sean Elliot's death?

'He could've eaten something on our walk,' Jamie says. 'But I'm always so careful, and he seemed off before we left. Not like his usual self. Quieter, didn't you think?' We get into the car and sit for a bit outside the vet's, unable to drive away. It feels wrong leaving Ziggy behind. I touch my stomach. There is only a slight swelling, barely noticeable, but I already feel an overwhelming protectiveness towards this baby. The future stretches in front of me, my earlier hope diminishing, instead replaced by all the dangers that could threaten our precious baby and I'm seized with anxiety so strong I start to shake. Will I be able to do this? What if something happened again?

'I don't want to leave him, Libs,' says Jamie, his voice sounding pitiful in the silence of the car. He collapses into tears then, and I stare at him in shock as his shoulders heave. I don't think I've ever seen him properly cry before, not like this, not these giant sobs that seem to consume him, and it scares me. I reach out and touch his shoulder, murmuring words of comfort, for myself and him, then he turns and pulls me into his arms, fiercely, and we hug awkwardly over the gear stick. Despite how uncomfortable it is, we stay this way for ages.

The sun is going down by the time we get home, and our side of the street is in shadow. I'm conscious of how puffy my face looks, how red-rimmed my eyes are, and I'm grateful that the street is quiet in the way it often is on a Sunday evening. It's cold in the shade and I shiver in my short-sleeved blouse as Jamie retrieves the door key from his pocket.

The flat seems so empty without Ziggy rushing to greet us. I feel a fresh wave of grief when I notice his lead on the floor where we'd left it in our rush earlier and I pick it up and hug it against me, inhaling his scent.

Jamie is bending down to untie his laces when I see an envelope, half-wedged through the letterbox. It definitely hadn't been there earlier. Had it? Even if it had, we wouldn't have noticed, we had been so focussed on Ziggy. I pull it out and open it, and straight away I wish I hadn't. The words blur in front of me. Those awful, awful words.

'What is it?' asks Jamie, peering over my shoulder. 'Why have you been sent your medical records? Did you request them?'

'It's . . . it's nothing.' I try to shove the sheets of paper back into the envelope but they refuse to go, bending in the wrong direction.

'Libby? What's going on?'

'Nothing . . . it's nothing . . . I'll put the kettle on . . .' I slip them under my arm and hurry to the kitchen but he's close behind me.

'Why are you being so secretive? Why did you request your medical records?'

How can I tell him that I didn't. I place them face down on the worktop and put the kettle on. When I look around he's holding them in his hands.

I snatch them from him, furious. 'That's private!' I snap. 'What the fuck do you think you're doing?'

He stares at me, his face full of hurt. 'Private? You're having our baby. Why can't I see your medical files? You're welcome to see mine – I've got nothing to hide.' His eyes are hard as he assesses me. 'Have you?'

No more lies. That's what I promised him.

'I'm sorry . . .' I say, swallowing down tears. I silently hand him the three sheets of A4, can only watch as his eyes scan down the first page, his expression growing darker.

When he's finished reading he looks up at me. 'You had an abortion?' I consider lying, telling him these are the real Elizabeth Elliot's medical records, not mine. But there is no point. The dates won't add up. He knows when I stopped being Karen Fisher. I nod and look down at my stomach, as though I've betrayed the baby growing inside me.

'Why?'

I sigh. 'I wasn't with the father. I met him in

Thailand. Thought I was in love. I didn't know I was pregnant. And then I came back here with a new identity, a new start. I'd only been at college a month when I realised I was pregnant. I couldn't . . . I couldn't keep it. It would have meant giving up everything.'

'Why didn't you tell me?'

I meet his eyes. They are dark with disappointment.

'Because . . .' Katie's voice comes back to me as clearly as though she's standing in the kitchen with us. *It doesn't mean you're weak to show that you're not perfect, you know.* 'Because I didn't want you to think less of me. I didn't want it to tarnish the version of me that you have in your mind,' I say, truthfully. 'I'm the person that loves kids. A teacher. And I aborted my baby.'

'And you really think that's how I would have felt? That I wouldn't have understood. I'm not anti-abortion. I wouldn't have thought less of you. It's the lies. I *asked* you. I asked you if there was anything else you weren't telling me. You could have told me then. But you didn't. I don't think you're perfect, Libby. I don't expect you to be.' He shakes his head, his expression perplexed. 'What the fuck is going on in your head, Libby? Karen? Whatever your real name is. Who the fuck *are* you?'

'I'm Libby,' I cry. 'I'm your Libby.'

His jaw is set hard as he says slowly, deliberately, 'No. No you're not.' He thrusts the papers back at me and I grip them to my chest. I screw them up, the paper rustling under my fingers. He storms out of the room and I follow, watching silently as he pushes his feet back into the trainers he's just taken off. And then he grabs his jacket from the peg by the door and wordlessly leaves the flat.

I cry myself to sleep that night, scrunched up in a ball, the duvet pulled tightly over my head. Jamie comes home late. I hear him crashing into things and wonder if he's drunk. Who's he been with? His mum? Hannah? When he doesn't come to bed I gather my dressing gown around me and pad into the living room to see him passed out on the sofa, snoring, still fully clothed.

I'm woken the next morning by the sound of the phone. I know instinctively that it's the vet. I listen as Owen gently breaks it to me that Ziggy didn't make it despite all his best efforts, that his heart gave out, and my mobile drops to the floor so that the screen cracks across the photograph I have as my wallpaper: of me, Jamie and Ziggy, together. One happy family.

37

I run to the bathroom and retch into the toilet, resting my head against the rim, the smell of toilet cleaner making me retch again.

Ziggy is gone. The enormity of it hits me afresh and tears career down my already puffy face. Then I wake Jamie, my heart heavy that I have to give him such awful news. He turns over onto his back. He smells of stale sweat and last night's alcohol. 'I don't want to talk to you,' he says, closing his eyes.

'Jay. It's Ziggy.'

His eyes snap open. They are bloodshot, sticky in the corners. 'What?' He sits up. 'What is it?'

'He . . .' I can feel the tears running down my face. 'He didn't make it.'

'No.' His voice breaks, and despite our differences I put my arms around him as he cries into my shoulder.

Later, after Jamie has showered and shaved, he sits on the sofa, as far away as he can get from me. The distance hurts. We always sat touching one another with some part of our bodies; our toes, our fingers, our thighs.

He clears his throat. 'Listen. While you were getting dressed I called Owen. We know Ziggy was poisoned.

But we don't know with what. It was obviously heavy-duty though. To kill him.' He winces as he says that last bit. 'I can't help but think someone did this on purpose.'

My scalp prickles. 'What?'

'It's more than him eating some berries or a foxglove, Libs. He had a large amount in his blood. Enough to cause a cardiac arrest. I told Owen about Sean. About everything. I'm worried that Sean wasn't acting alone.'

I can't take this in. 'But who?'

'Did Beth have any other enemies? Did you? Who else were you travelling with?'

I shrug. 'I hardly knew the others really.' Apart from Harry. Although after what he did with Beth maybe I didn't know him either. He wasn't the person I thought he was. 'We travelled together for a few months but why would they do something like this?'

He frowns. 'Are you sure? What about the guy who got you pregnant?'

His words are sharp, piercing my heart, and I wince. 'Harry wouldn't do something like this. Why would he?'

'You were pregnant with his child. You left him and had an abortion.'

I cast my eyes downwards, fiddling with my wedding band. 'He never knew. He probably doesn't even remember my surname. I was probably just one of many.'

He clears his throat and shuffles, avoiding eye contact. 'There's something else. Something I haven't told you yet. I only found out myself on Friday. I was waiting for the right time but then, with Ziggy . . .' He pauses, his voice cracking.

'What? What do you want to tell me?'

'I don't want to scare you. But I checked the bank. That money. It was taken *after* we got back from Cornwall. Sean was already dead then.'

'What?' I can't believe I'm hearing this. 'Sean didn't take the money?'

'He couldn't have. And the stuff from the catalogue. These things were done afterwards. The website, though, that was done before. That must have been Sean. Plus the website would have taken a while to set up.'

I clutch my head. It feels like it's spinning. This is supposed to be a happy time; our first year of marriage, expecting a baby. How can it have all gone so wrong?

Jamie fidgets, the way he does when he's worried about asking me something.

'What is it?'

'Is there any way . . .' He hesitates and runs a hand over his stubble. 'Do you think there's any way Beth *didn't* die in that hostel fire?'

I shake my head. 'Absolutely not.' I can't admit to him why I'm so sure. 'There is no way she could have survived it. I've told you before. She was in the room, fast asleep. I only survived because I was already outside.'

'But you said there were other survivors.'

'I rang around all the hospitals. I went back to the hostel the next morning. Nothing.' I wrap my cardigan further around my body, suddenly feeling cold. 'Look, Jay. I know you're feeling dreadful about Ziggy. I am too. But we can't assume Ziggy was poisoned on purpose, that somebody set out to kill him.' Maybe I don't want to believe it. I can't have Ziggy's death on my conscience too. 'The other stuff was more opportunistic. Maybe whoever killed Sean had a snoop about our flat and took some bank statements in order to rip us off?' I reach over and place my hand on his. 'I just want to put it all behind us, Jay. This has all been so awful; losing Ziggy, my job . . . but we're going to have a baby . . .'

He shakes my hand off and stands up. 'I can't. I'm sorry. I need time.' I'm seized by fear. He seems so angry, so unreachable. I'm losing him.

'OK,' I mumble. 'But I'm sorry. For the lies. I love you. I want to earn your trust back.'

He picks at something on his neck and doesn't look at me. Instead his eyes are trained on the beige carpet that could do with a clean, his shoulders slumped. He looks broken. I long to put him back together but he won't let me. 'I . . . I don't want to leave you on your own in the flat. But I need some time by myself. I'm going to work from Mum's during the day. I'll come back at night so you're not alone.' He folds his hands into his lap. He doesn't look at me as he says, quietly,

'But, Libs, I'm not sure I can forgive you for lying to me again.'

Low-level anxiety flutters in my stomach. It feels like grief, at losing Ziggy and Jamie, at losing my life; my lovely, happy life. And OK, it hadn't been perfect; we'd worried about money, I'd had to contend with his mother, Hannah, Katie. But they seem like such trivial things now. If he tells me our relationship has ended, there is no meaning to anything.

I try to keep busy during the day, but it's hard without the routine of a job to go to. I make an appointment with the GP, find out I'm about nine weeks pregnant. Still so early, she says, the risk of miscarriage raised until after twelve weeks. I try not to think about that as I walk home. It's a blustery, showery day, which matches my mood, and in the dull light the buildings look dingy, washed with grey. I keep bursting into tears, suddenly overcome with emotion about Ziggy and Jamie. I feel like I'm losing my grip on reality, find I'm unable to stop myself wandering past the school where I used to work. I watch the children in the playground from across the road, an umbrella covering my head and face so that they won't notice me. I want to run over and comfort little Zac McMurray when he falls over and grazes his knee, or when I see Katrina Simmons standing alone at the friendship stop, bravely trying not to cry, her little face pinched with worry. I miss them all so much that the feeling of hardness in my chest expands like a tumour, so that I have to gasp for air. I remember the panic attack I had in Sylvia's conservatory and I breathe deeply like she instructed. In through nose. Out through mouth. In. Out.

The flat feels so big and empty and unwelcoming. Every now and again I'll hear a crash, or a creak of floorboards from the flat above or the echo of voices, and wonder if there are viewings. We had plans to put this flat on the market, but who knows if that will happen now? If Jamie wants us to separate I'll have to find a flat on my own and when I think of this I have to forcibly push down my panic at the idea of being a single mother, with no money, living on benefits – if I'm able to claim them, that is. Where would I live? The future feels so uncertain.

Days pass, sliding into one another. I only see Jamie in the evenings. We eat dinner together, barely talking, and lie side by side at night, but it feels as though there is an invisible wall between us. He says he needs time and I try to be patient, to not push him. Some days I end up wandering the streets aimlessly, imagining that Ziggy is by my side, his tongue hanging out eagerly as he strains against the lead. I'm tempted to ring Cara but I'm too ashamed to speak to her, to anyone.

One day Florrie pops over with a home-made cottage pie. She sits with me and holds my hand while Jacob is engrossed in CBeebies, and tells me she'll always be my friend, whatever happens with her brother. Her visit raises my spirits, and for a few days afterwards I don't feel quite so alone.

I force myself to go out for a walk every day. Sometimes I'm sure that I hear the heavy tread of footsteps behind me, the hairs on the back of my neck instantly springing up, but when I look around the narrow streets are empty, except for a solitary person or an inquisitive tourist glancing up at a historic building, or peering into a shop window.

Jamie asks about the baby every evening. He wants to know if I feel nauseous, if I have any twinges, if I'm eating OK during the day. But when I try and probe him on the state of our relationship the barriers come up and his face goes blank so I give up.

On a Wednesday about ten days into my new routine, the sun is shining, the sky a clear, hazy blue. I can hear the sounds of a drill or a lawnmower as I leave the flat for my regular walk via the school. As I climb the steps I notice Hannah standing on the pavement, staring up at Evelyn's flat. It always takes me aback, how tall she is, almost as tall as Jamie. She's wearing a dove-grey jacket and a matching pencil skirt. She looks smart and attractive, her blonde hair falling in soft waves over her shoulders.

'Hannah,' I say as I reach the top so that we are level. 'What are you doing here?'

She looks startled to see me, as though she's forgotten that I live in the dark depths of the basement flat, my own personal dungeon. She stutters a bit. I notice she has a smudge of lipstick on her teeth and debate whether to tell her, oscillating between wanting to spare her pride but not wanting to embarrass her.

'Oh . . . yes, hi, Libby. Are you still calling yourself Libby?' she asks, a touch of smugness to her voice.

I nod, not trusting myself to speak.

She shifts her heavy-looking tote bag further up her shoulder and points to Evelyn's flat. 'I'm waiting to show somebody around. But they're late.' She looks cross, and I imagine she'd rather be anywhere else than here talking to me. Maybe she feels like a traitor, standing here making small talk with Jamie's estranged wife. She avoids eye contact; instead she stares straight ahead at Evelyn's flat. We've never had much to say to each other in the past but now the awkwardness sizzles between us as we stand on the uneven pavement. I notice a weed growing in the cracks in the slabs.

I hate myself for asking but I can't help myself. 'Have you . . . have you spoken to Jamie?'

She turns to me then, and looks at me levelly with her cool gaze. 'He's told me about the baby. Congratulations.' She says it through a clenched jaw, like it's taking all her effort to speak the words.

I fumble with the button on my jacket. 'Thank you . . . it's . . . well, it's difficult. You know, the worry after the first miscarriage. We promised we wouldn't tell anyone until the twelve weeks have passed. Things with me and Jamie aren't great . . .'

She purses her lips together. 'Yes, he's told me

everything. We have lunch together when he's working from his mum's house. I'm just happy that I can be there for him. With Ziggy and everything.'

It niggles me that he's told her. I can imagine the cosy lunches in her coach house, Hannah fluttering her eyelashes as he tells her how unhappily married he is.

'I suppose if you do decide to separate, then you won't need to divorce. He says he doesn't think you're even legally married, considering you were using a fake name.'

It's like I've been kicked hard in the stomach. Divorce? Are things really that bad? I'm hoping that Jamie will forgive me eventually. She continues relentlessly, 'And I can't deny, it's hard being a single mother. Felix is very full on, you know. But his father doesn't want anything to do with him.' I've never heard her talk so much.

My face grows hot. 'Yes, well, Jamie won't be like that. Even if we do split up,' I say.

'Oh, I know. Jamie will be an excellent father. I've always thought so. Devoted.' She smiles to herself as if reliving a private memory. 'Anyway, where are you off to?' She appraises me and I'm sure she's finding me lacking, in my denim jacket that I've had for at least seven years, my cotton trousers with the zebra print, my battered Birkenstocks and my chipped pink nail varnish.

'Just for a walk.'

'Yes, it's sad, what happened about your job. Suspended because those parents complained. Awful,' she says. I wonder how she knows. I've never told anyone apart from Jamie that some parents complained about me. Unless Jamie's told Hannah, of course. It wasn't a secret, after all, and it's beginning to sound like he confides in her a lot. 'Have you told them yet that you're not really Elizabeth Elliot?'

'Yes. I resigned.'

'They must have been disappointed. But they would have had to sack you otherwise, wouldn't they? And you, head of English or something, weren't you?' She's enjoying this too much and I have to bite the inside of my cheek to stop myself retaliating.

I nod. 'I've made some stupid mistakes. Haven't we all?' I say and then, to change the subject, I ask how the viewings are going.

She frowns and brushes a wayward curl out of her face. 'Not great. We've only had one or two. The place needs a lot of work. Rewiring and so forth. Now that the summer's coming though we hope to get a few more.'

'Shame, the place standing empty like that.'

She narrows her eyes at me. 'Oh no, it's not empty. Mrs Goodwin's niece is staying there. Just until it sells.'

'Oh . . . right . . .' Niece? I don't remember Evelyn mentioning a niece.

She glances at a chunky gold watch on her wrist. 'Anyway, must get on. I think my potential clients have arrived.' She shields her eyes from the sun as she squints down the street. A young couple are strolling arm in arm towards us.

I'm just about to turn and walk off in the opposite direction when I remember. 'Oh, Hannah,' I say in a loud whisper. 'You have lipstick on your teeth.' She looks rattled, reaching into her cavernous handbag to retrieve a mirror, and then she's all fake smiles, talking in exclamation marks as she's joined by the young couple, and I slink away, more determined than ever to win Jamie back.

38

I call Jamie's mobile while I'm walking. He answers on the second ring. 'Is everything OK with the baby?'

'Everything's fine. I just bumped into Hannah. She's showing people around Evelyn's flat. Apparently a niece is staying there. Evelyn never said she had a niece. A nephew, yes, but not a niece.' Talking while thundering along makes me pant and I slow down.

'So that's the noises you've been hearing?' he asks, but he sounds distracted, and I know I've probably interrupted his work flow.

I take a deep breath of fresh air. I can smell cut grass and petrol, the newly laid tarmac from a driveway that I pass. An old lady is weeding in her garden. The curve of her back and her silver hair reminds me of Evelyn and I feel a fresh pang of grief. 'Hannah said you've told her everything. About us. Our problems.'

There is a stunned silence and then, 'Have you only called for a row? Because we can do that tonight.'

'No, of course not. It's private though, Jay, what's happening with us.'

His tone softens. 'I know that, Libs. I've not said anything to Hannah. I wouldn't. It's no one else's business.'

He sounds sincere. But then how does she know about the baby?

'I miss you. What we had.' My eyes pool with tears, blinding me for an instant so that I have to stop and lean against the wall.

A pause. 'I just wish I could . . .'

'Forgive me?'

He doesn't answer, he doesn't need to. His silence says everything.

The flat feels different when I get back, as though somebody has been here. A chair has been pulled out from under the kitchen table, there is a glass on the side that wasn't there when I left. Has Jamie been here while I was out? I call his name while wandering in and out of the rooms, but the flat is empty. And he would have said when we spoke. There is a strange smell in the air. The same scent I recognised after getting back from Cornwall. Spicy, like someone recently lit a scented candle, although I have no candles with this specific smell.

Puzzled, I go into the bedroom and stare out onto Evelyn's overgrown garden. It's even worse now than it was the day we found Sean. The leaves of the neighbouring trees poke through the broken fence, ivy has wound itself around some of the plants, strangling them, clusters of weeds sprout from the ground and the lawn looks muddy and churned up thanks to the feet of all those policemen. And then I notice it: a dirty footprint on one of the cream patio slabs right outside my bedroom window. I feel a flutter of panic. It looks fresh, as though it has only been there a matter of hours. It rained last night, a sudden, violent downpour that had woken me about midnight. The print would have been washed away if it had been made yesterday.

Maybe it was the couple looking around Evelyn's flat earlier. Or Hannah? Perhaps she'd nosed through the window, to see the room where Jamie and I slept. Or maybe it was this mysterious niece who's living in Evelyn's flat.

I don't know what makes me do it. Maybe it's the absence of any mention of a niece, or the way Hannah behaved earlier, but I suddenly find myself rooting around in the kitchen drawer for the spare key to Evelyn's place.

Before I can change my mind I'm running upstairs to Evelyn's flat with the excuse of hearing a noise at the ready, just in case the niece is there. She doesn't need to know that I saw Hannah this morning. Feeling reassured, I turn the key in the lock and the door swings open. My heart is heavy as I walk into Evelyn's hallway, remembering the last time I was here, half expecting to see Evelyn in her chair by the window, knitting. Always knitting.

It's not until I reach the living room that I'm hit by the same smell that was in my flat earlier. A scented candle? Incense? Where have I smelt that before?

I scan the room. It's just as Evelyn left it, although there is now a layer of dust covering her ornaments, her mahogany coffee table and the picture rail. I wander into the kitchen. It's not like ours, which is open plan and encompasses our dining room; it's long and narrow, with units down either side and a single back door in the middle. I open the cupboards. Nothing looks out of place; a few tins of tomatoes and a can of tuna in one, a row of cups and glasses in another. I go back into the living room. It's all too tidy, too unlived in. Surely nobody is staying here?

With trepidation I make my way up the stairs and check the rooms that Evelyn hardly ever used. I pause on the landing. It's creepy up here and old-fashioned, with dark painted walls and wood panelling. The incense hasn't reached this level; instead the rooms smell of mould and damp. I check each bedroom. Where is this 'niece' staying? When I get to the box room I realise this is where she must be sleeping. The duvet is wrinkled and there is a book on the bedside table. I pick it up – it's a novel with a strapline promising a dark and twisted thriller – and a crumpled and well-thumbed photo falls out onto the brown patterned carpet. I pick it up and study it. It's a picture of a man with kind, dark eyes, but what strikes me most about him is the sorrow etched on his face. It's emanating from the photograph in such a way that it's almost tangible. He's holding a baby with a crop of dark hair in his arms, wrapped in a yellow blanket. The baby's eyes are tightly closed and by the waxy texture of the skin and the unnaturally pale colour I realise, with a sickening thud, that the baby is dead. I slip the photograph back inside the book, my heart heavy, and hurry back downstairs.

Who is this person staying in Evelyn's flat?

I feel uneasy being here. I'm just about to leave when I see a plastic folder on the mahogany sideboard. Intrigued, I pick it up, turning it over in my hands. It's A4-sized and transparent so that I can see the papers inside. I open it, disappointed that it's nothing more exciting than house brochures. It must belong to Hannah. I rifle through them anyway. And that's when I see the card. Frowning, I slide it out of the folder. 'To the One I Love' is emblazoned on the front, above the backs of two cartoon penguins, their arms wrapped around each other. Who would Hannah be sending cards to? I know I shouldn't, but I open it up anyway, and everything seems to stop. All I can hear is my heart pounding in my ears.

I think about you all the time.
Jamie xxx

I stare down at it, my hands trembling. Did Jamie send this to Hannah? Is he in love with her? Surely not! He seemed so sincere, so genuine when I asked him about it. But maybe I've pushed him to it, with my lies. The writing isn't in his usual scrawling hand, but block capitals, small and square and neat. I shove it in the inside pocket of my jacket. Maybe he'd given it to her years ago, when they were together, and she'd held on to it.

Although it doesn't look a decade old. But she could have kept it in a safe place where it didn't tarnish and yellow with age . . .

I'm just about to leave the living room when I hear the key in the front door. I freeze, unsure of what to do. I contemplate hiding but know it's ridiculous. I just have to stand and brazen it out, tell whoever is staying here that I'm a neighbour just checking on the place because I heard a noise. I replace the folder and walk into the hallway.

It's Hannah. She has her back to me as she closes the front door. When she turns around she starts when she notices me. 'Libby, what are you doing here?' She looks harassed but her eyes are cold as she assesses me.

'I should be asking you the same,' I say to win time.

She walks towards me, the square heels on her sensible shoes clipping the tiled flooring. 'I left my folder behind. How did you get in?'

'I have a spare key.'

'You can't just let yourself in here, you know.'

'I . . . I heard a noise.' I wonder whether I should confront her now. But I want to wait until I've spoken to Jamie first, given him a chance to explain.

She narrows her eyes at me in disbelief. 'I told you that Mrs Goodwin's niece is staying here. The family still own it. You're trespassing.' She seems distracted as she hurries into the living room and gathers up her folder. Clutching it close to her chest she retreats back down the hallway. 'Can you close the door after you?'

she says. 'I'm late to pick up Felix.' And then she's gone, slamming the front door behind her.

I breathe out in relief.

Tapping my denim jacket to make sure I've still got the card to show Jamie, I head towards the front door. I'm about to turn the handle when I hear a creak on the stairs.

I freeze. I know somebody is behind me, I sense eyes probing my back, boring into me. I turn slowly and there she is, standing on Evelyn's staircase. After all these years. She's changed considerably. Her hair is long and knotty, hanging almost to her waist. She has bags under her eyes and her face is pinched and hard. There is a faded bruise on her cheekbone, near her right eye. For a few seconds everything is quiet. I can hear a neighbour putting the bins out, birds singing and a cat yowls, but it all sounds far away, as though the world is only made up of the two of us.

'Well, well, well, if it isn't little Karen Fisher,' she says.

39

Beth

Her mouth is gaping open, her face ashen. She looks like she's seeing a ghost – a cliché, I know, but in this case it's true. So she really did think I was dead.

What had made her so sure?

'B . . . Beth,' she stutters. She's holding on to the radiator for support and there is a sheen of sweat on her top lip. She always was prone to sweating when nervous. I remember the fuss she made over getting that tattoo.

'Haven't we got a lot of catching up to do?' I say, walking down the stairs. She twists around to look frantically behind her, as though calculating her escape. Before she has a chance to move I reach out and grab her upper arm and squeeze it hard enough to leave bruises. 'I hope you're not thinking of going anywhere?'

'I'm . . . no . . .' She is staring at me as though unable to believe that I'm actually here. There is fear in her eyes too. It gives me a surge of energy, of purpose, like an electric charge. I've been waiting for this day ever since I saw her photo in the newspaper six weeks ago.

'Like seeing a ghost, huh?' I grin, enjoying myself. I

steer her into the living room. 'I think we need to talk, don't you?'

She opens and closes her mouth like a ventriloquist's dummy but no sound comes out. It actually makes me want to laugh. As always in our relationship, I hold all the power. I'm glad that nothing has changed there.

'Beth,' she begins but I shove her hard in the chest so that she falls back onto the sofa. 'I can explain.'

I sit opposite her, in the chair by the fireplace, underneath Evelyn's photographs. 'Good, because I'm listening.' I cross my legs, the chains on my biker boots chinking. She shoots a glance at them, her face puzzled.

'Have you . . . have you been following me?' she asks.

'For weeks.' I sit back, grinning. 'And yes, it was me that sent you the packages. And I cleared your bank account. It was easy considering we have the same National Insurance number. The same everything really . . .'

'Were you in my flat earlier?'

I shrug and pick at a rip in the knee of my jeans. 'I could have been.'

'H . . . how?' She looks appalled.

'I have my ways. Some advantages of being with Sean.'

She hesitates, her eyes sweeping over me as though still unable to believe I'm actually sitting in front of her. 'How did you know where to find me?'

'I saw your photograph in the newspaper. Right little hero, aren't you? Leading all those kids to safety. A shame that you couldn't do that for me and the other people who died in the hostel.'

She juts out her chin stubbornly. 'I thought you were dead . . .'

I lean forward, resting my elbows on my knees. 'What I want to know is, how did you escape?'

She doesn't look at me; instead she studies the pattern on Evelyn's rug. 'I . . . I was already out of the hostel.'

'I knew it,' I say triumphantly. 'I knew there was manipulation behind it. Oh I've underestimated you, haven't I? What did you do, Karen?'

She lifts her head. Her eyes are wary. She looks exactly like a trapped animal. Then something changes in her face, her expression hardens and she glowers, baring her teeth. 'I hated you after what you did with Harry. Did you know that I was pregnant?'

I didn't, although I suspected, later. She was so pale, so listless in Bangkok. I thought it was because she was lovesick for Harry. 'I found out from looking at your – or should I say my – medical records.'

'I didn't mean for things to end up like they did. I saw an opportunity and I took it.'

I glare at her. She hasn't changed. Still won't take responsibility for anything. 'So that makes everything all right, then? Because you didn't mean to do it. So tell me, Karen. How did you escape?'

She looks at her hands and I can see she's suddenly afraid again. 'I . . . I put drugs in the Coke you drank.

Who knows what they were. I found them in your bag. And then I left you there, knowing you'd be too out of it to follow me.'

'Drugged me?' I remember the feelings of wooziness when I woke in the bunk bed to the room filling with smoke. I stand up, my heart banging. 'So that's why you were so sure I was dead. Because you thought I was too drugged-up to escape. Well, you obviously didn't use enough, did you, because I did wake up. And I was rescued.'

She stands up to face me, her hands clenched by her sides, her face red. 'I don't know why you're acting like the fucking victim in all this,' she spits. 'They were your drugs. When I found them I realised what you'd done. To me. To Harry back at the party that night. You're evil, Beth. You ruined everything. I loved him. I loved Harry and you ruined it all. So when you went to the loo I drugged my can of Coke then pretended to fall asleep so you would drink it. And you did. You always were a skank.'

I feel a rush of anger and slap her hard around the face. She gasps and shrinks away from me, clutching her cheek.

'I loved him too,' I cry. 'I loved him too but you took him for yourself. You didn't give a shit about my feelings. You didn't even tell me you were seeing him. We were supposed to be friends, Karen. You knew I was running away from an abusive relationship. That I had been through hell. Harry would have been good for me. But you didn't care about that, did you? You're a selfish bitch. You pissed off the wrong person, when you fucked off with my passport, my identity and took on my life.'

She splutters, her eyes burning with fury. 'But I didn't take your life. You *had* no life! You were going to give up the opportunity to do your PGCE and I was desperate. What harm would it do? That's what I thought. You were dead and there was a place on a respected course going to waste.'

'That's nice. You thought I was dead and yet you couldn't wait to fill my shoes. If I had died it would have been your fault, Karen. Your fault!'

She collapses onto the sofa, tears on her cheeks. She looks crumpled and small and I realise with a sudden clarity that I no longer really care about Harry. Or about her. All of this was a distraction, to stop me thinking about Lilianna. What I really should be doing is going home to Spain. To Matteo. To try and sort things out. He phones me every day. I never answer but he leaves pleading messages, asking me to come home to him, to let him know that I'm safe, telling me that he still loves me, that we should be supporting each other through our grief. That we can try again for another baby. That it won't replace Lilianna, nothing will, but that we can be happy.

But do I deserve to be happy?

I sink onto the chair and light a cigarette. I inhale deeply, my hands shaking. What am I doing? I'm no better than Karen. I've done some bloody stupid things, some nasty things. Because I was bitter, jealous, unhappy. I'd spent my life being controlled, by my father, by Sean. And when a lovely man like Matteo comes along I think I don't deserve him. I've been so desperate to hurt her, to punish her, but now that I'm here, now that I've ruined her relationship and her career it all feels so . . . so *anti-climactic*.

Because it doesn't stop the pain.

It doesn't bring my baby back.

'I'm sorry. For what I did with Harry,' I say eventually.

Her head shoots up. 'You are?' Her mascara has run and her eyes are smudged with black. It looks like she's been punched in the face.

'I wasn't,' I admit. 'Not at the time. But afterwards. Yeah, I felt bad about it. I thought you were dead too, you know. I thought you were still in that room. I didn't realise you'd already done a runner before the fire had even started.'

'So the house swap? Did you set that up as revenge?'

I take another drag on my cigarette and exhale while shaking my head. 'No. That was Sean. We were still married, you know. He was a sick bastard . . .'

She laughs bitterly. 'Yes, I'm beginning to realise that.'

'He thought it was me in the paper. He wanted revenge. For leaving him. For running off with his money. So he set the whole thing up and then tried to frighten you and your husband – thinking it was me.'

'The taxidermy . . . the bloodied underwear. It was all him?'

347

'Taxidermy?'

She nods. 'Stuffed animals. Dead animals. In the freezer . . .'

I shudder. 'They're my fears. I have a phobia of stuffed animals. I know, it's weird, but I'm petrified of them. He knew that if it had been me staying at that house, I would have seriously freaked out at seeing them . . . and I suppose the underwear was a threat. If I'd seen all that I would have realised it was him. That he had found me.'

She brushes her fringe from her eyes. It suits her, that hairstyle. More than it ever suited me. Her cheek is still pink where I've slapped her and I feel bad for losing my temper.

'I can't believe he went to all that trouble,' she says. 'The house had been empty for months. He had a lot of time to work out his plan.'

I put the cigarette out on one of Evelyn's saucers. 'You'd be surprised what he was capable of. The things he did when we were together. He was going to kill me, you know. I turned up at your flat, expecting to find you. And he answered the door.'

'Oh, Beth . . .'

'I'm just so tired,' I say, realising that it's true. 'When I saw your photo in the paper I hated you. You had everything that could have been mine. A happy family,' my eyes go to her stomach, 'and a baby on the way.'

'How did you know . . .?'

'Evelyn told me.'

348

Her face pales. 'You met her?'

'She was nice to me. She'd seen me hanging around . . .'

'Ah.'

I frown. 'What do you mean?'

She chuckles. 'I think she thought Jamie had some fancy woman. She must have seen you hanging about and thought he was having an affair. She tried to warn me.'

I swallow. 'I was with her. When she died.'

'You were *here*?'

I nod, blinking back tears at the thought of it. 'I was just leaving and she had a heart attack. It was so sudden. So quick.'

'And Sean? Was it you that killed him?'

There is no point in denying it. 'It was self-defence. I was running from him. He would have killed me. It was me or him.'

'Oh my God,' she mutters, her eyes darting around the room. 'Oh God, Beth. What are you going to do now? Will you go to the police? Will you tell them about Sean?'

I suddenly have no idea.

40

Libby

I should have guessed she was back as soon as I entered Evelyn's flat. The smell – it's everywhere. In the air, on her clothes, in her hair, and I suddenly remember where I've smelled it before: that room in Koh Lanta. The heat, the sickly smell of incense, the undercurrent of sickness. Beth was always wafting joss sticks around as though she was about to perform a church service.

She sits in the armchair by the fireplace. She looks so vulnerable, even with her tough-looking leather jacket and biker boots. I wonder if she's suffering from some kind of breakdown. I realise that I don't actually know much about her, not really. I know her parents died when she was young but that's all. I remember the photograph that I found upstairs. She lost a baby.

My cheek stings. But I deserve that slap. I deserve everything that she's done to me.

'Beth,' I say gently, 'I saw the photo. Upstairs. Your baby?'

She turns to me, her eyes sad as she searches my face. 'I had to hide under the bed when you came into the room.' She looks exhausted suddenly, as though all the fight has gone out of her. 'But yes, that's my baby. Lil-ianna. There were complications. She died . . . she was already dead when I gave birth . . .' Her voice catches.

'Oh Beth.' My hands cradle my stomach. 'I'm so sorry.'

Tears pour down her cheeks. I've never seen her cry. It's so shocking, so unexpected, that I can only stare at her. She wipes them away as though embarrassed. 'It's been hard,' she manages.

'I can imagine. I had a miscarriage. I know it's not the same . . . but . . .'

She holds up a hand as she collects herself. 'Let's not talk about this. We're not friends, Karen. Not any more.'

'I know. I know that.'

She studies the rips in the knees of her jeans, picking at the frayed denim. 'So how has it been, living as me?'

I laugh, despite myself. 'Not as easy as you'd think. College was hard. Without a degree I really struggled to pass my PGCE. I had to work bloody hard. I couldn't learn to drive . . .'

She looks confused. 'Why?'

'Because you already had a licence. How could I go on a driving course when I was already supposed to have passed my test?'

'Couldn't you have just done a refresher course or something?'

I laugh. 'I never thought of that. I got behind the wheel once, but obviously I had no clue how to drive and nearly killed Jamie and me. I haven't tried since.'

She smiles but it doesn't reach her eyes, like she's not really listening to what I'm saying. 'What do we do now?' she asks. 'Where do we go from here?'

I suddenly have a dreadful thought. 'Did you poison Ziggy?'

She frowns. 'Ziggy?'

'My dog? He died. The vet said he'd been poisoned.'

She looks furious. 'Of course I didn't. Yes, I wanted to hurt you, to split you and Jamie up. To make you suffer like I've suffered, but I would never hurt an animal.'

I can see by her indignation that she's telling the truth. My stomach falls. So if she didn't kill Ziggy, who did? Or was it just a terrible accident?

She stands up and I follow suit, wondering what's going to happen next. She killed Sean. She's a killer. Will she hurt me too? Somehow I don't think so. And I believe she killed Sean in self-defence. I would have done the same, in the circumstances. Kill or be killed. I've noticed a change in her in the time we've spent together, as though it's slowly dawned on her that this is all so trivial in the grand scheme of things.

'What will you do now?' I say again. 'You know they've arrested someone for Sean's murder. I'm not sure if anybody's been charged, but Sean owed a lot of money, apparently. Was in with some dodgy people.'

'That doesn't surprise me. Knowing Sean.'

'So you can leave. I'm the only one who knows you were ever here and I won't say anything.'

She narrows her eyes. 'You'd do that for me? Why?'

'I did something awful to you. I drugged you. You could have died in that fire. I took your identity, I lied about my qualifications, I should never have done it. I deserve everything that's happened to me, Beth. I just want to move forward now. Try and salvage things with Jamie. Second chances.'

She looks sceptical. 'I stole from you.'

'Well, that makes two of us,' I say wryly. 'Let's call it quits.'

We stand and stare at each other. Then suddenly she takes me by surprise by giving me a brief, awkward hug.

I walk slowly out of Evelyn's flat. I can feel Beth watching me from the window as I descend the steps into my own flat. I wonder what she will do now. Will she return to wherever she was living? I hope she'll be happy. We've both wronged each other. I just want to put this whole nightmare behind us.

Because really, I owe her everything.

41

Beth

I watch her leave, all my resentment and bitterness and anger dissipating. Let her live her life as Libby Elliot if that's what she wants. Because I need to live mine as Elizabeth Perez, Matteo's wife. I need to go back to him. If he'll have me.

When Matteo asked me to marry him three years ago I told him I couldn't find Sean to get a divorce, but we moved in together anyway and lived as husband and wife. At last I'd found someone who loved me, who didn't want to abuse me, mentally or physically, like my parents, or Sean. A good man. I began to heal. And things would never have taken such a downward turn if it hadn't been for Lilianna.

When the midwife broke the news to me that awful day in hospital, that Lilianna had died in the womb, it felt as though all those prophecies my dad had flung at me while I was growing up, about being a bad person and having the devil in me, were true. Lilianna was taken from me because I was evil. She didn't deserve to have a mother like me.

When Lilianna died, my hopes and dreams died with

her; of being a mother, of taking her home to the nursery we'd painted bumblebee yellow, to the little white cot that Matteo had spent all afternoon putting together, the soft toys that awaited her, the babygros and vests, nappies and little socks neatly folded in her wardrobe. I'd never watch her take her first steps, or say her first words. I'd never see her ride a bike, or start school, or fall in love for the first time, or get married. It had all been snatched away and I yearned for her and the life she could have had.

Seeing Karen again, confronting her, talking to her, has been a therapy of sorts. A kind of closure. I'm not proud of my behaviour in Thailand, or what I've done to Karen since being back in England. But I have to forgive myself as well as her.

She drugged me so that I wouldn't follow her. She hated me that much. And I deserved it.

As darkness falls I sit in Evelyn's chair by the window and ring Matteo. Tears spring to my eyes when I hear his warm, sexy accent and I'm transported there, to our home near the beach with the veranda and the wooden floors, with our washing line full of colourful towels flapping in the sea breeze, and I suddenly want to be with him so much it hurts. 'Beth. Oh Beth, thank God you're all right. I've been out of my mind with worry,' he cries as soon as he answers the phone.

'I'm so sorry,' I say, my throat constricted by tears. 'I'm so sorry for running away. I just feel so sad. I miss her so much . . .'

'I know, baby, I know, please come home. I need you too.'

'I can't believe you still want me back. After everything I've put you through.'

'Of course I do, *hermosa chica*.' Beautiful girl. My heart takes flight and soars. 'I love you. If you need money I'll put some in your bank account, but please . . . please come home . . .'

And then I'm laughing through my tears as I tell him that I'll be home the next day, that I love him too. That I'm sorry.

He's waiting for me as I walk through the airport less than twenty-four hours later. He's grown a beard in the months I've been away and his dark eyes are wet when he sees me. I rush towards him and he picks me up, swinging me around, joy in his face as he plants kisses on my lips, my eyelids. He runs a finger along my cheekbone as if trying to heal the bruise and I feel real joy, so sudden and pure that it makes me catch my breath. Sean's gone. I never have to be scared of him again. I'm free to be happy, with Matteo.

I cling to him and cry and laugh, and then he leads me out of the automatic doors, his arms wrapped protectively around me as though worried I'll disappear again. At last I can stop running. I'm finally safe. *I'm finally home.*

42

Libby

I sit and wait for Jamie as the light is sucked from the day and dusk comes. Yet he still doesn't arrive.

I need to confront him about this card. I try to ring him but his phone goes straight to voicemail.

He's probably at his mum's. With Hannah.

I need to fight for my husband. For our relationship. Otherwise all of this has been for nothing. I ring for a taxi and ten minutes later I'm walking up Sylvia's path.

Her eyes are round with surprise as she opens the door to me. 'What are you doing here?' she says as I storm past her.

'Where are they?' I cry.

'Libby,' she says, her voice cutting. 'What's all this about?' She closes the front door calmly.

'Where's Jamie?'

She folds her arms across her ample chest. 'In the dining room . . . what's going on . . .?' But I've already stomped off.

They are all there in Sylvia's elegant dining room, with the duck-egg-blue walls and the chintzy curtains that frame the French doors to the garden, sitting around the oval table. Katie and Gerard, Hannah and Jamie.

Jamie's face when I walk in is such a picture of horror that I almost want to giggle. The rest all look up at me with expectant faces. Katie smirks. Hannah blushes, a forkful of pasta near her mouth.

'Ah, there you are, Jamie. Planning to come home tonight?'

His knife and fork clatter onto the plate and he stands up, pushing his chair away. 'Libby, why are you here?' He frowns. 'And what's happened to your face? Your cheek – it's all red.'

I put my hand to my face; my cheek feels hot to the touch. And in that moment I consider walking away from all this. From Jamie. Starting again. I've done it before. I reach inside my jacket for the card and slap it onto the table. 'I found this,' I say.

Hannah also puts down her fork and eyes me with dislike. Katie and Gerard continue to stare at me too, but there is excitement in their eyes. As though they're about to watch a good show.

'Where . . . where did you get that?' she asks.

Jamie reaches for it and picks it up. 'Wait a minute . . . this is . . .' He turns to Hannah, his face pinched. 'What are you doing with this?'

She shuffles in her seat, looking uncomfortable. She can't meet his gaze. She bites her lip and looks as though she's going to cry. I wonder, briefly, where her son is.

Katie and Gerard continue to stare at us openly. I can tell they are enjoying this.

Despite everything I feel sorry for Hannah sitting there while we all gawp at her. Judging her. 'Jamie. Hannah. Why don't we go into the living room and talk about this?' I suggest. But Hannah pushes her chair back so violently that it falls to the floor.

'Don't do me any favours,' she snaps. Sylvia, who is standing in the doorway, is visibly shocked.

'You really want to do this here?' says Jamie. Over her head his eyes find mine and an understanding flickers between us. I know, in that instant, that Jamie definitely didn't write that card.

'You sent those cards to our neighbour Anya, didn't you? You wanted me to believe that Jamie was having an affair,' I say.

She rounds on me, her eyes flashing. 'You don't deserve him,' she laughs cruelly. 'He should have married me. Not some scrawny jumped-up little scrubber like you.'

'That's enough, Hannah,' says Sylvia, her voice hard.

'And all the other stuff?' says Jamie.

I could speak up. About it being Beth who sent the leaflets, and backpack, who emptied our account. But I don't. I wait. The air in the room is thick with tension. And then Jamie looks furious. 'And Ziggy . . .?'

She hangs her head. 'I didn't mean for him to die. I just wanted to drive a wedge between the two of you. I thought then you'd come back –' she turns to him and

359

reaches for his hand but he brushes her off '– you'd come back to me.'

'Hannah, that's never going to happen,' Jamie says, his expression stony. I know it must be taking all his strength not to scream at her for what she's done to Ziggy. 'I'm sorry if I hurt you but it's Libby I love. It's Libby I want to be with. Me and you – that's in the past.'

For a brief, horrifying moment I wonder if she's going to lunge for him, or me. But instead she walks silently past us and out of the room. A few seconds later we hear the front door banging behind her.

43

I've taken a part-time job in the local café, cash in hand, no questions asked. No charges have been brought against me yet. Melanie thinks there will be something but she's hoping, if I plead guilty, that the worst I'll get is community service. I miss teaching and the future seems so uncertain that it scares me. But at least I still have Jamie and the baby, and for that I'm so grateful. We've put the flat on the market and are hopeful of a quick sale. A new start.

After Hannah admitted to writing the letters and hurting Ziggy, Sylvia told her she needed to move out of the coach house. That she needed to stay away from Jamie. I was impressed by how Sylvia handled the situation. We've grown closer as the weeks have progressed. I feel, at last, that she sees me as her rightful daughter-in-law.

Jamie and I have had long discussions about our relationship. All we seem to do at the moment is talk, our innermost thoughts spewing out of us, each of us desperate to purge ourselves. 'I didn't realise that by spending time with Hannah I was giving her false hope,' he admits one night as we lie in bed. 'It still shocks me to think she'd be capable of something like that. Poisoning Ziggy, the letters, the fraud. And did she send those things from the catalogues too? She's not admitted to that but . . . it's the sort of thing she'd do.'

I haven't told him the truth; to do so would mean telling him about Beth. And I want to keep that between us.

'I've known Hannah for years,' he continues. 'Since we were eighteen. How can we really tell what goes on in people's heads? It makes me not want to trust anyone.'

I snuggle up to him and try to reassure him. 'You know me, Jay. I know you. You can trust me. I promise. We have to look to the future now. To us. To Peanut. Put the past behind us.'

He turns his face towards mine. 'No more lies?'

I smile in response and reach up to kiss him. 'No more lies.'

I think it is possible to know someone, to know what's truly in their hearts. I've never trusted Hannah, I knew she was jealous; I'd seen how her eyes followed Jamie, I could tell she disliked me just because I'd married him. We go through our lives doing the best we can, we make mistakes, we inadvertently – and sometimes deliberately – piss people off. But how are we to know if people will retaliate? How can we tell how much, or for how long, someone will hold a grudge?

I watch as Jamie sleeps, his arm slung over his eyes so that I can only see his full lips, his chiselled chin, the hollow where his throat meets his collarbones. I know he loves me but how can I be sure he didn't encourage

Hannah in his own way? That some of this wasn't his fault, even if he wasn't fully aware of it? How accountable are we?

Lies. There will always be lies. The little white lies we can't bring ourselves to tell our spouses, our friends. Sometimes it's to protect them and sometimes it's to protect ourselves.

I know I promised to tell Jamie everything, to confide in him, warts and all, to stop trying to make out that I'm perfect. But I can't tell him about Beth. And I can't tell him that I have forgiven her. Because I'm partly to blame.

After I found the drugs that Beth had used to spike my drink, anger and resentment grew inside me like a weed, entangling itself around my insides so that I was consumed by it. It was her fault I'd lost Harry; she'd manipulated us both. I took the drugs and poured them into my can of Coke while she was in the loo. Then, when she returned, I pretended to be asleep. It didn't take long before she was out of it. I waited until I was sure she was in a deep slumber, before grabbing what I thought was my backpack, heaving it onto my shoulders and creeping out of the dark room. And then I started the fire in the women's loos, just around the corner from our bedroom. I lit one of Beth's matches and threw it into the wastepaper basket full of paper towels. It was supposed to be a small fire. Just enough to cause a distraction if Beth woke up. I assumed when the smoke alarms went off the hostel would be evacuated and the authorities would question her, as well as everyone else. That it would give me enough time to get as far away from her as possible. How was I to know the fire alarms at the hostel were faulty, that the fire would get out of control? That people would die? I've spent my life trying to atone for it. Trying to be a good person, a good teacher. And I'll be a good mother.

It wasn't until I was on the pavement outside that I saw the thick black smoke emanating from one of the windows on the second floor and realised my mistake. The fire took hold much quicker than I'd anticipated. I ran into a nearby hotel, screamed at them to call the fire brigade and could only watch in despair as the fire engines turned up, thinking of Beth in her drug-induced sleep, unable to escape.

The reason I'd been so sure that Beth was dead all these years was because I thought I'd killed her. It's my fault that people died that night. And I'll never forgive myself for that.

Consequences. We can't escape them.

Jamie turns over in his sleep with a soft grunt, flinging his arm across my chest. I snuggle into him, cradling my stomach, thinking of the new life growing inside me. We are safe, the three of us. This is my second chance and I'll do anything not to mess it up.

Epilogue

The flat was only on the market for a week before we had an offer. We've found a lovely little house not far away, in Saltford, near the river. It has a garden and when we move we're thinking of buying a puppy so that we can start training it before the baby arrives. Jamie's business has gone from strength to strength and I've had my twenty-week scan. We're having a boy. My T-shirts are now tight over my bump. I'll have to start buying maternity clothes soon. I feel excitement at my new life ahead. It's not what I thought it would be, I'll always miss teaching, but I'm looking forward to being a mum.

It's a warm summer's day, the sky a hazy blue, gossamer clouds hovering. I'm sorting out our paperwork so that we're more organised for when the moving date comes through. I'm sitting in the middle of the dining room with papers strewn around me.

Jamie wanders through, holding an empty mug. He has that tired, slightly distracted air about him that he always has when he's in the middle of working, as though he can't tear his mind away from figures and code and goodness knows what else he has to think about. He switches the kettle on. 'Coffee?'

'Decaf, remember,' I say, stroking my bump.

'I know.' He laughs because we have this conversation every time he offers to make me a drink.

When the knock on the door comes, it's so unexpected that Jamie and I exchange puzzled glances. Nobody usually calls around in the middle of the day. Not even Sylvia. She often waits until we visit her, not wanting to 'intrude'.

I go to answer the door and am surprised to see DI Hartley standing there. My heart jumps. I haven't heard anything more about charges I might face. Melanie Finch hasn't been in touch for weeks.

'Elizabeth Elliot,' he begins, holding up his police identification unnecessarily, as I know exactly who he is.

'It's Elizabeth Hall . . .'

'I'm arresting you on suspicion of the murder of Sean Elliot. You do not have to say anything but it may harm your defence if you do not mention when questioned something you later rely on in court. Anything you do say may be given in evidence.'

'What?' I splutter, staring at him incredulously. 'You can't do this. You've already arrested me for this once before and let me go. I thought you'd charged someone else . . . I thought . . .' My voice rises in hysteria. Jamie comes rushing into the hallway, his face draining of colour when he sees the detective on the other side of the threshold.

'Why are you here again?'

'We have new evidence to suggest that your wife is

responsible for Sean Elliot's death, Mr Hall. Now, Mrs Elliot, you can either come quietly or . . .'

I shake my head. 'It's fine. It will be OK. I know I've done nothing wrong. Please let me put my shoes on.' I slip my feet into ballet pumps and follow DI Hartley to the waiting police car.

'Libs, I'll call Melanie Finch. We'll meet you at the station,' cries Jamie, dashing out after me. He's standing on the pavement in his socks. I can only nod, a knot forming in my stomach as I'm helped into the back of the police car.

I can't stop the tears from flowing as Melanie Finch fills me in on what's been happening. We're sitting in an interview room in the police station. It's a different room to last time, smaller, windowless, the air stale. She sits across from me, her expression serious behind her glasses.

'They are in possession of an ornament from your property that they believe is the murder weapon,' she says. Her lipstick is too red and bright for her face so that her mouth looks almost cartoonish. I can't stop staring at it as she speaks.

'An ornament?'

'A Buddha.' She pushes a photograph across the table. 'Does this belong to you?'

I frown. It's the one Harry gave me, the one that was on my sideboard. I'd put it in the wardrobe, under a pile of clothes. How come the police have it? 'Yes. It does. Where did they get that?'

She blinks, her eyes look huge behind her glasses. 'I'm not at liberty to say at the moment.'

'Why? What's going on?'

'The shape of the ornament matches the wound to the head and your fingerprints are all over it.'

So Beth used my Buddha to kill Sean. And then what had she done? Wiped her prints from it and left it on my sideboard for me to find? If I'd never picked it up, if I'd just left it there, then this wouldn't be happening.

I sip water from a plastic cup. My hands are trembling. 'Well yes, they would be. It's my ornament. But I didn't kill him. You have to believe me, Melanie. It wasn't me. I was at the hospital in Cornwall with Jamie the day Sean died, remember?'

She sits back in her chair and assesses me. It's so hot in the room, so airless. My blouse is sticking to my skin and I can feel a wet patch forming on my back. She takes her glasses off and runs her fingers over her eye socket. She looks tired. 'Do you know more about this than you're letting on?' she asks, replacing her glasses.

I'm sorry, Beth. I take a deep breath and tell her everything.

When I've finished she regards me in disbelief. 'So you're saying that the real Elizabeth Elliot didn't die in the fire but came back here because she was angry with you for stealing her identity and then she killed her husband?'

I nod. 'Yes, that's exactly what I'm saying.'

'I need to ask you, Libby. Did you do it? Did you kill Sean Elliot?'

'No. I'm telling you. It was the real Elizabeth Elliot. Not me. I'm Karen Fisher.'

She consults her notes, her face darkening. 'Well it says here that the real Karen Fisher died in a fire. In Thailand. Back in two thousand and eight. Her documents were found in the clean-up operation. The fire is thought to have been started deliberately, Libby.'

'They were my documents. I took the real Elizabeth Elliot's bag when I ran away from the hostel. The real Elizabeth Elliot was here. A few months ago. She was staying in my neighbour's flat. I saw her. I had a conversation with her.' I can see it's falling on deaf ears and I realise with horror that she doesn't believe me. That she thinks I'm making the whole thing up.

'Leave it with me,' she says, standing up.

I sit and wait. Eventually Melanie returns with DI Hartley and DS Trott. She sits next to me while the two detectives take the seats opposite.

'We have enough evidence here to charge you,' says DI Hartley, his steely eyes flashing dangerously. 'And then it will go to Crown Court. It would make life a lot easier though, Mrs Elliot, if you confessed.'

'I'm not going to confess because I've done nothing wrong,' I cry.

'We've already established the ornament belongs to you,' he says.

'Yes . . . yes it does.'

'And it has your fingerprints all over it. Nobody else's. Just yours.'

I shuffle, sweat prickling my top lip. How can this be happening? 'Beth told me herself that she'd killed him. In self-defence. He was a total psycho. He was going to kill her. I found the ornament on my sideboard. I usually kept it in the wardrobe. I picked it up and put it back there. I just assumed Jamie had found it and put it there . . .'

'Who else can vouch for you? Who else saw this Beth? Did your husband see her? Did anyone?' asks DS Trott, her blonde bob falling around her young face. I decide to direct my answers to her. She's about my age, maybe she'll understand, be more sympathetic than Hartley.

I shake my head. 'No. Nobody. But you can check banks, can't you? Passports? I think she'd come from abroad. She'd recently lost a baby. She's a bit unstable . . .'

DI Hartley looks sceptical. 'I don't believe you. I think you killed your ex-husband and then concocted this whole cock-and-bull story of swapping identities in Thailand to get out of it. I believe you killed your ex-husband because he was threatening to expose you. That's the truth of the matter, isn't it, Elizabeth?'

'No . . . no it's not.' I feel like I'm in a nightmare. 'How could I have done it? We were in Cornwall. Jamie was in hospital.'

DI Hartley smirks. He looks like a fox with his sharp nose and beady eyes. 'Yes, we checked that out. You actually left the hospital at six thirty p.m. on the fifth of April. Sean Elliot was killed between three p.m. on the fifth and six p.m. the following day. So you had plenty of time to drive back to Bath, kill him, and then get back to Cornwall before meeting Jamie the next morning.'

I run my hand over my face, exasperated. 'But why? Why would I do that?'

'We have a record here that you rang Mr Elliot at approximately –' DS Trott consults her notes '– eleven a.m. that morning.' She slides a piece of paper under my nose containing a list of telephone numbers. I recognise mine straight away. 'For the benefit of the tape I am showing Mrs Elliot telephone records,' she adds without taking her eyes off me.

'Yes. But I thought it was Philip Heywood that I was speaking to. Not Sean Elliot.'

DS Trott remains impassive. 'I think you realised when you spoke to him what he was up to. I think that you then arranged to meet him in your flat in Bath and killed him,' she says. I was wrong to think she'd be the more sympathetic of the two.

'No. I had a broken arm. My right arm. I couldn't drive. I can't drive,' I wail.

'You have a driving licence and an automatic car, Mrs Elliot. I'm sure you would have been able to drive with a broken arm if you took off your sling and if the need was great, which in your case it was.'

'I . . . no . . . I can't drive. Karen Fisher can't drive.'

DS Trott surveys me quietly, unnerving me. Then, 'Are you prone to violent outbursts, Elizabeth?'

'No, of course not.'

She glances down at something in front of her, her hair swinging forwards. She tucks it behind her ear. 'We have a statement here from a James Penton. He says you assaulted him.'

James Penton? And then it clicks who they mean. Jim. 'Assaulted him?' I gasp. 'I didn't assault him. I prodded him because he was trespassing, lurking around the Hideaway. I just wanted him to leave us alone. I suppose you could say I pushed him, but not hard . . .' I look about wildly at Melanie Finch. At the detectives. But they just stare back at me, their faces grave.

I've been formally charged with Sean's murder.

And now I await trial. I've not been allowed bail, despite being pregnant, because of the seriousness of the crime. Apparently I'm a flight risk, which is ironic since I haven't been out of the country since Thailand.

Melanie Finch has tried to remain upbeat, telling me that we have a good defence. But I know she's lying. We have no proof that Beth was ever in this country. Melanie has tried to find her but there is no record of the real Beth Elliot living in England. If she's abroad she could be anywhere.

Jamie visits me often. He's the only one who believes me, but even I can see that his devotion is waning and it will probably disappear when he hears all the facts in court. Because if I was on the jury, I wouldn't believe me. I'm in so deep now, I've become Elizabeth Elliot to such an extent, that nobody accepts I'm really Karen

Fisher. I've asked Melanie to speak to old friends of mine from school – or the colleagues I worked with at the local supermarket – to ask them to make an identification. Surely somebody from my past will remember me? I wasn't that invisible. She's chasing it up for me but she did tell me gently that, really, it doesn't matter what I call myself because the fingerprints on the weapon are mine, whoever I say I am.

'But if we can prove you are Karen Fisher then your motive for killing Sean becomes weaker,' she explained. 'And your story will be more believable to a jury. So there is hope.'

Hope. It's all I have while I wait in prison. This is retribution. For Thailand. For the hostel fire. I might not have killed Sean Elliot but I'm responsible for the deaths of seven other people. I'm not innocent in all of this. That one night of madness has cost me so much. If I'm found guilty I will miss years of my son's life. I'll miss his first steps, his first laugh, his first words. And that would be the worst punishment of all.

I have too much time to think, to obsess, alone in my cell. How did the police get that one piece of incriminating evidence? Beth admitted being in my flat. Had she gone there to find the Buddha and then posted it to the police knowing my fingerprints were all over it? It's the only thing that makes sense. She'd spent a lifetime looking over her shoulder and selling me out was the only way to ensure her own freedom.

Beth and Libby. Libby and Beth. We are more alike

than we ever wanted to admit. I know if it had been the other way around I would have done the same to her to save my own skin. Because we are survivors. We've had to be. And I'll survive this. I'll prove my innocence. I refuse to let Beth win.

Acknowledgements

A huge thank you to my fabulous editors Maxine Hitchcock and Eve Hall who have made this book so much better than it would have been, and to Eugenie Todd for her eagle-eyed copy-editing. Thank you to the whole team at Penguin, who do such an incredible job, from the cover design to the sales department. I'm so grateful.

Thank you to the wonderful Juliet Mushens — the best agent in the world (with the cutest cats in the world!) and to Nathalie Hallam. You are both amazing and I feel so lucky to be part of Team Mushens.

Thank you to The Prime Writers for being such a lovely, supportive group and in particular to Sarah Vaughan for all the word races which kept me motivated and away from browsing Facebook!

To my writing buddies, Fiona Mitchell, Joanna Barnard, Liz Tipping, Gilly Macmillan and Nikki Owen for the chats, support, meet-ups and laughs.

To all the bloggers — I'm constantly in awe of how much reading and reviewing you all do and how much support you give to us writers.

To the readers who have bought, shared, borrowed and recommended my books and to those who have contacted me on Twitter or Facebook — your messages mean so much to me.

To all my lovely friends who have been so kind, reading and recommending my books and even choosing them for our school book club. You are all the best! Nicky Jones – the pink fluffy unicorn is for you!

Last but not least to my family. To my mum, Linda, and sister, Samantha, for being my very first readers and for all their support and advice. To my dad, Ken, for his faith in me which has never wavered, who always believed that I would one day be published. To my step-dad, John, and step-mum, Laura, (the best step-parents ever) and to my husband, Ty, for helping me brainstorm plot ideas, for telling me honestly if something isn't working and for always believing in me. I'm so lucky to call you my family and I love you all.

And finally, to my children, Claudia and Isaac, who I love more than anything in the world. Every day I thank my lucky stars that I have you both in my life. This book is for you (you just won't be able to read it until you're older!).

Last Seen Alive Reading Group Questions

1. 'He needs this holiday just as much as I do. Our first nine months of married life haven't been easy.' How do Jamie and Libby's marital problems affect their experience at The Hideaway? Would the events that followed have taken a different turn if they were a stronger unit?

2. Are Libby's insecurities over Hannah and Jamie rational or do they just distance her from Jamie and his family unnecessarily? Is Jamie's relationship with Hannah normal?

3. Karen and Elizabeth both suffer miscarriages. How does the trauma of this affect them both? Do their different stories leading up to this life event change the way they react?

4. Karen and Elizabeth's stories begin in Thailand. How does location affect the drives of the characters? Are we prone to act differently when taken out of our usual environment?

5. 'Lies. There will always be lies. The little white lies we can't bring ourselves to tell our spouses, our friends. Sometimes it's to protect them and sometimes it's to protect ourselves.' Is it sometimes best to lie in order protect ourselves and others? When should Karen

have told Jamie the truth? How have her and Beth's lies affected their lives?

6. How important is trust in a marriage? Is Jamie wrong to trust Libby again after he learns the truth? How long should Libby atone for her actions?

7. 'How can we tell how much, or for how long someone will hold a grudge?' Is Elizabeth's bitterness about Karen 'stealing' Harry along with her own later miscarriage enough reason to try and destroy Karen's life? Do you feel pity for Elizabeth?

8. In the novel a person's identity appears to sometimes be fluid and at others inescapable. How important is a name and legal identity?

9. How do Karen and Elizabeth's shifting circumstances and relationships change their personalities? How do they differ from one another? How are they similar?

10. While at The Hideaway, rhetorical questions run constantly through Libby's mind. What effect does this have on the reader? Does it give an impression of paranoia or of insight?

11. Karen and Elizabeth both lack a mother figure. How has that affected them, if at all? In what ways does Evelyn fulfil a maternal role for them both?

12. Where you happy with the way the novel ended? Do you feel that anyone was punished unfairly or not enough?

Read on for an extract
from Claire Douglas'
new novel . . .

Publishing Summer 2018

@DougieClaire

ClaireDouglasAuthor

Her long limbs are spreadeagled on our restored Victorian tiles, but with one leg bent, her neck at an unnatural angle. Blood is tangled in the strands of her pale hair, and looks too red, unreal somehow, as though my daughters have been busy with a paint brush. She's wearing a black jumpsuit in a silky fabric; elegant, even in death. One of her heels has slipped off, revealing her bare foot and the purple polish on her toe nails. It makes my eyes well up, that foot. So vulnerable, so familiar, with the soft fleshy sole and the elongated middle toe. I used to tease her about her middle toe being longer than all the others. She said it meant she was descended from a Roman princess. She was always coming out with stuff like that as a kid.

How long has she been lying here? How long?

Selena.

Her eyes are closed and her cheek is pressed against the cold tiles, her lips blue. I fall to my knees, leaning over her, the tips of my fingers pressing against her slender neck. There is no pulse.

A scream bubbles in my throat, but I can't let it out, I can't call for help. I look around, desperately. I don't know where the others are. Scattered, like the beads of one of Evie's broken plastic necklaces, around the house. The children. Oh, God. Ruby mustn't see her mother like this.

What am I going to do? I can't leave her alone here, in this draughty hallway, with the muddy wellies and the smelly trainers and the unseen footprints of strangers.

Selena.

And all I can think about is that I've failed her. I've let her down. Again.

PART ONE

I

Ten days before

It's my mother's idea. The bad ideas always are.

'We should invite Selena to come and stay,' she says, her piercing blue eyes lighting up behind her thick glasses as if she's just thought of it. Yet I know it has probably been brewing in her mind for days, like the sloe gin she still insists on making despite nobody in the family liking it. 'She's your cousin and she's had a hard time of it lately, what with her husband leaving her and –' she lowers her voice even though we are alone in the room '– all the problems she's had with the daughter.' She pulls *that* face. The face she always pulls when she speaks of The Daughter. Ruby. Apparently that's her name, although I've never met her. I haven't spoken to Selena for over fifteen years.

'I don't think it's a good idea,' I say, trying to keep my voice neutral while sweeping a cloth across the surface of the rustic sideboard in the front room. I've never told my mother – I've never told anyone – the real reason we fell out. It would have destroyed so many lives.

I stand back and glance around with a critical eye at the high ceilings and the open fireplace and the arched picture window with the mountains in the distance. I can see Crug Hywel from here, the top disappearing into diaphanous clouds. We've managed to make the place look cosy, not too formal. Comfortable, even, with squashy sofas and high-backed chairs placed strategically by a log fire. I spent hours sanding and waxing the floorboards and painting the walls in soft Farrow and Ball hues. Adrian's mood was lifted, his problems temporarily forgotten as he got stuck in to restoring the Victorian tiles in the hallway and getting the weeds in the garden under control.

My stomach contracts at the thought that we will be opening for business in just three days. In time for October half term. All the months of hard work, stress, renovations and upheaval will be finally worth it.

I can sense my mother watching me for a reaction. Then, 'You've got bedrooms to fill, my girl.' She still talks to me like I'm a teenager and not a woman in her mid-thirties. 'And Selena's got money by all accounts.'

I don't even know why we're having this conversation. There is no way Selena will want to see me again.

I know too much.

'She won't come,' I say as I straighten a cushion and then tweak the vase of tulips on the windowsill, the memory of the last time I'd seen Selena coming to the forefront of my mind; her eighteenth birthday party, her lies, those angry words that I threw in her face like a pint of the lager and black she was always drinking. I haven't seen her since.

'Of course she'll want to come.' There's an edge to her voice and I experience a cold, sharp lurch of dread.

I turn to face her. 'You've already asked her, haven't you?'

Mum dips her head, her perfectly coiffed hair doesn't move. There is a slight flush on her cheeks that reveals I'm right.

'She was thrilled to be asked, actually. She said yes.'

'She said *yes*?' The room tilts. 'But that makes no sense.' Why would she? After everything?

Mum bristles. 'I don't know why you're so surprised. You were inseparable growing up. It's sad, how you lost touch. She's family. And she's vulnerable right now. She has no one else.'

'What about Aunt Bess?'

My mum whistles through her teeth. 'She's a waste of space, that one.' Aunt Bess is an alcoholic. There was a time when I thought Selena might turn out the same way. But from the snippets of news passed down over the years it seems that Selena did all right for herself in the end, marrying, as my mum put it, 'into wealth' and devoting herself to her daughter, who was born with health problems, although I don't know all the details. I had to distance myself from Selena after what happened. It was the only way.

But before all that, before the secrets and the lies and the anger, we were close. More like sisters than cousins. I put it down to the fact there was only nine months between us, but really we just got on. We had the same sense of humour and, despite me being the older one, I looked up to her. She had this courage that I lacked back then. She threw herself into everything. She had no inhibitions and no fears, whereas I was shyer, more cautious. She brought me out of myself. She made me do things that I'd never have done otherwise, like smoke my first cigarette, drink cider in the park when we were much too young to do so and getting chucked out of a department store for putting knickers on our heads. Our dads were brothers and we were always in and out of each other's houses, living just streets away from one another in Cardiff. Happy. Content. Naïve. Or at least I was.

And then, in just one night, everything changed.

I'm not proud of how I acted afterwards, but shock made me flee. To university. To London. To Adrian.

Mum bustles from the room in her smart blouse and slacks. She always dresses like she's about to go to the office, despite having not worked for decades. She still has a good figure, I concede. Trim and tidy, as my dad would have said. I follow her as she weaves her compact frame into the small study off the hallway. It's the only room we haven't decorated yet and it's very 1980s, with yellow striped wallpaper and navy blue borders.

Mum leans over the desk and opens an A4 leatherbound diary with gold edged pages. My diary. The diary that I'd bought with such excitement only a few weeks ago from a little boutique, thinking of all the potential guests' names that would hopefully fill it. She flicks through it now, a tight smile on her face. 'Okay,' she says when she finds the right date. She picks up a scratchy blue biro and my heart sinks a little. I'd bought a fountain pen to use especially and had done so for the others that were booked in for next week, taking care to write neatly, so that we could look back in years to come and remember our first guests; the excitement, the nerves. Adrian calls me a perfectionist, a high achiever. And it's a good job I am because my husband is disorganised and messy. 'I'll stick Selena and Ruby in here then, shall I? It's the day before the first guest arrives. I think her daughter has a wheelchair so best to use Room Two.' She doesn't wait for an answer as she scribbles on the page.

'I don't want her here,' I shout, shocked by my strength of feeling, that the anger and resentment is still within me, even after all this time.

She jumps and breathes in sharply, sucking her cheeks in and holding her chest theatrically. 'Kirsty! There's no need for that. It's my home too and she's more than welcome to come and stay.'

It's happening already. She's taking over, just like I knew she would.

We hadn't planned on moving back to Wales. Not yet anyhow. Buying a guest house in the Brecon Beacons had been a long-held ambition of mine. Something to daydream about while I toiled away at my dead-end job in marketing, or when I was on maternity leave, surrounded by nappies and wet wipes. The Brecons held great memories for me, of picnics in the foothills, of family days out, my brother, Nathan, and I bickering in the back seat of the car, my dad barking at us good-naturedly. Of homemade egg sandwiches and milky tea. Of Frisbees. Of those endless hills and mountains that seemed to go on for ever. Adrian's parents had owned a guest house in Devon for a while when I was pregnant with Amelia, and the idea of doing the same, but in my beloved Beacons, took root and grew. It was something we imagined we'd do in the future, when both girls were at university, when we were in our late forties or early fifties and had had enough of our terraced house in Twickenham and the frantic London life. Then Adrian had his break-down and suddenly the idea of the mountains, the fresh air, the peace, became more appealing, more urgent than ever before.

It had been a dank February day during half term when we first saw the house.

We were staying in Brecon, driving through those same mountains that I had so admired as a child. Adrian sat shrivelled up in the passenger seat, quieter than he used to be, still shell shocked from all the torment that had happened, as if he were a war veteran or disaster survivor. The mist was like dry ice, nudging the hills and draping itself over the mountains in the distance. The land was spread out in front of us in varying shades of green, some of the grass in the fields was tufty so that it looked like wheat blowing in the breeze, our one solitary road zig-zagging through it all. There wasn't another soul for miles.

The girls were in the back seat, all elbows and knees as they fidgeted and fought over what DVD to watch on the iPad. I could see them in the rear-view mirror: our eldest, Amelia, sleek and dark like her dad, and Evie, with her rounded cheeks and mass of bushy blonde hair like mine. Five years between them and I could already sense that Amelia, at eleven, was moving away from her sister emotionally. She wanted to watch *The Hunger Games* (even though I wouldn't allow it) whereas Evie still loved *Sofia The First*. Every time they bickered I inwardly winced, as Adrian's shoulders hunched even further up his neck.

'Amelia, just let Evie watch Sofia. *Please.*'

She huffed from behind me. 'It's not fair. She always gets her own way.' I tried to shoot her a conspiratorial look in the mirror but she just glowered at me, her arms folded across her skinny chest, her bottom lip sticking out. But she relented, thankfully, and I was relieved to see them fasten their headphones over their ears and concentrate on the screen. I could sense Adrian uncoiling, his body relaxing with every beat of silence that followed.

'I can see why you love it here so much,' he said eventually. 'I feel like I can breathe properly.' He reached out and touched my knee. It was the most affection he'd showed me for months. His depression had turned up like a bully, pushing his bubbly personality, as well as his sex drive, into the cold. 'It must remind you of your dad.'

I nodded, my throat tight. It was my dad's favourite place.

Suddenly Amelia shot forward, straining against her seat belt and squealing. 'Look! Mum, look!' she cried. I nearly slammed the brakes on, but then I noticed what she was pointing at. Half a dozen ponies grazing by the side of the road. 'Oh, they're so cute!'

'They are, but sit back in your seat, honey,' I said. 'It's dangerous.'

'There's nobody else on the road,' grumbled Adrian. 'It's not dangerous. You're going twenty miles an hour.'

I ignored him.

Evie removed her headphones too and I slowed right down so they could get a better view of the ponies.

'Wow, this is a magical place,' proclaimed Evie seriously, watching a chestnut pony hoovering up the grass.

I laughed. Evie has a thing for fairies and magic. She lives in a dream world half the time. Normally, Adrian would have laughed too but he continued to stare ahead morosely. I shot him a sideways glance. I missed the easy, happy-go-lucky man he used to be.

It was when we were on the edge of a little market town that we saw it. Set back from the road, it stood alone amongst the overgrown foliage, ivy scrambling up the walls. A double-fronted Victorian detached; part white-washed, part stone, with a gabled roof and mullioned windows. It had a 'For Sale' sign propped up in the driveway. The tiles were falling off of the roof and the paint was flaking in places, but I could see the beauty in it even then. With a bit of TLC it could be magnificent.

I pulled over to get a better look. Adrian must have been thinking along similar lines, because he turned to me, his eyes bright. For the first time in a long time he looked excited.

We arranged a viewing for the next day, and as the four of us followed the estate agent through the crumbling, neglected house, the excitement hummed between us. I was convinced it was what we needed. A project. A change of direction for Adrian. A distraction. For all of us.

Our enthusiasm quickly turned to disappointment as we realised we didn't have as much money as we initially thought due to the fact that Adrian hadn't worked for months. Most of our savings had dwindled in the interim, and even if we sold our four-bedroom terraced house in Twickenham, we'd still be short of cash to complete the work that was needed.

So my mum stepped in. Despite my reservations, I'd fallen so deeply in love with the house that I found myself saying yes to her offer of help. She sold the 1930s semi that we'd grown up in, and divided the proceeds between Nathan and me, with the proviso that she moved in with us. I convinced myself we would get along fine – after all, I was the child who never really gave her much trouble. I left that up to Nathan. But since leaving home and only seeing her every few months when we were both on our best behaviour, I'd forgotten how strong-willed my mother could be.

I glare at her now, standing imperiously over the diary, her mouth set in a stubborn line. It's been less than two weeks since she moved in and already I could throttle her. I bite back a retort and walk from the room before I say something I'll regret. I can feel her eyes boring into my back. I can't bother Adrian with this, not after everything, so to take my mind off of it I go and find the girls. They're in the garden playing with their new lop-eared rabbits and my heart lifts at the sight of them. I stand at the back door and watch them as they sit on the grass, not caring that it's damp, both with a bunny on their laps and chattering away to each other. All this space, I think, surveying the vast garden. Now they have a trampoline and a swing set, things our postage stamp of a garden in London could never accommodate.

This is supposed to be our get-away from the stresses and strains of city life. Our new start. And I'm not about to let Selena swan in like the evil fairy in *Sleeping Beauty*, with her resentment over the past and her lies, messing things up for us. We've been through too much as a family. And I'll do anything – *anything* – to protect them.